Jessica Fellowes is an author, journalist and public speaker. Her bestselling The Mitford Murders series has been nominated for awards in Britain, France, Germany and Italy, and sold into eighteen territories. Jessica is also the author of five official companion books to *Downton Abbey,* some of which hit the *New York Times* and *Sunday Times* bestseller lists. She has written short stories for *Vogue Italia* and *L'Uomo Vogue,* and made numerous appearances on radio, podcasts and television. She lives in Oxfordshire with her family.

JESSICA FELLOWES
THE
MITFORD
SECRET

SPHERE

SPHERE

First published in Great Britain in 2022 by Sphere

1 3 5 7 9 10 8 6 4 2

Copyright © Jessica Fellowes 2022

The moral right of the author has been asserted.

A CIP catalogue record for this book
is available from the British Library.

Hardback ISBN 978-0-7515-8067-9
Trade Paperback ISBN 978-0-7515-8068-6

Printed and bound in Great Britain by
Clays Ltd, Elcograf S.p.A.

Papers used by Sphere are from well-managed forests
and other responsible sources.

Sphere
An imprint of
Little, Brown Book Group
Carmelite House
50 Victoria Embankment
London EC4Y 0DZ

An Hachette UK Company
www.hachette.co.uk

www.littlebrown.co.uk

FOR JULIAN AND EMMA

PROLOGUE

17 April 1941

Even after eight months of heavy bombing on London, Louisa Sullivan hadn't decided which part of hearing the bomb's whistle was the worst: the constant whine, which prevented any respite from fear and defied any guess as to its navigation, or the immediate black silence that came in the seconds when it stopped. In that dark spot was the moment of death and destruction, but you knew not where. Sometimes it seemed as if it had happened to you, only you weren't aware yet because pain travels more slowly than the speed of sound. You waited, breath held, to discover whether you were alive. And if you were, there was no relief, for then you would have to discover who had died. Of this one thing you could be certain: someone was now dead who had been alive only seconds before.

One saving grace of being down in the London Underground – as Louisa and her five-year-old daughter Maisie were, most nights, sleeping on the platform at Hammersmith – was that you couldn't hear the bombs as loudly. Guy, Maisie's father, was rarely with them as he was out at every opportunity, working all the shifts given to him and any extras he could take, as a private for the Home Guard. He and Louisa argued frequently about the fact that Maisie had not been evacuated. He saw it as the safest option for their only child, but Louisa could not bear to give her up to an unknown family in an unknown part of the country. Some children had been brought back to London during the Phoney War and she had heard one or two terrible stories of neglect, which she could not dismiss. Guy would remind his wife, to no avail, that the vast majority had been well looked after.

Lying on the concrete floor, her winter coat a paltry mattress, Louisa held Maisie to her a little tighter, breathing in the sweet smell of her freshly washed hair. In response, her daughter wriggled, shifting closer to her mother, adjusting her hands beneath her cheeks as she slept. A thin blanket was drawn over them both, although it did not cover Louisa below her knees. As she held her child, she thought about Deborah Mitford's wedding, due to happen in two days' time. Maisie was going to be a flower girl. Although Louisa had first known the Mitfords when she was their nursery-maid, just over twenty years ago, things between them now were very different.

The eldest of the six daughters, Nancy, was no longer a Mitford but married to Peter Rodd, commissioned into the Welsh Guards and currently abroad, fighting in Addis Ababa, much to Nancy's relief. Louisa knew that, recently, there had been a brief but intense love affair. Even so, Nancy had thrown herself into war work with a fervour that few might have expected from the woman who claimed to work only so she could afford to take taxis rather than buses. She had been an ambulance driver for the ARP, sheltered Jewish refugee families at her father's London house on Rutland Gate, and was now working for the Free French in London.

Louisa could imagine her, lying in bed, shivering with fear, running through the argument that was debated daily in every café, on every street corner: was it safer to leave your house and run to a shelter, to stay on the top floor of your house, or simply embrace death from the comfort of your own bed? It wasn't the screaming bombs Nancy said she minded so much as the sirens, the constant searchlights and the ominous red ropes at the end of a street. She lived only a few roads away from Paddington station, which she knew was a target. When it was light, she could get up and do good. In the small hours of the night, in the desperate blackness, she could do nothing.

Diana was in Holloway prison, locked up for her Fascist sympathies. Louisa pictured her lying in the dark, upon a thin single mattress, shivering fiercely not from fear but from a stark lack of heating. Nancy had told Louisa that, in spite of the privations, Diana wore a fur coat, an eccentric but vital luxury she claimed, because of the cold of her cell. In letters, Diana told them she thought all the time of her children, who were safely in the country with their aunt Pamela at Rignell House. Max, the baby, had been only three months old when Diana was arrested eleven months before. She'd missed his first words, his first steps. Alexander, at three years old, would feel his mother's absence harder, Louisa knew. He would remember her too well, and Pamela had described how he would cling to Diana desperately, sobbing when it came to the end of their permitted half-hour visit. Even Diana had begun to say that perhaps it would be better if they didn't come at all. Her husband, Sir Oswald Mosley, leader of the British Union of Fascists, languished in another prison. Even though their father's cousin was married to Winston Churchill, the prime minister, Diana and Sir Oswald remained imprisoned on no charge, with no trial.

Pamela, now in her late thirties, was as solid and doughty as ever. In her role as the ballast of the family, she had taken on Diana's young boys. Of course, no one knew how long it would turn out to be for. Pamela ran her own farm at Rignell House, while her husband, Derek Jackson, was in the RAF. Louisa worried about those boys: Pamela was fair and straight in her dealings with the world but she was not maternal. The old Guinness nurse, Nanny Higgs, was with them, too, and Louisa hoped she would be more fulsome with her affection. They would be safe, at least, in the country house.

Decca, as the family called Jessica, was far away from danger in Washington and absorbed in her new baby, Constancia. Her husband, Esmond Romilly, had signed up to fight, training for the Royal Canadian Air Force, now that he was reassured Britain was engaged in a war against Fascism. Life had been hard for them already in their short marriage, with the tragic death of their first baby girl from measles when she was a few months old.

Tom Mitford, brother to the six girls, was fighting somewhere in Libya. Louisa knew that their parents, Lord and Lady Redesdale, were terrified: Tom was their only son. But there were no special cases in war. It had been complicated by the fact that Tom did not want to engage in war against Germany, so a request had been made for him to fight in the campaign in Africa. But the nature of his engagement was unknown to them all, so distant and alien was it from their own war experiences.

He might as well have been engaged in battle on the moon. All they could do was hope and pray he would survive and come home safely.

That night, a bomb landed on Rutland Gate, where the youngest sister Deborah – Debo to her family – lay sleeping. The tremors shook her awake and the blast blew in all the windows of the ballroom where her wedding party was due to happen two days later. She leaped out of bed, pulled on her dressing-gown and ran quickly down the stairs, to find Muv and Farve in the hall. They could smell the acrid smoke and hear the sirens. Unity, her older sister and a confirmed Fascist, came down minutes later, her footsteps slow and heavy. On the outbreak of war, she had tried to kill herself with a pearl-handled pistol but the bullet had lodged in her brain.

'What was that?'

'It sounds as if a bomb has landed on our street.'

For the first time in the war, Deborah was truly frightened. Her father opened the front door and stepped outside. It was pitch black but they could hear the chaos of people in the street, ambulances arriving and shouts from the Home Guard, trying to keep people back.

Lord Redesdale came back in, his face as pale as plaster. 'It was number twenty-two,' he said.

'But that's only two doors down. Were Mr and Mrs—'

Lady Redesdale stopped her daughter. 'Yes, they were at home. They were supposed to be coming to the wedding.' Her voice cracked on the last word.

Unity knelt on the cold, tiled floor. 'I shall pray for them now. Our Father, which art in heaven ...'

On the morning of Deborah's wedding, 19 April 1941, the

newspapers reported that there had been over a thousand deaths and more than two thousand casualties in London alone from that single night of attacks. But death was a familiar spectre, and even in war, happiness finds a way to appear, as a single flower grows in a wasteland. Deborah wore her dress of white tulle and, with a wide smile, became Lady Cavendish that very afternoon.

CHAPTER ONE

17 December 1941

'Next station Hassop.'

At this prompt from the train guard, Louisa looked again through the window, though she hardly needed reminding of the landscape. She had barely taken her eyes away from the speeding view since they'd left London some hours ago, heading due north. In the last hour or so, the train had sliced through vast moors, with their deep browns and rich purple hues beneath a steel sky that made Louisa fancy she could hear Cathy shouting for Heathcliff. Even without the view, the names of the stations were enough to tell her that they were in another world: Matlock, Darley Dale, Bakewell.

Until a few weeks ago, this trip had not been in Louisa's plans, but over lunch with Nancy, Louisa had confessed that there were repeated rows with Guy over her insistence on keeping Maisie at home in London instead of sending their daughter to the countryside as an evacuee. As a solution,

7

or so it seemed, Nancy had invited her to Christmas with the Mitfords.

Deborah, said Nancy, keen to cheer everyone up – 'what with Diana languishing in Holloway, Muv and Farve barely on speakers, Decca stuck in America, all our men at the front and her own ghastly sadness with the baby' – had invited the family to her in-laws' house in Derbyshire. Apparently it was large, having been taken over by a school since the war began, but would be empty when the children and teachers went home for the holidays. Nancy said Louisa coming would do her a favour, to be there as someone on her side and keep everyone in check, although Louisa suspected it was a kindness. When she had first known the Mitfords, twenty years before, it had been as their servant; she knew the times had changed but the older stalwarts of the aristocracy, such as Nancy's parents, had not. Her being there as a guest in the drawing room might put the cat among the proud pigeons.

Maisie, now six, sat beside her mother, slowly turning the pages of her book, a Rupert Bear annual, the leaves crinkled from the many times it had been dropped into the bath or survived a spilled glass of milk. Maisie needed the reassuring comfort of the familiar pictures of the bear in his yellow checked trousers, as they hurtled towards somewhere unknown, leaving her father behind. Louisa brushed one of her daughter's dark brown curls behind her ear, and gave her a kiss, earning a brief smile. There was a whistle, followed by the screech of the train brakes and the clouds of steam that billowed outside the window. Louisa took Maisie's hand. 'Here we are,' she said. 'Let's begin our new adventure.'

When Louisa and Maisie disembarked, struggling slightly

with their two cardboard suitcases, hats, gas masks and Maisie's favourite teddy, Fizz, they didn't notice Deborah rushing up to them through the steam. She bent down and gave Maisie a kiss, then took one of the cases from Louisa.

'It's so wonderful to see you both,' she said, practically shouting to be heard over the noise of the other passengers getting on and off the train, soldiers home on leave, sweethearts rushing to greet them.

'It's very kind of you to meet us at the station. I'm sure we could have got a taxi.' Louisa felt suddenly rather formal and shy before this young woman. She had been the age Deborah was now when Deborah had been born, working for the Mitfords as their nursery-maid. There had been so much disappointment that she was a girl and not a boy – longed for after five girls and Tom – that the family had barely looked at her for the first three weeks. She was supposed to be the spare for the heir, Louisa recalled. But now here she was, smiling and chattering away, in the sort of clothes Louisa knew she was most comfortable wearing: a heavy tweed skirt and jacket, sturdy shoes and a felt hat. She looked ready for a long country walk, not a trip to the station.

'I wouldn't have dreamed of putting you in a taxi, and I need to pop into the village on the way back to pick up some bits. You'll see we're camping in the house, really. Everything is topsy-turvy and thick with dust in the rooms the school isn't using, but I'm just so happy that everyone is coming together for Christmas. There are no servants at all, except for some odd bods and a couple of dailies I've scrounged locally. I'm afraid it's all hands on deck,' said Deborah, talking at speed, puffing as she walked them to the car.

Maisie gripped Louisa's hand a little tighter and Louisa squeezed back. 'I'll be happy to help in any way I can,' she said. She marvelled at herself as she said this, but she knew she could confidently offer to help without being reduced to servitude. Louisa and Guy's detective agency, Sullivan & Cannon, was still in operation, in spite of Guy's commitments with the Home Guard. They had had quite a few missing-person cases, brought to them while relatives were understandably reluctant to ask the police to be diverted from war work. And there was always plenty of their bread-and-butter work: following husbands and wives suspected of adultery.

Maisie sat between her mother and Deborah on the front seat, excited gasps coming from her at all the toggles and switches – she hadn't been in a car many times before. This one was a black Bentley with a long bonnet, and Louisa felt pretty smart herself for being in it.

'She's a dear thing,' Deborah remarked, glancing at Maisie, as she smoothly pulled out of the station and onto the road. It was a generous comment. Now they were seated, Louisa could see Deborah's middle was larger than it had been when she had married. It was a sad reminder that the body didn't know what had happened to the baby it had birthed, instead betraying a terrible sadness. Rather than talk about her daughter, Louisa diverted the conversation.

'Where is the nearest village to the house?'

'Well, there's Pilsley, which belongs to the Devonshire estate. The Devonshires are my in-laws. Their surname is Cavendish but their title is Devonshire.' She seemed to wait for Louisa to acknowledge that she understood this arcane corner of aristocracy, forgetting Louisa had had to learn it long ago. 'Pilsley's mostly houses but there's a post office, which is quite handy. You can walk there. And a sweet little pub, the Devonshire Arms. Then there's Baslow, with a decent shop, and it also has Strutts Café, which I'm told does a marvellous ham and eggs. That's only twenty minutes on a bicycle, and there's plenty of those to borrow. But for knicker elastic, shampoo and that sort of thing, we go to Bakewell. It's a drive, not too long, and if you ever need to go there, do say. There'll be someone who can take you.'

'Where are we going now?' asked Maisie, who had her hands up before her, curled into fists at ten to two, mimicking Deborah's on the steering wheel.

'Perhaps you would be so kind as to take us into Baslow, Miss Maisie,' said Deborah. 'You need to turn left just here. Here we go, turn your wheel when I turn mine and we'll get there perfectly.' They giggled and steered in unison.

Baslow village was small and very pretty, with a brick bridge over the river that ran through the middle. After the fear and strangeness of London in the war, with its constant cacophony of ambulances and air-raid sirens, this felt like a Disney cartoon version of England. There were few men to see, which was unsurprising, and none of them in uniform, which was. The women walked rather than hurried, and only a few had a gas-mask box hanging from their shoulder. The buildings were made of pale grey stones, all of them unscathed. Louisa had grown too used to turning into a London street to see houses ripped in half, pictures still hanging from a wall, doors flapping uselessly, floors and ceilings gone. They followed Deborah, walking again at a brisk pace, and went with her into the village shop, Formby & Son painted smartly above the door. Inside, Louisa absent-mindedly looked at the postcards on sale while Maisie went to stare at the labels of the large, empty glass jars neatly lined in rows behind the counter. Their names alone were enough to make the mouth water: Sherbet Lemons; Buttermilk Toffees; Penny Chews; Humbugs. Louisa knew everyone bemoaned the scarcity of meat and eggs, foodstuffs one really needed, but the rationing of sugar sometimes seemed the hardest of all.

The shop was small and Louisa easily overheard Deborah's conversation with a man she presumed was Mr Formby, standing behind the counter and wearing a large brown cotton apron, his hair slicked neatly back. She was asking after his wife.

'She's not in a good way, Lady Andrew,' he said, in the attractive Derbyshire accent that Louisa had started to pick up on. 'She can't help worrying about our Henry. Every day without news from him is a bad day, so far as she's concerned, no matter what I try to tell her.'

Deborah clucked sympathetically. 'Yes, I know my parents worry terribly about my brother.'

'Aye, that's what I tell her. We're all in the same boat.'

'Still,' said Deborah, 'it's your own you fret for. That's only natural.'

Mr Formby flicked his eyes to Maisie. 'Would she like a sweet or two?'

Maisie turned to Louisa – could she? Louisa smiled and nodded her assent.

He tapped the side of his nose and bent briefly beneath the counter, returning with a paper bag. 'Don't tell, eh? It's our secret.'

Maisie regarded him seriously and took the bag. 'Thank you, sir,' she said.

'Where did you come from?'

'London. I came today on the train. With my mummy.'

'Ah,' said Mr Formby, and looked at Louisa. She gave a half-wave.

'And what is it you're doing here?'

The tone was direct, almost sharp. It certainly demanded an answer, which flustered Louisa. Londoners never asked such questions. She answered on her daughter's behalf. 'We're staying with Lady Andrew, for Christmas.'

'Ah, that'll be it, then. I wondered if this one might be one of those evacuees. We've got a few here.'

'No,' said Louisa, firmly, as she walked across to place her hands on her daughter's shoulders. 'We're here together. We'll have to return to London. I work, you see.' She knew it was silly to be defensive of her position but she couldn't help it.

'War work?'

What was this? The Spanish Inquisition?

'Not exactly. My husband is in the Home Guard but we have a private detective agency. I'll have to return to our ongoing cases in the new year.'

Mr Formby drew himself up and raised his eyebrows so high she thought they were going to meet his hairline. 'We don't get many of those around here, I must say.'

Deborah must have caught on to Louisa's discomfort. 'No, I dare say not,' she interrupted. 'But with luck, Mrs Sullivan won't be professionally employed up here. I think our part of the world is rather quieter on that front, don't you?'

'Aye aye, Lady Andrew.' Mr Formby tipped his imaginary cap, and they left him, doubtless wondering who to tell first of this exciting new visitor to the district.

CHAPTER TWO

❧

Louisa thought she had prepared herself for the size of Chatsworth. She hadn't. Deborah was chattering away as they turned off the main road and through a stone archway. At first Louisa assumed they had turned into another road but when she saw there was no other traffic and only vast parklands surrounding them, dotted with grazing sheep, she was forced to realise that they were on the drive. A very long drive. It was some minutes, in fact, before they even saw the house. And when she did Louisa couldn't help herself: she let out a gasp loud enough to make Deborah stop talking.

'It *is* rather daunting, isn't it?' said Deborah. 'I'm awfully glad we won't ever be living there.'

'Why not?' asked Louisa. This house – a word that in itself seemed laughingly incapable of embodying such a vast architectural structure – could surely accommodate any number of the Cavendish family.

'The duke and duchess will live here after the war, whenever the end comes. And then, eventually, it will pass to Billy, as the eldest son. Andrew and I are destined for poverty, I'm afraid. And, honestly, it's a frightful place. No one is sure it will even make it past the war. Everything is falling off, the roof is constantly leaking, there are too many—'

Louisa cut her off. 'I know it's probably full of all those problems, as you say. But it's also beautiful.'

They came closer now, driving over a narrow bridge that crossed a river, but not so close that Louisa couldn't take in the whole impressive view, bathed in a soft light as the sun began to set. Mature trees were dotted elegantly around sloping lawns, and Louisa spied a folly peeping out of the woods. There was what appeared to be a stone railing dotted with enormous carved urns that ran around the top of the house, itself built of bricks the colour of baked pastry. On the façade she saw columns, carvings and other things for which Louisa didn't know the proper terms. The tall windows glinted in the fading day, and the whole impression was of something huge and unyielding, ever present and completely contained. What it didn't look like was a home.

Deborah drove the car around to what Louisa presumed was the back of the house, though it looked no less grand than the side or the front or whatever it was she'd seen. Here were signs of domestic activity: a low wall, a gate that looked as if it might lead to a kitchen garden, a glimpse of a greenhouse, a wheelbarrow full of dead leaves and twigs. Deborah parked the car casually and they got out, fetching their bags and following her through a narrow door.

'I'll show you your rooms later,' said Deborah. 'We'll go to the library now and hope there's some tea for us. We're a little late, so fingers crossed.'

Louisa looked down at Maisie, who had been silently, happily, sucking a humbug for the car journey, and still had the paper bag clutched in one hand. She looked a trifle pale. Louisa held her other hand firmly and whispered that they would be staying together in one room, which seemed to bring some colour back into her cheeks. The only time Maisie had been to such a large interior would have been on their visit to the Natural History Museum.

They walked along the corridors, past rooms with doors tantalisingly ajar, and just as Louisa was beginning to think that if one got one's bearings soon enough, the house wasn't too terrifying in scale, they walked into a room that was, in fact, a museum. Possibly it was the Sistine Chapel. Louisa was in serious danger of believing she was in an H. G. Wells novel and had been magically transported to Rome in a flying car. Ahead of them was a wide staircase that went up to a gallery, the ornate black and gold of the banister circumnavigating the room as a balcony railing. The floor was black and white chequered marble, and a fire blazed in a hearth to the side – which did nothing to prevent the room from feeling freezing cold – and there were columns with marble busts atop. Rather mysteriously, a squat organ sat awkwardly at the bottom of the stairs. But all of this was as nothing, a mere sideshow to the main act, which was a gigantic baroque painting that lined most of one wall from head height to a ceiling that soared above their heads. It was painted with ornate scenes of clouds, swans, angels, naked ladies and men swathed in loose red cloth.

'I've only seen something like that in a book or the National Gallery,' said Louisa. Maisie was looking up too, mouth mid-suck on her thumb.

'It *is* rather extraorder, isn't it?' agreed Deborah. 'They've just mended it. A few years ago it was sagging and on the point of complete collapse. Can you imagine?'

Louisa couldn't.

'This is called the Painted Hall,' Deborah carried on. 'The school has been using it as a chapel, hence the organ. Everything sort of leads off from here so you can find your way around. The library is just up there, on the left.'

She headed for the stairs but before she had taken the first step, they heard a cough. The three turned to see, standing in the middle of the hall behind them, the formidable figure of a tall butler, who had apparently arrived as smoothly and quietly as a swan landing on water.

'Oh, Ellis,' said Deborah, though her voice wavered. 'I'm so sorry, we came in through the back door. I didn't want to disturb you.'

Ellis dipped his chin. 'There is no need for my lady to apologise. I am here to be disturbed.'

'Of course I shan't do it again. This is Mrs Sullivan and her daughter, Maisie.'

'Good afternoon,' said the butler, with a sweeping glance over Louisa that she did not feel was entirely welcoming. He almost certainly knew she used to be a servant and would not approve.

'As you can see, Ellis is the butler. We call him Ellis the Second but not every time. It is rather a mouthful.' She gave a nervous laugh.

'Why are you called Ellis the Second?' asked Maisie.

'My father's elder brother was the first Mr Ellis. He was butler to the duke's household from 1908 to 1929, when I became his most unworthy successor.' Said without a trace of the modesty implied in the statement, thought Louisa. But at least he had answered Maisie's question with a small smile.

'We're going to the library for tea,' said Deborah. 'I believe Lord and Lady Cavendish are due to arrive shortly.'

'We are prepared, my lady. The Wellington Room is ready. As is the Pink Room for Mrs Sullivan and Maisie.'

Deborah thanked him, and the three of them ascended the stairs. When Louisa turned halfway, Ellis the Second had gone but she hadn't heard a single footstep.

CHAPTER THREE

'Don't mind the dust sheets,' explained Deborah, as they walked into the library. 'We'll take them off when everyone's here but for the moment we've got a camp in the middle.'

The room was the length of the hall below and lined with what looked to Louisa like tens of thousands of books, rigid in their leather bindings, on dark-wood shelving stacked so high that a narrow gallery ran around the top, at just the right height below the ceiling for someone to walk along. Thick curtains were drawn the length of the wall opposite, but Louisa could see moth holes as big as her fist on all of them. In the middle of the unidentifiable lumpen shapes draped with white sheets were two dark red sofas, close to the fire, which was glowing a good heat. On one sofa sat Lady Redesdale, and on the other, Unity. Neither of them stood to greet the arrival of Louisa and Maisie.

'Here they are, Muv,' said Deborah, cheerfully.

Unity eyed Louisa balefully. 'Hello, Louisa. I pray to Jesus *every* night. Do you?' she asked.

Louisa, conscious of her daughter beside her, balked at answering but before she had managed to choke out a half-truth, Maisie saved her. 'I do,' she said, as direct in her response as Unity had been in her question, and went to sit beside her. Unity looked surprised but shifted her heavy frame slightly to accommodate the little girl. Before long, they were talking about prayers, seemingly happier not to have to talk to the others.

Lady Redesdale looked similarly grateful, and perhaps it was this that made her give Louisa a smile that could almost have been described as warm, were it not for the exhaustion that pulled the corners of her mouth downwards.

'Yes,' she said. 'Here you both are. I would offer you a cup of tea but I fear it's gone stone cold. And there's no one to answer if I ring for more.' She gave a child's sigh of frustration.

Louisa had almost forgotten the Edwardian diction of her former employer, a voice that prompted a servile response no matter who one was. Even Winston Churchill probably doffed an imaginary cap to Lady Redesdale.

'Ellis would answer,' said Deborah.

Lady Redesdale scoffed. 'Only if he happened to be in the servants' hall at the time one rang. I don't see how anyone can manage in a house this size when there's a war on. I must have been half crazed when you suggested Christmas here.'

For a brief moment, Deborah looked deflated, but she picked up the plate of bread and butter, so thinly spread as to be near-invisible, and handed it to Louisa and Maisie. 'Yes, there's a war on, and we're going to make the best of it.'

Louisa, fairly famished after the long train journey, tried not to grab at the remaining slivers, their corners beginning to curl.

The sandwiches she had packed that morning were inevitably eaten before they reached the outskirts of London. 'Who else is coming?'

'I've done terribly well,' said Deborah, beaming. 'Andrew and I—' She caught a look from her mother and addressed her. 'Muv, Louisa is here with us now and I simply cannot be getting on with long mouthfuls of titles every time we talk about my husband, or our friends.'

Deborah turned back, two pink spots in her cheeks, and Louisa knew it had taken her courage. She was grateful, even if rather uncomfortable at the same time.

'Andrew and I haven't had anything approaching a house party since we married, what with him training and us being so poor. I'd much rather he was here, and we thought he might be, but he got his orders a few days ago.'

She put the plate down, Maisie and Unity having taken some, and Louisa tried not to stare too hard at the one square of bread left.

'Let me see, who's coming? There's Kick Kennedy.'

'*Kick?*' asked Lady Redesdale.

'American,' said Deborah and her mother nodded – a satisfactory explanation. 'She's a terrific girl. We came out together, everyone was mad about her and somehow none of us were jealous. I'm sure she and Andrew's brother will marry, though not without a frightful scene – she's Catholic, you see.'

'Are you sure it's a good idea to ask her, if the duke and duchess are coming?'

'Yes. They can get to know her and they'll have to fall in love with her, too.'

Lady Redesdale looked disbelieving of this but said nothing.

'Then there's Lord and Lady Charles,' Deborah said coyly, catching Louisa's eye.

Louisa gave her a smile in return. She'd read about Lady Charles but hadn't dared to hope she would be at the same house party.

And finally, of course, all of us Mitfords. Or, rather, those of us we can muster, which is only me, Unity and Nancy. Out of seven, it's not the best showing, is it?'

Louisa totted up the absents: Pamela at home with Diana's babies and her Aberdeen Angus herd; Diana in prison; Tom away fighting; Jessica in America with Constancia.

'Lord Redesdale will be here tomorrow,' said Lady R, stiffly.

'Yes. I think Ellis has put him in one of the bedrooms on the north side. I was going to ask—'

But she was interrupted by a gust of air as the library door swung open and in marched Nancy, thinner than ever, her white skin making her look as fragile as bone china. Even so, her presence was no less fulsome than usual.

'What?' said Deborah under her breath. 'She wasn't due to arrive until tomorrow.'

'Nine!' the figure roared, as it advanced the length of the library.

Deborah flinched at her childhood nickname. 'I do wish—'

'You might be an old married woman now, but you'll always be Nine to me,' her sister snapped, before she could protest any further. Nancy went straight to Louisa, arms open. 'Darling Lou, what a treat to see you here. Now we can be absolutely sure of everyone behaving.' Maisie was given a firm kiss on the cheek, as was Unity, before she sat down on the sofa. Nancy hadn't kissed her mother but Lady Redesdale said nothing, merely smoothed her skirts.

'Yes, everyone, I am alive. And here. Did you completely forget?'

'You said you were arriving tomorrow, on the four o'clock.'

'No, it was today. But you are Nine so I'll forgive you. I found a taxi – don't you all start worrying about me. Oh, *no.* I forgot, no one worries about me at all.' She took the last square of bread on the plate. 'Ugh, that's old. But I suppose there's a war on. Is there any tea to be had? Or have I missed it? I say hopefully. I'll move things swiftly on to gin, if you don't mind.'

'Are you sure you should—?' began Lady Redesdale.

'No, Muv, not at all sure but I think it's rather late for you to be asking the question, isn't it?' Nancy turned to Louisa. 'Do you know, the records state that I was "in danger" for three days after the op and not one person from either my family or Prod's telephoned to ask if I was quite well? I rather fancy the in-laws looked up R in the deaths and were disappointed not to see my name there.'

'Don't say such things,' said Deborah. 'I sent you flowers.'

'Yes,' conceded Nancy, patting her knee. 'You did. There is a scrap of kindness for Poor Old Me after all. And now it's nearly Christmas, with love for all. Plenty of it to go around. Pour the gin, will you, dear? We'll begin.'

CHAPTER FOUR

In the middle of the night, Louisa was woken by something soft and flimsy brushing over her face. Startled she sat up and reached to turn on her bedside lamp, only to find it wasn't there. It took her a few seconds to remember she wasn't in her own bed but at Chatsworth, and then she heard Maisie's voice, small and tremulous in the pitch black.

'Mummy?'

'I'm here, little one.' Louisa felt around gently and soon had her arms around the soft body of her daughter, who reached for her and clung tightly. 'What is it?'

'I heard something . . .'

'I'm sure it was nothing.' Louisa wondered what time it was. There wasn't even a hint of light behind the curtains. She had the strange feeling of being wide awake but knowing that if she stayed up now she'd be exhausted by breakfast. She would have to get them both back to sleep.

'I think there were footsteps, and somebody was crying,' Maisie persisted. 'What if it was a ghost?'

'Shush now. There's no such thing as ghosts.'

'Yes, there is!' Louisa could detect the edge of a sob; her daughter would wind herself up into a state if she wasn't careful. 'Everything is so old here, and so big and very dark and . . .'

She could hardly blame Maisie for feeling like this. The walk to the Pink Room, following the stiff back of Ellis the Second, had taken so many confusing turns, going up two separate staircases and along corridors that were unlit because of the need for blackout. Ellis carried a torch before him, which threw alarming shadows. Statues loomed out of the darkness, and the paintings that lined the walls more often than not featured unsmiling people, long dead, their mouths clamped shut. Probably hiding rotten yellow teeth. The cold and the dark had given them both the shivers, and Louisa took the decision that they would unpack and she would get into bed with Maisie at the same time.

Louisa knew her daughter was being brave in the dark but she wondered if she had been foolhardy in accepting Nancy's invitation. There were no bombs, but the stark atmosphere of the enormous house made her feel completely adrift. She reached back, feeling around until she got hold of the lamp, and switched it on. The bed was flooded with a bright light and they blinked, stars in their eyes. 'Look,' said Louisa, her face turning to the empty room. There was the cream-painted wardrobe, in which they had hung their clothes and a hidden bag with Maisie's Christmas presents. In the corner there was a low red armchair, the arms worn bare, and a chest of drawers, with a washbasin and jug on the top. An old-fashioned touch, as there was a bathroom for them to use at the end of the landing. Pale pink curtains, lines of dust showing from the folds, were drawn across the window. The walls were papered with a pattern of pink and green flowers, which matched the green of the quilt on their bed. It showed moth holes but was very thick and soft. They were quite warm under it but the air around them was cold; earlier, Louisa had broken a thin layer of ice in the water jug. She turned the light off again and lay down, holding Maisie even closer. 'You see? There's nothing to worry about, and I'm here.' She kissed her head, smelling her hair.

'I miss Daddy.'

'So do I. But we must go to sleep.'

'What if the bombs are falling on him?' asked Maisie but she was starting to fade back to her dreams and Louisa left the question unanswered. She didn't know, was the truth, and she prayed over and over that Guy was safe, at home in their bed.

CHAPTER FIVE

⸎

O ver the next two days, the women in the house busied themselves to prepare for the arrival of the rest of the guests. Louisa didn't mind. Everyone was doing something to help – it felt like part of the war effort. There was Ellis to direct them, and Mrs Airlie, the cook, kept up their energy with thick vegetable soups and home-made bread. Louisa suspected the meat and egg rations were being saved for when the grander elements of the house party arrived and the date was closer to Christmas.

Tasks were divided. Nancy was put in charge of the finishing touches to the bedrooms. She won this job after she discovered the linen cupboard – 'Always my favourite place in a house' – and gathered huge piles of stiff, dusty sheets and pillowcases to be sent to a laundress in Baslow to be washed and pressed. In the meantime, she set about finding pretty bedspreads and moving pictures around to make a room more stylish. Louisa went to the room Nancy had spruced for Kick Kennedy and admired her knack: the space was bright and airy, with a pretty water jug and glass by the bed, a gleaming mirror on the dressing-table and a pile of novels on the window seat, beside plumped cushions.

'No cut flowers, which she won't understand,' said Nancy, 'but I'm afraid it's simply not done in the country at this time of year.'

Louisa didn't question this. She'd long learned that Nancy kept a list of things that were 'done' and 'not done', which followed no logical line of reasoning that she'd ever managed to discern. A 'sofa' was allowed; a 'settee' was not. The family ate dinner in the evening, never in the middle of the day (that was 'luncheon'). And from the way Lord Redesdale once reacted, you could believe that pouring the milk in before the tea was a crime punishable with a prison sentence. The awful thing was, it was contagious – once learned, it couldn't be forgotten, and Louisa would find herself adjusting her words according to whatever company she was in, which made her despise herself a little.

Deborah was rushing about in the manner of a headless chicken, not like her at all, but she took her lead from Ellis when all else failed. The difficulty was the chasm that lay between 'the way things have always been done here' – whether from the pull of nostalgia or normality – and the fact that there was a war on. There were no maids, only two girls coming in daily from the nearest village for the house party, but they didn't know their way around, and were often more hindrance than help. Simply trying to light enough fires to keep the rooms warm was a job that took up most of the morning. Mrs Airlie had to co-ordinate the different ration cards to get what she could, and little could be done until the rest of the guests gave her theirs. Unity had to be given a new task every half-hour because she would so quickly tire of what she was doing, yet insisted on helping. Lady Redesdale looked faint at every suggestion for a job, until Louisa whispered to Deborah that perhaps she could plan the place-ment settings, which worked very successfully.

Louisa found herself almost by default in charge of the daily maids when they weren't in the kitchen, setting them to work on the dusting, putting sheets on the beds, sweeping the bedrooms, the library (which had had the dust sheets removed), and a small sitting room, which had been found on the first floor in the private quarters. Lord Redesdale would be installed there, said Deborah, out of harm's way. There were shouts of delight when a room was discovered filled with boxes of Christmas decorations. Most were ancient, in danger of falling apart on touch, but there were charming brass candlesticks decorated with angels, and tangles of green silk leaves with berries that could be artfully draped on mirrors and pictures. Maisie was put to sorting out the boxes and was soon surrounded by painted wooden Father Christmases, piles of red and gold ribbon to tie into bows on the stairs, and boxes with tissue spilling out, protecting beauti-ful glass baubles. 'There's bound to be a tree on the estate that can be cut down for the hall,' said Deborah. 'I've been told they used to have them reaching all the way up to the ceiling.' Louisa thought Maisie might pass out with the promise of it.

The revelation of such a large house was that people kept randomly appearing, usually with some sort of threatening implement in their hand: a cooking knife, secateurs or a brass letter opener. She couldn't remember all their names – not everyone was introduced – but identified them in other ways, such as the gardener who popped up behind a large plant pot in the orangery wearing a flat cap, and another whom Maisie mistook for a scarecrow because he was seemingly never out of the vegetable patch. There was also a teacher, Mademoiselle

Dupont, seemingly left behind for the Christmas holidays. Louisa came across her in the footman's waiting room. She'd been looking for a place for Maisie to sit and read quietly that wasn't too formidable – or cold. Mademoiselle Dupont, cutting some cloth with a large pair of scissors, seemed delighted to meet them both.

'I'm a little lonely now the girls and other teachers have gone home. You see, I am not able to return to my own family for the *vacances*. We shall amuse each other, yes?' she said to Maisie, in her charming accent. She looked quite young, in her mid-twenties, and wore an emerald green silk scarf knotted around her throat, her blonde hair pinned up in a chignon. Having introduced herself to Maisie, Mademoiselle Dupont turned shyly to Louisa. 'Is it true you are a detective, madame?'

'Yes,' said Louisa, 'a private detective. I'm not in the police. And, please, call me Louisa. Madame makes me feel far too old.'

'That you are not,' the teacher replied. 'And you must please call me Lucie. You have just arrived?'

'Yes. We're finding our bearings, if not very successfully.'

Lucie laughed. 'It is *énorme*, this house. I am told nearly two hundred rooms.'

Maisie's eyes widened comically. 'What do they do with all those rooms?'

'I think they are mostly empty,' said Lucie. 'I explore sometimes. You can come with me and I'll show you what I know. Perhaps we will discover a secret or two.'

CHAPTER SIX

L ucie began by taking them around the servants' workrooms, which occupied the entire basement. Most lay in a dusty silence, clearly untouched for some time.

'Not just because of the war,' Lucie told them. 'The old duke, who died a few years ago, had a stroke in 1925 so there was nobody to take decisions. The estate lost money. The cook, she told me that the dowager ordered them to make nettle soup to save pennies.' She wrinkled her nose. 'The new duke has not lived here yet, because of the war, and so many of the servants have left to fight or do war work. And who knows when this war will end and how life will return afterwards? Can you imagine them using this room again?' She opened the door to a small windowless room, in which stood nothing but an ironing board.

'How strange. Do they not iron their clothes any more?' asked Louisa.

'Oh, yes, but this room was used to iron newspapers. Nothing else.'

'Why would they iron the newspaper?' This was Maisie's question but Louisa wanted to know, too.

'To dry the ink,' answered Lucie.

'How do you know all this?'

'From Mrs Airlie and Mr Ellis. They have been here a long time, and I find them interesting. This eccentric English way of life is most *amusant*.' She chuckled. 'I am collecting the stories to take home.'

Louisa couldn't disagree.

She remembered her own sense of wonder and awe when she had arrived as a young girl at Asthall Manor, where the Mitfords used to live when she first worked for them. Back then, that house had seemed grand to her, alien in its stiff, traditional ways, yet it was probably a twentieth of the size of Chatsworth.

As they navigated their way, making eventual sense of the corridors, Lucie showed them some of the rooms that had been converted for use by the schoolgirls. The butler's pantry was now a physics lab. Next door to that was the strong room, which allegedly held an Egyptian tomb's worth of gold and silver plate. When needed, Mr Ellis could generally be found in there, Lucie said, his sleeves rolled up as he polished away at the Sisyphean task.

Louisa looked at her watch and realised they had been wandering the basement for almost two hours. 'I'd better get back upstairs,' she said, 'I was only going to settle Maisie and then return to help. It's been such a pleasure to meet you, and thank you for the tour. I can't imagine finding my way around it all.'

'Oh, it's not so bad. It only took me about a month,' Lucie

deadpanned. They both started laughing and made a plan to meet up later for a walk around the garden to collect more holly and ivy to decorate the library and dining room.

Back above stairs, after Louisa and Maisie had found their way – somehow – to the Painted Hall, they were spotted by Nancy, who was carrying a large brown-paper package. 'There you are!' she called.

'Sorry,' said Louisa, 'we got distracted below stairs. We met a French teacher and—'

'Follow me.' Nancy's back was turned, but she had barely gone up two steps before there was an almighty clatter – a dog barking furiously, heavy doors opening, and shouting inside and out. 'What the hell?'

Nancy dashed down the side of the hall towards the front door, Louisa and Maisie behind her, unable to resist looking at whatever spectacle might lie ahead.

The scene that greeted them was quite unlike anything Louisa had seen before. There was Ellis, flustered as he tried simultaneously to hold open the door, announce the guests and prevent them from carrying their own luggage. The guests, in turn, varied in their response to his attempts at buttling. There was an elderly woman dressed entirely in stiff Edwardian black, who could be heard saying plaintively, 'One does miss the footmen,' as she stared at the luggage. The barking – *yapping* – dog was a Pekinese, as black as the ostrich feathers in its mistress's hat, with a face that looked as if it had run smack into a wall. It was presently halfway up Ellis's left leg. Deborah appeared to be trying to appease the old woman, whom she greeted as 'Granny Evie', but was also very distracted and excited by the arrival of a fresh-faced girl, who was shouting gaily in an American accent about how terribly thrilled she was to be there. Louisa liked her instantly. The old woman, however, looked as if she did not. Nancy piled into this scene and eventually, somehow, as if herding kittens, nudged everyone up the stairs to the library, leaving Ellis, red-faced and sweating, to bring in the bags and close the door.

The new arrivals, including the flat-faced dog, convened in the library, which had a modicum of heat now that the fire had been lit for three days in a row, as well as having regained its elegance with the furniture revealed, the tables polished, the mirrors shining. The old woman made her way to the fireplace, the Peke trotting beside her, jumping skilfully out of the way of the umbrella she used as a walking stick. When they were assembled, Deborah made the introductions.

'The Dowager Duchess of Devonshire,' she said, with a sweeping look to the rest of the party.

Louisa felt caught out – was she supposed to curtsy to a dowager duchess? She looked across to Nancy, who was doing nothing of the sort.

'Duchess,' said Nancy. 'How do you do?'

The dowager merely gave a half-smile at this greeting.

'May I introduce my sister, Nancy, Mrs Rodd?' continued Deborah, gamely keeping up her role as host. A tough call when this house had previously belonged to the dowager, who even now appeared to be judging the state of the mantelpiece, covered with holly, and finding it wanting.

'This is Miss Kathleen Kennedy, but we all call her Kick.'

Kick stepped forward but knew enough not to put out her hand. 'Delighted, Duchess,' she said, with a wide, toothy smile.

You couldn't say she was conventionally pretty but there was something undeniably warm and attractive about her. 'Wasn't it funny that we both arrived at the exact same time?'

The dowager gave a smile that didn't indicate she found the same level of humour in the circumstances.

'And this is Louisa, Mrs Sullivan, and her daughter Maisie,' finished Deborah, with a visible sigh of relief. Louisa decided to say nothing but smiled as warmly as she could. She probably looked half mad.

Maisie looked up at the dowager. 'May I stroke your dog?'

The dowager regarded Maisie for a moment. 'She'll probably bite, but you may try,' she replied, in a voice Louisa hadn't heard since before the last war, grander even than Lady Redesdale's.

Maisie bent cautiously, extending both hands, palms down, as Guy had taught her to do when they met dogs in the park. The Peke stepped towards her, sniffing. Everyone held their breath. Maisie remained completely still, making low clicking sounds, until the Peke began to lick her hands. Before they knew it, Maisie had the dog on her lap, preening as she stroked it.

'Well,' said the dowager, 'I've never seen that before. You must have a way with you.' She sat down on the sofa, or perched rather, and held her umbrella upright to her side, appearing to wait, although Louisa couldn't see what she was waiting for exactly.

Nancy rallied. 'Somehow, our mother seems to have missed this grand arrival. I shall fetch her and we'll proceed to luncheon.' She gave Deborah a look that seemed to say, *I'll arrange things.* Deborah smiled gratefully.

Louisa thought about Lucie, how kind she had been, and was

happy to watch her daughter playing with the dog in front of the vast fireplace, the dowager looking on. It was far removed from her own domestic scenes but she felt assured she could only look forward to the peaceful weeks that lay before them.

CHAPTER SEVEN

In the afternoon, Louisa and Maisie walked into Pilsley, the hamlet on the edge of the estate, to post a letter to Guy and breathe in great lungfuls of the bright, nippy air. She was a Londoner, born and bred, but the sight of a country landscape in winter always brought Louisa waves of hope for the future. It had been in the coldest months that she had first arrived at Asthall Manor so many years ago, the first time she saw mist rolling over a river and spiders' webs covered with frost in the morning, not to mention the first time she had felt free of her uncle Stephen and a life that had promised little but poverty or crime. Now she could see Maisie take in this fresh beauty, too, and, apart from the gas masks slung around their shoulders, they could forget the war was even happening. Which made it something of a shock when the two of them returned at dusk to the drawing room to find a particular visitor. Unity came over, dragging them to the sofa by the arm.

'Come and meet Group Captain Nesbit,' she said, breathless with excitement. The man in question, tall and white-blond, impeccably dressed in a blue RAF uniform, stood quickly, his hand outstretched. Louisa thought she detected a hint of relief in his face from the interruption that their arrival had brought. There was an empty space beside him on the sofa, which was presumably where Unity had been sitting. Lady Redesdale was on the other side, while opposite sat the duchess and Deborah. Kick was in an armchair at the side, watching with clear amusement, as if she was in the front row at the cinema. It was quite a formidable gathering.

'Is there any tea?' asked Nancy. 'I'm quite famished from a freezing walk around the gardens. I'm sure Group Captain Nesbit would appreciate it, too.'

'We're not being inhospitable,' said Deborah. 'Ellis is bringing some up shortly.'

'Good,' said Nancy, shaking the captain's hand before sitting between her youngest sister and the duchess. Whatever conversation had been going on before they had appeared had stopped. By arriving late, Nancy dominated the proceedings and nobody seemed keen to challenge this. 'So tell me, Group Captain Nesbit, what brings you here?'

'I'm stationed at Harpur Hill,' he said, in a voice that was attractively deep.

'It's near here,' said Unity, whose childish glee had not abated. 'Less than an hour by car. Do you think we can go there?'

Nancy gave her a silencing look, then waved a hand, urging him to continue.

'It's a courtesy visit,' he said. 'We're aware the school is stationed here for now, and I have visited them in the past, ensuring the blackout has been observed and so on. I thought I'd make myself known while the headmistress was away.

Occasionally we need to forewarn of a training exercise, so as not to alarm anyone.'

'The entire war is alarming,' said Nancy, crossing her legs and leaning forward slightly.

Nesbit gave a half-smile. 'Quite so.'

Ellis came in with the tea, followed by one of the kitchen-maids carrying a second tray. She had kindly played with Maisie earlier, and Louisa asked her now if she might take Maisie downstairs with her. It was easier for her daughter not to suffer the formality of the drawing room for too long.

'Are you married?' asked Unity, suddenly.

He probably knew Unity's story but it must have been unsettling to be asked such a direct question by a female who had the body of a woman, but not the manners.

'Yes, I am,' he replied, politely. 'Although, of course, Mrs Nesbit and I are kept apart for many months at a time.'

'Your wife can't live on the base?' asked Kick.

'Not during wartime,' said Nesbit. 'We have young children.'

Everyone nodded sympathetically.

'Are there any exercises we should be forewarned about?' asked Nancy, as Ellis handed out the cups of tea. The maid had left with Maisie already.

'No, thankfully not. Things are relatively quiet for us at the moment. That is, for me. I'm not a very good pilot, I'm afraid, so I'm mostly remaindered on the ground, keeping the base in order.'

'Have many of your pilots died?' asked Unity, and before anyone could stop her, she went on, as thoughtlessly as an apple rolling down a hill, 'Decca's husband is dead. He was a pilot and he crashed into the sea. Completely dead.'

'I think that's enough,' said Lady Redesdale. Her grey complexion had tinged with colour. 'Come with me. Time for you to have a rest.'

Unity knew better than to cause a scene with so many people around, but the fury was clear on her face. She stood and followed her mother, leaving the rest cowed into silence. At the door Unity stopped. 'Group Captain, sir, I mean, could one come and visit? I'd so love to see the base. I've never seen a base, or an aeroplane up close.'

'Really, miss—' began Nancy, but Nesbit interrupted.

'I don't really see why not,' he said. 'Perhaps not all of you at once. But I'm sure something could be arranged.' He gave a winning smile, and Louisa knew Unity would believe it was just for her.

Everyone's cups of tea were finished. There had been no offer of cake or even bread and butter. Louisa knew she was being treated very well in the house, as well as anyone else, but there was an almost constant low-level gnawing of hunger in this war. The certain knowledge that you couldn't indulge whenever you felt peckish, and that treats were to be saved for the children. She wasn't resentful of it, but that didn't mean she avoided the feeling of hollowness in her stomach. Without the sipping of tea to distract, the lull in the conversation was more of a ringing silence.

'I wonder if I might do a blackout check on the house,' said Nesbit. 'I know you'll do one every night but it's just for reassurance.'

'My father, Lord Redesdale, does a nightly check,' said Deborah.

'I'll accompany you,' said Nancy. 'Show you the way. Mrs Sullivan will join us, too.'

Louisa looked at Nancy questioningly – why would she join them? But there didn't seem much point in contradicting her, and Maisie would be perfectly content downstairs.

Group Captain Nesbit made his farewells, brief and polite, then followed Nancy and Louisa down the stairs to the Painted Hall. He stopped on the last step. 'My goodness,' he said, taking in the huge Roman paintings and ornate ceiling. 'I had no idea this was here.'

'No,' said Nancy, haughtily, as if it belonged to her. 'It's a funny thing. You stop seeing it after a while. Now, we'll go through here – there should be a torch on the table by the door.'

They had left their coats by the door from their earlier walk, but when they stepped outside it was clear the temperature had fallen as quickly as the darkness. Nesbit looked decently swathed in his RAF greatcoat and there was no doubting he cut a striking figure, tall and slim with broad shoulders. Louisa noticed Nancy watching him as they strode out from the front door. Outside, with no light coming from the windows and no moon, it was almost pitch black, only the merest hint of a lighter navy above the trees. They set off to walk the perimeter of the house, their feet crunching on the gravel. Nesbit asked questions about the household – who was staying, who the staff were, right down to the gardeners. It seemed to Louisa a touch on the intrusive side.

'You seem to have quite the house party planned,' he said.

'It was my sister's idea,' explained Nancy. 'Something to cheer everyone up.'

'Why did they need cheering?'

'Well, the war,' said Nancy. 'Among other things.' She fell into a rueful silence. They had reached the furthest end of the house now, near the orangery.

41

'It all looks to be in good order,' said Nesbit. 'Not a slice of light showing.'

'A slice of light!' laughed Nancy. 'You are a hoot.'

'I know it seems rather over-cautious but we don't believe we can be too careful. At best, Chatsworth could help German planes get their bearings. At worst, it would be a target.'

'You don't believe the story, then?' said Nancy.

'What story?'

'That Hitler has his eye on the grandest houses for himself and his top-ranking officials. Blenheim for him, perhaps Chatsworth for Göring. It's said to be the reason they haven't been bombed so far.'

'The war isn't over yet,' said Nesbit, seriously. 'But perhaps my visit is. I had better start making tracks back to base.'

'No, stay for supper,' said Nancy. 'We can't promise much in the way of culinary delight, I'm afraid, but there is good company on offer.'

Nesbit laughed. 'I'm sure your cook will produce something more delicious than anything I could get in the mess. And the company is certainly better.' He gave a small bow and Nancy took him by the arm, leading him back inside.

CHAPTER EIGHT

A t a few minutes past eight, with Maisie tucked up in bed,
and herself dressed in her second-best evening frock,
Louisa pushed open the door of the library. She could hear
the low murmur of people talking, and felt her throat constrict.
Nancy had noticed Louisa's nerves earlier but failed to quash
them with her brisk remark that this was 'only an ordinary house
party'. It was the first event of its kind that Louisa had attended as
a guest, and she wondered why Nancy had asked her. There was
no chance that Lord and Lady Redesdale, to say nothing of the
dowager duchess, were delighted to have a former maid sitting
alongside them at the dining table. It might be 1941 but they
were firmly stuck in their Edwardian past. She consoled herself
that Kick Kennedy might be more welcoming, and Deborah had
said to Louisa that she would ask Lucie Dupont to join them.

As she walked through the room, Louisa took in the scene.
The weather had turned earlier – the trees had bent in the wind
while the rain pelted against her window as she changed in her
room – but in here the outside world was banished by thick

velvet curtains. There was Group Captain Nesbit, sitting with Lady Redesdale and Unity on a sofa towards the back of the room, the three of them talking quietly. Deborah was standing by the fire with Kick, each holding a glass of champagne. Nancy was with her father, who must have arrived in the afternoon, and though he looked as shockingly tired and old as he had at Deborah's wedding, Nancy was making him laugh. The dowager was nowhere to be seen, and Louisa was rather relieved.

Deborah waved her over. 'Here,' she said, handing Louisa a glass.

'Thank you.' Louisa took a sip, the bubbles fizzing at the back of her throat.

Deborah looked very pretty, so young and clearly pleased to be in the company of her friend. Kick was wearing a simply cut but expensive-looking navy dress, with wide shoulders and a narrow belt on her small waist, the skirt flaring out below.

'We're very excited about Lady Charles,' said Kick, with a charming manner, as if she and Deborah had been waiting for Louisa to join them.

'Is she the one who–?'

'Yes! Adele Astaire, sister of Fred. They say she gave up a glittering career to marry Charles.'

'Who is Charles exactly?' asked Louisa.

'He's Andrew and Billy's uncle. He lives in Ireland, at Lismore Castle. He's the duke's younger brother. Technically he's Lord Charles.'

'Yes, she's marvellous by all accounts,' said Deborah. 'When she was first introduced to the dowager and the late duke, apparently her name was announced and then she did cartwheels across the floor. They've been in love with her ever since.'

'Even though she's American,' said Kick.

'Oh, Kick, the duke and duchess are going to love you, too.'

'In fairness, it's not that I'm American they hate, though I'm sure they don't love it,' said Kick. 'It's that I'm Catholic. And it's not as if my parents are any easier on Billy.'

'Which is why you're here now. To lobby for favours. I know you will.' Deborah turned to a sound at the door. 'Speak of the devil,' she whispered, and walked towards the two couples now coming in. Louisa recognised the Duke and Duchess of Devonshire, Deborah's in-laws, from the wedding. They were a handsome couple, in their mid-forties, the duchess wearing a rather heavy dress with a tatty fur trim at collar and cuffs. The duke had a cigarette clamped between his lips, the smouldering end dangerously close to the tips of his handlebar moustache. But their aristocratic grandeur faded to nothing when Lady Charles came into the room.

Louisa immediately saw her resemblance to her famous brother, Fred – something in those high, arched eyebrows and small mouths made them look like marionettes. Adele Astaire – Louisa could thereafter never think of her as the dry 'Lady Charles' – had dark brown hair that fell to her shoulders and was fashionably curled under, perfectly painted red lips and nails, and wore a glittering dress that looked as if it had sashayed directly from a designer's *atelier* onto her slender frame. She had the height of a ballet dancer yet walked into the room as if she were commanding the stage at the London Palladium. Probably she had, many times. Behind her, her husband, Charles, was a great deal taller, yet slouched slightly. He headed straight for the drinks trolley and poured himself a large whisky before he said hello to anyone. Ellis, whom Louisa had not noticed in the room before now, reached Charles a moment too late. She caught the butler withdrawing from the trolley with a dip of the head, as if humiliated.

There was a round of introductions, and how-do-you-dos, and then the dowager arrived, aided by Lucie. Louisa met Lucie's eyes, feeling bolstered by an ally in the room, although there were now enough people for her to feel that the attention need not be on her at all. In fact, there was a real party atmosphere, which she hadn't experienced for some time, certainly not since the start of the war. It felt both unfamiliar and reassuring, with the noise, the sloshing of drinks, the warmth from the fire and the gathering of the bodies.

'Who is that handsome man?' said Lucie to Louisa, one perfectly plucked eyebrow raised.

'He's stationed at the RAF base near here.'

'It's quite some time since I saw a man less than thirty years older than me,' Lucie whispered, and there was no doubt at the mischief in her voice. Louisa gave her a small smile and took another sip of champagne. She had better tell Lucie he was married or there would be trouble.

As she thought this, there was a change in the atmosphere, a lull or a silence that had fallen, and Kick was running to the door, shouting, '*Billy!* Is it really you?'

In the doorway stood a tall officer in uniform with a wide, foolish grin on his face that was quickly covered by Kick, whom he scooped easily into his arms for a long, impassioned kiss. Everyone watched, unable to stop themselves, until the dowager said, as loud and clear as the chime of a grandfather clock: 'Somebody's at the door.'

There was a roar of laughter as Billy put Kick down. 'Yes!' about three people shouted. 'Billy's at the door!'

'No,' said the dowager, thumping her umbrella on the wooden floor and startling her Peke. '*Listen.*'

Nobody had heard it before – except the old lady – but now it was unmistakable. A *thump, thump* at the front door, muffled by the stairs and walls between it and the library, but definite nonetheless.

'Well, Ellis, aren't you going to see who it is?'

Jolted, Ellis left the library as fast as his butler's ways would allow him, to discover who the unexpected visitor might be.

CHAPTER NINE

Louisa and Lucie managed to edge their way closer to each other, until they were on the periphery of the circle by the fire that included the duke and duchess, happy to see their son, Billy, home and safe. Kick was beside herself with glee. Adele was watching them with wry amusement as she chatted to the dowager, while her husband, Charles, poured everyone more drinks in the butler's absence. Lord Redesdale and Nancy were still gossiping together, now with Nesbit. Lady Redesdale and Unity were studying a jigsaw puzzle that had been set up in the corner. So engrossed was everyone that they quite forgot Ellis had gone downstairs to see who was at the door, or perhaps they had already decided it wouldn't be anyone important. It was quite a shock, therefore, when there was a brief power cut – the lights flickered and went out for two or three seconds – and when they came back on, an old hag was standing in the door, water dripping from her sopping coat onto the rug. Only the clap of thunder and flash of lightning were absent. Ellis rushed to Deborah's side, talking in an urgent whisper.

'Apologies, m'lady, I don't know how she got up here—'

Before he could get any further, there was a crash behind Louisa. They all turned to see that Charles had dropped the bottle of champagne. His face was pale, his jaw slack.

'Darling, what is it?' His wife was quick to his side. He said nothing but bent down, shaking, to pick up smashed pieces. Ellis, caught between two calls on his duty, hesitated.

'Please help Charles,' instructed Nancy, who had walked past Deborah, fatally hesitant herself.

Nobody else quite managed to resume conversation.

'Good evening, Mrs ...?' Nancy approached the hag, who remained as wet and unappealing as she had on arrival.

'Mrs Hoole,' she replied, in the local accent. 'I do beg your pardon to disturb but I have a message.'

'You're so kind, Mrs Hoole,' said Nancy, laying on the charm as thickly as royal icing. 'But, as you can see, we're all about to go in to dinner. It *is* rather late to be turning up, and frightful weather. How did you get here?'

'Aah,' breathed Mrs Hoole, loudly. 'I walked. It's a long, long way. May I?' Before she could be stopped, she had staggered to an armchair, and plopped down, without removing her coat. Louisa thought of the water soaking through the upholstery into the horsehair stuffing and metal springs.

'A car went past me on the drive. It didn't stop,' Mrs Hoole said accusingly.

Billy spoke, blushing: 'That was probably me. I'm very sorry. I was anxious to arrive in time for the dinner and was rushing. I didn't see you.' He took Kick's hand. 'I'd made the arrangement with Debo. I didn't want anything to go wrong.'

Kick slapped Deborah's arm playfully. 'I can't believe you kept

49

that a secret from me!' Deborah grinned, but Louisa thought she saw a flicker of sadness, too. She must have hoped Andrew would be arriving with his brother.

Mrs Hoole coughed, bringing the attention back to her. 'Perhaps I might have a drink? To warm the cockles.'

'Yes, of course,' said Nancy, evenly. 'Ellis, could you bring Mrs Hoole some brandy? Given that we have been unable to welcome her in the kitchen, where she might have warmed up.'

Her meaning was not lost on the butler. He blushed, and stillness dropped over the room, broken only by his shuffling and clinking as he fetched the drink and gave it to Mrs Hoole. She drank it in one, wiping her mouth with the back of her hand. Steam began to rise from her coat.

'As I say—' Nancy was cut off by an imperious wave of Mrs Hoole's hand.

'I have an important message for Lady Andrew.'

'That's me,' said Deborah, stepping forward.

Mrs Hoole looked her up and down. 'Is it?'

'Yes, I'm fairly sure it is.' Deborah gave a smile to the others in the room, as if she was in a skit.

Louisa felt a ripple move through everyone. Mrs Hoole had started as an oddity, become a nuisance and was now turning into an amusing story.

'From whom is this message?' That was the dowager, who had pushed through to the front of the circle that had formed around Mrs Hoole, her umbrella smartly moving them aside. 'Where are you from? I must say, this is all most unconventional.'

'There's a war on,' said three or four people, and everyone laughed. That explained everything from food shortages to delayed trains and strange women turning up soaking wet in the middle of the evening.

'I'm from the village,' said Mrs Hoole.

'Well, I've never heard of you. And I know everyone in the village.'

Mrs Hoole looked affronted. 'I was born there.' Judging from her wrinkles and grey hair, this had been a good number of years ago. 'Not Pilsley. Baslow.'

'Oh,' said the dowager. 'Well, go on. The message?'

'I can't say as it's *from* exactly,' Mrs Hoole started, with a sweeping look at all the faces around her – it was like watching an actress on the stage. Even Adele seemed transfixed. Charles had recovered the colour in his face. 'I receive messages . . .' She fluttered her fingers in front of her face.

'I'm sorry,' said Deborah. 'I don't know what that means.'

'Messages,' said Mrs Hoole, impatiently. 'They come to me. *Through* me, like.'

'I see,' said Deborah, although she clearly didn't. There was a stifled giggle that Louisa was surprised to realise came from the duchess.

'The message for you is: look in the vestibule.'

'*Vestibule?*'

'Yes,' said Mrs Hoole. 'In the vestibule. You must look there.'

'I don't know what a vestibule is.'

'That is the message,' insisted Mrs Hoole.

'What's in there?'

'I don't know.' Mrs Hoole held out her glass. 'More brandy, please.'

Nancy took the glass and gave it to Ellis. 'Isn't it funny,' she said, 'how messages from the other side never reveal the meaning of life, but are instead about how to find the missing egg cups in the cupboard under the stairs? Or in the vestibule.' This was too much, and there were splutters as everyone finally released the laughter that had been building.

Mrs Hoole stood up. 'You may all laugh. But I suggest you do as they say.'

'But who are "they"?' demanded Nancy.

Mrs Hoole was unmoved. 'The message was clear. That's all I'm saying.' She turned to Ellis. 'I think I'd better go down to the kitchen now.'

At their exit, Nancy turned to the room, a touch of the ring-master in her manner. 'Come on, then. Let's find the vestibule.'

CHAPTER TEN

N ow Mrs Hoole was safely out of earshot, the party broke out in a babble of questions and exclamations.

'That was the most extraordinary thing I've ever heard,' said Kick. 'And when I tell you my sister's in the madhouse, you'll understand I've heard some pretty wild things in my time.'

Billy gave her a worried look. 'Don't say things like that in front of my parents.'

Kick clamped her hand theatrically to her mouth. 'Sorry. Everyone else in the family is normal, I promise,' she whispered.

Unity was taken off by Lady Redesdale, when it looked as if hysterics might threaten. Lord Redesdale remained sitting on the sofa beside the dowager, the two talking quietly to each other, studiously avoiding the hullabaloo. Someone needed to take charge, and perhaps it was just as well that Nancy was the one to grab the mantle.

Louisa felt sorry for Deborah. It had, after all, been her idea to bring this party together, in a house that was not hers and never would be. Full realisation of the responsibility Deborah had brought on her own head was only now dawning on Louisa. Kick couldn't behave like a chatelaine when Billy had yet to propose, while Billy was a returning soldier on leave: he simply wanted to relax. The dowager couldn't make any decisions around the house because her husband had died and it no longer belonged to her. That left her son, the duke, and his wife, the duchess, but they had owned the house for just a few months since the previous duke's death when war was declared. Nor did it seem as if they were in any hurry to reclaim their stake. Neither seemed urgent about anything. The duke puffed languidly on his Turkish cigarettes, and the duchess sipped her champagne, staring into the middle distance. At any rate, they didn't look as if they could be called upon to make any urgent decisions regarding the house party, Christmas or Mrs Hoole.

Louisa poured a small brandy and took it to Deborah, standing momentarily alone beside the fire.

'Oh, thank you, Lou-Lou,' she said. 'Lou-Lou' was Nancy's pet name for Louisa, but the sisters used it when they were in childlike mode, as if wanting her to be their nursery-maid again. 'I'm just pulling myself together. We need to go in to supper, or Mrs Airlie will start spitting into the food.'

'I wondered if there was a plan for the house anywhere,' said Louisa. Her earlier tour with Lucie had been only below stairs, and not exhaustive, but she was certain they had not come across any 'vestibule'.

'I'm sure there must be. The duke will know. Why?'

'Because if there's a vestibule – it's a type of room, isn't it? – it might be marked on it.'

Deborah's face lit up. She went over to the duke, and he, unhurried, took her to a shelf and pulled down a large book.

She beckoned to Louisa. The lights in the library were not very bright, and the plans were old, made on thin paper, with thick black ink for the lines and blurry type for the numbers and room descriptions. Each floor plan was on a separate sheet, and the papers did not appear to be in order. Some of the plans looked to be a great deal older than others. Charles and the dowager wandered over, and soon they were all poring over the pages, the Cavendishes remarking on rooms that had changed name, or exclaiming over mistakes. Louisa thought of her own two-up, two-down home in London – a hundred of it would fit into this sprawling structure. (And how was Guy, alone? He'd be rattling around without her and Maisie.) West wing, state bedchamber, state closet, south sketch gallery, oak room, chapel, great dining room, great east library. They sounded like counties, not rooms.

'Vestibule!'

'Where? Where?'

Deborah pointed triumphantly. 'In the north wing. It's called the west staircase on another plan, but vestibule here.'

They all looked at the diagram on the page to which she was pointing. It showed a narrow space between two larger rooms, an ante-room of sorts, with staircases marked.

By this time, the rest of the party had gathered to look, too.

While their heads were bent, there was a cough from Ellis in the doorway. 'Beg pardon, but dinner is served.' He looked mutinous.

'Mrs Airlie will be having a fit,' said the dowager. 'What's the first course? I hope it's not a soufflé.'

'It's soup,' said Deborah. 'It will keep.'

'Probably for four days,' quipped Nancy. 'I think we should go and look at the vestibule while Mrs Hoole is still here. It's right next to the dining room – it won't take a moment.'

A fizz of energy ran through them and as one, including Lord Redesdale and the dowager, they headed along the hall, through the ante-library and the dome room, into the great dining room – now a dormitory for the schoolgirls, iron bedsteads and striped mattresses – and into the vestibule. It wasn't a large space, but they all crammed in.

'It's like playing Sardines,' said Adele, happily.

At that, Louisa saw Nesbit notice Adele and react; he must have realised belatedly who she was.

Everyone peered around but there wasn't much to look at. The space was effectively divided into three parts: two nooks to left and right, either side of the corridor between the great dining room and the sculpture gallery. On the right, a staircase led upwards, presumably to bedrooms; a tiny gallery overlooked it.

'It goes to the music gallery,' said the duke, as he relit his cigarette with a taper long enough to be a dressing-gown cord.

On the left there were cupboards, elegantly designed but cupboards nonetheless.

'What is this for?' asked Adele.

'The hot plates and dinner service are kept in here,' said the duke, 'not that it works. The kitchen is so far from the dining room that everything is cold and congealed by the time it arrives. I'm going to install an electric railway so that the food can reach us hot instead of tepid.'

Louisa looked to Deborah – 'May I?' Deborah turned to the duchess, who nodded in agreement. Louisa pulled open the cupboards, looking for she knew not what: something that linked

Mrs Hoole to the house, perhaps. Some clue that explained why the strange old woman had directed them there.

As the duke had explained, the cupboards contained the dinner service. Columns of painted porcelain plates, edged with gold leaf, too precious to eat from, surely. There seemed not to be any hidden walls or secret drawers, though Louisa self-consciously knocked on various surfaces, listening for a hollow sound. She returned to the side with the staircase, knocking again. Most of the party had started to lose interest and were chatting among themselves. Louisa didn't mind. She was focused on her task. Only Deborah had stuck to her side, perhaps wanting this done but also needing to shepherd everyone back to the dining room.

And, then, quite by chance, behind a panel that lined the bottom of the staircase, Louisa found what she had been looking for.

CHAPTER ELEVEN

⁓

The panel was the only one with a hollow sound, and Louisa had pulled it off. It came away easily, revealing only a black space behind it. The panel wasn't large, but the space behind it might be. It was hard to tell as it was completely dark. With some trepidation, Louisa put in her hand and felt around. She tried not to screw up her face in disgust as she did so, like Maisie refusing to eat spinach. Somehow, she knew something was there.

Something soft.

Without meaning to, she gasped in shock and jerked her hand back.

'What is it?' The duchess came over, stiff in her movements, like one of Maisie's dolls. She looked at the panel that had been pulled off. 'I've never seen anyone do that before.' She didn't sound entirely approving.

Louisa put her hand back in, steeling herself this time, and picked up the soft thing she had felt.

It was an old-fashioned housemaid's mobcap. Rather more

grey than white, with a decaying black velvet ribbon threaded through the edges. And dark red stains. Blood?

'Give it to me,' said the duchess. 'How curious. The maids don't wear these caps.'

The dowager looked at it. 'They were worn by the maids when we first arrived at the house, not long before poor King Edward VII's funeral.' She turned to the person beside her, who happened to be Lord Redesdale. 'We were there, you see.'

'Yes,' replied Lord Redesdale, matching her haughtiness. 'As were we.' He walked over to Louisa. 'Now, look here, what's going on? Every time you get mixed up with my daughters, something of this nature turns up.'

Louisa, who had been studying the cap, looked at him sharply. Everyone turned to regard her now, as they had Mrs Hoole only moments earlier in the library. 'I'm sorry—'

'Farve, do be quiet.' Nancy put herself between them. 'Louisa is a private detective. We *asked* her to get involved last time, to find Decca, which she did, if you remember. And it's been some years since there's been a murder among us.'

'Murder?' shrieked the dowager, causing her Peke to yap. 'Why are you talking about murder?'

'I'm *not*,' said Nancy, almost shouting back. 'We don't know anything about this cap. There's *possibly* blood on it. It might be there for any number of reasons.'

Louisa felt it was time she showed her mettle. 'Quite,' she said. 'This could be tomato sauce or wine. Perhaps there was an accident with one of the maids serving something, and she hid the evidence in here.'

The duke piped up: 'I'm afraid it's not that.'

'Why not?' asked Louisa.

'Because in my father's time a maid never went near the dining room to serve.'

Like watching a relay in a tennis match, everyone turned to Louisa again. 'The point is, we don't know if it's blood,' she said, hoping to calm things down. 'And there's a number of reasons this cap could be here. The question to ask is: did Mrs Hoole know this is what we would find?'

Blank faces looked back at her.

'We're going in to dinner now,' said Deborah. 'I must insist.' And then she blushed. 'I do apologise for this unruly beginning to our evening,' she said, more directly to Nesbit, who seemed at a loss for words to reply.

The rest of the party seemed to grasp that they had been misbehaving in front of a stranger. The dowager looked at her approvingly, the duchess too. The duke was staring at the tips of his shoes, which needed polishing. Louisa put the cap into her pocket.

After a rather more muted return through the house, they sat down in the small dining room, Lady Redesdale directing the placement. After Ellis and two housemaids served the soup – mildly congealed and definitely tepid – the conversation returned to their mysterious visitor. Kick asked if this sort of thing often happened at Chatsworth.

'I daresay it never happens in America,' said the dowager defensively.

'I wish it did but it hasn't to my family, so far as I know,' Kick replied. Louisa liked the naughty glint in her eye.

Nancy, as was her wont, drove the speculation to ever wilder reaches. 'It goes on all the time in families like ours. Missing maids, trapped governesses, daughters bored out of their minds running off with the groom ...' Kick encouraged her further and soon Nancy was regaling her and a wide-eyed Nesbit with ever taller stories. Deborah tried half-heartedly to quieten her but Nancy was always the most amusing person at the table and everyone at her end was thoroughly enjoying themselves.

Towards the other end of the long table, Lord Redesdale arched his eyebrows at his daughter but said nothing. His wife was sitting opposite him, looking sad. Whether this was because she was watching her increasingly estranged husband, their damaged daughter, or both, Louisa didn't know. Unity was eating silently, steadily, making no conversation with her father, nor he with her.

Lucie and Louisa were sitting opposite each other, somewhere in the middle. There weren't enough men for the usual arrangement – five men, ten women – but that wasn't unusual, these days.

'What do you think?' asked Lucie, and it was clear there was only one thing she could be asking about.

'I can't deny that I'd quite like it to be something mysterious for me to solve,' said Louisa. 'After all, that's my job. It'll be disappointing if the cap was stuffed behind the panel because the maid spilt some sauce.'

'If I can bring something to the investigation, please let me know. I've read a lot of Agatha Christie's books. I must have picked up a tip or two.' Lucie laughed at her own joke.

'You know your way around the house. That could be useful.' Louisa glanced around the table. Someone had to know what the connection was between Mrs Hoole and her mysterious message about the vestibule. Louisa intended to find out who it was.

CHAPTER TWELVE

Shortly after dinner, Louisa heard Ellis confirm to Deborah that Mrs Hoole had been returned to the village, driven by one of the gardeners; she had not wanted to wait until Ellis was off duty. The ten women had withdrawn to the drawing room, while the men – the duke, Charles, Lord Redesdale, Nesbit and Billy – remained in the dining room to drink port. Louisa had never been at a dinner where this was the form. At home, after supper (she could no longer call it 'tea'), she and Guy would move from the table in the kitchen to the armchairs by their fire, a distance of mere yards. It was rare to have anyone join them, and since Maisie came along and Guy's mother died, they went out to meet friends in restaurants or clubs only rarely. When they did, everyone would remain at the table together until they all left to go home. She was intrigued by this part of the proceedings at Chatsworth, as if some great secret would be revealed. What did these women – duchesses, dowagers and movie stars – talk about when they were left alone?

The reality was a touch disappointing. They talked about

entirely predictable things: friends, family, minor aspects of the war, which were proving complicated and dull. There was no heartfelt revelation, no deep insight to their inner souls. Rather, there was a lightness to their talk, a deliberate glossing over of true feelings – or so it seemed to Louisa – that was impressively, if dishearteningly, consistent. But Louisa wanted more. She was miles away from her husband, in a vast, strange house, in the middle of a war, her daughter asleep upstairs in an unfamiliar room. She would rarely be in such an extraordinary variety of company. Yet there seemed no way of getting beneath their perfectly polished skins.

Luckily, someone else seemed to have the same idea.

'I think we should play something,' said Kick, when she had put down her cup of coffee. 'I love your crazy English games. Charades?'

'What about Sardines?' suggested Louisa, prompted by the mention of it earlier.

'Sounds fun. How do you play that?' Kick's enthusiasm was high but not, it seemed, infectious.

Nancy sighed. 'Really, must we? The men won't want to join in.'

'We'll make them,' said Kick. 'We have champagne and kisses to offer.'

Nancy rolled her eyes, but Louisa could see the glimmer of her pleasure-seeking side begin to show. 'I suppose it is nearly Christmas,' she acknowledged, and with that, capitulation was complete.

When the men came into the drawing room, they were presented with the fact: any hue and cry was roundly shouted down by the women, although the Redesdales and the dowager, were excused from playing. In the interest of fairness, it was decided that someone who didn't know the house too well should be the first to hide, so Louisa was sent off. They would give her ten minutes before they started seeking.

'State rooms only,' said the duke, 'on the ground and first floors.' He looked a tad sheepish. 'We've played it here before.'

Louisa had walked through these rooms but did not know their intricacies. They were large, cold and barely lit. Every window was covered with blackout, and there were only sparse electric lamps along the corridors. In some rooms the furniture was entirely covered with dust sheets, and while others were elaborately decorated with red damask on the walls, they contained rows of single beds for the schoolgirls. Statues hid in the shadows, and Louisa had to remind herself that she did not believe in ghosts even as one thought looped insistently in her mind: if they *did* exist, this would be the place to find them. She hoped Maisie was sleeping soundly.

Treading lightly, trying not to let the floorboards creak, she went through the line of state rooms on the first floor, but there was no cupboard large enough to get into, no bed to hide under. The portraits weren't watching her, she knew that, but she resolved to guard her instincts and not flinch at every small sound, every flicker of light. Until she heard a quick patter of footsteps and realised her ten minutes were up. Quickening her pace, she ran down the staircase and into the Painted Hall, cavernous and freezing. And dark. Some light came from the top of the stairwell, and some from the corridor on the ground floor, but in this double-height room, it didn't go far.

The footsteps came nearer, heavy. A man.

Louisa knew it was only a game but her heart was thumping.

By sheer chance she found a space behind the staircase, more than large enough for her and the others to hide in. Sweating, she pressed herself against the wooden panels and listened for anyone close by. She was concentrating so hard, which was somehow more difficult when she couldn't see anything, that she nearly screamed when she someone close by whispered: 'Louisa?'

'Who is that?'

'Billy.' Deborah's brother-in-law, Kick's sweetheart. The heir to the dukedom. 'I'm glad I found you first.'

Louisa wasn't sure which was more discombobulating: the darkness and the whispers, or someone she didn't know saying he was pleased to have found her.

'Why?'

'This funny business, a madwoman from the village, saying she's getting messages from the other side. I think I know what's going on.'

There was an echo of a door slamming and Louisa jumped. 'What? What do you think is going on?'

'It'll be money. It always is.'

'But why did you want to say that to me before anyone else?'

'You're a private detective, aren't you?'

'Yes.' Louisa still felt a surge of pride in being able to say this. Not a nursery-maid, or a lady's maid, or a seamstress, or a housewife. She had been all of these things.

'This Mrs Hoole, she ...' He paused. They heard footsteps pass overhead. 'She probably thinks she knows something. But she doesn't.'

'Something about what?'

'Nothing that bears repeating. But she needs to be stopped.'

'Are you asking me to stop her?'

She could hear Billy's breath quicken slightly. 'Yes. No. Not exactly. I mean ... Perhaps there's something about her you could find out. I don't know why she's turned up now and I don't trust her.'

'So you don't think she's hearing messages from the other side?'

'No, I bloody don't.' This was said with some vehemence.

'This something she thinks she knows. Could it be anything to do with the maid's cap?'

'Just find a way to keep her quiet. Or I will. My grandfather's not long dead and there's a war ... Well, you know. The duke and duchess could do without this.'

Louisa nodded pointlessly in the dark. She couldn't see how any power lay with her to stop Mrs Hoole. Neither was she any closer to understanding exactly what she was trying to stop. Before she could ask anything more, there was a breathless giggle, and the scent of Chanel No 5 was tickling their noses.

'Kick? Is that you?'

'*Billy*,' said Kick. 'I found you.'

Louisa coughed.

'Louisa's here,' warned Billy, and Kick laughed again, shushing herself almost immediately.

'Hello,' she said, over-polite. 'You found a good spot.'

After that, it was only a matter of time. More footsteps and accidental gasps of delight as they were discovered. Nancy was the last, pretending that she'd not been looking. 'I was waiting till I knew I'd be able to hear you all. You forget I've been playing this game for a lot longer than any of you.'

The game over, everyone made their way back to the drawing

66

room. Louisa decided she'd had enough for one night and hung back on the stairs to catch Nancy. She wanted to tell her what Billy had said.

'What do you think he meant?' Louisa asked her.

'Sounds as if he suspects the potential for blackmail,' said Nancy. 'But she's only a mad old woman, isn't she? I can't see how much harm she could do.'

'Mad old women can be quite dangerous. You and I know that,' replied Louisa. She didn't need to remind Nancy of the detail, but they had encountered their first not long after they'd met, more than twenty years ago, when solving the case of the war nurse who was murdered on a train.

'Yes, I suppose I do. Even so, I don't see what he expects you to do about stopping it. The man's a fool because *now* you're interested, aren't you?'

'Yes,' Louisa admitted. 'Yes, I am.'

CHAPTER THIRTEEN

⁂

When Louisa went down to breakfast the following morning with Maisie, she was surprised to find they were alone. Today was the official first morning of the house party, marked by the maids now staying in the house rather than walking up from the village shortly after dawn. Hitherto, they had scratched for themselves in the kitchen, Deborah and Louisa carrying bits and pieces up to the dining room for the older guests much of the time. It was not quite eight o'clock when Lord Redesdale would make his punctual appearance; everyone else would probably be a great deal later. There wasn't much on offer, but it was still more generous than the usual tea and toast she had at home, with scrapings of margarine and not much else. This morning, the bread was homemade and the butter looked as if it had been hand-churned, with crystals of salt visible. Probably sent down from Pamela's herd. There were pots of home-made marmalade and jam, which must have been left over from previous years as no one could get enough sugar to make them during the war.

Louisa and Maisie tucked in, while Ellis poured them tea. A maid brought in more rounds of toast, which were cold but perfectly browned.

When Maisie had finished, Louisa gave her permission to go to her favourite window seat in the yellow drawing room for an hour of reading her *Beano* comic.

Alone in the room with the butler, Louisa decided that now was her moment.

'Mr Ellis ...' She hesitated. Only other servants would address him as such. Her former employers, not to mention Deborah, called him 'Ellis'.

He responded with a mere tilt of the head.

'I'm sure you're aware of what happened yesterday. I know you've worked in this house for a long time, and that your uncle was here for many years before that. You must have heard some tales.'

Ellis made the movement again.

'Do *you* have a theory about Mrs Hoole and the maid's cap that was found in the vestibule?'

Ellis straightened up, though Louisa hadn't realised there was any straighter to go. 'It is not my place to speculate, ma'am.'

'I think it's everyone's place,' said Louisa. 'I'm a private detective, but I used to be a nursery-maid for Lady Redesdale, then a lady's maid for— Well, never mind who for. The point is, I know how these houses work, and the discussions that are had below stairs. I'd be grateful for any insights you can pro-vide.' She realised something. 'The *family* would be grateful, I'm sure.'

'They have asked you to investigate?'

'Yes.' She thought about what Billy had said to her in the dark, under the stairs of the Painted Hall. It wasn't quite an official commission but it was enough.

Ellis seemed to think this through.

'Do you know Mrs Hoole?' Louisa asked. 'She said she was born in the village, so I'm assuming she is a familiar face.'

'One doesn't know everyone in the village, ma'am.'

'No,' said Louisa. 'But—'

'I have encountered Mrs Hoole previously.' Ellis tugged at his waistcoat, the last button left undone, as etiquette decreed. Looking at him, Louisa saw, with a small shock, that he was probably the same age as her. It was only his manner that was of someone born in the era when Queen Victoria was still amused.

'Can you tell me anything of those encounters? I'm curious as to how she knew about the maid's cap. I can't say I'm absolutely convinced that she received messages from the other side . . .'

Ellis allowed himself a small smile. 'Stranger things have been known to happen, ma'am. But as for those previous meetings, I cannot say much of interest. I may have seen her in the queue at the post office, or possibly waiting for a bus to Bakewell.'

'Does she offer services as a medium? Do people go to see her to have their tea leaves read, that sort of thing?'

'Possibly. I couldn't say. I'm not very involved with the village. My life is here at Chatsworth.'

Couldn't or wouldn't say? Ellis's face was inscrutable. She felt sure he was holding on to something she'd find useful to know but was at a loss as to how to provoke him into telling her.

'What about the maid's cap? Do you have any theories about that?'

He turned down the corners of his mouth. 'A maid may

have cut herself while she was working, and hastily cleaned the wound with her cap. If she heard a member of the family coming along the hall, she may have panicked and hidden it quickly. I see no reason for any more sinister explanation than that.'

'That *is* a likely explanation,' agreed Louisa. 'Nonetheless, it still begs the question as to how Mrs Hoole knew about it.'

Ellis picked up the teapot. She thought she saw it slip in his hands a little but he recovered himself fast.

'Are there rumours in the village about the family?'

But this was a push too far. Ellis took a step backwards. 'I'm very sorry, ma'am. I've told you all I either know or surmise. I'm not willing to speculate further. If you will excuse me, I believe others will be here for breakfast soon and I must fetch more tea.'

On his way out, Ellis crossed with Lord Redesdale coming in. He was a sorry sight, with his white hair and stooped posture. He didn't even have the heart to lose his temper any more, had snapped only a little at his wife since arriving at Chatsworth. He gave a small grunt in Louisa's direction, and sat down, silently helping himself to the toast and butter.

'Do you think Mrs Jackson sent the butter down, Lord Redesdale?' asked Louisa, attempting to strike up a friendly conversation but using the formality she thought would please him.

'Eh?' He looked down at his plate. 'Pamela? Yes, yes, I suppose so. Good to see the stuff.'

Then there was nothing to be heard but the scraping of his knife. A maid came in with a fresh pot of tea. There was no tension between Louisa and Lord Redesdale exactly, yet she felt she could have sliced the air between them with the butter knife. If she stayed, the silence would be too awkward to bear but to leave would be rude. Fortunately, after her solitary companion had begun to chew morosely, she was saved by the arrival of Lady Redesdale and Unity, and shortly after that by Deborah and Kick.

'Oh, good,' said Deborah, at the sight of the half-full table. 'I hope everyone slept well?'

To this she received only scowls from Unity and her father, and a noncommittal grunt from her mother.

'Yes,' said Louisa. 'Maisie and I did.'

'Are there plans for today?' asked Lady Redesdale.

Deborah looked panicked. 'Plans? Was I supposed to make some?'

'You brought us all here,' said her mother, coolly.

'Golly, yes. I hadn't really thought beyond getting ready and then Christmas Eve. I thought everyone could just go for walks and that sort of thing ...' She trailed off, avoiding the eye of her father, though he didn't appear to have been listening to any part of the conversation.

'The weather outside is filthy,' said Kick. 'Couldn't we explore the house? Hide and seek, even? I did enjoy that game last night.'

Nancy had come in just as Kick was saying this. 'Get the measure of the house before you marry into it, you mean?'

'Oh, no, I didn't mean that at all,' Kick protested, but the colour in her cheeks gave her away.

'Maisie would certainly enjoy some games inside, if you were happy enough to entertain her,' said Louisa. 'I can help Deborah with the last of the preparations. I'm sure there are still things to do.'

'Yes,' said Deborah, gratefully. 'There are.'

Louisa stood up. 'Let's go, then. I'll bring Maisie to the

Painted Hall in half an hour, if that's enough time for your breakfast?'

Kick nodded.

Louisa was pleased. There were things to do on her list, too.

CHAPTER FOURTEEN

~~~~~~~

Leaving Maisie playing with Kick and Unity, and Lady Redesdale supervising by sitting in the gallery of the Painted Hall with some sewing, Louisa and Deborah went down to the kitchen. 'I need to talk to Mrs Airlie,' said Deborah, 'but I'm nervous after last night. I think she was in a blind fury that we sat down so late. It's not as if it isn't hard enough with all the rationing. And I have an awful feeling that Adele is waiting for a tray in bed this morning. I forgot to ask Mrs Airlie to instruct the maids.'

'Then let's do her tray together and one of the maids can take it up. Will Charles come down for breakfast?'

Deborah shook her head. 'No. He never appears before noon, I'm told. He's been sleeping in the dressing room next to Adele. Which is quite normal for their generation. Andrew and I—' She flushed and didn't go on. 'Anyway, that answers your question. Was there something you wanted to talk to him about?'

'Nothing specific,' hedged Louisa. 'It's just that it all seems a bit fishy to me. That business with the old woman and her messages.' She didn't want to give Billy away, but she had rather taken on his commission and wanted to talk to the rest of the family. Starting with Charles: he had reacted to that first sight of Mrs Hoole by dropping the champagne bottle, and she wondered if there was a reason for that. And what grounds did Billy have to suspect the potential for blackmail? That had to be what he had meant by saying money would be at the root of it.

'It's only—' Deborah stopped.

'What?'

'I just want it all to go *well*, you see. I've always been the baby of the family – you know how they tease me. I'd like them to see that I can run a house party properly.'

'And me enquiring into a mysterious maid's cap doesn't really help?'

Deborah shook her head. 'Please forgive me.'

'There's nothing to forgive. I completely understand. I'll say no more about it.' Mentally, Louisa crossed her fingers behind her back. 'Now, let's go and see to Mrs Airlie and deal with that tray. I know cooks can be grumpy but we'll talk her around, I promise.'

Deborah gave her a wide smile of relief and they went into the kitchen. Mrs Airlie was there, beads of sweat already forming on her hairline, as she stirred another vast pot of murky vegetable broth. She didn't acknowledge either of them at first but Louisa, with her knowledge of the servants' quarters, was soon able to smooth the way. As promised, the tray was sent off and the menus for the next few days were confirmed to everyone's satisfaction. After the meeting, Deborah ran off, saying she owed Louisa heaps of favours, and when she had gone, Louisa was able to get down to brass tacks.

'Mrs Airlie,' she said, 'do you mind if I ask you a question or two?'

The cook wiped her hands on her apron, leaving faint smears of grease. 'If it won't take too long. What questions?'

'Mrs Hoole, who I think was given a little supper last night in here. Do you know her?'

Mrs Airlie pulled a bowl towards her that was filled with Brussels sprouts, and started peeling them, marking crosses on the bottom. 'Why are you asking?'

'She was a surprising visitor, and caused something of an upset. I'm fond of the Mitfords, and very loyal to them. I began my working life as their nursery-maid more than twenty years ago.'

'Oh?' There was a pause in the peeling.

'So if I can help soothe any difficulty, I'd be keen to do so. I'm sure you understand. I believe you've been here a long time.'

'Yes,' said Mrs Airlie, proudly. 'I began with the dowager, here as a kitchen-maid when I was nowt more than a sprat.' She put the knife down. 'Mrs Hoole isn't someone I know, though. I can't help you there.'

'You don't recognise her from seeing her about in Baslow?'

'No. Maybe her face but I'm not down there often. The suppliers come to me, you see. And I don't get much time off to go gadding about. When I get my week, I go back home, more than forty mile from here.'

'You couldn't explain how she knew about a maid's cap that had been hidden away in a secret panel under the stairs?'

'Hark at you!' laughed Mrs Airlie. 'Mr Ellis told me what happened last night, and seems to me you're all letting your imaginations run away with you.'

'But she seemed to indicate that someone—'

The knife was taken up again and pointed rather alarmingly in Louisa's direction. 'Mrs Sullivan, I'm sure you're a blessing to the family but if I was you I'd keep your nose out where it's not wanted. Leave that maid's cap well alone. Now, if you don't mind, I've luncheon to be getting on with. That's if everyone sits down when they say they will. After last night . . . ' She continued muttering under her breath, and Louisa knew she had been dismissed. She didn't mind because she was in possession of new knowledge: Mrs Airlie was hiding a secret. But what – and whose – was it?

Up in the Painted Hall again, Louisa saw Lady Redesdale sitting quietly on a window seat in the gallery, mending a skirt. Unity was beside her, tidying the sewing box. 'I'm awfully sorry,' said Unity, 'but Miss Kennedy is too loud for me. I don't want to play her silly game.'

'Never mind,' said her mother, 'you carry on.' She grimaced at Louisa, a trace of apology in the twist of her mouth.

There were faint echoes of laughter coming from the rooms that led off it, presumably Maisie having fun with Kick.

'I'd better find them,' said Louisa, keen to get away. She was rather relieved that her daughter wasn't playing with Unity.

Louisa followed the sound. They weren't in the library, or the ante-library. She climbed the back stairs to the next floor, which opened up into a vast empty room with nothing but a fireplace in it. There were faded squares on the walls, where paintings had been removed. Deborah had told her that the house's best pictures had been taken down for safety, while the school was there, and were stacked together in another room somewhere in the house. There was talk of Gainsboroughs and Renaissance paintings that wouldn't be out of place in a national gallery or a Venetian church. From this strange, vacant room a long corridor led to various state rooms: the state drawing room, the state music room (with its beautiful trompe l'oeil violin), the state bedchamber. Apparently they had been intended for a visit from Queen Mary, who had never turned up. Now they were large, ornate rooms with leather walls and china pots, and no obvious function. Perhaps that was a harsh judgement, when they were important art and historical relics—

'I don't understand why it's all starting up again now.'

Louisa was stopped in her reverie. The laughter and footsteps of her daughter and grown-up playmate had disappeared. Instead she could hear a conversation between two adults. A man and a woman. She couldn't quite recognise the voices but the man's was definitely English and upper-class.

'I didn't mean it to happen, you know that.'

Again, the faint sounds of a woman's reassurance, no words clear enough for Louisa to discern.

'But if anyone finds out now that I lied at the time, all hell will break loose . . . Supposing they go to the papers with the story? It's never going to be over, is it?'

Louisa stood still, her breath held, but nothing more significant was said, and slowly, quietly, she retraced her steps to the Painted Hall.

CHAPTER FIFTEEN

The rest of the morning passed uneventfully, Louisa and Maisie walking in the garden with Lucie, collecting more greenery to be used as festive decorations. They couldn't really gather enough – the house was so huge – but it was beginning to drizzle and Maisie complained of the cold, which was definitely of a different, more bitter quality than the cold felt in London. As they headed back towards the house, which was barely warmer inside than out before the fires were lit, they spotted the tops of the small greenhouses, peeking over the kitchen-garden wall.

'Let's have a look in there,' suggested Louisa. 'At the very least, we'll warm up a bit in the dry.'

'What is it?' asked Maisie.

'A glasshouse, for growing things that need a warmer temperature. Like tomatoes,' Louisa explained. 'But I admit that's the extent of my gardening knowledge.'

They stepped in and were hit by a delicious fug of warm, scented air.

'Herbes!' exclaimed Lucie. She ran over to some tiny-leafed

sprigs and pinched them between her fingertips, giving an appreciative sniff. '*Menthe.* My favourite, especially for tea. Why do your English cooks never use these?'

'Tea?' Maisie was confused but she went over and soon the two of them were sighing over *origan, basilic* and *romarin.*

'May I help?'

A man was walking towards them, dressed in baggy corduroy trousers, boots and a flannel shirt, all well worn and as scruffy as one might expect on a gardener. He wasn't smiling but he wasn't unfriendly. 'I'm so sorry,' said Louisa. 'We're staying in the house, and just came in out of the cold and wet.'

'As you were,' he said. 'If you don't mind, I'm just getting on with potting some seedlings at the back here.'

'No, no, of course not. We won't stay long.' Louisa felt awkward, as if they had interrupted something private. There was something about him that confused her and it took a minute or two to work it out. He looked young. Or, rather, younger than most of the men one saw, certainly out of uniform. But he was probably older than Louisa's own forty years; she could see some lines around his eyes, which were very blue, like a clear summer's day.

'I haven't seen you in the house,' said Lucie, suddenly, with her foreign directness. 'I sometimes eat with the servants when the rest of the staff are away. I'm a teacher, with the school that's here. My name is Lucie Dupont.'

'Right, miss,' he said, touching his ear. 'I eat with the head gardener at his cottage. We'll join the servants' lunch on Christmas Day, I expect.'

'What's your name?' asked Lucie.

He looked startled, then smiled. 'Max.'

'Nice to meet you, Max.'

'You too, miss,' he said.

'I suppose you must know the names of all these plants,' said Lucie, her hand gesturing expansively at the wide variety that grew in the greenhouse.

Max gave a wry smile. 'Yes. I've been lucky to learn from the best here. Mr Coates knows the Latin names of everything in these grounds.'

'Everything?' teased Lucie. 'From tiny flowers to tall trees?'

Max nodded but Louisa could see confusion in his face: he wasn't sure quite what he was being teased about.

'And there are one or two poisonous plants to watch out for, I expect?' said Lucie.

'One or two, yes,' Max replied, but evidently he no longer wished to continue this line of questioning. He touched his cap lightly, and walked back to the other end of the greenhouse. Something about his posture, the slope of the shoulders perhaps, reminded Louisa of Guy. She felt a sharp pang, missing him.

'I think we should put some of these decorations in the servants' hall, for Christmas,' said Lucie, as the three of them went out. Their trugs were full, it was true.

'No one ever decorated the kitchen or servants' hall in my time,' said Louisa, aware of how old it made her sound.

'No? But why ever not?'

'I don't think it was meanness. It just wouldn't have occurred to Lady Redesdale. There was always a servants' Christmas dinner and that sort of thing, though.'

Lucie rolled her eyes. 'And you had to be grateful for *that*?'

They were still laughing as they came around the corner from the greenhouse, when Nancy rushed up to them, followed closely by Deborah, who was shouting after her and panting. Even though they were all married women now, Louisa felt herself briefly transported back to being their nursery-maid. 'What's going on?'

Nancy's eyes had a familiar glittering mischief in them. 'I've invited Mrs Hoole back to the house tonight.'

Deborah had stopped, and doubled over, hands on her knees. 'I *wish* you wouldn't,' she gasped. She stood up. 'I've chased her all the way from the telephone.'

'How did you know her number?' asked Louisa.

'I didn't,' said Nancy, smiling. 'I gave a message to Ellis to deliver to her. She telephoned me.'

'We can't do a party so suddenly. I didn't warn Mrs Airlie. We haven't got the food!'

'Oh, blow the food,' said Nancy. 'There's a war on. Everyone will understand. It's all rotten, anyway.'

'That's jolly mean,' protested Deborah. 'I think we've done a very good—'

'Yes, yes, you've done very well.'

Louisa interrupted, just as she had when they were younger. Nancy's teases always went just a little too far for the younger sisters to bear. 'Maybe. Even so, why have you invited Mrs Hoole?'

'I know you're pleased. Don't even try to deny it.'

The two exchanged a glance, but Louisa saw Deborah looking desperate, and felt sorry for her.

'It's making trouble, and you know it.'

'Maybe,' Nancy admitted. 'But why not? I think we ought to get to the bottom of whatever she's doing. She says she's a medium, doesn't she? So let's have a séance. All the smartest houses do it, I promise you. We've got endless days and nights ahead with each other and this will liven things up. Either you believe in it, in which case she might say something of use, or you don't, in which case no harm done.'

'Lou-Lou, *please* tell her.'

Lucie and Maisie had stood by, dumbstruck. Maisie tugged at Louisa's skirt. 'What are you going to do, Mummy?' she whispered.

'Well, now that the invitation has been issued . . .' she began, and Deborah threw her hands into the air.

'I don't believe it. I'm simply not going to be allowed to do anything I want so long as any of my sisters are here, am I?'

'It's not that,' said Louisa, hurriedly, feeling bad. 'But something *is* going on. Don't you think we should try to get to the root of it?'

'No,' said Deborah. 'I don't. But I can see that my words mean nothing.' With a final, furious glance she stalked off.

Nancy had the good manners to look a little abashed. 'I didn't mean to make her so cross.'

Louisa sighed. 'Nonetheless, you did. I do think you might be a little kinder, Nancy. She's a newlywed and trying her best with the in-laws, and she doesn't even have her husband here to support her. She's only doing all this to cheer everyone up.'

'Yes,' said Nancy. 'You're right. I'll be nicer, I promise.'

'Could you invite Group Captain Nesbit, too?' asked Lucie. She wasn't even blushing as she asked.

Nancy looked at her a little askance but something in her understood the young woman. 'Yes,' she agreed. 'I shall. Perhaps it will help to make it even more of a proper party and Debo will see I mean well by her.'

Louisa didn't hold out much hope for this, but Nancy offered to take Maisie into the kitchen for a glass of milk and to see if the cook had a secret biscuit tin somewhere. 'I'll talk to Mrs Airlie about the dinner tonight, explain that it's my fault,' she said, contrition itself. 'Debo won't stay angry. She's not capable of it.'

'You're lucky,' said Louisa, following her out of the door. As she did, something made her turn and she caught sight of Max, watching them all leave, his expression unreadable – too much so, as if he was deliberately practising a poker face. He must have overheard them, but Louisa shrugged it off. Servants always knew far more about the family they worked for than the family ever knew about them.

CHAPTER SIXTEEN

Nancy was right, of course. Deborah couldn't stay angry for
long. The two of them decided to occupy a room in the
private wing that was used by the school's headmistress as her
study, chiefly because it was reasonably clean and had a large
round table in the middle. Books were stacked on a desk in the
corner, but it was otherwise fairly empty. A tall window reached
from the floor, but the ceiling was not so high as in the other
rooms and the walls were painted bottle green. With the fire lit
in the grate, it soon felt quite cosy. Chairs were found from about
the place, a cloth put on the table and Nancy stole candlesticks
from various rooms, placing them on surfaces high and low.
'We won't have any electric lights on,' she declared. 'I'm sure
the spirits will prefer it.'

'You're playing with fire,' said Louisa.

'Am I? Do you believe in dead people coming back to haunt
the living?'

'I don't *not* believe.'

'Spoken like a true heathen,' said Nancy. 'I'm a Christian, of course, and know it's all nonsense.' She paused, while she tidied the books on the desk. 'On the other hand, that maid's cap ... We want to find out what's behind it.'

'Everything is not fodder for one of your novels,' admonished Louisa.

'Well, there, you see, I'm afraid I'd have to disagree. Why else should I endure such misery, as is this life, if not to write about it?'

At five o'clock Ellis confirmed with Deborah that he had despatched one of the gardeners to collect Mrs Hoole from Baslow in the car, to be brought to the house for a light supper in the kitchen and thereafter upstairs for the 'special event'. Come the hour, when they had all changed for dinner, Louisa decided it would be politic to see Mrs Hoole first, and went down to the kitchen with Maisie, on the pretext of fetching her daughter a cup of warm milk to take to bed.

Their footsteps clattered noisily on the stone steps down to the kitchen, and Louisa noticed that the conversation she heard as she arrived stopped rather suddenly.

'I'm so sorry to interrupt,' said Louisa, seeing Mrs Airlie and Mrs Hoole sitting across the cook's small table in the kitchen. It usually had her papers and cookbooks on it but had been cleared for two bowls of soup. Mrs Airlie stood when she saw Louisa come in; Mrs Hoole remained seated.

'No trouble,' said Mrs Airlie, though she sat down again heavily, as if the effort had been rather too much.

Louisa felt Maisie retreat behind her skirts. 'Would you mind if I warmed some milk for Maisie?'

'Of course, ma'am. One of the girls will help you.'

Louisa protested, but she didn't know where the pan was or the milk. Or a cup. It was a reminder of how hard it was to cross the divide from upstairs to below. If she insisted on doing it herself, Mrs Airlie would be affronted at the invasion of her kitchen. But she felt awkward standing at the side. A maid appeared, magically summoned, and started to warm the milk.

The two women quietly ate their soup.

'It must be nice,' said Louisa, 'to have a house party here again, I mean.'

'If you mean by that I must like a lot of extra work, I can't say as I do,' replied Mrs Airlie, sourly. 'But it's nice to have the help for a bit.'

Mrs Hoole smiled to herself, dipping her head low over her bowl. She was dressed all in black, her grey hair flattened by a headscarf or hat, and her figure was large, spilling over the edges of the wooden chair.

Mrs Airlie looked to her companion. 'You'd remember what it was like, wouldn't—'

'No.' Mrs Hoole was sharp. 'What would I know?'

Mrs Airlie's already red cheeks deepened their colour. 'No, 'course not,' she muttered.

But it was too late. Louisa knew what she'd heard. 'Did you work in this house before, Mrs Hoole?' Nothing but innocent curiosity in Louisa's voice.

Mrs Hoole pushed back her chair with a noisy scrape on the stone floor. 'I need some quiet before going up,' she said to Mrs Airlie, as if she hadn't heard Louisa's question. 'Did you say the servants' hall was through there? If you don't mind, I'll have a nap.'

There was a shuffle of movement as she gathered her copious

skirts, the rest of them reduced to little more than bystanders. But instead of leaving the room, Mrs Hoole came and stood before Maisie. She bent down to the little girl and seemed to regard her closely for a moment too long before she spoke. 'Do you live here?' she asked.

'No,' said Maisie, eyes agog. 'I live in London.'

'Do you believe in ghosts?'

'I'm not sure—' Louisa began, but Mrs Hoole put up a hand, and she fell silent.

'Yes,' said Maisie, with certainty. 'Do you?'

'Yes,' said Mrs Hoole, with equal firmness, and left the room.

'What was that?' mouthed Louisa to Mrs Airlie. 'What was she trying to do?'

Mrs Airlie shrugged. 'There's nowt so strange as folk.'

'But you know her, do you? From before? Did she used to work in the house?'

Mrs Airlie wouldn't be drawn. 'If she were, I didn't know her. I were a kitchen-maid at the end of the last war, and the likes of me didn't talk to the others in the servants' hall then. Now, it looks as if your milk is ready and I'd best be getting on.'

'No,' said Louisa, with more force than she had intended. She didn't want another brush-off. Did everyone in this house have some closely guarded secret?

Mrs Airlie, Maisie and the maid all stood completely still.

'What's going on? Who is Mrs Hoole? Did she used to work in the house, Mrs Airlie?'

'I don't see what business it is of yours.'

Louisa softened her stance, smiled. 'It's not that I'm trying to pry—'

'Is it not?' But this was said with a wry smile, a softening, too.

'I was a maid to Lord and Lady Redesdale twenty years ago,' explained Louisa. 'I've been with the family a long time. Perhaps I'm being protective. But if you know what's going on, will you tell me?'

Mrs Airlie gave a quick glance at the door that Mrs Hoole had gone through only moments earlier. 'I don't really know. She's from Baslow, one of us. Her mother lives there still, though Mrs Hoole moved away a long time ago. I don't think she's out to cause trouble, though, if that's what you need to know.'

'I'm not sure I agree,' said Louisa, 'the way she's going about things. But thank you.' The milk was in the cup, there was no reason to linger. They would have to see what revelations the séance brought about, though she felt afraid at the very thought of it.

CHAPTER SEVENTEEN

A fter dinner, those who had agreed to attend the séance went up to the sitting room that had been prepared earlier by Louisa and Nancy. Lord and Lady Redesdale made their excuses, and Unity was not told. Her new fervent love for Jesus meant she would have been very angry at such a heathen plan – 'And she hates me enough as it is,' sighed Deborah. The event was also concealed from the dowager; it was felt that she might object to their summoning ghosts into her former home. Surprisingly, the duke and duchess were willing – they said they had attended many similar events in their travels and believed not a jot of it but generally found mediums to be good entertainment. Charles did not want to be there, but Adele persuaded him. That left Group Captain Nesbit, Kick and Billy, Deborah, Louisa, Nancy and Lucie. And, of course, Mrs Hoole, brought up by Ellis, his face resolutely revealing nothing. He was not permitted to stay in the room; only those sitting around the table in the circle could remain.

When they arrived, Mrs Hoole was already sitting at the

round table, her back to the window, facing the door; she offered no smile or words of welcome to greet them. Ellis, as instructed, lit the candles and stoked the fire so that as they came in there was a blast of warmth that felt quite unfamiliar. With the drawn velvet curtains and the dark walls, the atmosphere was perfectly set and, though it was rather dark, their eyes soon adjusted. In silence, subdued by the seriousness, everyone sat down.

Mrs Hoole took command. 'I know you went to the vestibule. Did you find what you were looking for?'

'Yes,' said Louisa, who had been nominated by Nancy to speak on behalf of everyone. She pulled out the maid's cap from her skirt pocket and put it on the table. Mrs Hoole picked it up and looked at it, then held it close to her face and closed her eyes briefly before putting it on her lap.

'Were you all there when this was found?' Her Derbyshire accent was still strong but the formality in her speech now was different.

'Yes,' replied Louisa.

Charles made an indeterminate sound and took a drink from a hip flask, fished from his pocket. There was a moment of heavy silence while Mrs Hoole waited for him to finish.

'I would like everyone to join hands,' said Mrs Hoole, eventually, holding her own outstretched on either side. Nancy and Kick sat either side of her and managed to maintain straight faces. Charles and Billy looked as if they might protest but their respective women soon put a stop to that with fierce glances.

'We will now alert the spirits to our presence,' intoned Mrs Hoole, 'by giving our names.' Around the table they went, the women giving their first names, the men, absurdly, giving theirs with their titles. Louisa wanted to laugh at the notion that even ghosts were expected to adhere to protocol.

When this was done, Mrs Hoole lifted her head and speaking slightly louder than before, said: 'I ask the archangels and gate-keepers to keep out evil spirits and protect us.' With a dramatic shudder she dropped Nancy and Kick's hands, and everyone else let go, too.

Louisa noticed a glass disc in the middle of the table. Mrs Hoole instructed them all to lay the fingertips of their left hands loosely on it, which they duly did.

'Spirit, when I ask a question, if the answer is yes, move the disc in a circular motion. If the answer is no, let there be no movement at all.'

'How do you know they're not busy?' asked Nancy, with faux-innocence. Mrs Hoole gave her a haughty look and did not answer.

'Spirit, have you a message for anyone in particular here present in this room?'

Louisa's arm was relaxed, so it was surprising to feel it move with the disc as together they kept their fingertips on it, now moving in a distinctly circular motion. She wanted to examine the faces of everyone there, to see who might be deliberately nudging it, but it was impossible to do so discreetly.

'Spirit, are you female?'

Again, the disc moved, jerkily at first and then in a circular motion. Louisa knew she wasn't making it move. At least, she didn't think she was. It was difficult to know exactly, because it was a natural shape to follow somehow. Could they all be urging the movement along, even without meaning to? Louisa took a breath and tried to concentrate on what was happening in front of her.

'Spirit, does this cap belong to you?'

This time, the jerk was strong, stretching Louisa's arm almost to its fullest reach, pulling everyone in turn as it completed its circle.

The half-smile that always lingered on Kick's face disappeared. Deborah looked worried, but she maintained her posture, her back beautifully straight. She was her mother's daughter in moments of crisis. Louisa and Lucie caught each other's eyes and raised their eyebrows simultaneously.

Whatever was going on, it didn't feel ordinary.

'Spirit, thank you for talking to us,' said Mrs Hoole. 'Please stay with us a little longer. Tell us, were you wearing this cap at the moment of your death?'

There was a pause, nothing moved, no one seemed to breathe, and then the disc slid gently to Louisa's left and moved in a circle again, smaller than before. Louisa tried to see if anyone's fingertips appeared to be pressing harder than hers but it was impossible to tell.

'Spirit, did you die by the hand of someone present in this room?'

'Now look here!' Charles stood up. 'This is too much. I don't call this a game any more.'

'I never did call it a game,' said Mrs Hoole. 'Please, sit down, or leave the room. The circle must be complete for the spirit to talk.'

'Then I'm leaving,' said Charles. 'Adele.'

'I'm staying,' said his wife.

'I—'

Charles's protests were cut off before they could start by something thudding to the floor. Each person turned their heads and saw a small painted china pot lying on the rug by the hearth. It must have been on the mantelpiece. Kick cried out and Louisa immediately started reasoning that it must have been caused by the vibrations of Charles moving so suddenly. The duke lit one of his Turkish cigarettes. Nesbit shifted in his chair.

'What have you done?' asked Adele, her American accent startling after Mrs Hoole's low tones.

'Nothing. I've done *nothing*.' Charles flounced out.

Mrs Hoole lifted her nose in the air, as if to find a scent. 'The spirit has gone,' she pronounced.

'What do you mean?' asked Nancy.

'They are delicate. If the spell is broken, so to speak, they don't stay.' She picked up the cap and held it, looking down at it. Louisa couldn't have said how she knew, but Mrs Hoole seemed suddenly terribly sad.

The duke and duchess stood up and thanked Mrs Hoole politely, as if they had been introduced at a drinks party, then left, summoning Adele and Billy as they went. The duchess put her arm around Adele's back, and tipped her head close, a gesture that looked well practised between the two sisters-in-law. It seemed that she must often require the touch of human comfort. Kick followed them, never wanting to be too far away from Billy. Then Lucie made her excuses and left, too. Nesbit looked uncomfortable, still at the table, and Nancy suggested he go down to the drawing room for some port. 'We won't be far behind you,' she promised, and he gratefully exited the room.

Nancy, Deborah and Louisa remained sitting at the table with Mrs Hoole.

'Mrs Hoole,' said Louisa, 'was that genuine what we saw there?'

She put the cap on the table and met Louisa's eyes. 'A young woman died, yes. There's nothing not genuine about that.'

'But what are you doing here exactly?'

'I'm trying to make her voice heard, as I have done for the last twenty-five years. But no one has listened. I hope now that you will, tonight.'

CHAPTER EIGHTEEN

ome of the candles were starting to burn dangerously
low, and one or two had snuffed out. Nancy stood up and
switched on a lamp, transforming the room's atmosphere from
eerily ghostly to a well-lit stage set, the fakery of the props all too
visible. Mrs Hoole no longer looked like someone possessed by
witchcraft, just a housewife in badly fitting clothes.

'*Did* someone die, Mrs Hoole?' asked Deborah, her voice
higher than usual. 'I mean, in some terrible way?'

Mrs Hoole's head dropped and when she spoke it was without
the portentousness of before. 'Yes,' she said. 'I don't know exactly
how, or even exactly when, but I know it happened. I just know.'

'What – because you're a medium?' said Nancy, sharply.

Mrs Hoole gave a small smile. 'No. Because I was her friend.
We worked together, here, as maids. I was older than her by
about ten years and I looked out for her. Her name was Joan
Dorries, and she came to the house when she was still a child,
practically. She had no family watching out for her, she never
went anywhere when we got a week off in the summer. She was

shy and very sweet. I didn't really have nobody then neither. She was a little sister to me.'

'Why didn't you simply say so? Why all this mysterious message business?' Nancy looked cross.

'Because I've been trying for more than twenty-five years to get someone to listen to me, and nothing's worked. Until now.'

Louisa sat up. 'Who have you tried to get to listen to you? Did you know anyone who was in the room just now?'

Mrs Hoole replied carefully, 'The duke and his brother. I knew of them when I worked here but I was a maid in the kitchens. We didn't see much of anyone upstairs.'

'Have you tried to talk to them about it? And they haven't listened?' Deborah asked.

'Not them so much, no,' admitted Mrs Hoole, 'because they were so young at the time, but I tried to talk to the police. Lord Charles was a boy of not much more than ten, the duke twenty, I suppose, but mostly fighting in the war. I wrote letters to their father, the late duke, but he never replied.'

There was a short silence while everyone absorbed this information: a dead maid, police, a family who didn't want to know.

'When did you work in the house with Joan?' asked Louisa, her private detective hat firmly on. She wanted facts, not messages through the ether.

'She first came to the house not long before the war started. The dowager was the duchess then and her husband was still fit and well. There was a large staff living in, and hundreds working on the estate. We worked long days but it had its rewards. We were proud to be in service, working for a grand family, and all sorts coming here to stay. We were never short of a story or two round the servants' hall. We had other servants coming to stay,

97

too, you see, when they accompanied their masters or mistresses. It made for a lively time. The war changed all that.'

'How?' Nancy and Deborah looked at Louisa when she asked this question. Perhaps the answer was obvious to them, but it wasn't to her.

Mrs Hoole gave a small shrug. 'The house parties stopped. The men who worked and lived here signed up to fight, as well as the men from the villages. The duke and duchess went to Canada during the war, but their older son, the current duke, who was here this evening, went to fight at the front. You may have known that men who worked together, or came from the same village, were put in the same regiments, and we lost a lot of them round here. You couldn't go down to the post office without seeing someone there in sobs.'

'But this girl, Joan Dorries. Tell us about her,' said Louisa.

'She disappeared one night. One day, she was here, the next she wasn't. The housekeeper who was here then, she told me Joan had decided to go, she didn't know why and there weren't anything any of us could do. But I didn't believe it.'

'Why not?' Nancy was at her most alert, her attention fully on Mrs Hoole.

'Because she wouldn't have gone without telling me. I know she wouldn't.'

'What about her things? Had she packed to go away?' Nancy asked.

'Some of her things were missing, but it looked as if it had been done by someone else, not her. It's hard to explain but she'd left things behind I knew she'd care about, little keepsakes she'd collected over the years, a pair of shoes she'd always said were her only comfortable ones. A photograph of a house.'

Louisa understood. These were the clues that mattered.

'Who did you try to talk to about it?' she asked.

'Everyone. But they all shut me down.'

'Do you think they knew something you didn't?'

'I don't know, maybe not. Maybe they'd all been told to keep quiet, maybe they just thought I was impertinent for asking. Like I said, I was a kitchen-maid, the lowest of the house.'

'What about the police?' asked Deborah.

Mrs Hoole gave a dry laugh. 'They certainly weren't going to pay attention to me. There was one young policeman in the village, and I met him one day and he seemed to listen to me but he said he couldn't do anything about it, not if the duke hadn't asked for an investigation. And without a missing-person report, or a body, there could be no investigation.'

'Can you remember his name?'

'Tucker. He had a nice face and I was hopeful he'd think on it, and act on it. But he never did.'

'What about this cap?' said Louisa. 'I assume you hid it in the vestibule. How did you get it? Did it belong to Joan? Is this her blood?'

Mrs Hoole looked away from them, and seemed to take in some breaths, to steady herself. 'Could I have a glass of water, please? Or something stronger?'

Deborah went to a table in the corner and poured some brandy. 'I asked Ellis to put it out,' she explained, 'in case we all needed it.'

'I'll have one, too, in that case,' said Nancy.

'We didn't share a room, because I was older,' continued Mrs Hoole, when she'd gathered herself. 'She was in with two other younger maids, and they were quite slatternly. We had to keep our rooms tidy because the housekeeper would check, but I knew they'd never do it proper. After she went missing, I sneaked in and looked around. That's how I knew she hadn't packed her things, and that cap was under the chest of drawers. It had been pushed quite far back so I wasn't surprised they hadn't found it before.'

'Did you ask the other maids in her room about it?' Louisa was beginning to wish she had her notebook on her.

'I can't remember. I might've, but I was so upset when I found it.' She stopped and took another drink of brandy. 'I suppose it means I can't be certain it's hers, but I don't see how it couldn't be.'

'Why are you doing all this now?' asked Nancy. 'Why not before?'

'I moved away not long after Joan went missing. I was uncomfortable in the house, and with the war on, it was easy enough to make the excuse. I moved to Manchester, and I stayed there. I've been lucky, like poor Joan wasn't. I married and I've got three children, all grown now. But I come back here as often as I can to see my mother. When I heard there was a private detective staying in the house I thought it was now or never.' Mrs Hoole exhaled deeply, as if she had finally let go of something she'd been holding tightly.

'But why the charade with the messages and the medium?'

'Who says it were a charade?' asked Mrs Hoole, with dignity.

'I thought, earlier, you said you didn't know she was dead simply because you were a medium ...'

'No. I know she's dead because I know she's dead.'

'Did you find her body?' Louisa asked.

'No,' said Mrs Hoole. 'But she vanished, completely. She would never have done that to me. She told me everything.'

'You don't know that,' said Nancy.

Mrs Hoole was indignant. 'I do.'

'No,' said Nancy, with force. 'You only think you know what you've been told or seen. If life has taught me anything, it's that people carry the most surprising secrets.' As if exhausted by her own worldliness, Nancy reached over and rang the bell for Ellis. Seconds later – had he been standing outside the door? – Ellis came in.

'Thank you, Ellis,' said Nancy. 'Could you arrange for a car to take Mrs Hoole home, please?'

Mrs Hoole stood. 'I'll go. I only ask that you don't forget this conversation. Don't forget Joan Dorries, like the rest of the world has. Whoever made her disappear still deserves to be punished for it. I owe her that much.'

'Why?' asked Deborah. 'Why do you owe it to her?'

'Because Joan was nothing but a kind creature. She meant no harm to anyone, and if someone was capable of hurting her, I don't believe they'd have stopped at that. What if she wasn't their only victim?'

'But it was such a long time ago,' said Deborah. 'Can't you let it lie?'

'No,' said Mrs Hoole, drawing herself up to her fullest height. 'A crime that happened a quarter of a century ago is no less a crime than if it happened last week.' With that, she turned and walked out of the room, a confused-looking Ellis hurrying after her.

CHAPTER NINETEEN

When Louisa, Nancy and Deborah came into the yellow drawing room, there were few left of the earlier supper party. The duke and duchess, and the Redesdales had gone to their respective beds, as had Unity. The dowager would have been driven home shortly after supper ended. Lucie was not there, and neither was Nesbit nor Adele. Only Kick and Billy were in the room, standing suspiciously far apart on either side of the fireplace, the fire reduced to embers, giving off little heat. Charles was slumped in an armchair in the corner, his back to the room, a quarter-full whisky decanter on a table at his side; he barely responded to their entry. At that moment Louisa missed Guy very strongly. The chilliness of the room, the distance of the people, were suddenly all too exhausting to bear.

'Is Muv not here?' said Deborah, to no one in particular, not quite knowing who to ask.

Billy and Kick looked at her, nonplussed. 'She'd gone to bed by the time we were down here, I think,' said Kick.

'I'd better go and see her. I'll feel rather badly if I don't say good night to her.' Deborah looked like Louisa felt. She left the room, the dutiful daughter.

'What's been going on?' asked Kick.

But Nancy seemed in no mood to share the curiosity. It was possible, hoped Louisa, she understood the mystery for the serious matter it was.

'Mrs Hoole is a complete charlatan,' Nancy said.

Or maybe not.

'Why?' asked Billy. 'Which isn't to say I disagree with you.'

'Some utter nonsense about things she thinks happened a quarter of a century ago. Even if they did, I don't see why it matters now. She's one of those strange types who need attention, I'd say. Mrs Nobody from the village, wanting to get into the big house.'

'What did she say happened?' asked Billy. 'She thinks she knows something, does she?'

'Don't upset yourself,' said Kick, rushing to his side. 'Every family has its secrets.'

'Not mine,' said Billy, forcefully. 'We have nothing to hide. But there's always a nasty meddler in the village, isn't there?'

'Ignore her,' said Kick, gently, and Billy seemed only too willing to allow himself to be soothed.

Louisa noticed Charles, largely hidden from view by the back of the armchair, pour himself another two fingers of whisky. Had he been disturbed by Mrs Hoole's séance? He'd certainly left in a hurry. Louisa wondered if he'd recognised her: he'd been a young boy during the war, and the children of a big house tended to know the servants better than their parents did.

There was a clap of thunder and they all jumped. Nancy went

to the window and pulled back the curtain. 'My goodness,' she said, 'that's a real storm out there. It's *pouring*.'

'At least it'll put paid to any air raids,' said Billy.

'Why?' asked Kick.

'No one wants to fly in thunder and lightning. It's not worth the risk.'

'That reminds me,' said Nancy. 'What happened to Group Captain Nesbit?'

'He wasn't here when I came in,' said Billy. 'I expect he's driven home. It was rather an odd evening.'

Nancy, partly responsible for the evening's so-called entertainment, could not disagree.

Kick gave an exaggerated yawn and stretched her arms upwards. 'Well, I'm tired. That was fun and all but it's time for my bed. Good night, everybody.'

Kick left, and about half a minute later, Billy said that he, too, was tired and made his excuses.

'It's as if they don't even try to be discreet,' said Nancy, when he'd left the room.

'You don't think they're . . . ?' whispered Louisa.

'Well, probably not. I expect there's just a bit of giggling in the dark. Who can blame them, anyway? We should probably all be living each day as if it were our last. However, I may assume I'll be around tomorrow, and I need beauty sleep, so I'm off, too. What about you, Lou-Lou?'

'I don't feel tired but I'd better get back to Maisie,' said Louisa. She was feeling grateful that Billy hadn't taken a chance to ask her if she'd found out anything more about Mrs Hoole. She wasn't sure what she'd tell him.

They heard a snore coming from the chair. 'I think we'll leave

Charlie boy,' said Nancy, in a half-whisper. Louisa agreed, and the two of them tiptoed out.

Louisa made her way to her room, in the opposite direction to Nancy's, and was horrified to realise that she was rather scared walking through the house alone at that time of night. She wondered if maybe all Kick had wanted was to be accompanied safely. Once again, she'd forgotten to pick up the torch that had been thoughtfully put in her room. She'd assumed it was in case the power went but the blackout in this house had been thoroughly done. At least tonight the darkness was penetrated occasionally by a flash of lightning, bright enough to cut through the blackout material pinned to the windows that had no curtains. She couldn't get used to the statues appearing in unexpected places, and the combination of their silhouettes and the flashes of light were enough to leave her seriously unsettled by the time she turned the last corner to reach her room. Gratefully, she almost ran the last few steps and put her hand on the doorknob. She hoped Maisie hadn't been woken by the storm, and she looked forward to cuddling her daughter in the night, it would help send them both to sleep. In that second as she started to turn the handle, Louisa heard a creak in the corridor behind her. It was pitch black and she couldn't see who, or what, had made the noise. Hurriedly, she tried to push open the door, her heart beating fast even as she tried to tell herself it couldn't be anything to worry about. And that was when she felt a hand land heavily on her arm.

CHAPTER TWENTY

B efore Louisa could scream, a torch was shining in her face. 'I do beg your pardon, ma'am.'

The hand was removed, and the figure holding the torch stepped back. Blinded by the light, Louisa waved her arm. 'What on earth is going on?' She blinked, trying to get her eyes used to the forms and shadows that were taking shape in the brightness. 'Ellis?'

'Yes, ma'am. I do apologise for surprising you.' He did sound sorry.

'What's going on? That was a horrible scare. What are you doing here? Why did you spring on me like that?'

'I didn't realise it was you, ma'am.'

'No, I should hope you didn't. But who did you think I was?'

It was so cold that Louisa could see the steam coming from her breath, and that Ellis looked rather pale and worried.

'I wasn't sure. I heard the footsteps. I was worried about Maisie, with the storm. I thought I'd check she hadn't woken and was frightened. I knew you were, or thought you were, still in the yellow drawing room.'

'Why didn't you put your torch on? Why grab me in the dark?'

'If it was an intruder, I thought the element of surprise was best.'

'I see.' Her breathing had returned to normal. 'Thankfully, I wasn't an intruder. If you don't mind, I'll go to bed now.'

'Yes, ma'am. Do beg pardon.' But he remained standing there.

'Was there something else you wanted to say?'

'No, ma'am. That is, there's only one thing, which is that Mrs Hoole is still here.'

'Still here?'

'She'll be staying for the night. The car wouldn't start and, what with the storm and the lateness of the hour, it was decided it would be better to try to repair it in the morning and then take her home.'

'Right, yes, I do see. Thank you, Ellis.'

'I've put her in the servants' quarters. She was asking to be in a room close to the family but that didn't feel correct to me.'

Louisa felt confused; did he want her to give him the authority to do so? Perhaps he needed it, if the rest of them had gone to bed. She nodded. 'I expect you're right and the servants' quarters are probably best.' Still, the butler didn't move. 'I don't want to be rude, Ellis, but I *am* very tired now. I think I'd better get to bed.'

'Yes, ma'am. Absolutely. Sorry to have disturbed. Sorry, again, for ... ' Without finishing the sentence, he turned and walked away, the torch on, this time. She had the vague sensation that there was something further he'd wanted to say to her, and that she had missed the opportunity. But she hadn't lied: she wanted only to climb into bed, find her daughter's warm, sleeping body and curl up next to it, for hours and hours, until the morning came.

Only, once Louisa was in bed, sleep seemed hard to reach. The curtains in their room were thick, which at least meant she was shielded from the sound of the storm if it was still going on. Yet there seemed to be myriad other noises, as if bad jazz was being played by a tiny travelling orchestra, a series of dissonant creaks and bangs. The longer Louisa lay there, the more awake she felt, and the more sensitive she seemed to become to the smallest nuances of sound and vibration. In a house so old and huge, she shouldn't have been so alarmed, she knew. She supposed she must have been lucky the previous nights, that she had somehow been tired enough to sleep through it all. Unless the rain and the storm *were* partly to account for it. More likely it was the fact of being so unsettled by Mrs Hoole, and her story of a missing maid. A young girl disappeared twenty-five years ago, with nothing heard or seen of her since – until the bloodied maid's cap was discovered in the vestibule. Charles had seemed visibly disturbed but not to the point of explaining what had upset him. The duke and duchess, the dowager, had all said nothing but their silence was definitely of the 'stiff upper lip' kind. Deborah was concerned about its effect on the success of her party. Nancy thought it was all a lot of rubbish. Billy was concerned about rumours and asked her to find out more about Mrs Hoole, but the little she had discovered this evening only seemed to throw up more questions. Mrs Airlie and Ellis each seemed to be bothered about something, but was it about Mrs Hoole or something else altogether?

The very thought of the long, dark, cold corridors that ran through the house gave her the shivers as she lay there. She saw herself running down them, for miles, as if they never ended, doors opening and closing by themselves, slivers of light briefly illuminating statues that had the heads of gargoyles, their anguished screams set in stone. Then the faces of the others in the house took on the same grotesque features, and it was only when the barking dog that ran behind her would not be quietened that Louisa realised she was waking from a disturbing dream. Maisie was shaking her shoulder, eyes wide open, frightened. The room was still completely black but she thought she could see a tiny glimmer of light coming through the curtains. The barking had begun to fade.

'What is it, darling?'

'Something woke me up. I don't know what it was. And then that funny dog ... I think it was outside our door. It wouldn't stop barking.'

Louisa wrapped her arms around her daughter. 'It seems to have gone away now. It must have been the dowager's Pekinese.' She said this and then remembered that the dowager would have slept in her own house. Perhaps she had left the dog behind.

'She's a very barky sort of dog, isn't she?' Maisie's voice was muffled, her face deep in Louisa's armpit.

'Yes, she is. I'm sure she knows this house well. Perhaps someone she likes stays in this room.'

Maisie pulled her head out, a tentative smile appeared. 'You mean she likes me?'

Louisa kissed her daughter. 'Yes, I think she probably does. Now, I expect it's time for us to get up.' She didn't feel rested, but if Mrs Hoole had stayed, she'd like the chance to ask her some more questions. A tepid bath – limited hot water meant no more than five inches – in a cold bathroom, left Louisa more shivery than before, and by the time she and Maisie came down it was nearly nine o'clock and the breakfast table was fairly crowded. Lady Redesdale was indiscreetly picking mould off the marmalade, ignoring Unity's endless inane questions. The duke was sitting back, gazing out of the window, drinking black coffee and smoking another of his odorous – and odious – Turkish cigarettes. Nancy was reading the paper, hardly looking up to say good morning. Lord Redesdale looked anxious to get away, indeed was pushing his chair back as Ellis came into the room. The butler stood in the doorway, a look of confusion on his face, and Louisa saw he was pale, too. Perhaps he hadn't had much sleep, either.

'Your Grace ...' he began, faltering, looking across at the duke.

'Don't mind me, man,' said the duke, tapping his cigarette ash onto a plate meant for toast and butter. 'I'm happily not in charge this week. Talk to Lady Andrew, would you?'

Ellis gave a dry swallow and took a step towards Deborah, who was fussing over the Pekinese on her lap. There was no sign of the dowager.

Ellis tried again. 'Your Ladyship ...'

'Yes, Ellis?' She wasn't really looking at him but into the vacant black eyes of the dog.

'Perhaps I could have a word?'

'You sound rather hoarse, Ellis. I do hope you're not coming down with a cold.'

'That would be most inconvenient,' said Nancy.

'I—' He coughed. 'No, it's not a cold. It's Mrs Hoole—'

'I know she stayed, if that's what you're here to tell me,' said Deborah. 'Mrs Airlie told me this morning. I heard the car wouldn't start last night. I hope it's nothing too difficult to mend. I need to go to Baslow today.'

'No, it's not about her staying,' said Ellis, rather more forcefully than he'd managed so far. 'It's about the fact she's dead.'

CHAPTER TWENTY-ONE

❧

Ellis's announcement certainly had an effect, whether desired or otherwise. Cups were noisily replaced in their saucers, newspapers rustled, chairs scraped. Deborah's hand was stilled on the Peke's head.

'In this house?' she asked.

'Yes. I put her in the housekeeper's bedroom. She appears to have died in the night.'

'She's in the bed?'

'Betsy, the maid from the village, found her not ten minutes ago. We'd wondered why she wasn't down for breakfast. I'd told her it would be at half past seven in the servants' hall.'

Louisa looked at her watch: a quarter past nine. 'Has anyone else been in to see her?' she asked.

Ellis shook his head. 'Not so far as I know, ma'am. I went in to check what Betsy had said was true – she was quite hysterical.'

Louisa took control. 'Don't let anyone else into the room. You need to telephone the doctor straight away.' She walked over to Deborah, and put a hand reassuringly on her shoulder. 'I'll see to this,' she said. 'But don't let anyone leave the house until the doctor has been.'

'What?'

'Just to be on the safe side.'

'What does that mean?' Deborah's hand automatically started stroking the dog again, but her pose was stricken.

'No more than that.' Louisa tried to sound reassuring. 'Would you mind taking Maisie down to the kitchen? She's quite happy there, helping Mrs Airlie peel potatoes.' She wasn't at all sure that was the case, but it was the best she could think of for the moment. She gave Maisie a kiss. 'Be a good girl. I won't be long.'

Nancy stood. 'I'll come with you, Louisa. Debo, you ring the doctor.' As they walked away, Nancy whispered in Louisa's ear: 'Don't tell me it's another murder. Farve will have a fit.' She giggled at her tease, but Louisa didn't. Whether it was her restless night, or Ellis's shocked face, something about the atmosphere worried her a great deal. Even as they walked along the corridor, following Ellis to the servants' quarters, through the baize door and up two flights of stairs, there was a feeling of everything being more hushed than usual. Nancy remarked on it. 'You'd think with the war, we'd all be used to death. But perhaps just knowing there's a body in the house is enough to make everything feel a bit odd.'

Ellis looked around behind him when Nancy said that but made no remark. When they reached the bedroom, he opened the door but remained standing outside it. 'I'd better go down and wait for the doctor in the hall,' he said, and left.

Louisa went in cautiously. The curtains had been drawn, presumably by the maid who had erroneously thought she would wake the late Mrs Hoole. The room was simple, with a few items to denote the seniority of the servant for whom it had been allocated. A cast-iron single bedstead, with a quilted counterpane over it, and a small sheepskin rug on the floor. Mrs Hoole's black clothes were draped on a chair, a pair of staid laced shoes neatly beside it. A narrow wardrobe, a long mirror, a chest of drawers in mahogany, a washstand: all unremarkable but polished and looked after. Two paintings hung on the plain cream wall, simple oils of rustic landscapes, not as pretty as the view from the window. Around the room were several candlesticks, with no candles in them but a lot of dripped wax gathered around the base of each. Louisa looked at one. 'I think they all burned down. What was she doing lighting so many candles? There's no book so it wasn't to read.'

'I think we know why,' said Nancy.

'A séance of her own.'

'Yes, and look.' Nancy pointed to the bed, where Mrs Hoole lay. She wore a petticoat and a thick woollen vest, both of which had become uncomfortably twisted, her legs at awkward angles and the covers wrapped around them. Her arms were outstretched, both hands clamped in fists, her mouth open, her eyes squeezed shut. There was a pool of something on the floor beside her. Cautiously, Louisa bent down and sniffed it. 'Sick,' she confirmed.

'However she died, it wasn't peacefully,' said Nancy.

'No,' agreed Louisa. She looked again at what had once been Mrs Hoole, the grey tinge of the flesh, the colourless lips. How strange a body looked with no life in it, as solid and heavy as a rock on the seabed. She wanted to recoil, an instinctive response to horror and death, but professionalism and pity made her look closer. 'Someone will have to tell her mother in the village,' she said. 'And I think she said she had children?'

'Yes,' said Nancy, not unsympathetically for once. 'She said they were grown now.'

'Too young to die, though. It was hardly old age that killed her.'

'No, but, Lou-Lou, you don't think it's anything suspicious, do you?'

Louisa didn't reply at first. She was too busy looking at what was in Mrs Hoole's left hand, so tightly gripped that at first she had mistaken it for a handkerchief. But even without prising open her fingers, Louisa could see it wasn't that: there was a thread of black ribbon in it. And blood.

Held in Mrs Hoole's cold, dead fingers was the bloodied cap that had belonged to her friend, Joan.

'Yes,' she said. 'I do think it's suspicious.'

CHAPTER TWENTY-TWO

⁕

Watching through the drawing-room window, Louisa happened to see the doctor's smart black motor coming down the drive at speed – she worried for any stray sheep that might be crossing – and was rather surprised when the figure that emerged from the driver's side was distinctly elderly. In fact, he fetched not only his case but a walking stick from the back seat before coming into the house. Ellis was ready and waiting by the front door, seemingly having got over his shock at the news of Mrs Hoole's demise. Given the necessary flights of stairs and the doctor's stick, it took at least fifteen minutes for him to be shown into the yellow drawing room, where they were all gathered. He seemed familiar with the house, and most of its occupants.

'Good morning, Your Grace and Your Grace,' he repeated, nodding as much as he was able at the duke and duchess. His head appeared to be fixed at a slight angle, preventing him from turning it to the side with any ease, and his suit had probably last fitted him properly before the Great War. It looked as if it might not have been cleaned since then, either.

'You're in time for elevenses, Dr Dunn,' said the duchess. 'We can't offer much but would you like a cup of tea?'

Dr Dunn took a few moments to sit himself down in an armchair that looked dangerously low. Finally he sank, like an egg yolk into a bowl of flour.

'Oh, no,' he said. 'I had better see the patient straight away.'

There was a silence, while everyone wondered whether he knew what he'd been summoned for.

'Who is the patient?' he queried, looking at those on his left.

The duchess maintained her poise, as did Lady Redesdale. Unity, however, did not.

'I don't know why Debo telephoned you,' she said, 'when the woman is dead. Nothing can be done for her.'

The doctor's white moustache twitched. 'Ah,' he said. 'Well, if there's no hurry, perhaps I will have that cup of tea.'

'No,' said Louisa. Everyone turned to look at her, even the doctor. 'That is, Dr Dunn, I do apologise. But I think the sooner you see her, the better. After all, isn't it necessary for any diagnosis you might need to make? As to how she died?'

Dr Dunn blinked twice, slowly. 'Given present company, I'm sure it will be natural causes. No urgency in that.'

Louisa felt a small fury bubble in her chest. 'Forgive me, Doctor. It's no reflection on present company but I do urge you to see Mrs Hoole—'

'I hope,' interrupted Lord Redesdale, 'that we aren't going to have any of your nonsense, Mrs Sullivan.'

'What nonsense?' whispered Kick to Deborah, though unfortunately not quietly enough.

'*Murder* nonsense,' said Nancy. 'Farve is convinced that Louisa is the root cause.'

'At some point, don't we acknowledge that Mrs Sullivan appears to be the common factor when it comes to murders and their unfortunate proximity to our family?' said Nancy's father, but he knew when to give up in the face of his daughter.

'Lord Redesdale, I assure you—'

But Louisa was interrupted once more.

'Not this again,' said Nancy. 'And, anyway, none of us are saying this is suspicious.'

'You think it's suspicious?' drawled Adele. She had been sitting so quietly, and elegantly, in a chair by the window that Louisa had hardly registered she was there. And yet, once noticed, it was impossible not to look and enjoy the gloss of glamour that no one else could match. She was wearing a pair of claret-red wide-legged trousers and a co-ordinating cashmere sweater, with huge pearls hanging from her ears: the ensemble was devastating. Dr Dunn had painstakingly turned his whole body around to see who had spoken and it was clear he felt justly rewarded.

'Or are you referring to my husband's reaction last night?' Adele added.

'No, we do not think it is suspicious,' said Deborah. 'I'm so sorry, Adele, this is not how the week was supposed to go. It's simply unfortunate. And of course it's terribly sad for Mrs Hoole's family. We'll need to let them know, as soon as the doctor ...'

'Yes, yes,' said Dr Dunn, gripping the arms of his chair and beginning his long haul up. 'I understand.'

Louisa picked up his case, and asked him to follow her. All along the corridors, which seemed twice as long as before while the doctor hobbled at his glacial pace, Louisa kept thinking of the opportunities that had been afforded to any potential murderer to clean up the crime scene so long as the room was empty. At the same time, she admonished herself: what if Lord Redesdale was right? Was she seeing something criminal, causing worry where there was none? Hopefully the doctor would settle the argument one way or the other.

When they finally reached the room, the doctor wheezing, Louisa was hit anew by the difference in the air to a room that contained a deceased person. There was nothing rancid – the rot would not have started yet – it was simply the absence of life. Mrs Hoole lay in her frozen, contorted position. So far as Louisa could see, everything in the room was as it had been when she had left it an hour or so before. The doctor made his way to the body, and carried out his various checks: a light in her eyes, a mirror to the mouth. He appeared to notice the vomit on the floor, congealed now.

'I know it seems a little over-cautious,' he said, 'but I'm an old man and I've heard too many tales of people being buried alive.'

Louisa didn't really know what to say to this. What a horrible thought.

He didn't take much longer. 'She's certainly dead,' he pronounced. 'I'll write out the death certificate when I get back to my surgery. We don't know the exact time of death, I suppose?'

'No,' said Louisa. 'She was found at nine o'clock by the maid. I think she would have gone to bed sometime around one o'clock in the morning, not long before me.'

'What was going on with all these candles?' asked the doctor. 'Was there a power cut last night?'

'I think she was conducting a séance.'

'Funny sort of thing to do.' He gave a big sniff and drew out a large handkerchief from his jacket pocket.

'Can you tell how she died, Doctor?'

'No. Was there any sign of illness last night, when she was here?'

Louisa shook her head. 'No. That's why I was thinking perhaps poison—'

'Young lady, be careful with your speculations. There will be a post-mortem, much as I don't like them. They're very upsetting for the family, delaying the funeral. I'm not an expert on these matters but there's no obvious sign of any struggle, no bruises on her that I can see.'

He looked once more at the for-ever inert Mrs Hoole. 'There's something familiar about her . . .'

'Her mother lives in the village,' said Louisa. 'I believe she moved away some time ago but comes – came back to visit quite often.'

'Hmm, yes. Perhaps that's it. Ah, well. People come and go in my line of business, as you can imagine.' He drew himself up as far as he was able – not very far – and gave Louisa a serious look. 'You're a private detective, are you?'

'I am.'

'Down from London?'

Louisa agreed.

'Don't go causing any trouble, young lady. This house might be a big one, but the place is small. You can cause ructions that go far beyond your mind's eye. It's not like London, where deaths and mischief are swallowed by the crowds.'

Again, Louisa was stuck for words.

He gestured to his case. 'Would you be so kind?'

Louisa picked it up. 'I'll take you back down to the front.' Her heart sank rather at the tedium of the journey ahead.

'No, no. Just hand it to Ellis, if you would, to take to my car. I know my way from here, and it's quicker if I leave by the back stairs. Don't tell the dowager.' He gave a small chuckle and went on his slow way.

CHAPTER TWENTY-THREE

Back in the yellow drawing room, where Maisie was content-edly reading her *Beano* for the hundredth time, Louisa was sitting with Deborah and Nancy on the sofa. There had been general commiserations for the events of the morning, before she admitted: 'I'm afraid there will be things that have to be organised.'

'Yes, I know.' Deborah was her mother's daughter, she knew how to mask her feelings well, but Louisa felt sorry for her. This was not the week she had planned, with a sudden death among the festive frivolities.

'Mrs Hoole's family need to be told, and the undertaker will have to come and remove the body,' Louisa explained, but before she could get any further, she was interrupted by Ellis appearing in the doorway.

'Sergeant Booth to see you, Your Ladyship.'

A young policeman came in, smartly turned out in an immaculate uniform and shiny boots. Louisa knew he wasn't a schoolboy but she did wish they didn't all look quite so young to her. It only meant that she looked old.

Nancy stood immediately and walked up to the policeman. 'Good morning, Sergeant Booth. How may we help?' There was an archness to her manner, like a cat toying with a mouse.

Sergeant Booth stammered and completely failed to hold his nerve. 'I believe there has been an unfortunate incident in the house, ma'am. Your Ladyship. Your Highness.'

'Ma'am will do just fine,' laughed Nancy. 'Yes, there has but we weren't aware it was a matter for the police.'

'It's routine, Your—' He stopped. Breathed, started again. 'Ma'am. If a person dies in a place that is not their home, and with no obvious signs of illness, I have to take a statement.'

'From whom?'

Wildly, Sergeant Booth looked around the room. There were Adele, Deborah, Nancy, Louisa and Maisie. 'The head of the household is the usual person,' he said. 'Do you know who that might be?'

'The Duke of Devonshire,' said Deborah. 'I don't know where he is but I can go on a hunt.'

The sergeant blanched but nodded. 'Yes, please, ma'am.'

'Actually, if you're talking to my sister, she is "Your Ladyship" but she's not stuffy about these things. Not like the duke. So no need to worry,' said Nancy, barely keeping the smirk off her face.

'Don't tease,' admonished Deborah. 'Sergeant Booth, I will bring the duke to the room where the unfortunate Mrs Hoole still lies. Mrs Sullivan will take you there.'

With Nancy left in charge of Maisie again – or it might have been the other way around, thought Louisa, as Nancy was the most likely to get up to mischief – Louisa took the policeman to the late Mrs Hoole. The sight of her in the bed was no less shocking than before, death having that peculiar ability to remain vivid and upsetting long after the fact of it had been established.

'This is ... was Mrs Hoole,' said Louisa.

Away from the drawing room and Nancy's teases, Sergeant Booth seemed to recover some professional confidence. 'And this is how she was found, is it?'

'Yes.'

He walked around the small room, hands behind his back. 'Who has been in here?'

'The maid who discovered her this morning, myself, Ellis and Mrs Rodd, whom you met just now. And then the doctor, of course. Why do you ask?'

'Standard question.' He kicked at crumbs of soil on the rug by the bed.

'Of course,' said Louisa, wondering a little at the earth that had been brought into the room. She hadn't noticed it before – had she?

Deborah came in with the duke, who looked bemused to be there, his hands stuck in his pockets, for once not holding a cigarette. He saw Mrs Hoole and looked away quickly, grimacing. 'Ah, there. Yes. I don't know that I have anything very useful to say on ...' He pulled a hand out, gesturing vaguely in the direction of the bed.

'I just need to confirm one or two things, sir.'

'Your Grace,' said Deborah.

'Eh?' The policeman looked at her.

Deborah blushed. 'You should address the duke as "Your Grace," not "sir".'

Sergeant Booth took this in. 'Right. Your Grace, if you could just ...'

124

Louisa sometimes wondered how two Englishmen managed to put their clothes on in the morning, let alone run governments, if these two shining examples were anything to go by.

The duke confirmed his name, and then there was some kerfuffle over the fact that he was the head of the household but not living in the house. He confirmed that he had met Mrs Hoole the previous evening, that she had appeared to be in good health and that he had been made aware of her death earlier that morning.

'Can you tell me why she stayed in the house instead of returning to her home?' asked Sergeant Booth.

'No, I can't,' admitted the duke.

'The car wouldn't start,' said Louisa. 'It was late by that time, and the decision was taken that she should stay here and be returned to her home this morning.'

'Except that she was dead when morning came,' stated the policeman.

'Well, yes,' said Louisa. 'Although I'm not sure any of us would have put it quite like that.'

'We shall have to arrange for the coroner to remove the body,' said Sergeant Booth.

'What about the undertaker?' asked Deborah. 'Can't he do it?'

'There will need to be a post-mortem to establish cause of death.'

'That seems unnecessary,' said the duke. 'Rather a lot of fuss and all that. I mean, one can see . . . ' Again he gestured towards the bed, without actually looking at the body there. 'Natural causes. Sergeant Booth, is it? Yes, my good man, I don't want the wrong sort of attention on the house. There is a war on, you know.'

'Yes, Your Grace,' said the policeman, evenly. 'We'll avoid any fuss. But the post-mortem is required by law. I'm sure there's nothing to be concerned about. As you say, anyone can see . . .'

Louisa wanted to scream. See *what*?

'If the duke's statement is sufficient,' said Deborah, gently, 'perhaps Mrs Sullivan could show you out.'

When they had left, Louisa knew she had to say something, it was now or never. 'Sergeant Booth, if the coroner does find something untoward in the cause of death . . .'

'It's not likely, though, is it?' The policeman chuckled, visibly relieved that he was no longer in the presence of dukes and snobs.

'Forgive me, I have no intention of telling you how to do your job, but I am a private detective, my husband was in the London Metropolitan Police, and the *likelihood* of something can be a poor indicator.'

'What is it you think happened, ma'am?' He had reverted to his blushing, earlier self.

She felt somewhat bad. Only a little, though. 'I don't know exactly. But she told us a story – that is, Mrs Hoole told Lady Andrew and Mrs Rodd, as well as myself that she had known of a young girl, a maid, who went missing in this house during the last war, and she was convinced that the girl's disappearance had been hushed up.' She took a step towards the bed. 'Look, she's holding the maid's cap, stained in blood, in her hand. She tells us this sorry tale, and then she's found dead in her bed the next morning. It's too much of a coincidence for me.'

'Right. And what are you asking of me, exactly?'

'Perhaps this room should be treated as a possible crime scene. I think you need a detective here.'

'Hmm.' Sergeant Booth rocked on his heels. 'I'll tell the detective inspector. It's coming up to Christmas, though, ma'am. He won't be keen.'

'Tell him,' said Louisa. 'What's his name, out of interest?' If they didn't hear from him, she'd contact him herself.

'DI Tucker,' said Sergeant Booth. 'And now I'd better get back to the station. We'll close this door, shall we? Can you ask that no one goes in here? The coroner should be here later today.'

'Thank you,' said Louisa. DI Tucker. She'd heard the name, but how could she have done?

And then it hit her.

Mrs Hoole had mentioned him. The sympathetic young sergeant, who knew about the missing maid. Yes, Louisa definitely wanted to talk to him. Because there was one thing she was certain of: if someone had killed Mrs Hoole, they were protecting Joan's killer.

Or they were her killer.

CHAPTER TWENTY-FOUR

'It doesn't exactly feel very festive, does it,' said Nancy to Louisa, over their cheese sandwiches at lunch, 'what with dead bodies, doctors and policemen all over the place?'

'You exaggerate.' Louisa sighed but she agreed. Maisie had got down from the table and was rather forlornly playing with a doll in a corner of the room. If a young child wasn't feeling the joys of Yuletide mere days before Father Christmas came down the chimney, something was wrong indeed. 'I think I'll ask Debo to drive us into Baslow. I need to find Mrs Hoole's mother, and Maisie can at least see some decorations hanging in the shops, perhaps spend sixpence.'

'I'll come with you,' said Nancy. 'I can be your assistant. We'd better change into black if we're going to meet the poor departed's mother.'

Less than an hour later, the four of them pulled up outside Mr Formby's shop. Louisa was heartened by the sight of it, on Maisie's behalf and her own. The curved window glowed prettily with a display of Christmas presents, and a red bicycle was propped up against the front, as if it belonged to an elf doing some last-minute shopping.

'Do you think he'll give me some sweets again?' Maisie asked.

'You'll have to behave nicely with Lady Andrew first,' said Louisa, with a wink to make her daughter laugh.

'We're off to the butcher first, and then we'll come back here,' said Deborah, extending her hand for Maisie to take. They walked off together, Deborah skipping and laughing with Maisie as if she was a little girl, too.

'I'll never have that,' said Nancy, watching them.

'What do you mean? It's not too late.'

'Yes, it is. And even if it weren't, the doctors removed my womb, so you see, it's impossible. Perhaps it always was. I didn't tell you but I had two miscarriages, each one around the time Diana's babies were born.' Nancy said this in a matter-of-fact tone, as relentlessly unsparing of herself as she was of others, but Louisa could see the unhappiness in her eyes.

'I'm so sorry,' she said.

'Don't be. And I apologise. I didn't mean to come over all maudlin. It's Christmas, endless talk of happy families. It's not as if I ever knew it as a child so I don't know why I should mourn it as an adult.'

'Of course you must grieve. You've not only lost your babies, but the hopes you had for the future.'

'Well, we've all lost that, haven't we? With the war.' Nancy turned her head away briefly, and took a breath before she looked back. 'It does us no good to think of it.' She touched Louisa's arm. 'But thank you. You're a darling for listening, and probably the only one I can really tell.'

'Anytime,' said Louisa, and knew there was no more to say

for now, but she felt very sad for her friend. Perhaps this was the real reason Nancy wanted Louisa at Chatsworth for Christmas: as a confidante if she felt low.

Inside, the shop looked much as it had when Louisa had arrived only a few days before, though there were colourful paper chains tacked to the ceiling, and snowflakes cut out of newspaper, which added up to a jolly effect. Mr Formby stood behind the counter, his hair neatly combed back, his large apron clean.

'Mrs Sullivan,' he said, as they came in.

'Goodness, you've got a good memory,' said Louisa.

'It's not often we get a private detective in Baslow.' He smiled. 'What would you like today? I'm afraid I'm all out of magnifying glasses, mind.'

'Very funny, Mr Formby. In fact, we haven't come to buy anything, although Lady Andrew will be along shortly and I know she has a list. I've come to ask a favour. I wondered if you might know where Mrs Hoole's mother lives.'

'Ah, God rest her soul,' said the shopkeeper, solemnly.

'You know what happened?' asked Nancy, sharply. 'The body's barely cold.'

'I can't say as what happened but, yes, we heard. It's a small place here, miss. Not like your London.'

'How do you know I'm from London?' said Nancy, with more than a touch of *hauteur*. Louisa knew she wouldn't be displeased that her black Dior was evident to a shopkeeper in Derbyshire, but Louisa didn't want Mr Formby to take offence.

'This is Mrs Rodd,' Louisa intervened, 'Lady Andrew's elder sister.'

'Pleased to meet you, Mrs Rodd,' said Mr Formby. 'Yes, I

know where her mother lives. Mrs Duffin's her name, but she's ninety-three if she's a day and lost her mind some while back. You won't get much sense from her.'

'I'm not investigating anything,' lied Louisa. 'We're going as representatives of Chatsworth to pass on our condolences.'

'I see.' He didn't look as if he believed her but he gave them directions.

As they were leaving, a thought occurred to Louisa. 'Mr Formby, my daughter will be in later with Lady Andrew. If I give you sixpence now, might you be able to give her some of those secret treats you had before?' She gave a nod in the direction of his counter or, rather, under it.

Mr Formby stiffened. 'It's not an illegal supply, if that's what you're implying.'

Louisa was confused. It was definitely what had been implied before. 'Of course not. Lady Andrew has my ration book. I know everything's above board.'

'That it is.' Mr Formby crossed his arms.

'Right,' said Louisa, unsure what she had done wrong. She put a sixpence on the counter. 'Might you be able to direct us to Mrs Duffin's house?'

Outside, Nancy pulled a face. 'That was odd. What a funny little man.'

'You never know what's happened in someone's day,' said Louisa. 'But I agree, he was protesting rather too much. Now, he said over the bridge, the third street on the right, and the cottage with the green door.'

In minutes, they were there, in the neat front garden of a small cottage with a thatched roof and a green door, recently painted. They could see shadows of people moving about inside. 'Perhaps we shouldn't have come so soon,' said Louisa.

'Doesn't Guy always tell you that the sooner you can ask questions in an investigation, the better?'

'Yes, but that supposes this *is* an investigation.'

To which, Nancy merely raised an eyebrow. Feeling found out, Louisa knocked on the door. It was opened by a short, stout woman, with grey hair in a bun and a hairy mole on her chin. 'You've heard the news,' she said, by way of a greeting.

'Well, yes—'

'Poor old thing, it would be the most terrible shock if she was able to understand. I just give thanks she doesn't know what day it is, let alone what's happened to her dear departed daughter.' She turned around, still talking, expecting them to follow her inside. 'Shocking it is, and in the big house, too.' She stopped and faced them. 'I don't recognise yer.' Her grey eyes squinted. 'Either of yer.'

'No,' said Louisa. 'I'm Mrs Sullivan, and this is Mrs Rodd. We were with Mrs Hoole last night, at Chatsworth. And we wanted to come with the family's cond—'

The woman drew herself up to her fullest height, which wasn't past Louisa's shoulders. 'As well you might!' she said fiercely. 'I said to my husband, I *said*, I wonder when they'll send someone up. They've had the police and doctors, and not a word down here. She had to hear it from the policeman. Did you know that? He was practically a child himself. He didn't know what—' She stopped herself and her shoulders sagged slightly. 'I suppose you're here now.'

'I do apologise,' said Nancy, smoothly, and Louisa was grateful for the switched-on charm. 'We had to make sure that everything was attended to properly at the house. I'm sure you understand. We had hoped, naturally, that someone closer to Mrs Duffin could have broken the terrible news to her, but it looks as if you have stepped into the breach *most* admirably.'

'I've done what I could,' said the woman. 'I've been her neighbour these past forty-three years.'

'Goodness,' said Nancy, as admiringly as if she'd been told she was standing before the inventor of the wheel.

'I'll take you through. But, like I said, she doesn't understand what happened.'

She showed them into the cottage's front room, very stuffy and hot from a fire that blazed in the hearth. Mrs Duffin was sitting in an armchair, covered with blankets, and only a crown of white hair was visible. Slowly, she lifted her head at their entrance, revealing a lined face with bewildered eyes, so pale they were almost translucent.

Louisa bent down before her. 'Mrs Duffin, I'm so terribly sorry about your daughter.'

'What?' The old lady peered around the room. 'Sorry for what?'

Louisa looked back at Nancy, who shook her head. Perhaps it was best not to go on with a conversation that could only distress her.

'Your daughter was a fine woman,' said Louisa, trying not to wince at her use of the past tense.

'Eh?' said Mrs Duffin.

Her neighbour came over and took Mrs Duffin's hand, finding it beneath the blankets. 'She's talking about your Eliza,' she said loudly. 'What a good woman she is.'

'Ah,' was Mrs Duffin's only response. 'I suppose so. She knows

133

how to make a good cake. I don't know what else she be good for. Caused me no end of trouble. Always poking her nose where it weren't wanted.'

Louisa knew better than to press this in front of the neighbour but she didn't have to. Mrs Duffin was happy to talk.

'Went off sudden to the city, I don't know what she wanted to do that fer. Left her sisters behind, us all struggling in the war, her brothers away fighting.' Her eyes turned watery. 'Our Arthur . . .'

'I know,' said her neighbour. 'I remember. But Eliza came home to see you as often as she could. She was a good girl to you.'

Mrs Duffin grunted at this and her head sank. She was clearly exhausted by the exchange. The neighbour kept a careful eye on her and whispered to Louisa, 'Things weren't always easy between them but, still, they were mother and daughter, weren't they?'

Louisa nodded sympathetically. 'Did you see Eliza on this last visit? I wonder if you noticed anything unusual.'

'No,' said the neighbour, 'only a friendly wave. Although I saw her getting into a motor-car last night. I presume she was being collected by the big house.'

There was the sound of a snore from Mrs Duffin.

'Yes,' said Nancy. 'One of the gardeners fetched her.'

'Oh, was that who it was? Funny that.'

'Why?' asked Louisa.

'No reason. There used to be stories, you know.'

'What stories?' Nancy's interest had piqued, too.

'I probably shouldn't say anything. They were only rumours. But it was said that Eliza knew something about the big house that they wanted kept secret. It's not many as has fancy motor-cars coming to fetch them.'

'That was me, actually,' said Nancy. 'I ordered the car to collect her.'

'Well, then,' said the neighbour, looking relieved that this awkward conversation could be brought to an end, 'that explains it. There's nothing for her to have known. It was a long time ago she worked there, wasn't it? And I'm sure whatever was happening then don't happen no more.'

'What?' asked Louisa. 'What was happening then?'

'I couldn't really say,' said the neighbour, her hairy mole twitching on her chin. 'But there were stories about the duke and his wicked ways. I dare say every duke has a story like that following them around.'

'Yes,' said Nancy, almost triumphant. 'Every duke has those stories and they are almost never true. Thank you so much for being so kind as to let us see Mrs Duffin and give her our sincere condolences.' With her inestimable charm, Nancy patted the neighbour on the shoulder and indicated to Louisa that they would be making a swift exit, stage left.

CHAPTER TWENTY-FIVE

The two women walked slowly through the village. Louisa needed to get back to Maisie but she wanted to think through the events of the last twenty-four hours. There was a lot to consider: Mrs Hoole and her séance; the angry reaction of Charles to her 'message' from Joan; her revelation that she had known Joan, and was certain she had been killed; Billy wanting to know what she had told them, seemingly hiding a concern that she might know something about the family that was a secret; Ellis surprising her in the middle of the night; and then, of course, Mrs Hoole's sudden and unexplained death. The doctor seemed almost adamant that it would have been from natural causes – what was he afraid Louisa would uncover if she asked too many questions? She knew country people were suspicious of interfering Londoners, and the fact she was a private detective was probably enough to put them on edge, but it didn't explain enough for her. Was Mrs Hoole's death connected with Joan's, and if it was murder, how was it done? The doctor said there were no obvious signs of a struggle, but he couldn't rule out poisoning, could he? Or smothering with a pillow. The young policeman said there would be a post-mortem: she hoped that with Christmas coming so soon the results wouldn't be delayed.

Louisa felt a jab in her side from Nancy. 'I'd give you a penny for your thoughts,' she said, 'but I'm flat broke at the moment, so you'll have to tell me for free.'

'Sorry,' said Louisa. 'I didn't mean to be so quiet. I've just been thinking about Mrs Hoole, trying to work out what happened.'

'There might not be anything to work out. Heart attacks happen, and she didn't look like the healthiest person to me,' said Nancy. They were turning onto the high street now, a little busier than usual with shoppers holding two or three bags each, jostling each other on the narrow pavement.

'Maybe.' Louisa stepped off the pavement to let a harassed young mother push past, bags hanging off the handle of her pram. 'I don't want to pry where it's not wanted but things aren't adding up.'

Nancy hooked her arm in Louisa's. 'That schoolboy of a policeman, he said there would be a detective inspector on to it, didn't he? Let's leave it to them for the moment. Now, it's nearly Christmas and we should do a good deed.'

'You're suggesting a good deed?' laughed Louisa, willing to lighten the mood.

'I do the teasing around here, thank you,' said Nancy, mock-crossly. 'Let's find my Nine and Maisie. We'll treat them to a cup of tea and a sticky bun.'

Instinctively, they walked towards Mr Formby's shop, the

beating heart of the village. 'Like Piccadilly,' said Nancy, 'where you're guaranteed to see someone you know if you stand still for five minutes.'

'Presciently said,' Louisa remarked, pointing straight ahead.

'Is that the French teacher?' asked Nancy, as they approached. Lucie was coming out of Formby's, her head bent against the cold breeze. She was holding something small close to her chest, almost bumping into them.

'Oh, hello,' she said. 'I didn't realise you were in the village.'

'We've been to pay our condolences to the mother,' said Nancy, with an edge of superiority in her tone.

'Yes, that was terrible news this morning. Very shocking.' She clasped her gloved hands around the small parcel she was holding even more tightly and made to move. 'So sorry but I am in a little bit of a rush—'

'What's that you've got there?' asked Nancy.

'Here?' said Lucie, her fingers still wrapped close.

'Nancy . . . ' Louisa warned but it was no good. Nancy had the bit between her teeth.

'Have you been Christmas shopping?' Nancy glanced at Mr Formby's shop, the decorations in the bay window.

Lucie looked trapped, and two pink spots appeared on her cheeks. 'Yes . . . that is, for me.' Embarrassed, she opened her hands partway to reveal a glass perfume bottle.

'Are you looking to impress someone?' Nancy smiled, but it didn't reach her eyes.

'It does no harm, does it?' Lucie retaliated. 'I thought that RAF officer was quite handsome.' She gave Louisa a knowing look. 'Now, I really must be going.'

They watched Lucie walk away and Louisa could feel Nancy

stiffen beside her. 'She's got another think coming if she imagines he'd be interested in a flibbertigibbet like her.'

Louisa knew the best way to manage Nancy's jealous fits was to ignore them and, luckily, she could see Deborah and Maisie coming down the high street, all smiles and glad tidings of joy.

CHAPTER TWENTY-SIX

When they returned to Chatsworth, it was to the rather distressing scene of Mrs Hoole – albeit beneath a shroud – being carried out of the front door and into the coroner's van. Ellis oversaw the proceedings with a distinct look of displeasure on his face. The porters did not acknowledge any of their party but asked Ellis to sign a piece of paper, which he did, holding the pen as if it might stain his fingers.

'What's been going on, Ellis?' asked Deborah, as the coroner's men drove off.

'Isn't it obvious?' said Nancy. 'At least the body is off the premises now. It needn't be our concern any more.'

Louisa bent down to Maisie, telling her to walk around to the back of the house and go into the kitchen. 'I'll see you there in a few minutes,' she said to her daughter. To Nancy, she said: 'Would you please be a little less abrupt about bodies in front of Maisie?'

'She's got to know the facts of death and life.'

'Not at six.'

Nancy shrugged, as if she didn't agree, but Louisa knew she had won the point. For now.

'I'm afraid that Miss Unity has been rather distressed by the incident this morning,' said Ellis.

'Oh dear,' said Deborah. 'That means Lady Redesdale will be upset, too. Unity can't stand the sight of me, but even so I had better go and see to them. Ellis, take the shopping out of the car to the kitchen, would you?' She went in.

'I'm exhausted from all the emotion of the day,' said Nancy. 'I'm going for a lie-down.' And she went in, too.

Louisa stood alone on the steps. She hadn't quite taken in the view from that vantage point, and it was rather spectacular. The rolling lawns, the clipped hedges, the woodland that climbed the hill behind the house. Everything was perfectly landscaped, as if each tree had been deliberately planted in its place. There couldn't be the usual number of workers on the estate, thanks to the war, but whoever was managing it was doing so admirably well. The gardener they had met a day or two before must be one of them, although it looked as if he was more in charge of the kitchen garden than the grander elements of the grounds.

He'd said there were one or two poisonous plants, and although there was nothing unusual in that, it made Louisa think about the cook, who must know what grew in the kitchen gardens. She could ask Mrs Airlie a question or two about Mrs Hoole. Louisa wanted to piece together exactly what Mrs Hoole had been up to in the house, not only the night before but on her previous visit, too. Whom had she talked to? It was true that there was no evidence as yet to suggest that her death hadn't simply been very unfortunate, a terrible coincidence of timing. But Louisa couldn't quite believe that.

In the kitchen, Maisie was peeling carrots, slowly and with a look of great concentration on her face. 'Look, Mummy,' she said, as Louisa came in. 'I can do this.'

'Thought I'd put her to use,' said one of the young maids, with a grin.

'Thank you,' said Louisa. 'It's a good idea. She's much happier when she's got a task to occupy her.'

'I've got five younger brothers and sisters,' said the maid. 'I know what it's like.'

'I can imagine. Is Mrs Airlie about?'

The maid nodded towards the servants' hall. 'Think she's in there. We've got a rest before we get started on the dinner proper.'

In the servants' hall, a simple room with a long table and a few chairs, a dresser at the side and the merit of a small fire in the hearth, Mrs Airlie was sitting with a newspaper on her lap but she wasn't reading it.

'Excuse me,' said Louisa, quietly, not wanting to startle her. 'I'm sorry to interrupt your rest.'

Mrs Airlie's shoulders shuddered, as if she was waking. 'No, no. What can I do for you?' She moved to get up.

'Please, stay where you are. I'll sit beside you, if that's all right?'

'Be my guest.'

Louisa pulled a chair up beside the cook, who folded the paper and put it on the table. She sat back but there was something in her posture that was not relaxed. 'I wanted to ask you about Mrs Hoole,' said Louisa.

'What about her?'

'It was a shock for everyone in the house, of course,' Louisa began.

'Yes, yes. A terrible business.' Mrs Airlie had the red cheeks and hands of a good country cook, but Louisa could see she was pale beneath.

'The police are investigating the cause of her death, naturally.'

Mrs Airlie gave a tight nod to this. 'So I understand.'

'On the face of it, there's nothing suspicious. It seems to have been a natural death.'

Mrs Airlie exhaled deeply. 'Yes, yes. Let's hope for all our sakes that were it. Just bad luck that it happened here.'

'On the other hand,' said Louisa, 'she could have been poisoned.'

The cook looked up at her sharply. 'What makes you say that?'

'She'd been sick.'

'It wasn't anything from my food,' said Mrs Airlie, flustered. 'She was fine when she ate, and I ate the same thing. Has someone said something to you? What are they saying?'

'No one is saying anything. I'm only trying to rule things out. I know there are poisonous plants in the garden.'

'As there are in any garden.'

'Of course,' said Louisa, as reassuringly as possible, though Mrs Airlie's fright was plain to see. 'But mistakes have been made.'

'If you're going to accuse me of something,' said the cook, 'I'd appreciate it if you would speak plainly.'

'No, no. There are no accusations. It's just that it'll take some time for the post-mortem report to come back, and there's Christmas slowing things down ... I thought I could be useful and try to find out what exactly occurred while Mrs Hoole was here.'

'By poking your nose into all our business?'

'I'm a private detective, Mrs Airlie.' If the cook was going to

143

spar, Louisa could parry with the best of them. 'The family have asked me to make enquiries.'

A white lie, perhaps, but Mrs Airlie said nothing.

'Mrs Hoole was having supper here with you last night. It seemed perhaps you knew her already.'

'It was only leftovers. I wasn't using up rations.'

Louisa was quickly getting the sense that the people here didn't like a private detective from London asking questions about their business. She seemed to be getting on their nerves in an alarmingly short space of time. 'No, of course not. I just wondered if you formed any impression of her.'

'Can't say as I did. I didn't know what she was up to last night but, as of today, I can say that I didn't like it.'

'What? The séance?'

'Messing with the dead. It's a dangerous business. You don't know what you stir up with things like that.' Mrs Airlie moved to stand. 'Now, if you don't mind, I've supper to be getting on with.'

'Just one more thing,' said Louisa. 'Were you here during the war?'

'Towards the end of it,' said Mrs Airlie. 'Scrap of a thing I was then, if you can believe it.'

'Can you remember Lord Charles and the duke as they were then?'

'Not really. Lord Charles was a small boy. He'd sometimes hang around the kitchens, hoping for a biscuit or two. His older brother, the current duke, was a young man. We wouldn't see him downstairs.'

'What about the other servants? Is there anyone here now who was here then?'

'No, I'm the only relic. There was Ellis the First, of course, Mr

Ellis's uncle. He was a very nice man. Not your typical snooty butler, always very kind to the children.'

'I'm sure you've heard about the cap that was found a few nights ago. Mrs Hoole seemed to think it belonged to a maid who went missing here, during the war. Do you know anything about that?'

'No, I don't.'

'And no one mentioned it? You never heard the story about Joan Dorries?'

'I came here after she'd gone. And even if they did, I'd know it were none of my beeswax, Mrs Sullivan.' And with that peremptory end to the conversation, Mrs Airlie returned to the kitchen. But Louisa was clear: Mrs Airlie had something to hide, and she was going to make it her beeswax to find out what it was.

CHAPTER TWENTY-SEVEN

Luncheon was corned-beef hash in the dining room. Nobody's favourite, and another reminder of the war that continued unseen and distant. It was hard sometimes to remember the reality of the fighting, the brutality and fear that shadowed the lives of millions. Daily, one heard news of another son or brother killed at the front, yet the war felt distant from Chatsworth. It wasn't like being in London, where the constant scream of air-raid sirens and bombs would regularly send everyone into a state of fear. All the same, it was curious how the silence could be equally unsettling.

Nonetheless, some things carried on as usual.

'It's like a buffet at an hotel by the sea,' sniffed Nancy, at the meagre spread, and her mother rebuked her for it. Unity was not there: she was being kept away from everyone until she recovered from the shock of the morning's news, or so Lady Redesdale said. She did her best to maintain a stoic pretence that nothing was terribly wrong with her daughter, a level of denial so deep Louisa thought Lady Redesdale might believe it. After everyone had desultorily swallowed their mouthfuls, various excuses were made to leave the room. They each needed a little time alone.

All, that was, except Kick, who was more muted today than she had been on arrival, while remaining the jolliest of the bunch. As Louisa was sitting with Maisie by the window, Kick came over. 'I was wondering if we could explore the house,' she said to them. 'I feel like I've only seen a quarter of it.'

Louisa knew Kick could never admit to any of the Cavendishes that she wanted to look around the place that she hoped would one day be hers to live in. And Louisa wanted to see more, too. A house of this size surely held a thousand secrets but she wanted to know only two: what had happened to Joan and Mrs Hoole.

'I feel the same,' said Louisa, and saw the gratitude in Kick's face. 'Let's do it. We can play I Spy with Maisie as we go.'

The school occupied rooms in the servants' quarters below stairs, as well as several of the state rooms on the ground and first floors, but the occupancy was awkward. Battered school desks stood, strangely lonely in the grand spaces. Several upright pianos were scattered through the house, and in other rooms, beneath double-height ceilings, rows of iron beds had been stripped and left with nothing more than their striped mattresses. Some of the more important rooms had been closed off entirely, apparent by the dust sheets thrown over the furniture and the pictures taken down. Nothing was locked.

'That will be so the night watchmen can check every room,' said Kick.

'Night watchmen?'

'There's two, Billy told me.'

'Why haven't I seen them? Or heard them?'

'I guess because they sleep in the day. They're awake all

147

night, every night, patrolling the whole house. It's not because of the war, although they are useful to keep an ear out for raids and warnings. They're here all the time, he said. It's such a big ol' house, they must worry about people getting in and hiding. Someone could disappear here for months, couldn't they?'

Kick was pushing open a door as she said this, and they tentatively stepped into the gloom. A lot of the rooms were dark because it was less work to leave the blackout blinds permanently up. Right now they were in the private wing, which stretched some distance from the yellow drawing room and the dining room they had used. The private rooms were smaller and cosier, relative to the state rooms elsewhere. They were also dustier, having not been used in some years. Maisie was sneezing her way around.

'What goes on in here?' said Louisa, as they entered one. The furniture looked modest in size, which was all they could tell of it, with the sheets draped over everything. Kick turned on a lamp and a bright glare dispelled the gloom. The walls and ceiling had been painted with an elaborate, if dark, mural of what looked like a Roman scene of a war. There were soldiers in armour wielding swords, horses rearing in terror and women half draped in white togas, attempting to flee the scene. Above them all was a grey and stormy sky, and imposing buildings with Corinthian columns, which more soldiers were attacking.

'I can't say I'd get a good night's sleep in here,' said Kick. 'It's gruesome.'

'I think I'll stick to flowers printed on wallpaper,' said Louisa, which made them both laugh.

The room next door was no more welcoming, even without the war scenes. This one had thick brown and gold curtains that hung long and heavy, flock wallpaper in dark brown and a large carved wooden bed. There were dust sheets over what looked like a side table and chair by the window, and the rugs were rolled up. Maisie lay on the bed, covered with a bedspread that looked like a medieval tapestry. 'It's like lying on the floor,' she said. 'Who sleeps in here?'

'No one,' said Louisa.

'But what about those?' Maisie pointed behind Louisa and Kick.

A pair of men's shoes was tucked beneath a chest of drawers. Louisa pulled them out. They were plain brown leather, with laces, and they could have belonged to Guy for their size and shine – as a former policeman, his shoes were always extremely well polished.

'They've been cleaned,' she said. 'Not dusty, not forgotten.'

'Perhaps one of the school teachers sleeps in here,' said Kick.

'That might be it, but the school hasn't been given use of the private wing, has it?' She put the shoes back, her interest piqued. The top of the chest was completely bare, a thin layer of dust on it, but the top left drawer contained some items: a handkerchief, slightly dirty; a glass and a bottle of whisky, almost empty. The right top drawer was empty, as was the one below, but the bottom contained an old navy woollen jumper, with moth-holes. Under that was an exercise book, the type schoolchildren used. Louisa took it out.

'You might be right about the teacher theory,' she said.

Kick took it from her and opened it. 'It's old, though. Look.' The paper had yellowed and the writing was immature, not a child's, but the script was tight and overly cursive, hard to read. Louisa tried to decipher it but it was too difficult: the pages were covered and she could only make out certain words that meant nothing without context – 'saw', 'Mother', 'school', 'hat'. If she could have, she would have taken it away to study more closely but she wasn't sure what Kick would think of that, so she put it back, beneath the jumper.

'Someone must have forgotten about it,' she said. 'I expect the rooms are full of things like that.'

'Billy's father, the duke, says when the war finishes they'll probably have to give the house away to an institution that can use it, and apart from the books and paintings, and some of the furniture, everything will get chucked on a fire.'

'Wouldn't you mind?' asked Louisa.

'Why would I mind?'

'If you marry Billy . . .'

'I'm not marrying him for this house, that's for sure. And I'm American. We look to the future, not the past.'

'That's true,' said Louisa. 'I admire you for it. We could do with more of it over here sometimes.'

Reluctantly, she closed the drawers, leaving the items inside. 'Well,' she said, suddenly feeling rather guilty and rattled by the clean shoes, 'we probably shouldn't be nosing around the family's rooms. Let's go down – we'll be in time for tea.'

CHAPTER TWENTY-EIGHT

When Louisa, Maisie and Kick came into the yellow draw-ing room, the curtains had been drawn and the lamps switched on. With the fire in the hearth, holly on the mantel-piece and the small Christmas tree covered with ornaments, shiny or painted, the mood was quite lifted. A tray of tea had been put on the table, and the sight of the pot with cups and saucers, a pretty jug of milk and a plate of plain biscuits, which was passed round, reassured Louisa somehow. She was missing Guy very much indeed, as she knew Maisie must be, but to be somewhere things were done so differently made it feel more like a holiday and less like an escape from London. She deter-mined that, in spite of the investigation, she would try to enjoy herself and give Maisie no reason to feel anything other than happy and Christmassy, as a young child should.

Nancy was sitting on the sofa, writing in a notebook. She paused as Louisa came to sit down beside her.

'I'm not disturbing you, am I?' asked Louisa, having decided to disturb her nonetheless.

'No,' said Nancy, looking rested after her nap. Her hair was curled and she wore a red lipstick that co-ordinated perfectly with her twinset. Adele Astaire was the undoubted Hollywood star but Nancy had a quiet style that Louisa always admired, everything beautifully chosen and well made. She knew how to look after her clothes to make them last, too.

'What are you writing?'

Nancy closed the book with a slightly embarrassed smile. 'I've got an idea for a novel but it's not one I think anyone here will like much.'

'Why not?'

'Because they're all in it, and not at their most flattering.'

'Are you in it, too?'

'Of course,' said Nancy. 'But when I was much younger, and I was sillier and more stupid then, too.'

'I don't remember that,' said Louisa, leaning into her, a playful nudge.

'Darling Lou,' said Nancy, 'you make me feel quite sentimental, remembering our past. And nobody else here does that.'

Unity came over to them. She was not the embodiment of chic, as her sister was, dressed in clothes chosen by her mother: thick woollen stockings and what looked like a scratchy tweed skirt, with a checked cotton blouse. Her hair had been brushed back, and her face was scrubbed clean, completely free of any make-up. 'What are you two talking about?' she demanded.

'We were remembering the past,' said Nancy. 'When Louisa first came to Asthall Manor.'

'Oh, yes,' her sister replied, without any suggestion of knowing what Nancy meant. 'I mean to say, we're going to church tomorrow. Would you like to come?'

'No, thank you.'

'I want to talk to the vicar. I haven't met him yet. I want to ask him if he sleeps in the same bed as his wife.'

Louisa thought she might splutter her tea.

'I'm not sure that's a very good idea.' Nancy signalled to their mother on the other side of the room, who saw but did not immediately move. Louisa pitied her: she looked exhausted, as well she might. Unity had the form of a grown woman, but the carelessness and restlessness of a young child who needed constant attention.

'You see, I can't find anything in the Bible about whether a vicar might sleep with his wife, and I feel he will know the answer.'

'Can't you think about something nicer?' said Nancy. 'Like Father Christmas coming down the chimney?'

Unity put her hands over her face. 'Oh, no! He's not coming into my *bedroom*.' On the turn of a sixpence, hysterics threatened. Louisa was worried but Nancy looked merely bored. 'Now, miss, you're being a perfect nuisance. I was talking to Louisa. Go away.'

Rather to Louisa's surprise, Unity reacted to this immediately. 'Yes, I shall,' she said, and she walked over to her mother.

'It's never going to get any better, is it?' said Louisa.

'No, it's likely to get a great deal worse. Let's think of other things. Have you heard from Guy?'

'We had a letter a couple of days ago. The thing is, he'd never say if there was anything to worry about so I don't even know if he's telling me truthfully how he is. I suppose one can only be grateful he's still alive, and our house is still standing.' But she felt an ache behind her eyes, a familiar sensation when she was holding back the tears. 'I dread reading the newspapers or hearing the radio in case there's been an air raid in our part of London. When we're here, we can almost forget the war is happening.'

'I know,' said Nancy. 'I feel the same. I have no idea where Peter is and I'm grateful. If I could picture it too easily, I think it would be tormenting.'

'You miss him, then?'

Sadness bloomed in Nancy's face. 'I do. We're not happy together, and I don't know what will happen when the war is over. But I want him back, alive and in one piece. It seems selfish, I know, when children are missing their fathers every day. And yet there's also a terrible part of me that worries it would be too difficult to leave him if he came back seriously injured. I'll admit that to you, but I wouldn't dare to do so to many others.'

Louisa understood. How strange it was, this war, the ripple effects it had on so many lives, not just those at the front. Deborah came over to them at that moment, carrying a plate of bread and margarine. 'I'd offer another biscuit,' she said apologetically, 'but I feel we ought to ration them, if you can forgive me using the word.'

'How did Mrs Airlie manage to make them, with all of the shortages?' asked Louisa.

'I have a feeling Mr Formby has his uses,' said Deborah.

'What do you mean?'

Deborah looked embarrassed. 'I don't want to sound as if I'm accusing him of anything. But one hears about these black markets in the war . . .'

'You think he sells things that are not strictly . . . above board?' pressed Louisa, wondering what else he might procure. The sweets they knew about, but might those be a cover for something more dangerous?

'I actually came over to tell you some news,' said Deborah, deliberately changing tack. 'Muv has had a letter from Decca. It seems she met with Cousin Winston in Washington, and he's told her that Esmond is very definitely dead.'

'It's not as if we didn't know,' said Nancy.

'Well, it seemed the most likely explanation but I think she must have held out hope to the very last second. It does seem awfully hard on her,' said Deborah, 'what with the baby, and everything. I don't know what to say to her but I must write.'

'Will she come back to England?' asked Louisa.

'I doubt it,' said Deborah. 'In the letter she said Winston tried to say something to her about Diana's conditions improving in Holloway, and she replied that the Mosleys should be put up against a wall and shot.'

'Christ,' said Nancy.

'I know they disagree violently, but I do think it's rather hard on Muv to read that in a letter. She frets terribly about Diana, too.' They all looked across to Lady Redesdale, sitting with Unity, and wearing a look of patient forbearance as her daughter chattered on. Looking across they saw, on the other side of the room, Lord Redesdale in an armchair with the newspaper.

'Lady Redesdale is very alone, isn't she?' said Louisa. 'The two of them have hardly said a word to each other since they got here.'

'I don't know what I was thinking,' said Deborah. 'I sort of hoped they'd see each other and remember they loved each other.'

'What am I always saying?' Nancy put her hand on Deborah's

knee, a rare affectionate touch. 'You've got the brain of a nine-year-old.'

In some ways it had been something of a sad conversation but Louisa was grateful for the company and sympathy of these women. No one could wish for the tragedies of war, but there was a sliver of comfort when people refused to be divided by it.

CHAPTER TWENTY-NINE

The following morning, after breakfast, Lucie kindly offered to take Maisie for a walk in the gardens so Louisa had a chance to write some Christmas cards and a letter to Guy. She would have preferred to telephone him and hear his voice, but they didn't have one in their house in London. He wouldn't ring her at Chatsworth from a telephone box, in case he called at the wrong time. Still, it was lovely to receive letters from him and she probably put more detail in than she would in a conversation that always threatened to be cut short by the pips after three minutes.

Sitting at a bureau in the yellow drawing room, with the bright wintry light coming through, Louisa wrote to Guy about the shocking death of Mrs Hoole. She included the revelation that a maid had been murdered and the killing covered up by a person, or several persons, in the house. It helped to set out the details as she knew them so far, although she held back from speculation on the people she was staying with. She thought about what she had just written and added: 'I wish we could be together to solve this. Maisie and I miss you terribly.' She didn't want him to feel guilty, so added that their daughter was very happy nonetheless, enjoying the sights and sounds of the coming Christmas as well as the huge gardens with a maze for hide and seek. Louisa finished by saying she hoped he was feeding himself properly, and that she loved him. There had been no definite date for their return to London, and she knew that, although she and Maisie missed him, there was no question that without the fear of air raids her equilibrium was greatly restored. She had no desire to rush back.

Just as Louisa was licking the envelope, she felt someone come into the room and turned to see Ellis standing there. She wished he didn't have the habit of gliding up behind her but she knew from her own working days with the Mitfords that servants never knocked on doors.

'Yes?' she said, turning in her chair, squinting as he stood in the sunlight.

'Beg pardon, I was looking for Lady Andrew, ma'am,' he said.

'I'm not sure where she is. Perhaps in the kitchens. I know that, with Christmas so close, she and Mrs Airlie are working hard on the preparations.'

'Yes,' said Ellis, but didn't move. 'I have looked in several places. The difficulty is, ma'am, that Mr Tucker is here, a detective inspector, and he wishes to talk to you.'

'To me? Did he ask for me by name?'

'He asked to speak to the person who claimed to be a private detective, yes.'

'Claimed? I *am* a private detective.' Louisa stopped herself: it would do no good to go on the defensive before she had even spoken to the man. 'Perhaps you had better show him in, then,' she said, with as much calm authority as she could muster. It didn't come naturally, asking butlers to do her will, but she knew better than to muddle things by talking to Ellis too informally.

'Very good, ma'am.' With what she was sure was a supercilious sneer, Ellis went to fetch the detective.

Louisa had braced herself but when Ellis came in, leading DI Tucker, she saw at once that there was nothing to worry about. He was short, not much taller than Louisa, with neatly trimmed red hair and a kind, ruddy face. He wore a well-pressed suit and carried his hat in one hand, the other outstretched to shake hers.

'So, you're the talk of the town,' he said, as she accepted his friendly greeting.

'What do you mean?'

'Oh, you'll have to forgive our provincial ways,' said Tucker, in the handsome local accent. 'A private detective down from London is quite exciting for us.' Without invitation, he sat on the sofa, hitching up his trousers at the knees. 'Mind you, I'm not as sure about the dead bodies turning up with you.' He gave a dry chuckle.

Louisa liked him but she wasn't quite up to laughing about the death of Mrs Hoole just yet. 'I gather you knew Mrs Hoole from quite a long way back,' she said, sitting down on the opposite sofa.

'I know everyone here,' Tucker replied. 'I grew up not three miles from this house.'

'Yes, but when you were a young policeman, you knew Mrs Hoole? She went by the name of Eliza Duffin then.'

DI Tucker gave her what her mother would have called a sidelong look. 'You've been busy already.'

'I won't deny I've got my instincts,' said Louisa. 'I run an agency with my husband, a former policeman for the London Metropolitan. I wasn't expecting to work up here, but as you know, Mr Tucker, when the call comes, you have to answer it.'

'Aye. I do know that. Tell me what more you've dug up.'

'Mrs Hoole came to this house a few nights ago, when it was raining very heavily. She said she had a message for one of the house's occupants, and that the message had come "from the other side".'

'Did you believe her?'

'I neither believed nor disbelieved, I think. She seemed a little strange but, then, her arrival was unexpected.'

'She were a busybody,' said Tucker, rather forcefully.

'Why do you say that?'

'Like I said, Mrs Sullivan, I know the people around here.' He reached into his pocket and pulled out a notebook and pencil. 'Now, you've set to work, so I'd better do the same. My sergeant took the statement from the duke so this is a little extra on the side, really. I'd heard you wanted to talk to me, and I was curious. Why do you think Mrs Hoole's death is suspicious?'

Relieved to be able to talk her ideas through, Louisa listed her reasons: the fact that Mrs Hoole had talked about the maid going missing and was found with the bloodied cap in her hand; the vomit on the floor; the fact that people seemed to be hiding something.

'Who is hiding something?' asked Mr Tucker.

'Someone in the family seems to think Mrs Hoole might have had reason to blackmail them,' said Louisa, thinking of Billy and his alarm at what Mrs Hoole had revealed after the séance to her, Deborah and Nancy.

'I see. Well, there are always rumours, but that's to be expected when you've got village gossips, and who hasn't got those?' said the detective. 'Anyone else?'

Louisa wanted to be careful. Charles had reacted badly – dropping the champagne bottle – when he had first seen Mrs Hoole, and she hadn't managed to catch him sober enough yet to ask him why. 'The cook,' she said. 'She seemed disturbed at my suggestion that poison might have been involved, and that there were poisonous plants in the garden.'

'You can understand why she might be nervous about that,' said Tucker. 'The last cook was sacked for serving up a lunch that made a whole table of guests sick. Mrs Airlie was working under her at the time.'

'Oh,' said Louisa. 'But you don't think Mrs Hoole's death is suspicious?'

'No, I don't. From what the doctor told me, there's no reason to, neither.'

'What about the case of the missing maid? Joan Dorries.'

'What case? There's no case. I was sympathetic to Mrs Hoole's point of view back then, but we were both very young.'

'She told us she couldn't get anyone to find out what had happened to her.'

'Maybe because there was nothing to find out. She was a young girl, not from here so far as I knew. She took off, probably with a sweetheart, maybe just went home. It was the war, everything was topsy-turvy, like it is now. What I knew was she'd packed a case and the family here weren't worried. There was nothing to go on. She used to stop and ask me about it, if she saw me in the street. Mrs Hoole, I mean. But how was I to know? I went off to fight in the war not long after, and when I came back, some things had changed, others had stayed the same. Like I said, there was nowt doing.' Tucker flipped open his notebook. 'Now, I'd better get a few details right. The coroner might ask.'

'So there will be a coroner's report?'

'There has to be, because she didn't die in her own home and she hadn't seen a doctor in the two weeks before, so far as her family knows. But the results of the post-mortem won't come through for some time, what with Christmas in the way. And as I say, I'm not expecting anything significant. I'd stand down, if I was you, and enjoy your time in the big house.' He broke off and stood up: Deborah had come into the room with the duchess.

CHAPTER THIRTY

'I'm so sorry, Mr Tucker,' Deborah began. 'The duchess and I were talking in her room and it took Ellis some time to find us.'

'That's quite all right, my lady,' said Tucker. He did not seem in the least fazed by the arrival of the two women, neither shy nor obsequious in his manner, which made him all the more likeable.

'Is this about that poor woman?' said the duchess, in her diffident way. She was dressed in a plain skirt, with a shirt that had a well-worn collar, a faded blue cardigan and several strands of pearls. There was nothing glossy about her, unlike Adele, and she moved with the peculiar brand of confidence that only the very rich and grand possess. But Louisa liked her, though she said very little – Deborah had confided her relief in having a mother-in-law who did not interfere or criticise. Louisa enjoyed the duchess's air of amused detachment, content to let others get on with whatever they were doing so long as she could pursue her own interests, which mostly revolved around sheep, from what Louisa gathered.

'Mrs Hoole, yes,' Tucker confirmed. 'Your husband, the duke, gave a statement to my sergeant. I would like to confirm a few other details for the coroner's report. But I wouldn't be concerned, Your Grace.'

'It takes a lot to concern me,' said the duchess, with a smile. 'But I'm not really on top of things in the house this week. I'm sure Lady Andrew is far better placed to give you whatever you need.' She stopped and sniffed the air, a finger held up warningly to keep everyone quiet. 'Ah. Excuse me.' They watched as she pulled a small hammer out of her pocket and started to bang it on the bookshelves, right by where she had been standing. 'Woodworm,' she said, by way of explanation. 'Do carry on.'

'Yes. Right,' said the detective, momentarily thrown. 'Lady Andrew, could you give me the names of everyone present in the house the night Mrs Hoole died?'

'Of course, do sit down, Mr Tucker.' Deborah took the other end of the sofa from Louisa and ran through the list of people in the house. It took some time, explaining the various titles and how everyone was related. 'Mrs Sullivan, of course, and her daughter, Miss Maisie Sullivan. I think that's it for the guests. I suppose you'll need the staff, too?'

'If you would.'

'Mr Ellis, the butler, Mrs Airlie, the cook. There's a teacher from the school, Mademoiselle Lucie Dupont. Two night watchmen, who we never see, but Ellis can show you their log. There are two maids who generally come in from the village, but they're staying here for this week. Their names are Betsy and Anna. I'm afraid we'll have to ask Mrs Airlie for their surnames.'

'I think I know who they are, but I'll check with the cook. What about estate staff?'

'There are only two gardeners at present, thanks to the war, but they don't sleep in the house. There's a gardener's cottage on the grounds. Mr Coates and, oh, goodness, I'm not sure what the other one is called.'

'Max,' said Louisa. 'We met him in the greenhouse the other day.'

'That rings a bell,' said Deborah. 'There's usually a Mr Shimwell, the duke's comptroller, but he's gone home for Christmas. I think that covers everybody.'

'Who looks after the cars?' asked Tucker. 'Sergeant Booth mentioned that the car that was supposed to take Mrs Hoole home broke down, so she stayed here unexpectedly.'

'The usual chauffeur has gone to fight in France,' said Deborah. 'I think the gardeners and Ellis share the responsibility between them so far as they can. For anything serious, they'd have to telephone the garage in Baslow.'

'So I should talk to Mr Ellis to find out what happened to the car that was supposed to take Mrs Hoole home that night?'

'Yes, I suppose so,' said Deborah. 'I assumed someone mended it. It was working again by the time I needed it.'

'For the coroner, I have to rule out any possibilities of deliberate sabotage,' Tucker explained. 'To clarify, so far as you are aware no one had any prior knowledge or friendship with Mrs Hoole? She had turned up unannounced a few nights ago – the eighteenth of December, I believe – to give a message to a member of your household.'

'It's true we weren't expecting her arrival,' said Deborah, but she looked unsure as to how to proceed. 'She said the message was for me, but I had never met her before.'

Louisa stepped in. 'As you know, Mr Tucker, Mrs Hoole

worked here as a maid, before the war, and remained here a little while into it. She left in 1916, shortly after the maid Joan Dorries went missing. What she really came for that night was to tell us that she believed Joan's disappearance should be investigated. She knew I was staying here, and thought she might be able to interest me in it.'

'You being a private detective,' said Tucker, with a trace of a smile. 'Well, I think that covers it. Thank you for your patient assistance, Lady Andrew. I'll ask Mr Ellis about the night watchmen's log and the car. If someone could show me the room Mrs Hoole was staying in, then take me to the butler's pantry, I'd be most grateful.' He stood, smiling, waiting for the offer of help.

'I'll take you,' said Louisa, standing quickly. She wanted to talk more to him, although she hadn't yet decided if she wanted the extra help he might provide. His manner was obstructive when it came to finding out what had happened to Joan, even though he was one of the few people around who could remember her going missing. Perhaps she could persuade him otherwise, unless she decided to do the investigation by herself.

In Mrs Hoole's room, which had been left untouched since the body was taken away, the detective inspector had a good look around, opening cupboards and drawers, looking under the bed. 'Bit odd, all the candles everywhere,' he muttered.

'I think she was conducting a private séance of her own,' said Louisa. 'When we found her, she was holding the cap that she believed had belonged to Joan Dorries.'

'Huh.' Tucker peered out of the small window, high up in the house and overlooking the kitchen gardens.

'The strange thing is, she said to us that she wasn't a real psychic. Her explanation was that she told us about messages and so on because she thought it was her best chance of getting everyone to take notice of her friend's disappearance.'

'Takes all sorts,' said Tucker. 'And there's plenty round here who will say ghosts aren't real but won't walk under ladders. Call it superstition or sixth sense, it's all the same heathen nonsense, if you ask me.'

Louisa said nothing to this. She was probably the same, preferring not to take too definite a stance in either direction.

'Did she explain why she thought her friend's disappearance was suspicious? Other than that she left suddenly? I expect she told me herself but it was so long ago, I can't remember the details.' His hands were in his pockets, making his question seem informal.

'She said that although a suitcase had been packed, there were personal items left behind that Mrs Hoole knew Joan wouldn't have forgotten to take with her.'

'That doesn't say much.' Tucker shrugged. 'If people are in a hurry, or can't carry much, they have to be ruthless about sentimental objects.'

'And she couldn't believe her friend would go without telling her, Mrs Hoole, what her plans were.'

'Again,' said Tucker, with a newly patronising edge that made Louisa grit her teeth, 'there are lots of possible reasons for that. She might have been planning something she thought her friend would disapprove of, or she might not have wanted to put her in the position of having to cover for her with a lie.' The detective inspector put his hands into his pockets and nodded towards the door. 'I think we'd better see about that car, though, don't you? I'd like to talk to Mr Ellis.'

CHAPTER THIRTY-ONE

Rather than ask the butler to come to the drawing room, where he might feel uncomfortable talking to the detective, Louisa decided the two of them would go and find him. It also meant she could be at the interview. At that hour, she knew he would be in the dining room laying the table for luncheon, the war having done nothing to lower his high standards for polishing the silver or ironing the napkins. (Deborah had not inherited her mother's inclination to do without.)

Ellis looked up as Tucker and Louisa came in, the usual pinched look on his face, his mouth closed and turned down at the corners, like a cartoon. Louisa found she was wearying of this expression. She recognised the look but was yet to know what she had done to merit it, other than be someone who was once a maid. It was 1941, for Heaven's sake.

'The detective inspector would like to talk to you about Mrs Hoole,' Louisa began, watching his expression darken.

'I don't know that I have anything useful to add but I shall 'endeavour to be of help,' he said, in a tone that suggested quite the opposite to his words.

'Sergeant Booth told me that the car broke down, which meant Mrs Hoole could not be driven home that night and had to stay,' said Tucker. 'I gather you are responsible for the maintenance of the car.'

'My knowledge of the motor-car engine is limited,' said Ellis. 'I do what I can.'

'Who else helps?' asked Tucker.

'Occasionally the gardeners have a look but more usually I'll telephone the mechanic in the village.'

'Can you tell me what happened when the car was discovered to have broken down?'

Ellis carefully put down the knife he had been holding. 'Yes. I had asked Max to take Mrs Hoole home but he came and told me that he was unable to start the car. By that time, the hour was late—'

'What time was it?'

'I think it was around midnight.'

'And you were still up?'

'Yes,' said Ellis. 'I was aware that some of the guests were not yet in their beds, and I prefer to be the last to retire, in case anyone should need something. It was late by the time she came down the stairs. We were waiting in the kitchen. I went across to the gardener's cottage to tell them she was ready to be driven to Baslow. But by the time I brought her to the back door, Max was there to tell me that the car wouldn't start.'

'What happened then?'

Ellis gave an impatient sigh. 'I decided she'd better stay. Mrs Hoole said she'd like a nightcap before she went to bed, so I left her in the servants' hall while I went to find a suitable room for her.'

'And to check on Maisie, in the storm?' Louisa watched him carefully as she asked this.

'Yes.' There wasn't a flicker of concern on his face, no hint of a lie being told.

'That was very kind of you, Ellis.'

Something seemed to relax in his features. 'My uncle told me that the young duke and his brother were always afraid of storms when they were boys. I endeavour to follow *all* of his guidance in buttling.'

'I'm sure you do. Can you tell me anything about how Mrs Hoole was when you took her to the room? Any sign of illness?'

'None that I was aware of. She seemed a touch upset but the brandy seemed to steady her.'

'Did she ask you to help her find some candles?'

Ellis seemed taken aback by this question. 'No, she didn't. But they aren't hard to find, if needed. There's always one or two in every bedroom, in case of a power cut.'

'You didn't check the car to see what was wrong?' Tucker was making notes in his book, and Louisa wished she could do the same but felt he might object.

'No. As I said, it was late. I knew we could accommodate Mrs Hoole easily. I felt it would be easier to look at the car in the morning.'

'Did Max offer any theories as to why the car had broken down?'

'No.' Ellis picked up the knife again. 'If that's all?'

'I'm afraid it's not,' said Tucker, in his amenable way. 'The next morning, what was the verdict on the car? Did you look at it yourself?'

'I did, and it appeared that the HT cable had come away from the distributor. It's nothing unusual – it's happened before.'

'I see, thank you,' said Tucker. 'I believe there are two watchmen who check on the house each night?'

'Yes, they take it in turns.'

Louisa was watching Ellis carefully but he was as inscrutably calm as ever.

'I imagine they sleep during the day,' said the detective, 'but I believe there's a logbook that records their night. I'd like to see it, in case anything anomalous shows up.'

'I check it myself every morning and there was nothing untoward in the logbook about the night Mrs Hoole stayed.'

'Nevertheless, I'd like to see it for myself.'

Ellis dipped his head a little. 'Of course.' He left the dining room and the two of them followed him down to the kitchens and thence into the butler's pantry, which held his desk. On it was the log, a handsome leather-bound book, with 'Chatsworth House' embossed in gold on the front. Tucker flicked through it and Louisa could see that dates were written, with timings next to locations, all initialled. The same initials showed throughout: DL and ML. Tucker closed the book and handed it back to Ellis. 'Thank you. That all seems to be in order.'

'If you'll excuse me, Mrs Sullivan, Detective Inspector. Everyone will be going through for luncheon soon, and there are things I need to do.'

Tucker took a step back. 'Yes, absolutely. Thank you, Mr Ellis. You've been very helpful.'

When Ellis had departed, Tucker closed the door behind him. 'I don't like the sound of this at all.'

'Of what?' asked Louisa, feeling she probably agreed with him but couldn't say exactly why.

'Call it policeman's instinct,' said Tucker. 'But the broken-down car seems too convenient for me. I think we're looking at the possibility of murder, Mrs Sullivan.'

'You think it's Ellis?'

'I don't know who it is. There's no motive yet, no weapon, no obvious suspect. But with Christmas coming so soon, we can't afford to waste time waiting for the inquest.'

CHAPTER THIRTY-TWO

Tucker believed there was a possibility of murder. Without a weapon or obvious signs of injury to the body, Louisa knew the likeliest methods were poisoning or smothering. One required forethought and planning, the other required strength. What she needed to discover was motive and opportunity. She was sure the answer had to lie in the link between Mrs Hoole and Joan. Mrs Hoole had been killed hours after telling them about Joan's disappearance: who might be afraid of this story getting out? Why would it matter after all this time? Joan had gone in the late summer of 1916 – twenty-five years ago.

So far, all they knew was that it was possible the car had been tampered with, to ensure that Mrs Hoole couldn't get home and had to stay at Chatsworth. That suggested planning, which tied in with the poisoning theory, and a certain amount of mechanical knowledge. Tucker, however, had told Louisa that he did not want to go down the route of looking for a connection with Joan, a case that – so far as he was concerned – was long over, and that there was nothing to merit any further investigation.

He was going to interview everyone who was in the house that night and look for holes in their alibis. 'Good old-fashioned policing,' he'd called it.

Louisa considered the fact that Billy had been so unnerved by Mrs Hoole, seeming to believe that she might have information about the family with which to blackmail them. What could that information be? And what did the neighbour know about people being 'shipped out'? That 'information' could be the same as the rumours that were going around the village; it was hardly unusual for people to hear a lie so often they started to treat it as fact. Then there was Mrs Airlie and the scandal after a whole luncheon was devastated by food poisoning: could there have been more to it than that?

Louisa knew that only three people had been in the house when Joan was still alive: the dowager, the duke and Charles. She decided she needed to try to get to the heart of the matter as quickly as possible. The dowager was old and rather frightening: she'd rather not talk to her first. Charles would have been a young boy during the war. She needed to talk to the duke but she couldn't do it alone; men like him didn't talk to women like her. Luckily, she knew the person she needed.

An hour later, Louisa, the duke and Nancy were taking a stroll around the gardens. Maisie was with them, too, but engaged in a new favourite pastime of spotting birds with a pair of binoculars that the duke had kindly lent her.

'You're very kind to Maisie,' said Louisa, as they walked along the path towards the rockery.

'Well, I'm rather missing our two girls,' said the duke.

'Where are they?'

'Staying with cousins in Scotland for a few weeks, but if the trains are running we hope they'll be down here in a day or two, in time for Christmas. They love staying there and it helped to keep the numbers down. We were keen that Deborah should have a good shot at a successful house party, as a new bride and after everything that's happened.'

Everything meaning the stillbirth, Louisa assumed. It was a rather unexpected and sympathetic move on the duke and duchess's part, and a reminder that though these grandees could present rather cold exteriors, their hearts beat a regular pulse just like everyone else's.

Nancy had been fully apprised of the reasons for the walk with the duke but they had agreed they would have to move slowly. The pretext had been that Louisa and Nancy wanted to know more about the names of wildflowers, a subject on which the duke was passionate. ('I couldn't wish to know about anything less,' Nancy had remarked.)

'Someone said there were one or two poisonous plants here,' said Louisa.

'Yes, common enough,' replied the duke. 'Hemlock, of course, easily mistaken for cow parsley, which is quite harmless. Foxgloves. Devil's helmet is nasty but not difficult to miss, with yellow and white flowers, growing on tall spikes in the summer. Laburnum, not many people know about that one.'

'Can you identify them all?' Nancy looked at the garden with different eyes.

'Well, you know, one or two,' said the duke.

'Do you think that's what happened at that luncheon,' asked Louisa, 'when all the guests were sick? Something was picked from the garden?'

'Who told you about that?' he asked sharply, before answering his own question. 'It must have been the cook. Mrs Airlie wasn't to blame. At least, my parents didn't think so, and kept her on. I wasn't here at the time but I know it was the most frightful scene. People vomiting on their shoes.'

'Ugh,' said Nancy, who had always hated the sight of anyone being sick.

Moving off the subject, the duke started to explain about some of the smaller wildflowers that grew through the crevices, mostly mosses, talking about their ability to survive in a harsh climate.

'Rather like growing up in this house, I should imagine,' said Nancy.

'You're right,' said the duke, with surprise in his voice, 'but how did you know that?'

'I grew up in much the same atmosphere. I recognise the signs.'

'Did you?' The duke gestured to a bench, indicating the three of them should sit there.

'I don't think I can recall my mother ever telling me she loved me,' said Nancy. 'When I see Louisa with Maisie, it makes me realise what I missed out on.'

'Yes. I dare say one never thought about it until we had our own children. My mother always used to find reason to make me cry on the first day of the holidays. School was rotten but I came to dread going home.' He glanced at Louisa and blushed slightly. But perhaps the knot had loosened. 'Do you know, when my parents left for Canada during the war, in 1916, they left their children behind? I was in the war by then, but Charles was only a young boy. I wonder sometimes if—' He stopped himself.

'If?' asked Nancy, gently.

'It's not the sort of thing one talks about outside the family,' he said. 'But there's no hiding it any more, and especially not while you're both here this week. Charles's drinking. It's very worrying.' He took out a packet of cigarettes and offered them to Nancy and Louisa, they both refused, before he lit one for himself.

'Do you think Adele minds?'

'One thing I know for certain,' said the duke, 'is never to get involved in other people's marriages.'

'Yes, that's true,' said Nancy. There was a pause, but a comfortable one. The three of them watched Maisie as she belly-crawled silently on the path, trying to get closer to a bird.

'It must be a relief to have your son home for Christmas,' said Louisa, after a while.

'Yes, although Andrew's away, of course, one doesn't know where. So I can't say one is entirely relaxed.'

'Our generation remembers the Great War,' said Nancy. 'It makes it all the harder to bear, knowing what the men are going through. At least there was a kind of innocence about it before.'

'That's true,' said the duke. 'I dare say that's why one's parents departed. They hardly knew what they were leaving behind.'

'What were they doing in Canada?' asked Louisa.

'My father was the governor, sworn in on the eleventh of November 1916. I remember the date because I had come home from Egypt and then returned to France when he left for Canada. It was an important post for him. He was there as the monarch, which is to say he was the king in one of Britain's most important dominions. Naturally, he became very involved in the politics because of the war. Indeed, he argued strongly the case for Canadian conscription, much objected to at first but he got it pushed through.'

Louisa couldn't tell if he was proud of his father or not. It sounded as if he had been a significant person, but how would one bear the guilt of having sent so many young men to their deaths? Deaths that ultimately ensured Britain's freedom but seemed to have led almost inexorably to this next war, with more – and more – deaths. It was a depressing thought.

'Could you tell me something of life in the house before the war?' she asked. 'It must have been so different then. I know we all feel as if that life was another era, only twenty-five years ago. Before telephones and radio—'

'Before jazz, and nightclubs and women dining alone in restaurants,' said Nancy.

'Before electricity everywhere, cars clogging up the streets,' said the duke, chuckling with them. 'Yes, before the war was another planet altogether. Indeed, Chatsworth was a very different place then, too. Secure and solid, or so it seemed. As if our way of life would never change. There were hundreds of servants and estate workers. My parents gave frightfully grand house parties, stuffed to the gills with royalty and politicians. I know we oughtn't to hark back too much but one does feel as if the Edwardians had the most terrific fun.'

'I know what you mean but I expect they'll say the same about today in the future. In the past, the grass is always greener,' said Nancy.

While they were in the mood for reminiscing, Louisa knew she had to take her chance. 'The maid that Mrs Hoole mentioned, Joan Dorries, do you remember her?' she asked.

'Well, you know, it was as one said. There were so many more servants then,' said the duke, not quite looking her in the eye.

'But gossip spreads upstairs as well as down. Are you saying you never heard about anything untoward happening with a kitchen-maid?' said Nancy.

'I'm not quite sure what you're insinuating, but I don't think the dowager would thank you for it,' said the duke. 'My mother ran a tight ship.'

'Mrs Hoole said that at the time she tried to make a fuss about Joan's disappearance. I wondered if you remembered anything about that.' Louisa had to keep pushing at the door, now that she had got her foot in.

'You don't seriously believe Mrs Hoole was getting messages from a dead maid, do you?' asked the duke, sternly.

'No,' said Louisa, 'I don't. But I do believe there might be something in her suspicion that Joan met an untimely death.'

'And why do you believe that?'

'Because the morning after Mrs Hoole told us about Joan, she was found dead.'

The duke stood up. 'I think we should leave the police to their investigations, don't you?'

'No,' said Louisa, 'I don't.'

'But even if you're right, what good would it do to find out what happened to Joan, all those years ago? What's done is done. It's in the past, like corsets and spats.' He smiled but his attempt at levity failed.

'Because I strongly believe that whoever killed Joan is being protected by whoever is responsible for the death of Mrs Hoole.' Saying it out loud made Louisa realise what a dramatic thing she was saying. Nancy was staring at her, clearly rather appalled. But Louisa knew she had to do it: bring them to the point from which there was no going back.

'However certain you want to sound, you don't actually know

that,' said the duke. 'And my family does not need someone digging around, trying to find something that would otherwise be long forgotten.' With that determined statement, he walked back alone to the house.

CHAPTER THIRTY-THREE

With the household at something of a loose end in the aftermath of Mrs Hoole's death, Nancy announced that she had telephoned Group Captain Nesbit to request they arrange the visit to the base. He had responded, she reported, with alarming alacrity.

'If he's not flying, he might be quite bored,' suggested Deborah.

Lord Redesdale reacted to this with a grunt but made it clear he expected to be among the party. Billy excused himself – 'Rather too military an activity when one's on leave' – and Kick said she would stay behind with him. The dowager, the duke and the duchess showed no interest in going, and neither did Lady Redesdale. ('It will do Farve good to see what it takes to look after Bobo,' Nancy said to Louisa, in a surprising show of sympathy for her mother.) Adele said she wanted to see 'the Brits at their flying best', which meant Charles had to accompany her. Thus it was a fairly considerable group that set off in two cars. Lord Redesdale drove the Bentley, with Charles and Adele, Nancy and Unity. Deborah drove the other car, accompanied by Louisa, Maisie and Lucie, who had asked if she, too, might see the RAF base.

Seated at the front, her daughter and Lucie in the back, playing Would You Rather?, a thought occurred to Louisa. 'If there's more than one car, why wasn't Mrs Hoole driven home in another?' she asked Deborah.

'Everyone had gone to bed, I suppose. It was too late to wake anyone and ask permission to borrow their car. Besides, I don't see Farve letting one of the gardeners drive his prized Bentley, do you?'

The drive took less than an hour, the road slicing through the sprawling Derbyshire landscape, its colours rich and varied even in these wintry days. Louisa was enamoured by the sheer size of it, let alone the beauty. In London, one's view was always limited by the buildings, narrowing all horizons. What was more, since the war had begun, the sky was terrifying: you never wanted to look up for fear of seeing a bomber. Their entry to the base was fairly smooth, a few questions at the gate, their names checked against a list and then they were in. Louisa had never been inside an RAF base before and the sight of the grey military buildings, the men in uniform, the complete lack of prettiness – no hanging baskets of flowers such as you might find in a railway station, or the ornate architectural detail of a school or hospital – made her feel both safe and terrified. Safe because she could see this was an operation established with the sole purpose of protecting Britain and its citizens. Terrified because it was a forceful reminder that they were a country at war.

Their group was ushered to a squat brick building and asked to wait in a room that contained nothing but a few wooden chairs and a table. Nothing hung on the plain walls, not even a clock. They were all rather muted, even Unity, feeling uncomfortably like suspects in a police station. But after only a minute or two Group Captain Nesbit came in, as tall and blond as ever, perhaps even more imposing in this setting where his uniform was so much more apt than their civvies.

'Welcome,' he said. 'I'm delighted you came. I can't promise you a great deal to see, but I would hope this outing gives you some reassurance.'

'Reassurance?' barked Lord Redesdale.

Nesbit gave a small bow in his direction. 'That we are fighting the Hun, my lord.'

'Huh,' said Lord Redesdale, but he seemed appeased.

Louisa thought he was probably rather rattled to be there. Tom was flying planes on the other side of the world; his son-in-law, Esmond, had been killed in a flight over the North Sea. She was gripped by the worry that they had done completely the wrong thing in coming here. What were they expecting? A jolly outing with a picnic? She looked at Nancy and Deborah, but both seemed unperturbed, merely interested in their surroundings and listening to Nesbit describe where he was going to take them.

'There are, naturally, sensitive areas we shall have to avoid,' he was saying. 'This base was built as an armoury, so there are miles of tunnels below us in which ammunition is kept.'

Unity kept trying to interrupt him with questions, but Lord Redesdale had a tight grip on her arm, pulling her back every time she opened her mouth.

Having given his introductory address, Nesbit looked at them all. 'I know I can trust you all not to say anything of what you see here today once you leave the base,' he said.

Everyone shook their heads, like school children in class.

'Thank you,' he said. 'Now, please follow me. There is something rather exciting I'm able to show you first.'

In a crocodile file, they all trooped out. Louisa hung back, discreetly waiting for Charles. He was the quietest of all, and looked very much as if he did not want to be there. By the time they were walking along behind a line of hangars, Louisa and Charles were in step together, a short distance from the rest of the group.

'I'm pleased to have a moment with you,' said Louisa, bravely. She didn't feel at all confident in striking up a conversation with him but decided that he was the type who would respond best to a direct approach. He was pale and red-eyed as usual, as if he hadn't had a full night's sleep for years, but for once the smell of whisky was not strong.

'Oh, yes? Why is that?' Charles looked at her as if he didn't fully recognise her.

'Well, I—'

He cut her off. 'Most people want to talk to my wife. The Hollywood star. Or my brother, the duke-in-waiting.' He gave a feeble attempt at a chuckle.

'Yes, I can imagine,' she said, as sympathetically as possible. A cold breeze was whistling through, and Louisa pulled up the collar of her coat. 'But it's you I'd like to talk to. It's about Mrs Hoole.'

'Who?' he said, and then almost immediately followed it with, 'Oh. Yes, I know who you mean. What about her?'

'She told us that she had a message from "the other side", which we know now wasn't true—'

'Do we?'

184

'Well, after the séance, she admitted she wasn't a medium.'

'I knew there was something not right about that woman.' A flash of the fury Louisa had seen that night came back to his face.

'She worked in the house before the war, and believed there was a deliberate silence around the disappearance of another maid, Joan Dorries. She was using the cover of a séance to get me interested – in investigating the case, that is.' Louisa wanted to watch him hear this, but he was so much taller than her, it was difficult. In any case, he possessed an aristocratic *froideur* that successfully masked his true feelings. 'You see, my lord, I think Mrs Hoole must have known you as a boy.'

'Yes, it seems she must have done.'

Louisa could see the group beginning to stop and walk towards the front of a hangar. She didn't have long to keep his attention. 'Do you remember her? She was called Eliza in those days.'

There was a tiny change in the rhythm of his walk, the only indication she had that he had registered the question.

'I was a young boy then.'

'This was in early 1916,' said Louisa, pushing for clarity on his part, to be absolutely certain of what he did or didn't know. What he might or might not be hiding.

He stopped and his hand went back into his pocket. 'I remember that year,' he said. 'My parents went to Canada in the summer, and they didn't take me with them. I was eleven. My brother was at war. My nanny, I'm afraid, was not a nice woman. Whenever I could, I would go down to the kitchen to see Eliza or Joan. They were kind to me.' He blinked slowly, before looking at Louisa again. 'I don't know why I'm telling you all this.'

'Because I asked,' she replied. She knew this by now, the power of simply asking questions. It was amazing how few people realised it. 'Do you remember Joan going missing?'

The group had stopped now and some of them were looking back at her and Charles, waving them to come on.

Charles turned to go ahead, but before he did, he faced Louisa. 'Yes,' he said. 'Yes, I do. Come and find me later and I'll tell you about it. I'll be in my dressing room at six. Ellis will tell you where it is.'

CHAPTER THIRTY-FOUR

ouisa was encouraged: for whatever reason, it looked as if
Charles was prepared to open the door to her investigations
into a link between Mrs Hoole and Joan. It wasn't much for her
to grasp at, but she needed to talk to those in the family who
had been there when Joan was alive.

Musing on this, Louisa followed the group around the hangar,
not paying much attention to the Spitfire, although she could see
Maisie out of the corner of her eye hugely enjoying the spectacle.
Group Captain Nesbit, resplendent in his uniform, was in the
cockpit, telling them what the various buttons did. Unity was
gasping with delight at everything he said, unaware of the irony
that this plane was one of many designed to drop bombs on
Germany, the country she had once loved to the point of near-
fatal obsession. Oddly, this sensation seemed to affect them all.
Singing patriotic songs and praying for the soldiers to come home
safely was one thing. Seeing the instruments of war up close
was quite another. When another RAF officer came around the
corner, a stern look upon his face, Louisa felt saved by the bell.

The officer motioned to Nesbit to disembark from the cockpit immediately and beckoned him to one side. They weren't able to hear the conversation but it was obvious from their gestures that Nesbit should not have issued such a generous invitation to the base. He came over when the officer had marched off.

'Terribly sorry, chaps, but I'm afraid that's the end of the tour. I've got to go and do something and there isn't anyone else to show you around. I hope you don't feel it was a wasted trip.'

'Oh, no!' said Unity. 'We *loved* it. Didn't we?' She turned to look at everyone's faces but did not seem to notice the looks of mild relief.

'It was awfully kind of you,' said Deborah. 'I'm sure it was far too much trouble for you to have taken on our behalf.'

'No, no.' Nesbit made vague protestations as he started to walk them back to the squat building at the entrance, his pace too fast for any of them to keep up with him.

'What was that all about?' said Nancy to Louisa.

'I think we must have come here without permission. I did think it was a little odd that we were all allowed in, given the circumstances.'

'I suppose I always assume I'm allowed anywhere,' said Nancy, with a wry smile. 'The question is, why was he trying to impress us? What favour is he trying to gain in return?'

'We don't know yet,' replied Louisa, 'but I'm sure we will.'

When they reached the cars, Deborah suggested that Louisa, Lucie and Maisie go with her to Baslow to break up the return journey. 'Otherwise it's rather a short outing for Maisie, isn't it?' she said sweetly, cupping Maisie's chin in her hand. Maisie smiled back at her gratefully.

Louisa knew that Baslow, for her daughter, was firmly fixed as the place that provided sweet treats. The sun decided to come out a little more brightly, which made the thought of a walk around the village quite appealing, even if there was still a stiff breeze to do battle with.

Christmas Eve was the following day, and in spite of the war and rationing, there was a feeling of heightened jollity in the air in Baslow. Mothers and children jostled on the pavements, carrying bags of shopping or delivering presents, and shouts of 'Merry Christmas' could be heard. Deborah said she had to go to the post office, so Louisa, Lucie and Maisie said they would meet her at the Formbys' shop in half an hour.

'I said I would collect some medicines for the dowager duchess from the chemist,' said Lucie.

'We'll come with you,' suggested Louisa.

They walked over the bridge to get there, playing a quick game of Pooh Sticks with Maisie on the way. Lucie told them that she was running an increasing number of errands for the old duchess, 'but I'm happy to do it. She's quite entertaining in her own way, and I think she enjoys practising her French with me.'

'Where in France are you from? Not that I know it terribly well,' said Louisa.

'We moved around a lot, mostly small towns that nobody has heard of, not even the French,' answered Lucie. 'Ah, now, here it is. I'll be only a moment.' She went into the shop, while Louisa and Maisie waited outside, playing a game of counting red hats. Louisa enjoyed these moments with her daughter, which she knew were brief in the context of a lifetime, but she couldn't stop her mind wandering back to her conversation earlier with Charles. She needed to find out what he remembered of Joan.

Absorbed as she was, she didn't notice DI Tucker until he was standing right before her, head on one side with a questioning smile. 'Mrs Sullivan?'

'Oh, Mr Tucker, I'm so sorry, I was playing a game with Maisie.'

'Ah,' he said, bending down to the child. 'What were you playing?'

'Counting red hats. I've seen seven, Mummy has only seen two,' said Maisie, triumphant in her win.

'Definitely a detective's daughter, then.'

'Go into the shop and find Lucie, darling,' said Louisa. She wanted to discuss murder with the policeman, but not in front of her daughter.

'I'm glad to have run into you,' said Tucker, when Maisie had gone in.

'Why is that?'

'We had the results of the post-mortem this morning. It's not really for me officially to tell you anything, it's for the family, but I thought you'd like to know.'

'I appreciate it. What was the conclusion?'

'Frustratingly inconclusive.'

'What does that mean?'

'It means what it says. They can't rule out either natural or unnatural causes as the cause of death. That is, she died of a heart attack but it might have been brought on naturally or unnaturally. There was some bruising but it was light, and could have been caused by any number of things. This means a toxicology report is needed and that will take some time.'

'Did she have a history of heart problems?'

Tucker's demeanour became more serious. 'That I can't tell you, even if I knew. Her doctor was not the local one but in

Manchester. We've written to him but had no reply as yet. With Christmas, he may have gone away.'

'Thank you for telling me. I know I have no real right to be told.'

Tucker pushed his hat a little off his forehead and pinched his nose. 'Maybe. But now that you're here, there *is* something that bothers me.'

Louisa didn't say anything. Sometimes it was better to wait for an answer than to push for one. But she was intrigued. If she'd been sitting down, she'd have been on the edge of the seat.

'I feel a bit ridiculous saying this,' Tucker said, after a moment. 'In novels, it's always the butler who did it. But I do wonder about Mr Ellis.'

'What about him?'

'I don't know if you're aware that his uncle used to work in the house, also called Mr Ellis.'

'Yes, I knew that,' said Louisa. 'It's why the present Mr Ellis is known as "Ellis the Second".'

'Ha, I see. Well, I believe there was some history between him and Mrs Hoole. I'm not saying anything definite here ... I probably shouldn't be saying anything at all, and I might not have done if I hadn't seen you ... ' He trailed off rather uncertainly.

'You think something might have happened between the uncle, Mr Ellis the First, and Mrs Hoole, that somehow implicates Mr Ellis the Second?'

'Yes,' said Tucker. He pulled a face. 'I say this to you as someone who knows how to look at these things. It's only a vague hunch.'

'Where did the hunch come from?'

'Oh, I'm long in the tooth around here. It was something someone happened to say.'

'I'll ask around,' said Louisa.

'Yes, but not officially, if you please.'

Lucie and Maisie came out of the chemist's at that moment, prompting Mr Tucker to touch the brim of his hat to them both, and bid them goodbye.

'Was that the policeman who came to the house?' asked Lucie. 'Was he talking to you about Mrs Hoole?'

'Yes,' whispered Louisa. 'And I think he may have given me an idea as to how our missing maid and the death of Mrs Hoole are connected.'

'Goodness,' said Lucie. 'You sound as if you are plotting a novel.'

'If only I was,' replied Louisa. 'Truth, as you know, is always stranger than fiction.'

CHAPTER THIRTY-FIVE

A t the appointed hour, Louisa went to Charles's dressing room in the private wing. She knocked softly on the door, and heard him tell her to come in. She was mildly relieved to see that it had more the appearance of a study than a dressing room, with a leather-topped desk in the corner and two small armchairs in front of a fire. A single bed was made up, a moth-eaten teddy propped on the pillow. Charles was wearing a smoking jacket and had poured two glasses of whisky.

'I'm glad you've come by yourself,' said Charles. 'Not that I mind your daughter in the least – she's a charming little thing.'

'Thank you.'

'We tried to have one of our own but we couldn't.' He seemed to sink a little further into his chair. 'She died, you know. After only a few hours. Frightfully sad and all that. Nothing to be done, the doctors said.' He gave a funny smile and his chin sank onto his chest.

'That is very sad,' said Louisa.

'And twin boys. Same thing happened. No one to blame, of course. Everyone blames Adele but I don't.'

'No.' She really did feel terribly sad for him, this long and lanky figure, who usually said so little and now, trying to say so much, could still only do it in phrases devised to keep his feelings at bay.

'It must be difficult for you both, at this time of year,' said Louisa.

Charles shook his head. 'Nothing to be done.' He indicated the bottle. 'Would you like some more?'

'No, thank you.' She hesitated because he was drunk but he almost always was – and she needed to have the conversation he'd promised earlier. 'You said that you remember the maid who went missing, Joan.'

'Yes, I do.'

'Can you tell me anything about her? What was she like?'

'Ah, well.' He blew out through his lips. 'I don't really know what she was like. She was a maid. I was only a small boy then, still in short trousers.'

'But you remember her?'

He waved a finger at her, the movements slow, slurred like his speech. 'Yes, yes, I do.'

'What is it you remember?'

'She was pretty. Or I thought so then. Small boys like pretty maids, don't they?' He didn't wait for her agreement, or otherwise. 'And she was nice to me. She used to talk to me. Hardly anyone did, really. Nanny was a brute, always telling us off. I got sent to bed without supper so many times I think I forgot what it was.' That hollow chuckle again. A line trotted out that failed to cover the pain. 'But Joan, you know, she would give me a kiss

194

when I came back from school and say she was pleased to see me. That can do a lot for a small boy, don't you know?'

'I'm sure,' said Louisa. 'I used to be a nursery-maid.'

'Did you? Did you?' He reappraised her, it seemed, but somehow she knew it would be a positive reappraisal. Certain members of the upper class felt much more comfortable with her working-class background. Whatever it was, it gave Charles licence to talk to her freely.

'Well, then, you do know,' he said. 'But it seems I wasn't the only boy she kissed.'

Louisa waited.

Charles tipped his head back and closed his eyes. 'I saw her with my father.'

'How do you mean?'

'I used to walk around below stairs, hoping for a biscuit from the cook, I suppose, or a piggyback with one of the footmen. And I pushed into a room and saw her in there . . .' He paused, his eyes still closed, his hand holding the glass beginning to droop.

'What did you see?' Louisa willed him to tell her. *Come on.*

'I know now what they were doing but at the time, little me in my short trousers, I thought my father was killing her. Those noises and the look on her face, and his . . . It was dark so I didn't see much. But I knew it was him – I saw his moustache. He'd taken the only thing that was mine in that house. The only person who'd cared for me.'

'I'm sure it didn't change her feelings for you,' said Louisa, but as she said it, she knew she'd made a mistake. She'd gone too far. His eyes snapped open.

'Rot. I was just a brat who walked in on something I shouldn't have.' He drank the last of the whisky in his glass.

'And how soon after that did Joan disappear?'

He shrugged. 'I've no idea. I had nothing more to do with her after that, and then she was gone. And so was he.'

'Your father?'

'Yes, my loving parents. Saw fit to leave us in the middle of the war.'

He put the glass down and hauled himself up. 'Right. I think it's time for a . . .' He shook his head. 'Can't remember quite what but I'm off. Merry Christmas and all that, eh?'

'Wait,' said Louisa, surprising him.

'What?' He stood in the open door.

'When Mrs Hoole first arrived, you seemed to recognise her. Her appearance made you drop the champagne bottle.'

Charles gave an embarrassed laugh. 'I'm afraid that happens rather too often.'

'Did you think she'd reveal something about your father and Joan?'

'No,' he said quickly. Then there was another pause. 'Perhaps. It was only at that ghastly thing she did, around the table, that I realised I recognised her.'

'You were angry then.'

'Yes. I didn't like what she was implying. What my father did was a terrible thing but I'm afraid he wasn't the only one of his kind. He didn't kill the maid. The worst he probably did was forget about her.' He looked exhausted, his skin ashen.

Louisa felt terribly sad for him. But she hadn't finished. 'Do you agree with me that there's a connection between Joan's disappearance and Mrs Hoole's death?'

'I don't want to think that,' he said. 'I don't want to think about much any more. I need another drink. I'm going downstairs.'

CHAPTER THIRTY-SIX

Louisa thought it all through. Who was willing to protect the late duke's secret to the extent that they would kill for it? She ruled out Charles on the grounds he had confessed to what he knew about his father and the maid: if Mrs Hoole had known, he couldn't have been afraid of her knowing. What she needed was something definite that determined the threat against Mrs Hoole. Was she afraid for her life that night? Was that why she had had to do it under the cover of a séance? The séance had protected her own identity for one thing: Mrs Hoole only revealed herself as a maid who had worked at the house before the war when she was talking alone to Louisa, Nancy and Deborah. Was there someone else in the house of whom she was afraid? And, if so, when she received the news that she was not going to be driven back to the village that night, did she fear for her life then? Could that have been the reason for the strange candlelit ritual?

In the drawing room, gathered before supper, Lady Redesdale appeared without Unity, explaining that she was tired and taking supper on a tray in her room. Lord Redesdale started to say he wished he could do the same but when he caught sight of his wife's face at this remark, he stopped. Nancy saw it.

'*Now* you must have sympathy for Muv,' she said. 'You've been exhausted by Unity, haven't you?'

'I have every sympathy, as you well know,' replied her father. 'Don't you dare try to tease me on this.' And in spite of the fact that Nancy was some decades past being a young girl, she blushed as if she had been scolded and was duly quiet.

The atmosphere was threatening to turn rather frostier than the lawn outside. Deborah motioned to Louisa to join her on the sofa by the fire. She was sitting with Kick and Billy, and they budged up to make room. 'We think we should do something fun for the grown-ups tonight,' said Kick. 'Tomorrow it's Christmas Eve and Billy's sisters will join us. And we want to do fun things for Maisie. Billy has agreed to dress up as Father Christmas.'

'Have I?' said Billy, but he was grinning.

'What about a game now, before supper?'

'Why are you asking me?' said Louisa.

'Because you're the bridge between us and the oldies,' said Deborah. 'You're the only one who somehow keeps things sensible. Look at Nancy and Farve, already winding each other up like carriage clocks.'

'Do you mean to involve them, too?'

The three young things looked at each other. 'It's friendlier, isn't it? But Granny Evie might be best left out.'

They looked across at the armchair where the dowager duchess was sitting, the Peke on her lap, umbrella leaning against the arm. She was stroking her dog thoughtfully, while Lucie sat on a low stool beside her, apparently chattering away.

Louisa glanced at her watch. 'It will be supper in an hour. What are you thinking?'

'Racing Demon,' said Deborah. 'I got the idea because I came across a hoard of playing cards in the library earlier. Tens of packs, unused.'

Louisa remembered the game from her days as the Mitford nursery-maid, when Diana had developed a passion for it and inveigled them all into playing night after night. 'Where is there a big enough table to play on? Or, rather, is there a table in a room that isn't too cold and dusty?'

'Yes, in the music room,' said Deborah. 'I asked the maids to give it the once-over, and Ellis has lit a fire. I thought that even if we didn't go in there, it's no harm to warm these rooms up now and then.'

'Ah, the haunted room,' said Billy.

'What?' said Kick. 'I don't want to go in there, then.'

'Oh, tosh,' said Billy. 'If we avoided rooms in this house where we thought ghosts had been spotted, we'd be left with nothing but the bathroom on the third floor.'

'What do you mean?' asked Louisa.

'There are ghosts everywhere, if one believes everything one has been told.'

'I know I'm Catholic,' said Kick, 'but the thought of unhappy spirits walking the hallways gives me the shivers.'

'Halls, not hallways,' said Billy.

'What?'

'I know you're American, darling, but I have to tell you these things or you'll have duchesses flinching all over England.'

Kick slapped him on the arm lightly. 'You silly. Fine. Halls. But what ghosts?'

'Bess of Hardwick is our grandest resident ghost. She and her husband bought the land in the 1580s and built the Hunting Tower. You can still see it, on the hill behind the house,' said Billy.

Louisa knew the tower he meant: she'd seen it peeping out of the trees, an elaborate folly, she had assumed.

'But why is her ghost here?'

Billy shrugged. 'I don't know what her unhappiness is supposed to have been about, if that's your question. She married four times altogether, and her final husband was grand enough to be appointed to keep Mary, Queen of Scots imprisoned here once or twice. Her rooms were on the east side of the house, though they've been completely changed now. Bess was regarded as the second most powerful woman in England, after Elizabeth the First, so one would have thought she was quite happy in the scheme of things.'

'Perhaps she never wanted to let Chatsworth go,' suggested Kick. 'What other ghosts are there?'

'I'm not sure I like this,' said Deborah. 'Can't we play cards instead?'

Billy ignored her, as did Louisa and Kick. They wanted to hear more. 'There's a woman who is supposed to cry at the bridge, the small one you see on the drive, over the River Derwent. Her baby was thrown into the water by a violent lover, so it's said, and she cries for her lost child in eternity.'

Deborah stood up. 'That really *is* quite enough of that,' she said.

'Oh, God, I'm so sorry. I didn't mean—'

'No, of course you didn't. It's not that,' said Deborah, her smile a little too fixed. 'But I'd rather play a game than talk about ghosts. It's almost Christmas and I'm not Scrooge.' With this, she lightened the mood effectively and Louisa was impressed. Deborah displayed an emotional maturity and charm that hadn't been much in evidence before, but then again, she had been through so much in the last year: marriage, the tragedy of her stillborn baby, her husband at war.

Deborah got up and Kick followed her, but as Billy remained on the sofa, Louisa took her opportunity. 'I know I've not had a chance to talk to you since—'

'We were playing Sardines?' He smiled sheepishly. 'I feel rather badly about that, asking you to look into Mrs Hoole.'

'There's no need. You weren't to know what would happen. But I *have* found out a little more. She worked in this house before the war, for one thing. And she was a friend of the maid she says went missing.'

'Whom she claims went missing,' he corrected.

'Hmm, maybe.' Louisa wasn't prepared to doubt her that much. 'But I want to know what you were afraid of. Why did you want me to look into her background?'

'I was protecting my family. She seemed a pushy intruder, and I didn't believe all that guff about messages from the other side.'

'I don't think that's enough of a reason, if you'll forgive me.' Louisa was beginning to feel the heat of the fire on the back of her legs, just a little too hot for comfort. 'I think there's a secret you're all keeping. Mrs Hoole knew it, didn't she?'

Billy stood up. 'Mrs Sullivan, I have no wish to be rude to you, so I'm going to end this conversation here. There is no conspiracy, and I would remind you that you are our guest for Christmas. Don't bite the hand that feeds you, and all that, eh?' With a patronising smirk, he walked off.

Louisa was less hurt than she ought to have been. He was young, the heir to the dukedom, and likely felt he was his family's knight in shining armour. And, anyway, she hadn't the slightest inclination to believe him. There was a conspiracy, she was sure of it.

CHAPTER THIRTY-SEVEN

Why would Joan suddenly disappear? Rather than make the assumption that Mrs Hoole was right – that she was killed – perhaps she should try to eliminate the possibility that she really did run away of her own accord. If she had had an affair with the duke, what might have made her leave, so suddenly, without telling anyone?

Louisa almost smacked her forehead. Pregnancy, of course.

A kitchen-maid, pregnant and unmarried, would not have had many options. She might not have told the duke, if she was frightened of him. And she might not have told anyone else, either, for fear of them revealing her secret. Unmarried mothers had few places of refuge today, let alone in the middle of the Great War. There were nursing homes where they could give birth, but the mothers were frequently forced to part with their babies for adoption. Nor was adoption then a legal process: a baby given away might never be traced. If the duke did know, he would have been afraid of his wife discovering, of his older sons. And who knew how far his fear would have taken him in defence of his family? Joan would certainly have been afraid. Louisa felt it was likely that Joan would have kept any baby secret from him. But could the presence of a real, live baby be kept a complete secret? Someone must have known. But who?

The other maids she had shared a room with might have known but Louisa didn't have a hope of discovering who they were. The dowager would probably have known little of their existence, let alone their names, and they would likely have married since they'd worked at the house so would be untraceable anyway.

The baby of an unmarried mother might not have been baptised, and any church records would be hard to find. It all depended on where Joan had had the baby, but with no money and no support, there were few options. She might even have delivered the baby alone, in a field somewhere. All this supposition was getting Louisa nowhere. What she needed was some kind of record of Joan or the possible baby that might determine her tracks. Who might have known about Joan and the duke? Who would also have recognised Mrs Hoole and been afraid that she would expose this long-buried dark secret?

There was only one person who had been in the house then, who had known Joan and the duke, and who was in the house now: the dowager. She was supposed to have gone home but supposing she hadn't? If the car had broken down ... And Maisie had heard her dog, hadn't she?

The dowager had a room permanently made up in the house, and she hadn't been at the séance. Could she have prepared something, a poisonous tincture for Mrs Hoole to take to bed, once she heard the car had broken down? Or might she have arranged for the car to be sabotaged? Did she have an accomplice?

It felt a stretch but it wasn't impossible.

But where to start asking? If Louisa was wrong, she could be telling the dowager a sordid piece of her husband's past that the old lady had no clue about. If there were no records, no facts, then could she see if there were rumours? Any smoke that might lead to the fire?

CHAPTER THIRTY-EIGHT

Louisa was woken by small hands fiercely shaking her shoulder. Her head felt heavy – she'd drunk rather more wine than usual last night – but she pulled herself up onto her elbows, slowly opening her eyes and smiling. Before her was the face of a small and excited child. 'Mummy, you have to get up. It's Christmas Eve.'

'What time is it?'

Maisie picked up the clock on the bedside table and scrutinised it. 'Eleven past six,' she said, after a moment or two. Then she looked crestfallen. 'That's too early, isn't it?'

'No, darling. It's actually five to seven, so it's not too bad. Though goodness knows what you'll do to me tomorrow morning.' She pulled her daughter to her and lightly tickled her under her arms, sending them both into giggles. Louisa loved it. Christmas as a grown-up had never been much fun. She and her mother mourned her father, who had died when Louisa was barely out of school, and after that Louisa had been working or just ... well, sensible, she supposed. With Maisie around, the atmosphere was delightful, an infectious state that everyone caught. Louisa had the sneakiest suspicion that Maisie was a big part of the reason the others had allowed Nancy to invite them. A child at Christmas helped make sense of the whole thing somehow, allowed everyone to go overboard with the decorations and games. And if that was the reason, she was very pleased.

After breakfast, several of them descended to the Painted Hall, where a fire was glowing in the hearth. It didn't throw much heat into that cavernous space but it had a cosy effect, making it feel more like a home than a palace. As Louisa had become more accustomed to Chatsworth, she began to see how it could be a home. She said so to Deborah, who sighed. 'I agree, I think it's a wonderful place. But everyone else seems to think that the time for these houses is over, or it will be after the war.'

'Don't the duke and duchess want to live here?' asked Louisa.

'I don't know that they do. They seem to love their farm and the house by the sea. They're not terribly grand, as you know.'

'And the duke doesn't have too many happy memories of this place, either,' said Louisa, remembering what he had said about his mother making him cry every time he came home for the holidays from school.

'No,' said Deborah. 'Let's hope we're making some now. I really do want to put all that horrid business behind us.'

Louisa took this as another tacit plea for her to drop her questions into the death of Mrs Hoole. It was clear no one believed it was murder or they'd be behaving a lot more carefully in a house where any one of them could have done it.

'Of course,' said Louisa, not really certain if she was lying or not. 'So tell me – what's happening now?'

'We've got some children coming up from the village. Granny Evie told me it was a tradition when she was châtelaine here, and I thought it would be a cheerful thing to do for them. Most are probably evacuees, so I'm not very certain how many are coming. It used to be around fifteen, but it might be twice that today.'

Louisa looked around the hall. Apart from the fire and a six-foot tree – dwarfed by the room – there wasn't much to indicate that a party was about to happen.

Nancy came up to them at that moment. 'Are we giving the children anything?'

Deborah looked flummoxed. 'Well, no. Do you think we should?'

'They're walking up from Pilsley. I think they might at least like a cup of water,' said Nancy, at her most imperious.

'Oh, goodness. I didn't think of it. I mean, with the war and everything, it's not as if we can lay much on,' spluttered Deborah, looking more anxious by the second. 'Do you think we should cancel it?'

'When are you expecting them?'

'In twenty minutes.' Deborah's shoulders sagged as she said it.

'I think you've answered your own question.' Nancy stood in the middle of the hall looking about her, hands on hips. Louisa liked her in this mode. No one saw it often, as Nancy liked to pretend she was incapable; she had told her sisters when they were still in the nursery that the reason she'd only lasted a few weeks at art school was because there were too many knickers on the floor of her bedsit with no one to pick them up. In truth, she was not shy of graft. She had already run the house in Rutland Gate as a refuge for a Jewish family and done a great deal of voluntary war work. Louisa knew that for all Nancy's brittle quips, she had a generous heart.

'Louisa, Kick, you go to the kitchens, ask the maids for as many small glasses and cups as they can gather and bring them up here, with jugs of water. Ask Mrs Airlie if she has any bottles of cordial stored somewhere. The maids can bring up tea, one big pot will do. Charles, please could you find a table we can set up here? Billy and I will go to the tree upstairs and take off its decorations. We can give one to each child to put on the tree here, so they feel as if they've been part of it. Duke and Duchess, could you stand here and welcome them in? It'll make them feel frightfully grand . . .' And on she went, until everyone had been assigned a duty of some kind. Even the dowager was to sit in the corner and allow the children to pet her Peke, the only task Louisa felt might be a challenge too far. Soon, the sight of the children coming up the drive was visible through the hall windows, and everyone jumped to their allotted positions as smartly as if ordered by a sergeant major. Ellis the Second opened the front door and directed them to the duke and duchess standing at the entrance to the hall, the duke in his shabby jacket, the duchess in her pearls.

They had arrived more or less all at the same time, so it wasn't long before the hall was echoing with the sound of delighted children. Kick and Deborah handed out water and cordial for the children, the maids poured tea for the adults, while Charles and Adele were instructed to talk to the villagers and make them feel welcome. Louisa wondered how many of them would guess at Adele's exotic past. Judging by the whispers going on between a few of them, it seemed that one or two definitely had. Lady Redesdale and Unity were out of sight: Unity kept from being the freak show at this particular circus. Lord Redesdale was chatting to the dowager, the Peke sleeping peacefully at her feet for once.

Louisa and Lucie were helping with the children, talking to them and pointing out things for them to look at on the walls and ceiling, while Billy and Nancy handed out the Christmas decorations. It was jolly and innocent, full of festive cheer, and Louisa was glad of it – it would help to turn around the atmosphere in the house, which had lately been in danger of gloom. She was especially glad for Maisie, who had barely seen a child since they'd left London. Now she was chatting away to another little girl, dressed in what looked like her Sunday best, but with dirty knees and her hair in ragged bunches.

Thirsty, Louisa went to the table for a glass of water, now the children had left to crowd around the tree. One or two of the parents were standing around.

'Is it true, what happened here?' The woman asking the question had a headscarf knotted beneath her chin, she looked more of a grandmother than a mother.

'What happened here?' asked Louisa, while wondering which of the many happenings she could be referring to. Mrs Hoole? Joan Dorries, the pregnant maid? The philandering duke?

'If you knew me, you'd know I don't like to gossip,' said the woman, 'but they're saying that someone came here and saw a ghost right before she died.'

'Are they?' said Louisa, wondering why ghosts were coming into so many of her conversations. 'How very interesting.'

'That didn't happen, then?' The woman looked around. 'Aren't there any sandwiches? They had them last time, delicious they were, very thin cucumber. I was looking forward to them, on the long walk up.'

'I'm so sorry,' broke in Deborah, 'but we couldn't manage sandwiches this year.'

The woman gave a harrumph but didn't seem too put out, and Deborah moved off to the children, encouraging them to admire the tree.

'Tragically, a woman died here not very long ago,' said Louisa. 'But as for the ghosts, I couldn't tell you. Who knows what she saw?'

'All sorts seem to go on here. But I'm not surprised. A big place like this, anyone could get lost in it, couldn't they?'

'Are you referring to something in particular?' asked Louisa.

'Oh, no. I've heard a thing or two, but I know better than to repeat nonsense like that. There's one thing I will say. The current duke standing over there, he doesn't seem to have the sins of his father.'

Louisa checked no one was listening in on their conversation. 'What were the sins of his father?'

The woman leaned in, as if she was about to share something powerful. 'Why would I tell you?'

Louisa was taken aback, but she felt a direct question deserved a direct answer. 'You're right, madam. You needn't tell me at all. But I'm a good friend of the family. If there are any unsubstantiated rumours going around out there, you would be doing them and me a favour to give us a chance to correct anything that's wrong.'

The woman nodded seriously. 'Yes, yes, I do see that. Well, I'd be happy to help. As I said, I'm not one of those busybodies.' She dropped her voice a notch. 'They say, the late duke, he got a young girl into ... you know ... trouble.'

Louisa knew what 'trouble' was code for. Pregnancy.

211

'And who was the young girl?'

But the woman looked worried she'd said too much. 'I think someone who worked at the house. But not a local girl, like.'

'Why do you say that?'

'Because if she was local, she'd have gone home, wouldn't she? But no one knew her. Like I said, it's only stories. And there's always plenty about lords and that, having their wicked ways with maids.'

Louisa knew rumours were stories: unquantifiable, probably highly exaggerated, tales designed to make a mockery of someone's life. Even so, the duke disappearing during the war, shortly after being caught *in flagrante* by his young son; a maid in trouble, not from round here. 'What happened to the maid?'

'I don't know. I suppose she weren't ever heard from again. That sort never are, are they? Trouble like that, with a duke ...' She seemed to lose interest. 'I'd better go back to my boy. He'll get lost in this place, and that would never do.'

Louisa was about to ask the busybody another question when there was a minor kerfuffle, just beyond the entrance to the hall. Several people were standing between her and the duke and duchess, as well as children running around, a little overexcited now that they had hung the decorations. If they weren't organised into a game soon, they would start haring up and down the stairs and running onto the balcony—

Louisa stopped and looked again at the person who was talking to the duke and duchess. It surely couldn't be?

But it was.

'Daddy! Daddy!' Maisie was running towards her father, who had set down his case and was bending, arms wide open, ready to receive his daughter, who struck him with an audible *whump*, making everyone around them laugh.

Louisa laughed with them, and ran over to her husband. Guy stood, one hand on Maisie's head while she clutched his leg, his other arm open for his wife. 'Merry Christmas, darling,' he whispered into her ear.

'It is now,' said Louisa, kissing him happily. 'It is now.'

CHAPTER THIRTY-NINE

'What happened? How did you get here?' Louisa had managed to pull her husband away from the fray, and Maisie rejoined her new friend, content now she knew her father was near. They were sitting on a window seat on the balcony that ran around the Painted Hall, the mêlée going on below them.

'Aren't you pleased to see me, then?' he teased.

'You know I am. I've been missing you – it was just the last thing I expected. I thought you had to do shifts for the Home Guard.'

'I did, but someone agreed to swap with me. I've never asked before, always worked through every posting they've given me, so the major was generous. And, honestly, I just couldn't stand the idea of not being with Maisie on Christmas Day. I took a train, but I didn't know which one I'd catch, and then I thought it would be more fun to surprise you both, so I walked most of the way from the station. I hitched a lift for some of it. It wasn't too far and it's beautiful around here, isn't it? I enjoyed the view.' Guy smoothed his hair back, slightly ruffled from his hat. Warm sunlight was pouring through the window. She was always thrilled to see her husband, tall and reassuring, his kind eyes measuring her up from behind his glasses. 'Enough about me. How are you?'

'It's been a strange time,' Louisa admitted. 'And, now I think about it, I should have expected you to surprise me. Remember when you turned up on the ship that time?' They smiled at the shared memory. 'Just like then, I'm rather relieved to have you here. I've been trying to puzzle something out and not getting very far on my own.'

'Have you heard any more about the woman who died? Mrs Hoole, wasn't it?'

'Yes, there's been quite a bit on that front,' said Louisa. 'The detective inspector and I agree the circumstances of her death look suspicious but there's nothing concrete yet.'

'What about the post-mortem results?'

'Inconclusive. She died of a heart attack, but whether that was brought on naturally or unnaturally, they don't know yet. A toxicology report is on the way but—'

'It will take weeks,' said Guy, knowledgeably. 'Anything else, any bruising?'

'Nothing obvious.'

'It doesn't rule out poisoning or smothering then,' said Guy.

'I had thought of that but hadn't got very far with the theory,' admitted Louisa, both annoyed and pleased that she and Guy could work together like this. 'The only thing that makes it look like a deliberate death so far is that the car apparently broke down, which meant she had to stay. It's just too convenient. That and the fact that she told us about the maid who went missing during the last war.'

'You think the connection is there?'

'Yes, but I can't quite pin it down. Whichever way I turn, people are keeping some kind of secret and I can't tell if they've got something or nothing to do with either Mrs Hoole or the missing maid, Joan.'

'Perhaps I'll have a fresh eye on it, but I can't stay long. I need to get a train back on the twenty-seventh.'

'Just three nights?' said Louisa.

'Yes, but we'll make the most of them. Let's go down now and fetch Maisie. I'd like you both to take me on a tour. It's quite something, this house. You said it was big but I still hadn't an idea it was *this* big. No wonder there are so many secrets.'

'Someone else said something similar.' Louisa stood and took her husband's hand. She could see the party was coming to an end now, the children putting on their coats and scarves, flushed with the excitement of what was still ahead of them.

'Come on, then. I'll show you our room. We'll have to find a camp bed for Maisie but there's bound to be one somewhere. She won't want to sleep in a separate room, I'm afraid.'

'Not that I mind, but why not?'

'Too many strange noises. I think the thought of all those rooms beyond the door is quite spooky for her at night,' said Louisa, knowing that she felt rather the same as her six-year-old daughter.

Louisa and Maisie took Guy through the house to their room, Maisie pointing out all the things she had discovered during her stay: a favourite painting of a child with her dog, the room with leather lining the walls, a chair that no one was allowed to sit on because it was too fragile. In the bedroom, Guy put down his bag and whispered to Louisa that he'd managed to pick up one or two extra presents for Maisie.

'What was that?' asked Maisie.

'Get away, Sharp Ears,' teased her father. Louisa was laughing, enjoying being with her own family, when there was a rapid knock on the door. She opened it.

Deborah was on the other side. 'I hoped you'd be here,' she said. 'I'm so sorry to disturb.'

'What is it?'

'We've had a message from Group Captain Nesbit. He says there's likely to be an air raid tonight.' She was brisk – everyone knew not to make a fuss about that sort of thing. But it was nerve-racking.

'Was he allowed to give us an early warning?' asked Guy. 'Seems rather unusual.'

'I don't know,' said Deborah. 'I'm not even sure I'm all that grateful. Sometimes one would rather not have too long to think about it. But I was wondering . . . I know it's silly but if we have to spend Christmas Eve in the air-raid shelter, we might make it look more cheerful. Could you do it for me?'

'Yes, of course, good thinking,' said Louisa.

'Ellis and the maids aren't available to help but you could ask Max, the gardener. He's very accommodating with extra jobs.' Deborah thanked them again, then excused herself, dashing off down the landing.

Louisa closed the door and turned to her husband and daughter. 'Right,' she said, 'no rest for the wicked. Let's get to work.'

CHAPTER FORTY

The air-raid shelter was in the cellar. Deborah assigned the gardener Max to show them the way, and Louisa asked Lucie along, too. The shelter was accessed by a flight of steep, narrow steps into a space that was dark and fusty. It appeared to run almost the length of the house, though it was really another series of divided rooms, with archways rather than doors. There were no windows at all, the place lit only by a few bare light bulbs, throwing corners of the cellar into pitch darkness. It was cold, too, their bones soon chilled by the damp.

'I'm sure it's sensible to be here,' said Louisa to Guy, 'but if the whole of Chatsworth collapsed, wouldn't we be trapped?'

'I don't fancy it myself,' said Guy. There were frequent arguments in London about whether it was better to be at the top of a house than in a basement when it was bombed. But from what he had seen, there was no definite right answer. It seemed to be nothing more than luck that decided whether or not someone survived.

'It's horrible,' said Lucie, with an exaggerated shudder. 'I never like coming down here.'

'Have there been many air raids?' asked Louisa.

'Not too many. The girls get frightened, but I think more of the cellar than the siren.'

Guy was carrying a box of decorations pilfered from upstairs, and Max brought some more branches of holly and trails of ivy from the garden. But the task of making this bleak, dank cellar into a festive place of joy seemed laughable. Like asking the Grim Reaper to wear a clown's mask. After a minute or so they turned a corner, Max switched on another light and they saw twelve huge wooden casks lined along the cellar walls.

'These hold the beer,' said Max. He never said much, and was brusque when he did, but he appeared to be a decent man. 'A hundred gallons, so they say.'

That was the extent of the guided tour. At the end of the line-up of casks, a wall supported a few shelves, which looked to have been hastily put up. On them were jars of Bovril, several chipped mugs, teaspoons, large tins of crackers, a first-aid box: the essentials. A camping stove stood on the lower shelf, with a bashed-up tin kettle and a jerry-can. Guy picked it up and something inside it sloshed about. 'Hopefully that's water not petrol,' he said.

'Thank you, Max,' said Louisa. 'You needn't stay. We can find our way out.'

'I have a couple of things to look at down here,' he replied. 'Take as long as you like.' He moved out of the corner that was designated the air-raid shelter and soon they heard him tapping on a pipe close by.

Guy set the box on the floor and the three of them pulled out various decorations. 'We should have brought a hammer and nails,' said Guy, after trying and failing to get one end of a paper chain to hitch onto a corner of the shelf. In the end, they weighted the ends down, and propped the branches and the ivy on the shelves. It wasn't much but at least it showed some kind of willing. Throughout, they heard the occasional tink-tink of Max at work.

'Are you enjoying your work here, as a teacher?' asked Guy.

'Yes, I like it very much,' Lucie replied, disentangling two baubles from each other. 'The girls are bright and, on the whole, well-behaved.'

'Must be tough for them. Away from their families. Where was the school moved from?'

'Wales,' said Lucie. 'It's true. It's a long way from their home. They miss their parents very much, but they know this is the safest place for them to be.'

'Do they like being here?'

'Yes, I think it's an adventure. *Mais* they do complain about the cold. The beds are in the corridors, the coldest of all, and it is creepy with the night watchmen.'

'What night watchmen?' asked Guy.

'Two men, every night, they walk around the house, check that it is safe and so on,' said Lucie.

Guy was interested. 'Do they have that system here, where they turn keys?'

'What system is that?' asked Louisa.

'It's quite usual, in this sort of house. I came across it a few times in my policing days and it could be useful for us. There are various points around the house where a night watchman will turn a key, and the time at which it's turned, as well as the location point, is recorded in a central place. Each time they turn the key it's to say that everything is fine, as it were,' explained Guy.

'So if a point is missed, you would know that the night watchman hadn't been there, or something had happened to them?' Now Louisa was interested, too.

'Exactly. I solved a burglary once, that way,' said Guy, past triumphs still a pleasure to recall. 'Have you not seen them here?'

'No,' said Louisa, 'I knew there were night watchmen, and we don't see them because they presumably sleep during the day. I assumed they simply walked around with torches – I had no idea a more sophisticated system was in place.'

'Has the detective talked to them?' asked Guy.

'I know he was shown the record, so I assume everything was in order,' said Louisa. 'But, of course, I haven't looked into the detail of this turnkey system.'

'Perhaps that's an idea, then,' said Guy. 'I hoped I could help.'

'And now you have. You're not just a pretty face.'

'Please!' said Lucie. 'It's not fair for a lonely girl like me to listen to this.' Which made them all laugh.

CHAPTER FORTY-ONE

A few minutes after six o'clock, dovetailing with the fading peals of the house's clocks, Deborah suggested that they all go down to the shelter, asking Ellis to summon the servants. 'It seems better than waiting for the siren,' she said, and everyone agreed. All afternoon, Louisa had felt anxious: in the week since they had left London, she'd almost forgotten about that awful anticipation of an air raid. Two minutes of a low moan that hailed only panic and death, a sound that filled one's head and pushed any good thoughts away.

Quickly, calmly, they put down their cups, picked up their gas masks, with their books or knitting, and made their way down the stairs to the Painted Hall, then along to the door that would lead them below. Everyone's face was set, devoid of the earlier Christmas cheer.

Maisie gripped Louisa's hand so tightly her knuckles were grinding. Her little face was pale and worried beneath her glossy curls. Louisa's heart broke just to look at her, a child who knew of war, of the very real chance of bombs falling, bringing nothing but destruction and injury. Guy had his arm around his wife's shoulders. He looked less frightened, perhaps more inured to the sound, or perhaps the solid walls of Chatsworth seemed less likely to tumble, marble, stone and brick that had been standing for hundreds of years.

But what if Group Captain Nesbit had had intelligence that Chatsworth was a target? Was that why he had forewarned them?

Louisa looked at the paltry Christmas decorations they had put up earlier and wondered what they had been thinking. In the harsh light of the bare bulbs, exposing the damp on the bricks, the cobwebs and the holes in the walls big enough for rats, the wilting branches of holly and the curling paper chains were pathetic. She knew everyone would rally soon enough, if only for Maisie, but for the next few minutes, she could see only the ashen, frightened faces of maids and duchesses alike. Maisie sat between Louisa and Guy, her head snuggled into Guy's waist, his large hand on her shoulder; she was quiet, her eyes open, fidgeting with the buttons on her doll's dress.

Deborah lit some candles and turned off the harshest light directly above them. 'That's a bit better,' she said. 'Now, would anyone like a cracker or two?' She opened one of the tins and passed it around.

Louisa took some for Maisie, though she could feel that they were stale, would crumble to nothing in her mouth. Betsy and Anna sat beside Mrs Airlie, Betsy smiling at Maisie as if willing her to feel better. In the cellar nothing could be heard of the world above – they wouldn't even know if a plane flew overheard. Would they hear a bomb drop? She supposed they'd feel it.

Gradually, everyone seemed to come out of the torpor that had descended on them when they sat down. The maids whispered together, while Mrs Airlie and Ellis were busying themselves around the gas stove, putting the kettle on to boil and setting out cups. Billy and Kick were huddled together. Unity's head was bowed, her hands clasped in prayer. Lady Redesdale sat beside her, eyes closed, mouth pinched together. Lord Redesdale and the dowager were talking together as if they were still in the library upstairs. Charles had propped himself in a corner, head on his chest, and was snoring lightly. Lucie was flicking through an old magazine.

'What's that?' asked Nancy. 'What are you reading?'

'Vogue,' said Lucie, showing them the cover. 'But all the dresses in it are hideous.'

'You don't like modern couture?' asked Adele. She was sitting between Louisa and Nancy, immaculate as ever in a navy wool dress that was nipped in at the waist, pleats on the skirt, and flowers made of felt on the collar. 'I thought the French were obsessed with it.' Her American accent dragged out the word, making it somehow onomatopoeic.

'Maybe in Paris,' said Lucie, licking her thumb to turn another page.

Ellis began to hand out mugs of Bovril for those who wanted one. Louisa didn't usually like it but there was some comfort in holding a hot drink, so she took it. Guy and Maisie were talking together, looking through a book that Maisie had managed to pick up on her way.

She felt a nudge in her side, from Adele. 'Have you been continuing your investigations?' she asked, her voice low, her head bent to Louisa.

It still made Louisa a little dizzy to be so close to such a well-known face. 'How did you know?' she said.

'I'm more than a foolish former film star,' Adele teased. 'And I've seen that something's up with my husband.'

'I'm sorry if I've upset him.'

Adele brought out a packet of cigarettes but kept it in her hand, turning it over. 'I know my Charles is not a happy man now, but he was when we were first married. Did you know we met in a nightclub in New York?'

Louisa shook her head mutely, not trusting herself to say anything and she didn't want to admit that any knowledge she did have was gleaned from the gossip column of a magazine.

'Anyway, we did. He was very gay, then, the proverbial life and soul. And so English ... charming, witty and – well, all those things that appeal to an American gal like me.' She gave a rueful smile. Louisa said nothing in reply, but it didn't seem to matter. Adele only wanted someone to listen. In the low light, and the warmth that was starting to build from their bodies in the room and the lit gas stove, the mood turned intimate. War was a leveller at times like these.

'You know, Louisa,' said Adele, still turning over the cigarette packet in her hand, 'I've been privileged enough to meet many different people in my lifetime. I've dined with presidents and cabinet ministers, danced with gangsters and high-court judges. There's something they all have in common.'

'What is that?' asked Louisa, intrigued.

'Everyone believes themselves to be an outsider at some time. Most get over it, or accept it. But some never lose that feeling of isolation, a fear of being abandoned, no matter who they surround themselves with. Those are the ones in danger of turning to drink.' She looked across at her husband, asleep in the corner. 'I knew he always believed that Eddy was the favoured son. Stupidly, I thought my American ways would convince him there was no shame in being a second son, because we have no need of titles to proclaim our importance. But it's too entrenched, you know?'

Louisa wasn't aristocratic but she was British enough to understand how deep-rooted the conventions of her country could be, how they could limit your expectations unless you deliberately broke away. And she understood the feelings of being an outsider.

'Nothing makes me sadder than the fact that I cannot make my husband happy. It's taken me a long time but I've finally realised that he doesn't drink because of me, or in spite of me. The only person who chooses to continue to pick up the glass, and who can choose to stop, is him.' She put the cigarettes back into her pocket. 'I apologise. You are a young mother and wife. This is a very disheartening conversation.'

'Not at all. It's a privilege to talk to you and I understand much of what you say. I'm sympathetic. It must be hard for you.'

'It's lonely at times, but I know how lucky I am.' She closed her eyes and leaned back against the wall.

Louisa hesitated but she couldn't let this chance go. 'Dare I ask, has your husband told you his memories of the missing maid?'

Adele opened her eyes. 'Do you mean the one whose cap we found that night?'

Louisa nodded.

'I thought the woman who said she was receiving the messages was a fraud.'

'She wasn't a real psychic, but I don't think she was a fraud as such. She knew the maid and she wanted to make us interested

226

in her disappearance. She believed there was a cover-up of some kind.'

'I see. And do you agree with her?'

Louisa looked around the room, everyone sheltering together from the war that raged above them. It seemed almost churlish to believe that one of them had wilfully disguised the real reason for Joan's disappearance a quarter of a century ago. What was more, that she believed one of them was responsible for the death of Mrs Hoole mere days ago. How much did she *really* believe it?

'I think a house like this inevitably holds a lot of secrets,' she said at last.

'And you are discovering them now?' Adele gave her a mischievous glance. Louisa would have said conspiratorial if it wasn't ridiculous to believe that a famous movie star could enter into a conspiracy with her. 'It's the English way,' Adele continued. 'That's how it feels to me. My brother and I ...' she gave Louisa another knowing look '... we talked to each other all the time. Less so, now we're divided by the Atlantic Ocean. But I'd like to think he'd answer any question I asked of him truthfully.'

There was an intimacy here that Louisa couldn't ignore. Honestly, she thrilled to it. But she also wanted answers to some questions of her own.

'I'm sure what you say is true.' Louisa took a breath. 'Do you think your husband knows something about the missing maid?'

'Yes,' said Adele. 'I do.'

Louisa listened. Beside her, Maisie was starting to wriggle in childish frustration at sitting down for so long. Any second now she'd demand Louisa's attention.

'He thinks his father had something to do with it, doesn't he?' said Adele.

'I know he walked in on . . .' Louisa dared herself to confide.

'Imagine what a horrible shock that was for a small boy. And then his father left the country suddenly.'

'Do you think the dowager knows anything?'

Adele looked at the old lady, petting her Peke as she talked to Lord Redesdale. 'She's the definition of inscrutable. It's impossible to say what she knows. She believes in protecting the family name, that's for sure.'

'She'd go to any lengths, you mean?'

Before Adele could answer, Maisie had clambered onto Louisa's lap, and was pulling at her sleeve. 'Mummy, when can we go back up?'

Adele gave her a sympathetic smile but she looked away, pulling a book out of her bag and opening it.

'Not until we hear the all-clear,' said Louisa, stroking her daughter's hair.

'But what about Father Christmas? How will he give me my stocking if I sleep down here?' To which Louisa and Guy came up with a stream of inventiveness involving magical reindeer that knew how to avoid German planes, until their daughter finally began to nod off, her head resting on her mother's chest.

At five o'clock in the morning, with no siren having sounded, Deborah decided that they could risk going back upstairs to the comfort of their beds. Stiff and cold, they straightened themselves out from their uncomfortable positions, necks and knees creaking. A camp bed had been made up for the dowager but the rest of them were had spent the night on chairs of varying levels of comfort, there not being quite enough cushions to put on the floor for makeshift mattresses. Louisa was grateful to have the warmth of Maisie and Guy beside her but even so, she had barely slept. Deborah told Ellis and Mrs Airlie that breakfast need not be put out until ten o'clock, giving everyone time to catch up on some sleep first.

'There will be a service at midday for those who want to go,' she added, addressing the room.

'What about Christmas dinner if everyone's at church?' whispered Guy to Louisa.

'They don't do it at luncheon,' said Louisa, resisting an eyebrow raise. 'They have it in the evening.'

Guy pulled a face. 'Typical.' He gathered up his daughter, still sleeping, her head flopping onto his shoulder. 'Let's go and see if Father Christmas has filled our stockings, shall we?' Maisie mumbled something but her eyes stayed shut. Slowly, everyone made their way out of the cellar, Ellis at the back, the last to turn out the lights.

CHAPTER FORTY-TWO

C hristmas Day, thankfully, went without a hitch. Although Guy and Louisa didn't manage to sleep – Maisie's excitement would not allow for it – it meant they had a few precious hours all to themselves as a little family, before the rest of the household gathered by the tree in the drawing room. Father Christmas had managed to track Maisie down at Chatsworth and delivered a jigsaw puzzle, a spinning top, a new Rupert Bear annual and chocolates covered in shiny gold paper to make them look like new pennies, which Guy pretended to pinch and was severely reprimanded by his daughter. 'You don't steal, Daddy!' she said, finger pointing.

'I most certainly do not.' He laughed, handing her back the precious coin.

After everyone returned from church, there was a bottle or two of champagne, which cheered Nancy up, and presents were exchanged. Paper had been rationed so nothing could be wrapped, although there was some inventiveness with silk scarves by Adele. Nancy gave Louisa a bottle of lily-of-the-valley eau de toilette. 'It's charming,' said Louisa, delighted, dabbing it on her wrists and behind her ears.

'I found it in Mr Formby's of all places,' said Nancy. 'I didn't ask him where he procured it but it seems rather nice, doesn't it?'

'Absolutely,' Louisa replied, handing over her own present, a box of lilac handkerchiefs she had made from an old dress. She had stitched Nancy's initials in the corners.

'You are a dream,' said Nancy, giving her friend a kiss.

The rest of the afternoon passed in the usual blur of walks and reading new books, playing games with Maisie and even some singing of Christmas songs around the piano, when it was discovered that Adele could play. At six o'clock, the party dispersed so that people could bathe and change. Maisie was exhausted by the day, and Louisa suggested to Guy that he might like to give her a bath and an early supper. Deborah asked Louisa if she might accompany Lord Redesdale on the blackout check. 'I don't like him to do it alone,' she said, 'and I've got to do one or two things for the grand feast . . . Well, it won't be all that grand but Mrs Airlie and I are doing our best.'

'Of course,' said Louisa. Darling Debo, she was always doing her best.

It was cold outside but on Christmas Day, a frost in the air felt entirely right. Lord Redesdale and Louisa walked beside each other, not saying much, but she took no offence. She knew that he was comfortable enough in her presence, and he took his blackout check very seriously, looking up at all the windows. They had gone all around the front and along the sides, with the entrance to the kitchens, which took quite some time. Louisa was beginning to stamp her feet to get some warmth back into her toes, when Lord Redesdale called, 'There's a light on. Dammit, what sewer has done that?'

It was only a small window, fairly high up. 'It must be one of the servants' rooms,' said Louisa. And then she counted along. She counted again, but she was sure.

It was Mrs Hoole's room.

CHAPTER FORTY-THREE

Taking the steps two at a time, Louisa raced up to Mrs Hoole's room – as she had come to think of it – and saw the small bedside lamp was on. She drew the curtains and looked around. Who had been in there, and for what purpose? It was hard to discern anything different about the room since the body had been taken away. The unmade bed had a rather disturbing aspect to it now, a combination of abandonment and neglect. Pulling back the bedspread to strip the sheets, she prepared herself for a revealing clue: a bloody knife, an empty pill bottle, a container of weedkiller. There was nothing, of course. She bundled up the sheets and empty pillowcase, throwing it into the hall to take downstairs.

Mrs Hoole's clothes, and the cap she had been holding, had been taken away by the coroner's undertakers. As she had not been expecting to stay the night, there had been no other personal effects that might have told something of who she was or her intentions: no book or toothbrush. Where, though, had all the candles come from? Louisa couldn't think why she hadn't asked herself that question before. She looked in the drawers to see if there was a collection of them that Mrs Hoole had come upon but found nothing. The drawers were completely empty. Louisa counted them: nine candles, burned down to the ends. One or two might conceivably have been in the room already. Fearful of power cuts or an air raid, people always made sure to have candles to hand, with matches. But not *nine*.

Louisa went into the bedrooms along the landing, servants' rooms that appeared to have been lying empty for a long time, their curtains drawn, a thin layer of dust on all the furniture, the beds stripped bare. Each had a candlestick and candle in it, bar three, which had none. So Mrs Hoole might have taken those. With one in the housekeeper's room already, that left five to find. Had someone helped her gather the extra candles? No one, so far as Louisa knew, admitted to having any more to do with Mrs Hoole beyond serving her supper in the kitchen or showing her to her room, let alone knowing that she was planning a séance in her room. Surely it was the sort of fascinating detail that would make good downstairs gossip. If they didn't tell, they meant to hide it: why?

Louisa turned off the lamp and closed the door. The landing was dark and she was momentarily blind until her eyes adjusted. A shaft of light was coming up the stairs from the floor below and she was able to see the bundle of sheets she'd put out earlier. Just as she was picking it up, she heard a bang, not especially loud, like a door slamming, whether by force of hand or a draught. It startled her but she told herself it was nothing and started to walk towards the stairs, following the light. But she had the unsettling sensation that something was at her back. There was a coolness on her neck and the niggling bother that she was being watched, though it was hardly possible in such darkness. Even if someone was there, they surely couldn't see much. She paused, wondering – had she checked *all* the rooms? She was definite she had but perhaps there had been an open window in one, and she hadn't noticed because of the closed curtains. A childish wariness of the dark spooked her and she scuttled to the stairs quickly. Whatever it was, she had no inclination to discover it while she was on her own.

CHAPTER FORTY-FOUR

On Boxing Day morning Nancy told Louisa that she'd asked Group Captain Nesbit over. 'I thought we could do with the distraction,' she said. Louisa suspected it was Nancy who wanted to be distracted by him but she knew to keep her counsel. Lucie would be pleased at any rate.

'Group Captain Nesbit,' announced Ellis, half a second before the officer walked into the drawing room. Unity had been sitting quietly in the corner with a jigsaw puzzle, but now leaped up and practically ran over to him.

'Oh, I had no idea you were coming. Nobody said you were. Why didn't anyone tell me? That would have been the best Christmas present ever. Better than the book I got.' She looked around the room, an accusatory stare at each occupant.

'We didn't keep it from you deliberately,' said Deborah.

'Yes, you did. I hate you,' replied Unity, but it was said without emotion, a statement of the obvious. Deborah smacked her hands onto her thighs but stayed quiet. Everyone had learned that there was little point in entering into an argument with Unity.

Nesbit gave an apologetic cough. 'I didn't mean to cause any trouble.'

'You haven't,' said Nancy, smoothly. More quietly she said, 'We did keep it from Unity, I'm afraid, as we wouldn't have heard the end of it otherwise.' She walked towards the sofa, expecting him to follow her, but he didn't. Instead, he went over to Unity, whom Lady Redesdale had beckoned back to the puzzle table. Soon he was bent over the jigsaw, picking up pieces and inspecting them, chatting quietly to Unity as he did so.

'Goodness,' said Nancy. 'You don't think he really means to keep her company, do you?'

'I think it's rather kind,' said Kick. Louisa suspected that Kick thought some of the family cold towards Unity, but she hadn't known the young Mitford in her days of Hitler adoration. It was hard to love someone who had signed off every letter 'Heil Hitler', and moved into an apartment in Munich that had previously been occupied by a young Jewish couple. Louisa had not believed Unity's faux naïveté that they had wanted to move out.

'Hmm.' Nancy crossed her legs and looked into the fire. If she minded, she wasn't about to let anyone know.

Unsettled by the shift of dynamics, the group sat silently by the fire for a while. Maisie was thankfully occupied with her new Shirley Temple doll, which Guy had found for her. For the last few years, when it was only her, Guy and their daughter, Louisa liked the days after Christmas, before the world got going properly again. Deborah and Nancy, who liked to return often to their familiar childhood theme of boredom, had been complaining that morning that the war made things worse because there was no hunt, which had, according to them, been the only thing that made life worth living after Christmas. (If not for the fox, thought Louisa.)

Uncertain of how to entertain their guest, the Boxing Day luncheon was a rather stilted affair. The duke and duchess were not there, having made their excuses to dine with the dowager at Edensor. Lucie had also gone there, to assist the dowager in an unspecified way. She'd made the plan before Nesbit's arrival was announced and it couldn't be undone. So far as Louisa understood, there was an aged butler in the dowager's house but no other servants, and it seemed likely that Lucie was providing something of a lady's maid service, if only temporarily. At least they both seemed to be enjoying the arrangement.

After the coffee had been served, there was another lull in the conversation, during which only the occasional clink of cup against saucer could be heard. Bravely, perhaps, in this void, Group Captain Nesbit turned towards Lord Redesdale, seated at the head of the table. 'I wonder if I might be taken out for a turn around the garden?'

Lord Redesdale looked as if he had been shaken from a stupor, as indeed he probably had. He said less and less these days, to the point at which Louisa almost missed his rages. At least they had shown some life in the old boy. 'Eh? Yes, I wouldn't stop you.'

'I think, Farve, what Group Captain Nesbit means is that he'd like to be accompanied in his walk,' prompted Debo. 'I'm terribly sorry it can't be me, but I promised Mrs Airlie we'd go over the ration books this afternoon.'

Nesbit gave another of his apologetic coughs. 'Actually, I was hoping I might walk with Miss Unity.'

This was met with a shocked silence. Afterwards, Louisa

wondered which was more shocking: a married man asking to escort a single girl around the garden, unchaperoned, or the fact that someone was interested in Unity's company.

'Not unchaperoned, I hope,' said Nancy, with a laugh that fooled no one.

'No, of course not.' The back of his neck, a thin strip between collar and immaculately trimmed hair, went a deep red.

'I can't,' said Nancy, though she did not deign to give an explanation. 'And Lady Redesdale must rest. Mrs Sullivan will have to go with you.'

Louisa shot Nancy a look but she knew it was hopeless. 'I should be happy to come along,' she said graciously. 'Maisie will enjoy the fresh air, too.' She knew Guy was tired, having already requested a snooze after lunch.

Nevertheless, Louisa privately conceded, it was a rum thing. Nesbit had to be after something – something he believed Unity could give him – but what could that be? Her childish ways, which could hardly fail to be noticed by even the densest of personalities, could only mean he felt surer of his ability to manipulate her. In short, Louisa could not bring herself to think well of his motivations. But no one seemed to be stopping him. She knew the sisters were very fond of Unity, in spite of everything, and there was a certain level of denial about how damaged she was, if not by Louisa. The difficulty for her was that any possible sympathy for Unity's situation was blunted by the remembrance of her passion for Hitler, which had continued unabated, even as the certain outbreak of war had come closer and closer. It was not that Louisa felt Unity deserved her fate exactly but, well, perhaps a tiny part of her did. It made her feel ashamed of herself, of such base and violent thoughts, but this, too, was what war did to humanity.

Stepping outside, Louisa hoped the cold air would blow away some of these ill feelings. Maisie was beside her, a touch grumpy at being dragged into the garden, away from her beloved new doll. But the grounds were huge, and even Maisie knew she hadn't explored all of them. Louisa suggested that she walk ahead of Nesbit and Unity, to show them the way.

'Don't listen to what we're saying, Lou-Lou,' demanded Unity.

'I shan't,' said Louisa.

Nesbit had the grace to look embarrassed at this exchange. 'Mrs Sullivan may join our walk, if she wishes,' he said.

'No, she mayn't,' replied Unity.

It was entirely possible that Nesbit did not quite realise what he'd done.

They set off, first along the lawn in the front of the house and around the fountain – dry in these winter months – down through the rockery, along the narrow path back towards the house and then a final loop that took in the boundary of the maze before reaching the kitchen gardens and greenhouses.

As much as she admired the grandeur of the landscapes, it was this smaller walled garden that Louisa liked most. She and Maisie had become accustomed to coming out here on their own, and they often saw the gardener, Max. He said little, whether shy or stand-offish Louisa wasn't sure, but he would occasionally find some treat from the hothouse and give it to Maisie: a tiny purple flower, a sprig of pungent rosemary. There wasn't much growing at this time of year, but for a London girl, these tiny delicacies were as prized as jewels. It was not yet four o'clock, and still light, but the sun was muted and the clouds dark. Louisa and Maisie started to play hide and seek around the vegetable patch and greenhouses, while Unity and Nesbit continued their conversation. They were walking slowly, pausing to stop and inspect a label or berries on a holly bush, so far as Louisa could tell. What on earth could their conversation consist of?

At last, having found Maisie behind the bay tree, under a bench in the greenhouse – where Max was potting seedlings – and twice in the corner where the compost was piled, Louisa called an end to the afternoon. She approached Group Captain Nesbit and Unity. 'I think we'll go inside now,' she said. 'I'm rather cold and I'm afraid I've done all the hiding and seeking I can stand.' She gave a smile to show there were no hard feelings. Unity pouted but she seemed to understand that she had been given enough of a treat. Nesbit, Louisa couldn't help noticing, looked relieved.

They walked around to the side entrance, which led through to the Painted Hall. Ellis was already there, waiting for them, ready to take their coats. 'If it's all right, I think I'll take my leave,' said Nesbit to Louisa, assuming her a superior rank over Unity and the butler. 'I drove myself here. Will you say thank you and goodbye for me to the rest of the family?'

'Of course,' said Louisa. Unity was already halfway up the stairs, and Ellis was walking away with her coat. Nesbit turned back towards the door. 'I can't help but wonder . . . ' she started, and wondered how she'd go on before deciding she could only be direct. 'Why is it that you wanted to take Miss Unity out for a walk?'

'Why not?'

But his face revealed uncertainty. She knew he was being disingenuous, and it made her cross. 'Group Captain, don't make me spell it out. Miss Unity is not her previous self, and even if you didn't know her before, it's surely clear that though she has the body of a young woman, she has the mind of a child.'

He blushed then. 'It's nothing untoward, if that's what you are implying. I'm a happily married—'

'No,' said Louisa. 'At least, I'll give you the benefit of the doubt, though others mightn't, and you should be clear in your mind about that.'

'Truly, Mrs Sullivan, I was embarrassed about my false alarm on Christmas Eve, not to mention that there was such an abrupt ending to the visit at the base. I knew Miss Unity had been particularly looking forward to it, and I wished to make amends. Is the desire to right a wrong so suspicious?' He had gained the moral high ground again, forcing Louisa to concede.

'Absolutely not. Forgive my intrusive questions.' Louisa took a step back.

'Goodbye, Mrs Sullivan. I hope we meet again. You and the family are pleasant company, a welcome respite in our current situation.' With this charming farewell, he tipped his cap slightly at her, and left.

CHAPTER FORTY-FIVE

'That was different,' said Guy to Louisa, as they stood on the railway platform, 'but delightful.' He bent down and kissed Maisie, with an affectionate ruffle of her hair. To their surprise, she squirmed and ran off down the platform.

'Maisie!'

Louisa ran after her and slowed as she saw her daughter was talking to another little girl, the one she'd befriended at the children's party before Christmas. She could see they were playing at being grown-ups, standing stiffly opposite each other and shaking hands, giggling at the silliness of it. Guy came up beside her and she leaned into him, enjoying the moment, the two of them watching their daughter. But then they got a shock.

'*I bin nine forty eiderdown,*' said Maisie. '*Lie man borkenjar.*'

The other girl gave Maisie a final handshake, stifling her laugh with her other hand, before running off to her mother.

Louisa touched Maisie on the shoulder. 'What was that you were saying to your friend? Sounded like a funny language.'

'Miss Unity and Captain Nesbit were talking it,' said Maisie.

'When we were in the garden. I was hiding and they didn't see me and I heard them talking with funny words like that.'

Louisa bent down. 'Say it again, what it sounded like.'

'For mine din lard der, jar bink zie–'

'All right, that's enough,' said Louisa, gently. She turned to Guy. 'Did you hear that?'

He nodded, his mouth set.

'Well, we did all wonder why he was so interested in Miss Unity,' said Louisa, her voice low, conscious of the people around them on the platform.

'And now we know.'

'To talk German. Is that the whole story?'

'An Englishman who misses the chance to practise speaking another language,' said Guy. 'It's a possibility, I suppose. A risky one, you would think. Could he trust Miss Unity to be discreet?'

'I don't think he could, and he must know that.' Louisa exhaled. 'You're right. It can't be anything more worrying. I'm letting my mind spiral into absurd places.'

'And we don't have much time left . . .' Guy gestured to the view around them. Soldiers in uniform were kissing their mothers goodbye, a few lovers parting, the hiss and steam of the train urging them to get a move on. In the background, the large pale skies and brown fields of Derbyshire.

'No,' agreed Louisa, pasting a smile onto her face. 'It's goodbye but we won't be far behind you.'

'Won't you? I'll miss you both but I don't miss worrying about you. You're so much safer here. I don't know that you should rush back.'

'We're a family.'

'And we won't be any less of one for being apart, just as

244

millions are at the moment.' Guy kissed her and picked up his bag. 'I love you. Write soon.'

Louisa and Maisie stayed on the platform until the train was out of sight, along with the other women. When the sound of the wheels had faded, it was soon replaced by the hiccuping sobs of those who feared they'd never see their men again. Louisa knew that she was lucky, with Guy only off to London and not to France, but it wasn't as if he was completely free from harm there either. Still, there was no good to be done thinking about it. Deborah had invited them to stay until New Year's Day, after which they'd all have to leave because the school would soon be returning. It was only a few days more.

CHAPTER FORTY-SIX

From Bakewell, the four rode in the sprightly Morris Minor, Deborah at the wheel with Kick beside her, Louisa and Maisie in the back. They chatted amiably, Kick showing Louisa the hair grips and cocoa powder they had been delighted to find in the town.

'But I still need to pick some things up from Mr Formby's in Baslow,' said Deborah. 'If you don't mind?'

'Of course not,' said Louisa. Her mind was on the newly revealed fact about Nesbit. Plenty of people spoke German and she knew she should be wary of leaping to wrong conclusions, but there was something in the fact of him talking in that language with Unity that unsettled her.

Parked outside the now familiar shop, Maisie transparently happy to see it, the four piled in together. Inside, the decorations were still up, but the shelves were looking considerably emptier than before. It looked as if there had been a run on all the tinned goods and there was no bread to see, barely even any vegetables. A few wizened carrots lay at the bottom of one box, a single cabbage in another. Maisie let go of Louisa's hand and ran to the counter, where a commotion of some kind was going on. A second or two too late, Louisa realised they had interrupted something.

Mr Formby took a step further back from the counter, as if distancing himself from it, while on the other side stood a housewife, her cheeks blazing, pulling a cloth over the top of her basket, in which Louisa was sure she had glimpsed tomatoes and onions. These were hard enough to find at the best of times, but especially after Christmas, when the cupboards were otherwise bare.

'Well, Mr Formby,' the woman was stammering, 'I think that'll be all for today. I'll be sure to come again soon.' She made a quick exit, with a guilty glance at each of them as she went.

Mr Formby recovered his composure quickly. 'It's very nice to see you, Lady Andrew,' he said. 'I trust you all had a pleasant Christmas.'

'Yes, thank you,' said Deborah, confusion on her face. Louisa could tell that she knew something had gone on but couldn't guess exactly what. 'I was hoping you might have some tinned peas but I can see others have beaten me to it.'

'I'm afraid so. Christmas, you see.' There was a moment's silence, not an entirely comfortable one. Mr Formby did not offer anything else to replace the peas.

'How is Mrs Formby?' Deborah asked politely.

'Oh, very well, thank you. Our son Henry is coming home this afternoon. He missed Christmas Day, of course, so we've held on. We'll be eating our roast chicken with him tonight. Mrs Formby's most pleased, as you might imagine.' He stepped forward to the counter again, his hands in his apron pocket. Whatever the minor crisis had been, he had averted it.

'Oh, I am glad for you. It's a relief when we know they're safe and well, isn't it?' said Deborah. Louisa thought she detected the smallest catch in Deborah's throat as she said this. It had been some days since she had had a letter from Andrew.

Louisa and Kick were busying themselves by looking at the stand of postcards as Deborah and Mr Formby talked. Maisie was patiently standing by, waiting for the moment when sweets might appear but knowing well enough not to say anything about it.

'It is that, Lady Andrew,' said Mr Formby. 'I take it all that business at the house is over now?'

'What business?' asked Deborah.

'The lady who . . . ?' He dipped his head, as if it would be too rude to say her name out loud, let alone what had happened to her.

'Yes, yes,' Deborah replied, a little flustered.

Someone else came into the shop then, a broad-shouldered man in uniform, removing his cap as he entered.

'Dad?' He gave them all a grin as he set down his pack. 'It's good to be home. I thought I'd never get here.' He had the distinct Derbyshire accent of his father, and his face was friendly and open. In unison, the three women and Maisie made their way towards the shop door, leaving father and son to a happy embrace, Mr Formby calling for his wife to come out from the back and join them.

Outside, they stood on the pavement, wondering what to do with themselves, as if they had witnessed something private they shouldn't have seen.

'What was going on in there?' said Kick. 'With that housewife, I mean.'

'I suspect Mr Formby has suppliers that are not entirely declared to the government's rations department,' said Louisa.

'Ah.' Kick nodded. 'I know that sort of thing must go on. It is kind of shocking, though, isn't it? It's a form of theft, to take extra food in wartime.'

'War makes people do things they never thought they would,' said Louisa. 'I don't think we can judge them for it. We don't know that woman's story. She might have a sick child at home.'

'Yes, she might,' said Kick. She had a kind nature and was always good-humoured. Louisa suspected she was never able to stay suspicious or cross with anyone for long. It boded well for her marriage to Billy. 'I say,' Kick went on, 'Henry was rather delicious, wasn't he?'

'Henry?' said Debo.

'The shopkeeper's son.'

'You're not supposed to notice that sort of thing now you're engaged!' But Deborah's shock was feigned.

'Until the ring's on the finger, a gal can look.' Kick winked. 'He's awfully tall and blond, not like most of the Englishmen around here. He might be good for that nice teacher, Lucie.'

'I think she's rather interested in Nesbit,' said Louisa, feeling a little on the old side for the conversation but enjoying it nonetheless.

'Do you think she's even interested in that sort of thing?' said Deborah, giving Maisie a nervous glance. 'Men, I mean.'

'Does she bat for the other team?' Kick giggled.

Maisie was listening to all this, her head turning to each one as they spoke, as if she was following a tennis match. 'Who bats, Mummy?'

'Cricketers, darling,' said Deborah quickly.

Which made them all laugh and dispersed their worries for a moment longer. In this way, thought Louisa, war could be borne: with tiny sips of fun.

CHAPTER FORTY-SEVEN

The person that Louisa could not talk to about Nesbit was Unity so she decided to go to Nancy – it was playing on her mind too much. Nancy was incredulous but she had a novelist's mind. 'So what do you think?' she said. 'That he's a spy?'

'When you say it out loud like that it sounds absurd,' said Louisa, 'but it is wartime. It's not all that far-fetched. The question is, how do we find out?'

'If we ask him, he'll deny it. If we report it and we're wrong, we could cause a whole lot of problems. It feels like a dangerous place to meddle.' Nancy perched on the end of her bed, smoothing her stockings. 'I could ask Cousin Winston?'

'The prime minister?'

'Well, yes. One might as well go straight to the top. He's in the White House for Christmas, though. I won't be able to get a message to him very quickly. I hardly dare telegraph it.'

'It seems rather extreme, but I can't think of another solution,' Louisa admitted. It made her nervous but at least she wasn't sitting alone with the information.

'Obviously, Winston won't know if he's a spy but I expect they have their ways of checking information, don't you think?' Changing the conversation, Nancy stood before the full-length mirror. 'I understand why we're doing this,' she said, as she buttoned her black crêpe dress. 'But it seems at odds with things.'

'Why?' Louisa was sitting at the dressing-table, watching her.

'We didn't know Mrs Hoole, or any of her family.'

'She died in this house,' said Louisa. 'It was Debo's idea, and I think it was a good one. It shows sympathy.'

'Yes, but do *all* of us need to go to her funeral?'

Louisa didn't reply, only pulled a face. She knew Nancy understood. Her petulant mood was more likely related to the letter she'd received that morning from Peter, which made no mention of his getting leave in the near future. Nancy suspected that he had leave lined up, he just didn't want to make plans for them to meet when he was back in London. It had been months since they had last seen each other.

In spite of the relatively short notice for the funeral, the church was almost full by the time they arrived. The duke and duchess, with the dowager, sat on the front pew, permanently reserved for the Devonshires. Lord and Lady Redesdale were off to the side with Unity, a defence position they automatically assumed whenever they were with their daughter in public view since the outbreak of war and her attempted suicide.

'We'll have to sit near the front,' said Nancy to Louisa. 'Everyone will know who we are and it will look as if we're shirking if we're at the back.'

The first five or six rows were not too crowded and Nancy was right: plenty of heads turned and low whispers could be heard as they made their way down the aisle. Deborah was the familiar face – she raised a hand and gave a small smile in acknowledgement to a few villagers – but it was not as if the rest were entirely unknown. Nancy sat down, preening slightly, as others moved up in the pew to make room for her and Deborah, with Kick and Billy. Louisa went into the pew behind, realising as she sat down that she was beside Dr Dunn. His suit looked no cleaner than when she had last seen him but his white hair was brushed back, and there was calm about him that she found reassuring. His bedside manner, perhaps.

'Hello, Dr Dunn. We met at Chatsworth, just before Christmas.'

He took her hand and shook it, more firmly than she'd expected from his gnarled knuckles and liver spots. 'Of course I remember. And now here we are, where the sorry story ends.'

'Hmm, yes,' said Louisa. They watched other people come into the church, everyone in black, hats pulled down low against the cold, heard the shuffles and coughs as they moved to accommodate others. 'It's nice of you to come to the funeral.'

'Unfortunately it's usually a sore reminder that I failed at my job,' he said, with a wry smile. 'But, yes, I do attend the funerals of those in the village. They're more restful than the births, if not quite so uplifting.'

'I can imagine.'

A hush descended over the congregation and a few stiff notes were played on the organ as Mrs Hoole's family came down to take their seats on the very front pew, on the other side of the aisle to the duke and duchess, and the dowager. Louisa identified the man who must have been Mr Hoole, with two women who looked to be in their twenties, red-eyed beneath their modest hats, handkerchiefs clutched in their hands.

'I hear her son is away at the front,' whispered the doctor. 'They're not entirely sure he's received the news.'

Before Louisa could reply to this, old Mrs Hoole's mother was pushed down the aisle in an antique Bath chair, a ludicrous sight, its wheels squeaking. The stout neighbour was holding the handles, propelling Mrs Duffin at a speed that looked to be on the cusp of foolhardy. She was deposited at the end of the aisle, while the neighbour took a seat beside the dowager, who could be seen giving her a thin smile.

Dr Dunn must have followed her eyeline. 'You know, I was at the duke's birth,' he said. 'Their usual doctor was delayed on his way down from London, and I was called in at the last moment. They weren't too pleased about it but we got the job done. Breech, you see.'

'Goodness,' said Louisa. This harmless-looking old man always seemed to leave her at a slight loss for words.

'Yes, well. He looks hale enough now.'

The organ had stopped playing its desultory, out-of-tune notes and the vicar stepped forward, looking nervously at the dowager. Louisa remembered that Lord Redesdale used to time the vicar's sermons: if they ran a second over ten minutes, he'd collar him afterwards. Louisa couldn't see old Mrs Duffin's face and wondered if she knew what was going on. Her behatted head was wobbling, only just visible above the back of the chair. The vicar made some general remarks about Mrs Hoole that could have applied to anyone who had been alive and reasonably normal, before the congregation were asked to turn to their hymn books and stand for 'Jerusalem'. Slowly, the doctor heaved himself up but showed no interest in singing; instead he muttered things to Louisa about various members of the congregation and their

254

ailments that he had treated. She was only half listening when he said something about having been at the birth of someone or other's father, when a thought occurred to her.

'Did you ever hear anything about a maid at the big house?' Louisa asked him, when they sat down. The hymn was over and the vicar was reading a passage from the Bible as drearily as if it was a shopping list.

Dr Dunn eyed her warily. 'There have been many maids at the big house.'

The woman in front turned around and Louisa mouthed an apology. 'This was during the last war,' she whispered to him. 'She got into trouble.'

There was a shuffle, while everyone stood again – the vicar must have announced another hymn. This time, Dr Dunn remained seated. Feeling she had better sing, Louisa dutifully did her bit and stood, too, but halfway through, not wanting to lose her chance, she sat down beside him again. 'Do you remember?'

He squeezed his eyes shut briefly. 'There was a pleasant young girl I worried about. She was quite far along when I saw her, but I never heard about her again. I have thought about her once or twice over the years. You never quite knew with those girls on their own.'

'She was on her own?'

He nodded, tapping his nose. 'These things can't be done *all* on one's own.'

There was another lull and Louisa waited for one of Mrs Hoole's daughters to take to the lectern and start reading a passage from the Bible.

'Would you still have the maid's notes? If you saw her, I mean?'

'I've never thrown anything away,' he said proudly. Then he paled. 'There's rather a lot of notes but, you know, I can't even remember her name.'

'Was it Joan Dorries, by any chance?'

'Are you meddling, Miss Private Detective? All this was a long time ago, you know. It does no good to raise bodies from the dead.'

'But, Doctor,' said Louisa, 'how do you know she's dead?'

CHAPTER FORTY-EIGHT

For the rest of the service, Dr Dunn said no more to Louisa, but he wasn't going to get away with it as easily as that. When the vicar thanked everyone for coming and said that close family only would be moving outside for the burial, Louisa leaned in to the doctor.

'I'll come to see you tomorrow, Dr Dunn, and we'll look at Joan Dorries's notes.'

'I'm not sure I'll be able to find them,' he said, looking pitifully old, his pale eyes querulous.

'I think you will,' replied Louisa, firmly.

Outside the church, she waited for the rest of her gang to come out. The wind had died down a little but the day was still grey, giving no warmth of sunlight. Louisa saw one or two other familiar faces: Mr Formby, with a stout woman who must have been his wife, and their son, Henry. The neighbour, self-importantly pushing Mrs Duffin's chair, gave Louisa a half-wave, pulling her hand back as soon as she seemed to realise it was too cheery for the circumstances.

Quite a few people stood about in the graveyard afterwards, waiting for the burial party to finish before they went on to the wake at the Dog and Duck, taking the opportunity to catch up on Christmas gossip, passing humbugs to suck or cigarettes.

'We're going for tea at Strutt's Café,' said Nancy. 'Come with us. Kick's never had ham and egg with chips.'

'Not together,' clarified Kick, with her irrepressible grin.

'You can dip a chip in the yolk,' teased Nancy. 'At least, that's what I hear. I've never tasted that particular gourmet fancy myself. Have you, Louisa?'

'Many times,' she replied. 'But I'll meet you there, if that's all right. There's something I want to do first.'

Before she could question what she was about, Louisa found herself heading off in the direction of Dr Dunn's surgery. A passer-by on the street obligingly gave her directions, along with a pinch of detail on the doctor's domestic situation: 'He's on the corner opposite the butcher's, big black front door, you can't miss it. His wife'll be there – she nivver goes out.' Louisa calculated that the doctor would be at the wake for at least an hour, possibly more, given how slowly he walked, and that the villagers would doubtless line up, hoping for a bit of free medical advice on their latest aches and pains. Louisa banged on the door three times and, after a minute or two, she heard the obliging sounds of the lock scraping back. The door pulled back only a few inches, restricted by a chain. Louisa couldn't see who was behind it, she could only hear an old woman's thin voice. 'The doctor's not at home. He'll be in tomorrow. Sorry, dear.'

The door started to close again but Louisa put her foot into the gap. 'I do beg your pardon, Mrs Dunn, but the doctor sent me. I've just seen him at the funeral, and he told me to come here.'

She withdrew her foot, and the door closed but there was a scrabble and then it opened again, revealing a very small, stooped woman, as pale as paper and with wispy grey hair held back with a velvet ribbon. It was affectingly girlish and Victorian.

'Why did he do that?' she asked. She didn't sound afraid but Louisa wondered why she had a reputation for never leaving the house if not for fear of the world beyond her big black front door.

'Well, you see, I'm a private detective down from London, and I'm investigating a case, but it's quite an old one. It concerns a maid who worked at Chatsworth.'

At this, Mrs Dunn startled and her fingers tremulously went to her cuffs, her eyes darting from the door to Louisa, as if she hoped she could close it with telepathy. 'You're from the big house?'

'Yes,' said Louisa. 'I work for them.'

'You'd better come in.' The door was held open a little wider, if not much, and Louisa sidled in. There was a wide hall with three chairs, and a dark-wood sideboard that bore various leaflets exhorting reminders that 'Coughs and Sneezes Spread Diseases.'

They stood awkwardly, the bright electric light above them.

'Joan Dorries was a patient of your husband's,' said Louisa, 'during the war. She went missing, we don't know where, and I'm looking into it.'

The doctor's wife continued to fidget with her cuffs, her nails bitten to the quick. 'Why? Wasn't it a long time ago?'

'Not so long,' said Louisa. 'You and I can both remember the war, can't we?'

'Oh, yes,' said Mrs Dunn. 'It was ... I don't ...' She stopped and, as if remembering an instruction, took two breaths. 'My two brothers were killed in it. We lost ... the village lost a lot of men, in one battle. They sent them out at the same time, you see.'

'I know,' said Louisa. 'I'm so sorry.'

Mrs Dunn's eyes darted about again but she seemed faintly reassured.

'Mrs Dunn, I hate to press but I need to look at Miss Dorries's medical records.'

'But Dr Dunn isn't here, he—'

'I know. He's at the funeral. But, you see, it's not possible for me to return another day and it's an investigation. You can understand there's a time pressure on it.'

Not strictly true. Quite a lot of it was rather loosely true, in fact. Dr Dunn did say he was going to show her the records if he could dig them out. It was only that she didn't believe he'd tell her whether he found them or not, so she had to do it now, before he could get back and tell her he couldn't find them or, worse, destroy them.

'Could you tell me where the records are kept for patients during the war? I expect they're in boxes quite hard to find, aren't they?'

'Well, no. I know where everything is,' said Mrs Dunn. 'I manage the records because it's very important they are kept in good order.'

'Yes, I imagine it is,' said Louisa. 'If you would be so kind?'

With one final nervous look at the closed front door, Mrs Dunn took Louisa through a door that led down to the cellar. She was spending so much time underground, these days, she was beginning to feel like a mole. This cellar was large and clean, with black boxes lined and labelled along the wall. She could see they were three deep and at least eight high. Each one showed the year and letters of the alphabet, 'A–C, D–F' and so on. It took some shifting and moving about, with one box nearly making a perilous fall on top of Mrs Dunn but eventually Louisa had '1916 D–F' on the floor beside her. She looked at her watch: she didn't have long. With a firm thank-you, Louisa dismissed Mrs Dunn and set to work, illuminating the records with the light of the single bare bulb that hung overhead.

It wasn't an easy task. The records were not in strict alphabetical order, the Cs and the Ds roughly lumped together but no other order beyond. And sometimes initials were used, or a note would be scribbled about the house address. Not to mention that Dr Dunn displayed the characteristic handwriting of his profession: largely illegible. Louisa knew doctors did this deliberately, to disguise the name of a medication or write in a code understood only by them and the local chemist. Louisa tried to keep herself calm as she worked through the records, when she heard the click of the front door opening overhead, Mrs Dunn rushing to the hall, and then voices: the doctor was home and his wife was letting him know who was in their cellar, looking at the records. It was at that moment she pulled out a sheet of paper with the heading 'Joan Dorries, Chatsworth'.

Unmarried. Pregnant, estimated seven months. Father: unknown. Symptoms: fainting, occasional bleeding. Prescription: iron tablets for forthcoming boat trip to Canada.

The note was dated 20 August 1916. The same summer the late duke had been appointed Governor of Canada.

CHAPTER FORTY-NINE

Louisa could hear the doctor at the top of the cellar stairs, calling her name. She put the lid on the box and restacked as best she could. She knew he'd hesitate to come down those steep steps.

'I'll be up shortly,' she shouted back. It bordered on insouciant, but she'd deal with it. She had what she wanted. Joan had definitely been pregnant, and there was a planned trip to Canada. Had she made it there? Once she was back in the hall, Louisa saw Dr Dunn sitting on one of his hard-backed chairs, Mrs Dunn standing beside him, hopping from foot to foot, the bow in her ribbon quivering. 'I do apologise, Doctor,' Louisa began but she didn't get far before he was thundering at her that she had no right, it was breaking the law to do what she had done. She let him exhaust himself before she talked.

'You did say that you would show me the records,' said Louisa. 'I apologise for coming sooner than expected but I will have to return to London before long, so time is not on my side.'

'That is precisely my point,' the doctor wheezed. 'You will

do this, cause trouble, and then return to London, leaving despair behind.'

Louisa stood still. Then, she realized . . .

'She had the baby, didn't she? She was seven months pregnant when you saw her, so you know she had the baby, don't you? "Father, unknown" it says on the record but someone must have helped her. Was it you?'

Dr Dunn was slumping on his chair. It was possible he'd had a whisky or two at the wake: his breathing was irregular and his cheeks were flaming. Mrs Dunn was fussing over him, or trying to, but he waved her away.

'Was it you?' Louisa repeated.

'Please, Mrs Sullivan. Don't ask any more questions. You don't know what you're doing. It happened a long time ago—'

'Why do people always say that, as if a crime lessens with age? If she was killed and the person who did it is still out there, and possibly killed Mrs Hoole too, I don't think time has anything to do with it.' Louisa was aware she was yelling, and Mrs Dunn was looking more and more distraught.

'Whose secret are you keeping, Doctor? Is it the late duke's?'

'All doctors hold secrets,' he wheezed. 'And we keep them.'

'But she went to Canada? Did she have the baby there?'

'I can't tell you anything. Don't ask me any more questions.'

He shuddered as he breathed, and Mrs Dunn mustered every ounce of courage she could find to ask Mrs Sullivan, please, to leave at once.

Out in the street, Louisa took in gulps of air, unnerved by the exchange. She felt in her pocket for the piece of paper: Joan's record. She still had it. Somehow Dr Dunn hadn't seen it or asked for it in all the confusion and shouting. Was it legal to have a dead person's medical record? She wasn't sure. Louisa knew she must hurry to meet the others, if they hadn't given up on her already and begun the walk back to Chatsworth.

And what of Mrs Hoole? If Joan had been seven months pregnant when she saw the doctor, chances were she must have had the baby. If circumstances had been hard, it was possible that the baby didn't survive the birth. But what if it had? Someone had to have helped Joan in the rest of her pregnancy. Louisa must assume that she managed to conceal it that far, and either someone had told her she had to see a doctor or some pain or feeling of worry meant she had taken herself to him. A doctor's visit would have been expensive for a young maid but perhaps she had had enough put aside. Or someone else had paid: someone with money. Someone like the late duke.

Louisa stopped herself. She was going too far down the road of speculation and Guy would not approve. What she needed was facts. The doctor wasn't going to talk, not yet, anyway. The detective inspector was not inclined to assist without hard evidence. She needed to sit down and think it through. And then she was going to have to talk to the dowager. All of the fingers were pointing at her late husband: might she know the truth?

This was tricky, though. She couldn't risk accusing the late duke of something so scandalous if it hadn't happened, and even if it had and the dowager hadn't known, was it Louisa's place to cause such upset at this stage in her life? It wasn't a story the Devonshires would want out there, she knew that. Even if she did confront the dowager, how likely was she to admit to it? Not at all. From what Louisa had heard and seen so far, anything that could possibly incriminate their family was hushed up, with the complicity of everyone, from doctor to policeman. It enraged Louisa the more she thought about it as she stalked through the pretty streets of Baslow. A young woman, working class and insignificant – in their eyes – who makes a wrong turn and is punished for it with her life, and no one interested in finding the culprit. Well, damn them. She wasn't going to let them get away with it. She was going to find the truth.

But – where?

Nancy, Deborah and Kick were in Strutt's Café, scraped plates before them, boredom having induced them to start twisting the paper napkins into badly shaped swans. 'What happened to you?' asked Nancy, but Louisa made only a vague noise in response, not wanting to get into it at that moment. Deborah was already pushing her chair back, bustling them together, leaving coins on the table and saying they needed to press on. She wanted them to drop in on the dowager at Edensor to let her know of the arrangements for supper.

'Why don't you telephone?' queried Nancy, never missing a chance to prod her baby sister. 'Why must we stop?'

'She doesn't like the telephone,' said Deborah, placidly. 'It will only take a minute.'

'It won't. That generation can't do anything quickly.'

Nancy was proved right. They arrived at the house, mildly complaining about having to do a detour on foot, but before they even reached the step, the front door was opened by a maid who asked them to come in. 'No hope of sitting it out while Debo goes in,' muttered Nancy, but she knew her Ps and Qs, pulled off her gloves and brushed down her skirt. Inside, the dowager was in her smaller sitting room, her dog lying by the fire. Lucie was there, too. Louisa was a little surprised to see her, or perhaps it was more that Lucie looked very much at home. Her blonde hair was neatly tied back as usual, her green eyes made brighter by a red sweater. They were drinking a dark liquid from very small, fragile glasses.

'Sherry,' said the dowager. 'Rather an indulgence, but Mademoiselle Dupont has persuaded me that a daily glass is good for the heart.'

'*Absolument.*' Lucie smiled, raising hers as if in a toast.

'This young girl has been a treasure.' The old lady tipped her glass back and drank the rest. 'I shall find it terribly hard when the school returns and you can't come and see me so often.'

'Is it true your husband was the Governor of Canada?' Louisa said, knowing this was a rather abrupt change of topic but unable to think of another way to ask the question.

The dowager, however, was not easily perturbed. 'Yes,' she said, 'he was. It was a marvellous time. It was the war, of course, but one felt one was doing something terribly useful over there.' She took another sip. 'It was another life. I know times were hard for so many but one travelled in such style, and it was all paid for by the government. I had my ladies' maid, much missed now. The duke had his valet, and we had our butler, naturally.'

'Mr Ellis the First?' asked Louisa.

'Why, yes,' said the dowager, looking at Louisa as if for the first time. 'You don't miss a thing, do you? Sharp.'

The praise earned Louisa a look from Nancy, who had been browsing the dowager's bookshelves.

Louisa wondered if the old lady was tipsy. Deborah looked nonplussed by this uncharacteristic conversation and sought to move them off it. 'Granny, I came down to let you know that it's only us for supper tonight . . . ' She drifted into a meandering explanation of who was doing what. Kick, keen to be seen as a potential family member, ensured she wore her most engaged face as she sat beside Deborah.

Louisa plucked at Lucie's sleeve. 'Have you been coming here every day?'

'More or less, yes. I enjoy her company.'

Louisa felt doubtful about this. Lucie was a young woman, the dowager in her seventies. 'Really?'

'*Vraiment*. She tells me about the village, what life was like before the war in the big house. And sometimes I talk to the gardener – he's a very gentle man and knows so much about flowers. It's these typical English ways, they fascinate me.' Lucie tipped her head in the direction of the window, and there Louisa saw Max, digging in the flowerbed. His hair was falling into his face, his forehead dirty and sweaty. He didn't see them looking at him and seemed wholly absorbed in his task.

'Ah,' said Louisa, smiling. 'Have you discovered anything about him?'

Lucie laughed. 'Only a private detective would ask that question. Do you think there is something to discover about him?'

Louisa felt caught out. 'No, of course not. I didn't mean in that way.'

'I know you didn't. I tease. But, no. He remains a mystery, like the crimes in my favourite books.'

Louisa saw a copy of Agatha Christie's *The Thirteen Problems* on the table beside them, its cover faded with age, the pages well thumbed. She'd read it some years before. 'Miss Marple,' said Louisa, as if absent-mindedly. 'The innocent old lady who sees everything that's going on with the eyes of a worldly detective. I could do with her myself.'

Lucie put her empty glass on top of the book. 'Maybe. But it's just a story, not real life.'

'I wonder,' said Louisa.

CHAPTER FIFTY

'I s there a plan for New Year's Eve?' asked Louisa, as they walked back

Kick jumped at this. 'We must do something! Billy has to leave on the first so it's our last chance.'

'I loathe New Year's Eve,' said Nancy. 'It's frightfully common to kiss someone at midnight.'

'Don't be a spoilsport.'

They were walking the first furlongs of the drive, the house not yet visible, the vast parklands stretching out before them.

'Kick's right,' said Deborah, 'everyone will be gone soon. What about if we had supper in the Hunting Tower?'

'What on earth is that?' asked Nancy.

'There, look.' Deborah pointed to a peeping turret in the woods behind the house. 'It looks like a folly but it's got a kitchen and bedrooms. It'll be too cold and damp to stay in – it's been empty for years – but it might make for quite an amusing supper. Something different, that's all.'

'The oldies can't get up there but that's all right,' said Nancy.

'I'm not sure I can do any more dinners with Muv trying not to fall asleep onto her plate and Farve scowling at anyone who says anything frivolous, which is everything that isn't actually about the war.' Nancy was warming to the idea. She loved anything that put her in with the young.

'We can't do New Year's Eve without the oldies,' said Deborah. 'But I'd like a young supper in the hunting tower. Let's do it tonight. There's nothing else planned. The dowager will be happy to eat with the duke and duchess, and Muv and Farve. Oh, and Charles and Adele, too. That will leave the way clear for the rest of us.'

Less than two hours later, with the efficient bustle that makes a plan happen fast, there was a packed picnic supper with plates, glasses and cutlery, wrapped in tea-towels and loaded onto a wheelbarrow by Mrs Airlie, who fortunately looked only mildly put out at having to change her plan for the evening meal. 'Sausages, bread, butter, boiled eggs, bottles of wine, salt and pepper ... ' Deborah checked everything off. 'Delicious.' She beamed at the cook, who looked surprised at the compliment, giving a grunt in reply and heading off back into the warmth of the kitchen.

Wrapped up in their jerseys, coats and scarves, stamping their feet lightly and blowing out visible breath into the cold night, Billy, Kick, Deborah, Nancy, Louisa, Maisie and Lucie set off for the Hunting Tower. Unity was with them, too: Deborah's concession to her parents for leaving them to dine at the house. Max had been asked to push the loaded wheelbarrow and lead the way to the tower. It stood not far from the house, but the path was steep and not always entirely visible once they got into the woods. Nancy took charge of Unity, who kept trying to go ahead of Max, bumping the wheelbarrow. He didn't say anything to her, was neither friendly nor unfriendly, keeping his eyes on the path that would soon be hard to see in the fast-falling dusk. He was initially resistant to Deborah's plan when asked to push the goods and lead the way, pointing out that it would be dark when they tried to walk back and that the tower itself would be cold and damp, but she dug her heels in. Louisa wasn't sure why she was so determined to pull off this plan but it seemed that she was, and she reasoned that her subconscious must be at play. About halfway along they heard the sharp yaps of the dowager's Peke.

'What's that?' said Nancy, as the barks came closer.

'Oh,' said Lucie, apologetically. 'It's Rosie. She must have followed me, I'm afraid I always have a treat in my pockets for her.' Sure enough, the little dog was soon at Lucie's ankles, turning around excitedly, duly rewarded with something from Lucie's hand.

Just as the chill began to set in, they arrived at the tower. It looked spooky enough for Maisie to squeeze Louisa's hand harder, with the dark woods around it and the faint hooting of an owl. It was tall and oddly shaped, like four lighthouses grouped together on the top of the hill, each turret topped with a round metal hat. The brickwork was grey and faded, covered with creepers trying to reach the windows, and there was a flight of several narrow steps that looked too large and grand for the unassuming front door, its white paint long peeled. Max pulled out an old iron key and unlocked it, disappearing inside for a moment until they saw an electric glare from his torch and they all piled in.

'Remind me again why we're doing this,' said Nancy. They were standing in what must have been the kitchen, small and curved inside one of the columns, an old wooden table and two chairs in there, and a range that looked as if it hadn't been lit for decades. Cobwebs thickly covered the corners and the stone-flagged floor had a damp sheen. There were no boards for blackout, so the curtains were drawn and only candles were lit. The Peke was nosing happily, making snuffly grunts at all the new smells she could discover.

'Let's unpack the food. There's hot coffee in the flasks to warm us up. We'll explore and play a game or two,' said Deborah, taking matters in hand. There was nothing she disliked so much as a failed plan. Max was already unloading from the wheelbarrow, which he'd left at the bottom of the steps, carrying several things at once in his capable arms, Lucie ready to lift them from him.

'Fun,' said Nancy. 'That's why we're doing this. Naturally, I do not disapprove. Let the games begin.'

CHAPTER FIFTY-ONE

There was a general commotion while the rest of the picnic was fetched from the wheelbarrow, until Deborah called everyone back. They stood and ate quickly, not bothering with cutlery but wrapping the meat in bread, eating boiled eggs salted and whole, drinking coffee to warm themselves.

'Is there much to look at upstairs?' asked Nancy. Billy and Kick had snuck off while the picnic was being brought in.

Billy and Kick met each other's eyes and laughed. 'We don't know,' said Kick. 'We only went up to one room and we were . . . talking' – there was another shared glance – 'when we heard you call for us. It's dark up there but not as scary as it seems from the outside somehow. It's abandoned and grimy more than anything.'

'It's the same down here,' said Nancy. 'Faded furniture and not much of it.'

'Shall we play hide and seek?' said Deborah.

Louisa felt Maisie tugging on her hand then. 'No, Mummy. I don't want to play hide and seek here.'

'You don't have to, darling,' whispered Louisa. 'We'll stay here together, in the kitchen. You can help me clear up.' She saw the relief on her daughter's face. It suited her, too, truthfully.

While Max and Louisa started to clear away the remnants of their supper, Maisie and Lucie counted to fifty. When they got to the end and Lucie shouted, 'Here I come, ready or not!' Louisa thought Maisie would run and hide in her skirts but it seemed excitement about the game took over. Grabbing Lucie's hand, Maisie started to pull her out of the room, Rosie the Peke yipping after them.

A piercing scream broke the quiet, followed by shouts and, then, just as Louisa was wondering what had happened, laughter. The dog came running into the kitchen, a dark flash that went under the table, hotly pursued by Kick and Lucie.

'What's going on?' asked Louisa.

Lucie was down on her hands and knees, pulling Rosie out, futilely trying to grip onto the stone floor with her back legs, growling from the back of her throat, something clamped between her teeth that she was refusing to let go.

'Mon Dieu,' said Lucie, pulling at it. Eventually, it came free and they all stared at it. A scrap of cloth, half the size of a handkerchief, ragged and dirty.

'Why did the dog want that?' asked Louisa, instinctively reaching out for it. Lucie handed it over, and she saw: it was covered with blood. Soaked in it. But it was old and filthy, the rag stiff in places, only softened where the dog's saliva had got to it. 'Ugh.' She put it on the table, not knowing what to do with it. 'Where did she find it?'

'We don't know,' said Kick. 'We were just in the room over there and Rosie came in and started sniffing and then she disappeared.'

'Disappeared where?' asked Louisa.

'I don't know. After only half a minute or so, she came back and she had that in her mouth.'

By now Deborah and Nancy had come into the kitchen, Billy standing behind them, Maisie pushing almost through their legs to get to Louisa, full of childish excitement for the game she was playing and longing to tell her mother all about it.

'I'd like to have a look,' said Louisa. She went into the other room, across the hall from the kitchen. It wasn't much, sparsely furnished, with a large armchair, stuffing coming out of the side of one arm. The others had followed and watched her from the door, while Louisa looked to see where the dog could have disappeared to. On the face of it, there was nowhere in this room to hide. She ran her hands along the wall, aware that she was being observed and trying to look as if she were deploying a professional skill. Then, behind the chair, she found it: a hole.

'Look,' said Louisa, pushing the chair out of the way. The hole was neat, and large, big enough for her to crawl into – though at this time of the night, she didn't want to. She leaned down and smelt the damp, with sour notes of rotting animal, a mouse that had died in there probably.

'Not quite right to be a priesthole,' said Billy. 'I had no idea it was there.'

'What if that cloth's got something to do with the missing maid?' suggested Nancy.

'Why would it?' asked Louisa.

'Quite,' said Deborah. 'Don't be such a troublemaker, Nancy. This place has been empty for ever, and that horrible bit of cloth could be anything.'

'Why don't you get it tested, then?' said Nancy. She'd got the bit between her teeth now.

'No,' said Billy, suddenly. Louisa had almost forgotten he was there, but he came forward, looking over the tops of everyone's heads. 'I think you should leave well alone. We've had our games now. Let's head back.'

'Absolutely,' said Louisa, not wanting Maisie to be upset by it. Still, Nancy had given her pause for thought. When Billy's back was turned, she picked up the cloth again and put it carefully into her skirt pocket. She could feel Max watching her do this, and she knew it must look a little odd, but what of it? She was past embarrassment these days, especially when it came to detective work. And this was detective work, or it would be, when she gave the scrap to DI Tucker tomorrow.

CHAPTER FIFTY-TWO

The walk back to the house in the dark was rather more subdued than their walk to the tower earlier, the discovery of the bloodied cloth having unsettled them all somehow. Max shone a torch carefully to light the path, and although Louisa knew Maisie was quite used to the darkness, with everywhere blacked out since the war had begun, it was nonetheless a relief when they got in. Tired from the evening's events, she and Maisie went off to bed straight away.

The following morning, Louisa telephoned DI Tucker and asked him to come to the house. Work was slow, he explained, when he arrived promptly less than half an hour later. 'Not that it's ever too fast around here.'

'Would you like a cup of tea?' Louisa asked. She was alone with the detective inspector in the Painted Hall, which was freezing cold again. They hadn't lit the fires in there since the Christmas party for the village children.

'No, thanks. I'll be on my way soon. What was it you were calling about?'

Louisa showed him the cloth. 'This was found last night in the Hunting Tower.'

He turned it over, then held it from one corner, pinched between thumb and forefinger. He gave her a questioning look.

'I was wondering if you could test it, see if the blood on it matched the blood on the cap.'

Tucker pushed his hat back and scratched an itch on his hairline. 'I suppose we could. What for?'

'Because if there is a match, it would mean it belonged to the missing maid. It's a clue.'

'It doesn't mean anything of the sort,' said Tucker. 'We can check if it's the same blood type but no more than that, and plenty of people share the same blood type.'

Louisa pushed back against his deflating remarks. 'I know it can't be anything definite. But it might point us in the right direction.'

'And what direction is that, if you don't mind me asking?' He wasn't stern, or even particularly unfriendly. She knew Guy would probably have said the same things.

'She was seven months pregnant at one point—'

'How do you know that?'

Louisa tried not to cross her fingers. 'Because Dr Dunn showed me her notes. She saw him, at least once, when she was seven months pregnant. He prescribed her iron tablets for her planned journey to Canada.'

'So she wasn't killed? She went to Canada? It was as I thought, then. She went of her own accord.'

'There's only evidence to say she planned the trip, not that she made it. What if the baby came early? I think she was hiding somewhere close to the house, and this scrap of cloth might confirm it. It might mean she had the baby here. I want to know who helped her.'

Tucker regarded her thoughtfully. 'She might have had the baby alone. People do.'

'Maybe, but she'd have to have gone somewhere. She must have had some assistance in getting the baby the things it needed, or travelling to the next place. And why have the baby here? So close by? Why didn't she go before she was due, to somewhere further away where no one knew her and she could ask for help? It makes me think someone from the house was with her.' She looked behind her then, as if one of the Cavendishes might suddenly appear on the staircase, ready to silence her. But it was empty. Just her, Tucker and the enormous painted gods.

'And the doctor told you all this? Why didn't he tell anyone before?'

'One day, if this gets resolved, I'll tell you but not yet. I'm asking you to help me here. You remember her. You know something isn't quite right about her disappearance. I'm not asking you to compromise your position at work. It's just a simple laboratory test.'

Tucker pursed his lips as if he was going to reply but thought better of it. With the smallest of sighs he put the cloth away, wrapped in his clean handkerchief. 'It'll take a couple of days, but I'll let you know. Don't keep asking favours of me just because I'm in a good mood today.'

'I won't. Thank you, Mr Tucker.' With an amiable handshake, she took him out to the front door and said goodbye. He had left a bicycle propped against the wall, and she watched him cycle off for a minute or two, lost in her thoughts and the prettiness of the landscape. It was cold that morning, and the frost still glittered in patches on the lawn. As she was about to turn back into the house, she saw Lucie and the dowager making their way along the path towards the kitchen garden, Rosie the Peke trotting along behind them, her flat nose almost parallel to the ground. They must have gone out for an early perambulation, and she decided to go across and say hello.

'Good morning, Mrs Sullivan,' called Lucie, as Louisa approached them.

'Good morning. You're up and about with the larks.'

The dowager gave Louisa a faint smile. 'Forgive me, my dear. I wasn't feeling well this morning and asked *Mademoiselle* if she would aid me with some fresh air. It always revives me to go around this garden.'

Louisa looked at her. 'You do look rather pale. Have you seen Lady Andrew? She might be able to help.'

'No, I don't think she will,' said Lucie, rather forcefully. 'We have tried very many avenues but a mixture of fresh air and rest is the only cure. My grandmother was exactly the same.'

'I see,' said Louisa. 'I won't interfere, of course. Let me go ahead and ask Mrs Airlie to make a fresh pot of tea for when you come into the house.'

Feeling puzzled by this encounter – Lucie had exhibited an ownership of the dowager that didn't sit quite right with Louisa – she went into the kitchen. As usual, Maisie was there with Betsy.

'I don't know what I'd do without you,' said Louisa to the maid, gratefully. 'Is she being helpful, or a nuisance?' Maisie was splashily stirring a big bowl of nondescript creamy liquid.

'Oh, very helpful,' said Betsy, ruffling Maisie's hair. 'Did I see that detective inspector arrive here earlier?'

'You don't miss a trick, do you?' Louisa smiled. 'Yes, you did. I've given him something to test.' She had to talk to someone. She was missing Guy dreadfully, and felt as if she had only half a brain without him. But she didn't get far with this thought: Mrs Airlie had practically jumped into the air where she was standing by the stove.

'Test? The police? What are they testing?'

Louisa decided she needed to tread carefully. Betsy was one thing but the cook had been edgy ever since Mrs Hoole had died. 'Something I found that I hope might give us a clue as to what happened to Mrs Hoole, as well as the missing maid.'

'I thought it was natural causes. The police, they said, didn't they, nothing happened to that poor woman?' said Mrs Airlie, talking fast and looking even redder in the face than usual.

'They haven't ruled out anything yet,' said Louisa, 'although I think—'

But Mrs Airlie didn't stay to hear the rest of Louisa's theories, and fled the room. 'What's up with her?' asked Louisa.

Betsy checked that the cook really had gone. 'I don't know. She was funny before Christmas but I put that down to worrying about everything that needed to get done, because it was a lot, what with the extra people here. But since we heard that it was natural causes, she's been . . . different. If you didn't know better, you'd have to call it relief.'

'And why do you think she was relieved?'

'I thought it was because, you know, she's similar to what Mrs Hoole was, in't she? If someone was going around killing women of a certain age, then . . . '

'So you think she felt in danger?'

Betsy twitched her nose. 'I suppose that must be it.' She

barked a laugh. 'Beats me, though. She only needs to put poison in the soup and she'd be the safest one here, wouldn't she?' There was another guffaw. 'I shouldn't go saying things like that to a private detective, should I?'

Louisa smiled to show she didn't take the remarks seriously. But then again ... maybe she did.

CHAPTER FIFTY-THREE

'Louisa, darling, have you seen the papers this morning?' Nancy, on the sofa in the drawing room, the paper open across her lap.

Louisa shook her head. 'No, I've not had a chance yet. Why?'

'Another terrible bomb raid two nights ago. More dead, more in hospital. Children. Just as one thinks one has some sort of equilibrium about it, not thinking about it too much ... I don't know. I feel as if I've slammed into a wall.'

'Where was it?' Louisa couldn't help it: she felt her heart squeezed by a vice whenever London and bombs were mentioned.

'Hammersmith. They think they were targeting the brewery.'

Louisa sat down beside Nancy, grabbed the paper. 'Hammersmith? Are you absolutely sure?'

'What? Oh, God.' Realisation dawned on Nancy's face. 'You don't think—'

'How do I know?' Louisa tried to stop her voice turning shrill, panic flooding her veins like a burst dam. 'I haven't heard from

Guy since he went home. We don't telephone every day, we write, but with Christmas the post has been slow. That was what I thought, if I thought anything at all. I stopped worrying, for one tiny moment, somehow I forgot to worry – and *now* ...'

'You don't know anything now,' said Nancy, pragmatism taking over. 'You only know to worry where you didn't before. There's no change in the facts of the matter.'

'What facts of the matter? Hammersmith has been bombed, more dead, you said. I must telephone the hospitals.'

Nancy stood. 'Yes. Come on. We'll do it together. We'll find him. He'll be fine. It's *Guy*. Nothing ever happens to him.'

Maisie heard this. She'd been playing with her doll on the window seat – they'd almost forgotten she was there. 'What about Daddy? What happens?'

'Nothing, darling,' said Louisa, her voice watery, trying to stay composed. 'I just need to make a telephone call. Can you stay in here for a bit? I won't be long.'

Maisie, reassured, nodded, returned to her solitary game, while they went to the telephone in the hall.

Placing calls to hospitals to find a person was not an easy thing to do. Louisa was grateful to Nancy, who was always good at the bigger crises of life. Messages were left, people were called back again and again; everyone was overstretched. After an hour, they were no further in finding out where he was.

'It's quite possible he's not in any hospital at all but is perfectly safe and well at home,' said Nancy. 'That's probably why we can't find him.'

Louisa tried to believe this. Failed. She knew he would have found a way to let her know he was alive after such a heavy hit. All her worst fears kept rushing in, refusing to be held back.

Stupidly, she kept thinking that if she were not so distracted by Joan's case, or had been in London, she would somehow have prevented this from happening. As if by not thinking about Guy, it had exposed him to danger. Deborah came into the hall and Nancy told her what they were doing.

'Oh, Lou, that's awful. Can we telephone someone at the Home Office? We must know someone.'

'I don't see what they could do,' said Louisa.

'No.' Deborah's face was pained. 'I'll ask Ellis to fetch some tea.'

Louisa thanked her. Perhaps tea would help: she felt slightly faint, a trembling sensation that seemed to bubble just below the surface of her skin. When the telephone suddenly rang, the sound was shrill and shocking.

Nancy answered. 'Hello? Yes, Mrs Sullivan is here. Yes, yes. I will ... Thank you.' She put the receiver down. 'He's in the Hammersmith Hospital.'

'Oh, God.'

Deborah was at Louisa's side, her arm around her waist, holding her up.

'No, it's all right. He's all right. Injured but not too badly. He's resting now and they're going to try to get him to the telephone as soon as they can. They had no way of contacting you. He had mild concussion and couldn't seem to remember where you were.'

Louisa nodded, hearing the words but not yet able to understand what they meant. She had been prepared to hear that he was dead, or unconscious, or had lost his limbs. The fact of his being 'all right' seemed incorrect, or too good to be true. 'I need to pack. Maisie and I will catch the next train to London.'

'No, Louisa,' said Nancy. 'Wait. Let's hear from him first. We don't know—' She stopped.

'Know what?'

'We don't know if your house is still standing, do we? Let's go and sit down, drink tea. He will call.'

Numbly, Louisa agreed, allowed herself to be led back into the drawing room, sat upon the sofa. She called Maisie to her, and held her daughter for a few minutes, until she felt herself breathe again and the trembling receded.

In the end, it was two hours before Guy telephoned. Most of the household was in the drawing room by this time, each person caught up in the drama, discreetly occupying themselves, trying not to look as if they were as tense as Louisa. When the sound of the telephone bell was eventually heard, Adele was teaching Louisa and Maisie to play backgammon. Louisa ran to the hall and picked up the handset before it completed three rings.

'Is that Guy?'

'Louisa—'

She heard the sob catch at the back of his throat. She knew then that he had been frightened, too. 'Are you all right? Where are you?'

'I'm in the hospital, and I'm fine. I had a nasty shock, and my left arm is broken but otherwise I'm in one piece.'

'We were so worried, I thought—'

'I know. But it's over now. I wondered if I might come to you, to Chatsworth. They're discharging me today.'

'Yes, please. As soon as you can. But, Guy, what about our house? Is it still there?'

There was static on the line, and she lost him for a second.

In that small space, Louisa remembered the photograph of her mother in a pretty silver frame, on the mantel above the fireplace. The only picture she had of her.

'Yes, it is. All the windows have been blown out but it's there.'

The pips went.

'Just get the very next train you can. We'll come and meet you.'

'I will.' The line went dead.

Louisa went back into the drawing room, where several expectant faces were looking at her. 'He's fine,' she said, still feeling a touch shaky. 'He's going to come down here, as soon as he can. He's being discharged from the hospital today.'

'And is he intact?' asked Nancy.

'Yes. A broken arm, shock. But intact. And so is our house, no windows but it's standing. I'll have to telephone somebody to go and board them up.'

'Marvellous news,' said Lord Redesdale, unexpectedly. When Nancy and Deborah turned to look at him, he put on an expression of mock surprise. 'What? I wish Mr Sullivan well. I'm glad to hear the good news about your husband, though I'm sorry about your house.'

'Thank you, my lord,' said Louisa. 'I think I could do with some fresh air after all that. Maisie, let's go and get our coats. Anyone is welcome to join us – it looks quite mild out there.'

CHAPTER FIFTY-FOUR

The knowledge that Guy was alive and on his way to see them gave Louisa a rush of renewed energy. Outside, with Maisie and Deborah, she decided on a whim to visit the night watchmen's cottage.

'Do you know where it is?' Louisa asked Deborah.

'Yes, of course. It's on the estate – there's a group of workers' cottages, all tiny and rather sweet. I think they're hundreds of years old.' A doubtful look came over her. 'I'm not sure we should go there now, though. They sleep during the day.'

'Maybe, but maybe not,' said Louisa, not in the mood for changing her plan. 'Who lives in the other cottages?'

'The gardeners. I think there are two more, where the groom and herdsmen lived. We don't have either there at the moment, of course, and the duke thinks they'll never come back.'

'Why not?'

'Well, he says it happened before. The men go to war and, awful as it is, it gives them a taste of life beyond the estate. Many workers won't come back here but will probably find jobs in the bigger towns, go after the bright lights.'

'They've never appealed to you, have they?' said Louisa, feeling a surge of affection for Deborah. She was so often dismissed when she was a little girl, the baby of the family, never interested in going to school, always happiest at home or on horseback.

'No,' said Deborah. 'I like going up to London for parties now and then, to see friends, but no, I'd much rather be here. It's not just the servants wanting different jobs, though. Everyone thinks the old way of life for these houses is over. It won't come back and they'll just become shells.'

'What do you think?'

They were far enough away from the house to look back and see it in its full glory, the warmth of the stone reflecting the sunshine, the windows winking back at them.

'The duke may be right about the old way of life but I don't think that should mean the end. I don't see why a new role isn't found for the house, and others like it. They've provided employment and entertainment for hundreds of years – surely they can still do that. We should share the house, not keep it just for family. That's what I think.' She stopped and grinned, her fresh wide smile that was always infectious. 'Not that it matters a penny farthing what I think. Andrew and I are going to live in a matchbox, very poor and very happy. Billy and Kick will be the ones who have to work it out.'

After ten minutes or so, Maisie skipping alongside them, singing 'The Grand Old Duke of York' over and over, they reached the workers' cottages. Smoke was coming out of two chimneys.

'Looks as if they *are* up,' said Louisa, triumphantly. 'One of them anyway.'

Deborah didn't share the enthusiasm. 'I don't know them,' she said. 'Why don't we go and talk to the gardeners instead?'

'Why would we? I haven't got a question for them.'

'Oh, Louisa,' was all Deborah said, but she gave up the fight.

There was no front garden to either of the cottages, just a scrub of grass between the faces of the houses and the path that ran alongside them, from the big house down to the river. They looked tidy, a few pairs of boots lined up outside, curtains drawn in all the windows but for one room upstairs. The two cottages that were empty had a shuttered look, windows that weren't shining, front doors that needed repainting. After checking which was which, Louisa knocked gently on the door of the night watchmen's cottage. It took only a minute before it was opened by a short man in his early fifties, she guessed, grey hair sticking up at the back, looking slightly sleepy.

'I'm so sorry,' said Louisa, realising what her impetuousness had done. 'I've woken you up.'

'No,' said the man. 'I'm up. I was just reading the paper, see.' Louisa remembered her father, then, that she would tease him when he said he was going to read his book: it meant he was planning to catch forty winks. He looked behind her. 'Lady Andrew.'

'Hello,' said Deborah. 'We didn't want to disturb.'

'Yes, we do apologise but I have a question or two. My name is Louisa Sullivan and I'm a private detective.' She felt she might as well get to the point. 'I'm looking into what happened the night Mrs Hoole died, up at the house.'

'Aye,' said the man. 'That were a bad business.'

'Really? Why? The police are saying it was natural causes.'

'I didn't mean it weren't that. I only meant it happening at the house and not at her home. Bad luck all around.'

'Yes,' said Louisa. 'Would you mind telling me your name?'

He rubbed his chin, scratching at the greying stubble. 'Derek Lancaster, ma'am. I expect Lady Andrew's told you what I do.'

'She has. Would you mind telling me what you know of that evening?'

'The police have looked at the logs already, and we've spoken to that detective inspector.'

'I know, and everything was recorded as normal. Do you mind me asking, what is it you look for on your rounds?'

Derek seemed to relax a little, putting his hands into his pockets and scanning the horizon. 'It's more a case of being alert to anything different. We check the blackout, of course. But when you walk around a house like that, night after night, and I've been doing the job for four year now, you get to know its patterns, its breathing almost. You know which stairs squeak, what noises the building makes after a wet night and it starts to dry out.'

'And on that night, the night Mrs Hoole died, you didn't notice anything?'

'No, nothing. I turned the key at each point, regular as always.'

'And what about the other watchman? What's his name?'

'Matthew Logan.'

'What did he see?'

'Well, he didn't see anything. He weren't there.'

'I thought there were two of you, that you both did it at the same time?'

'We do normally.' Something about the way he looked at Deborah alerted Louisa. Shamefaced?

'But on that particular evening . . . ?'

It was getting cold standing outside that front door, and it struck Louisa as odd that an employee of the house didn't invite Lady Andrew inside. She felt a shiver at the back of her neck and wished she'd remembered to put on her scarf before coming out.

'He was waylaid . . . It happens now and then.'

'Mr Lancaster, please, it's important that you're straight with me. What was different that evening?'

'I don't want to cost Matthew his job. He's a good man.'

'I'm not in a position to promise anything, but I'll do what I can.' Louisa kept a firm stance before him. Deborah hovered behind but she was distracted by Maisie, who was trying to show her a pebble.

'He sometimes has a glass of stout too many in the afternoon and falls asleep before the shift.'

'But the records were initialled by both of you. DL and ML. Are you telling me that you forged his initials?'

'No, ma'am, I didn't do anything like that. It was ML but not Matthew. It was Max – Max Landesman.'

'The gardener?'

'Yes, ma'am. He covered for Matthew. He's done it before. And, like I say, he saw nothing unusual.'

Louisa gave it one further try. 'You discussed it with Max? That you both saw nothing unusual that evening.'

'Aye, ma'am.'

They might not have seen anything but Louisa had: Max Landesman was in the house that night, the only person she hadn't talked to about Mrs Hoole.

CHAPTER FIFTY-FIVE

When they got back to the house, it was to the news that Guy would be arriving on the last train of the night. 'I spoke to him,' said Nancy, 'and he seems quite well. I expect he's happier knowing he'll be seeing you both soon.'

'Yes,' agreed Louisa. 'I know it's not a long time since we said goodbye to him, but it feels it, having gone through that worry. I know I have no right to complain.'

'Don't be silly.' Nancy's tone was brisk. 'We understand.'

Louisa knew she meant it, and she also knew the Nancy Mitford way was not to dwell on things. Glad of the chance to be busy, Louisa set to work, with Maisie and Deborah's help, to ready a camp bed in a dressing room close to her and Maisie's room, in case Guy's injury made it uncomfortable for him to sleep beside her. Maisie drew a picture for his bedside table, of the three of them holding hands in front of a Christmas tree. While her daughter was drawing, her tongue slightly sticking out as she concentrated, Louisa and Deborah tucked the sheets into the bed.

'What do you know about Max, the gardener?'

'Nothing,' said Deborah. 'I mean, he's been here for ever, as I understand it. He's been doing some extra work for Granny Evie, hasn't he? Perhaps she'll know more. But what exactly do you hope to find out?'

Louisa stood up, straightening her back. 'I don't know. Whether there's a connection between him and Mrs Hoole.'

'I think you're clutching at the paper straws Maisie likes so much,' she said, when they were interrupted by the door opening.

'Beg pardon, ma'am,' said Ellis, as he came in. 'Mr Tucker is here. He wishes to see you and Mrs Sullivan. I've kept him in the kitchen—'

'Send him up to the drawing room,' said Deborah. 'We'll meet him in there.'

'Shall I prepare a tray for tea?'

'No, I don't think so. Hopefully whatever he's got to say can be said quickly.' Deborah gave the sheets a final smooth and left the room. There was a confidence and authority in her manner that Louisa admired, for she knew it was hard won.

They reached the drawing room only moments before the detective inspector, who came in with his usual ebullience, holding his hat in one hand, the other outstretched. Louisa shook it, Deborah did so rather more faintly.

'I always like an excuse to come up to the house,' said Mr Tucker. 'It's such a pleasant ride on my bicycle along the drive. The view never wears, does it?'

This endeared him to Deborah. 'No,' she agreed, 'it doesn't. I'm sorry we're not offering you tea but—'

Mr Tucker waved away her words. 'No trouble. I'm only stopping briefly. I came to let you know I had that scrap of material tested, as you asked, and it's the same blood type as that found on the cap.'

'What's this about?' Deborah looked at Louisa.

'It's from that night in the Hunting Tower,' she explained, feeling unaccountably guilty. 'The cloth the dog found. I asked the inspector to see if the blood on it matched the blood on the maid's cap.'

'I see,' said Deborah, unsmiling.

'Well,' said Tucker, getting the measure of the atmosphere, 'it's the same blood type, A. It's not the most common but I can't say as it tells you much more than that. I don't know what you were hoping for it to tell you.'

'I knew it wouldn't be anything certain,' said Louisa, 'but it changes the balance of things, doesn't it? I mean, the chances of that blood having come from the same person are increased, aren't they?'

'I don't know that they are. Unless you know that Miss Dorries was in the Hunting Tower at the end of her life.'

'Miss Dorries?' quizzed Deborah.

'I knew the case,' said Tucker. 'Her friend, the late Mrs Hoole, tried to get us on to it at the time but there was no doing. No suspicious circumstances. Or, at least, she was the only one who thought there were.'

'I suppose you already knew this, Louisa,' said Deborah.

'Yes, I did.' There wasn't time to explain, thought Louisa. 'Mr Tucker, do you know anything about Max Landesman?'

The detective inspector repeated the name slowly. 'No, can't say I do.'

'He's a gardener here – he's been here for some time, I believe. It was his initials on the night watchman's log, the night Mrs Hoole died. It so happens his initials are the same as the usual watchman, hence the confusion.'

'Right.' He looked at her questioningly, but openly, too.

'The logs say that everything was fine, I know that. I wondered if you'd interviewed Max.'

'Yes, to confirm he was at the house that night. He was the one who reported that the car wouldn't start, and couldn't see the cause for it. The following morning, Mr Ellis reported that he'd repaired it and he thought no more about it.'

'Did he tell you that he was the night watchman on duty that night?' asked Louisa.

'I'd have to check my notes but what you say confirms his alibi. The logbook shows exactly where he was at what time, if those are his initials.'

She noticed that he hadn't answered her question. Louisa knew she would have to be careful. Professional men did not take kindly to women like her telling them how to do their job.

'But it's no more than protocol, is it? To talk to everyone who was in the house the night someone was killed.'

'We don't know for certain she was *killed*, Mrs Sullivan. I have every sympathy with your trying to find out what happened to Miss Joan Dorries, although it was a long time ago and I see no sense in it myself. But there's still every chance Mrs Hoole died of natural causes. My job is to rule out the possible unnatural causes of death and, so far, that's what I've done. There is no one who was in the house that night with motive or opportunity.' His affability had disappeared, and Louisa was not hopeful it would come back. With a quick movement he returned his hat to his head and dipped it slightly in Deborah's direction. 'Goodbye, Lady Andrew.'

When he had left, Deborah looked at Louisa. The entire interview had not lasted long, and none of them had sat down but remained standing by the fireplace.

'I don't think I made a friend there,' said Louisa, trying to lighten the mood.

'No. I'm going down to the kitchen now to discuss the rest of our menus with Mrs Airlie, such as they are.'

Louisa felt chastened. And yet, even as she watched Deborah leave the room, she knew the bit was between her teeth still. With Guy beside her soon, she'd have the support she needed to find out the link between Joan and Mrs Hoole once and for all.

CHAPTER FIFTY-SIX

L ouisa went over all the different scraps of information that were flying around in her mind. The blood type that matched on the two pieces of cloth: she believed that this connected Joan Dorries to the Hunting Tower. What could she have been doing there? If she had still been around when she was seven months pregnant, and seen by Dr Dunn, but not working at the house, could she have been hiding there in order to have the baby? That could only mean that someone from the house was with her, or helping her, perhaps keeping her near enough to be able to smuggle food to her. Perhaps keeping her near enough in case medical attention was needed. But who could that person have been?

Was it the late duke? Helping the mother of his illegitimate child?

As an impressionable young boy, Charles had walked in on his father and Joan Dorries *in flagrante*, and it was surely no chance that the duke had left for Canada at precisely the moment his misdemeanours threatened to be exposed by Joan's burgeoning pregnancy.

So much supposition, and Louisa knew Guy would remind

her that what they needed was facts and evidence. There was one person who could give her the answers and Louisa had been afraid of talking to her before but now she had no choice: the dowager duchess.

Thankfully, Deborah was still in the kitchen when Louisa went back in, finishing her conversation with Mrs Airlie. Louisa took her to one side. 'Guy is arriving on the ten-thirty,' she said.

Deborah's earlier froideur disappeared completely, of course. 'Oh, that is good news. You must be pleased.'

'Yes, I am.' She couldn't hesitate too long. 'I have a favour to ask.'

'If it's whether you need me to drive you to the station to collect him, I'd be delighted to do it.'

'Thank you. I was wondering if you might come with me to see the dowager on the way.'

'Really? Why?' Deborah's shoulders were pushed back, her posture stiffer than usual.

'There's something I need to ask her. I can't explain what, but I need you there.'

'If you need me there, then you have to explain.' She wasn't smiling.

'You have every right to say that. It's just that certain things don't make sense, and I think she can tie it all together in a way that means ...' Louisa fell silent. In a way that meant – what? 'I think she has the answers.'

Deborah maintained the stare for a second or two longer but then her shoulders dropped slightly. 'Fine. We'll go now, or it will be too late for her, and we'll have to come back for supper. It's rather a push on the petrol front but if you insist ...'

Louisa nodded. 'Thank you.'

*

Fifteen minutes later they pulled up in the dowager's drive, and knocked at the door. There was no reply, so Deborah knocked again. With the blacking in the windows, it was impossible to tell if anyone was in. A bicycle was propped up against the side of the house but the garage was closed – they couldn't tell if the car was there or not.

'She can't have gone out,' said Deborah. 'I'm sure I would have known. Let's go to the back door. Perhaps they just didn't hear us.'

At the back door, it was the same, but when Deborah tried the handle, the door opened easily, and when they went in, they could see a light on in the hall, coming down the stairwell. There was no sign of anyone in the kitchen as they passed by.

'We can't go any further,' whispered Deborah. 'If she's not here, we're trespassing, aren't we? And if she *is* here, perhaps she doesn't want to see anyone.'

'Call,' said Louisa. 'Someone must be in.'

At the top of the stairs they came out into the main hall, where the table lamps were on. Everything was in its place – the stand filled with several umbrellas, stamped envelopes waiting to be posted on the console table – but it felt too quiet. None of the lights were on for the rooms leading off the hall: the dining room, the drawing room. Then Louisa realised what was missing: the Peke wasn't barking, hadn't come running to the door to greet them.

'The dog's not here,' said Louisa. 'Perhaps she's not here, after all.'

'Hello?' called Deborah. 'Is anyone at home?'

There was a sudden shuffle and a light went out; it caused only the slightest change but Louisa noticed it. Without saying anything, they went quickly up the stairs. Deborah headed straight for a set of double doors on the first landing, and Louisa followed her in. The room was dimly lit and it took a moment for her eyes to adjust. As they came in, they heard the dowager's groans. She lay on her bed, sheets and blankets tangled, her head back on the pillow, her long grey hair undone, her face wet with tears. She didn't appear to notice, her head tossing from side to side, her eyes shut. On the bed lay her dog, completely still, its eyes wide open, its jaw slackened.

Dead.

CHAPTER FIFTY-SEVEN

'**G**ranny Evie,' said Deborah, quickly at her side, taking her hand. 'It's me, Debo. Can you hear me?'

To this, the dowager made no intelligible response. Louisa saw a bowl of something on the bedside table, half eaten, greenish in colour, and an empty sherry glass. And then she realised that the dog had been sick on the bed: the vomit was green, too. There was a smell in the room that turned Louisa's stomach. She put one hand over her mouth, and with the other she took the dowager's, squeezed it. She was alive, but weak: there was no pressure in return.

'We need to get the doctor here immediately,' said Louisa.

'I'll go,' said Deborah. 'Telephone Charles and the duke. Tell them to get here straight away. They can use Farve's car.'

With Deborah gone, Louisa ran through what had happened as she tried to clean up the vomit. She found a clean flannel and soaked it in cold water to lay on the dowager's forehead – she didn't know if it could possibly help. All the while she wondered: what had she missed with the old lady? She'd looked pale and tired the last time Louisa had seen her but if she'd thought about it at all she would have put it down to her advanced age and the rather strained circumstances in the house. Was it possible that whoever had poisoned Mrs Hoole had also tried to poison the dowager? The only link between them was that Mrs Hoole knew that the late duke, the dowager's husband, had had unorthodox relations with Joan. Why would someone want to kill the dowager for that reason? Louisa couldn't come up with an answer.

The only thing she could do was think about who had access to poison.

The current duke.

He knew which wildflowers and plants in the garden were poisonous. Could he be afraid the dowager would reveal something about the affair that might harm him? That there was little love lost between him and his mother had been clear, but Louisa had attributed that solely to her absent mothering when he was a young boy, as he had told her and Nancy. Could it be that he was angrier than that? That he believed she had somehow worked with the late duke to ensure that Joan 'disappeared' in Canada?

There was another possibility. That Joan had had a son, and the dowager knew about him. Did the duke feel betrayed by his parents?

There was motive, there was opportunity, and there was a weapon.

Louisa telephoned Tucker and told him to come to the dowager's house. Then she telephoned Chatsworth and had an urgent message sent to the duke and Charles, telling them the same.

A quarter of an hour later, the doctor was with the dowager. He administered an injection of something that seemed to revive her slightly but she was still incapable of speech. Her skin was completely leached of any colour. As Louisa and Deborah stood by the dowager's bedside, watching Dr Dunn quietly attend to his patient, they heard the commotion of three men coming up the stairs.

Charles burst in first and glared at Louisa. 'What is the policeman doing here? Why did you telephone him?'

Following fast behind him were Tucker and the duke, for once walking quicker than his usual ambling pace. At the sight of their mother, the two brothers rushed to her, Deborah immediately dropping the dowager's hand, to allow them to take over.

The duke turned to Louisa. 'What's happened? Ellis gave us a message but all it said was to get here as fast as we could. So we have.'

'Oh, my God.' This came from Charles, who had seen the dog, now wrapped in a towel, the shape unmistakable. It didn't take him long to reach the same conclusion as Louisa. 'Did the dog eat something that was meant for my mother? Something that's killed it?'

Dr Dunn was listening to the dowager's heart with a stethoscope, which he unhooked from his ears. 'She's alive,' he said, 'but more than that, I can't say. It's clear she's been poisoned but I don't know what with.' He indicated the bowl of greenish stuff on her bedside table. 'Mr Tucker, I suggest you have that taken away and analysed.'

Louisa stepped forward. 'Yes, I'd agree,' she said. The men, and Deborah, looked at her in surprise.

'She hasn't been feeling well these last few days,' said the duke. 'It could just be an unfortunate coincidence.'

The dowager hadn't acknowledged the arrival of her sons: her eyes were closed, her breathing shallow and ragged but, somehow, she was clinging to life. Charles was sitting on the bed, staring at his mother. He hadn't taken her hand. The duke was standing, lighting a cigarette, also watching her. Louisa could not see much love between them all, even at this extraordinary time.

After a few moments, the doctor asked them to retire to another room while he ministered to the dowager. Reluctantly, they moved to the drawing room downstairs, gloomy and cold. Charles poured a whisky for himself and his brother, before slumping down onto the sofa. No one, it seemed, knew what to say. Louisa could hear the tick-tock of a clock in the hall outside. She broke the silence. 'I believe the duke is responsible for this.'

'What the hell?' said the duke.

Louisa addressed the detective inspector. 'He knows what flowers in the garden are poisonous. He's the only person here capable of this. And he has good reason—'

'Now, look here—' the duke began.

'His father had an affair with the maid before the war—'

The duke turned to his brother sharply. 'Is this your doing? What have you been saying?' Before Charles could reply, the duke spoke to Louisa, his tone harsh: 'If she wasn't already dying, your question would have finished her off completely. How dare you talk like that in front of her?'

Charles got up, for once looking steady on his feet. He took a slow step and stood before his brother. 'Our father took the only person from me who showed me any kindness in this house, and you know it.'

'Stuff and nonsense,' said the duke, but he'd lost some of his bluster. 'And you're talking about things that happened a thousand years ago. What's the bloody point of bringing it all up now?'

'You didn't care, did you?' There was no stopping Charles.

Whether it was whisky or emotion, his tongue had been loosened. 'He took Joan, and then she ...' he motioned to the ceiling, above which his mother lay '... *she* went with him to Canada, leaving us all behind. You were at war. You knew you were leaving me to a rotten life at school, but you never thought about me again.'

'As if I had a choice about going to war,' cried the duke, distressed now at this argument, the raking up of the past.

'Your Grace,' interrupted Tucker, 'I apologise for this accusation at such a difficult time. I wasn't aware that that was why I'd been brought here.' He faced Louisa. 'You're a Londoner so you wouldn't know, but for those of us who have grown up in the countryside, we're taught which plants are poisonous at our mother's knee. You've made quite a leap there, and I suggest you don't go any further or I'll have to arrest you for slander.'

'Don't you see? The dowager is the connection between Mrs Hoole and the missing maid. Her late husband—' But she got no further. Deborah had grabbed her by the arm and started to pull her out of the room.

'What do you think you're doing?' Deborah was angry and upset, tears threatening to spill down her reddening face. 'You cannot start throwing these vile accusations around. Please, Louisa, just stop.'

Louisa was shocked into silence. She realised she had gone too far. Tucker came out, closing the door behind him, leaving the two sons behind.

'Explain yourself,' said the detective inspector.

Louisa took a deep breath. 'I'm sorry,' she said. 'It came out wrong. I've been thinking about all this for so long, and I felt so certain.'

'Evidence. Facts,' said Tucker. 'Arrests are not made because of feelings.'

'I know.' Louisa felt like a chastened child. 'It just all made sense. The duke's knowledge of poisonous flowers, his difficult relationship with his mother, the affair his father had had with the maid, the disappearance to Canada.'

'What affair?' said Deborah. 'Actually, no. Please, don't tell me. I don't want to know. I don't believe it.'

'But why would he want to poison his mother?' asked Tucker.

'I don't know.' Louisa had never felt so foolish. 'I thought he might know something about her, or was angry that she'd colluded in some way with it all.'

Deborah threw her hands into the air and, without another word, went back into the drawing room.

Louisa and Tucker stood there, and after a moment he said kindly, 'We all make mistakes.'

'Thank you.'

'But if the dowager duchess was poisoned, and it looks as if she was, who would have done it?'

'If Mrs Hoole was poisoned—'

'We don't know that she was,' Tucker interrupted.

'No, but it's a possibility. And if this has happened not once but twice, it has to be intentional and it has to be the same person, doesn't it?'

'I'm not sure how willing I am to explore this with you,' said Tucker.

There was a creak on the landing above, and they saw the doctor standing there.

'How is she?' asked Louisa.

'I shall arrange for her to go to the hospital in Bakewell where they'll be able to do some tests. I'm afraid that what she needs is beyond my powers.' He looked tired and frail but eyed Louisa sharply. 'I seem to remember telling you from the start that you should be careful of stirring up trouble.'

Louisa chose to ignore this. However badly she felt, she was not going to be treated like a naughty schoolchild. 'Your notes on Joan Dorries reveal she was pregnant and planning a trip to Canada,' she said. 'Did you know about the affair between her and the late duke?'

The doctor would not rise to the bait. 'I have no obligation to say anything to you, Mrs Sullivan. Right now my most pressing concern is the dowager duchess. I've only come out here to ask Mr Tucker to come back inside and check for any evidence he may need.'

They went into the bedroom, and Louisa was left behind, alone.

CHAPTER FIFTY-EIGHT

⟞⟍⟋

Disheartened, Louisa began the walk back to Chatsworth, not far but night was falling already. It reminded her that Guy's train was arriving in a few hours. She hoped Deborah would still agree to take her to the station to meet him. In the meantime, Maisie had been left for too long in Betsy's care. Yet another thing she had got wrong that day.

In the kitchen, when Louisa arrived and found her daughter there, she was thankfully engaged in her favourite activity: licking out a bowl of cake mixture. She gave her daughter a kiss. 'Thank you again, Betsy,' she said. 'I'm sorry I was gone for so long. I was with Lady Andrew.'

'What's happened with the dowager?' asked Betsy. 'We heard there was a message for His Grace and Lord Charles to get to her house.' Anna was there, too, washing up, and Louisa could see her listening.

'She's not well.' Louisa decided it would be best not to go into detail. It was already apparent that gossip spread fast. 'The doctor is with her now, and she'll need to go into hospital for some tests, I believe.' She looked around the kitchen. 'Is Mrs Airlie not here?'

'Having a nap,' said Betsy, nodding in the direction of the servants' hall. 'Do you need her?'

'No, no. Perhaps you could let her know that Mr Sullivan is arriving back here later tonight so there will be one more for breakfast in the morning.'

'That'll be nice for you, to have him back here.' The maid smiled.

'Yes,' Louisa agreed. 'I'm sorry to ask more of you, but could you keep an eye on Maisie for a while longer? I'll ask Mademoiselle Dupont if she can put her to bed. Guy's train is coming in too late for her to stay up.'

'Can't I see Daddy?' said Maisie.

'No, darling. You'll see him in the morning, as soon as you wake up. I'm going to find Lucie now. Back soon.' She gave Maisie another kiss and left the kitchens.

She hadn't been to Lucie's room before but was fairly certain she had been put close by in the servant's quarters. Thankfully, Louisa spotted Ellis on the back stairs and asked him to take her to Lucie's room. It was about the time that nearly everyone was in their room, bathing and changing for dinner.

Naturally, he enquired after the dowager, and again, Louisa was careful not to say too much. As they walked along the narrow corridor towards the bedrooms, a thought occurred to Louisa. 'Ellis, did you say your uncle worked for the late duke?'

'Yes, he did,' Ellis said proudly. 'He was with him for almost twenty years, and trained me up. I do everything exactly as he taught me. I know the old ways are not—'

'Do you know if your uncle travelled to Canada with the

Duke? When he became governor?' Louisa was not willing to listen to a lecture on Ellis's buttling theories.

'Yes, he did,' said Ellis. The pinched face had returned at Louisa's interruption.

'Then do you know if the maid, Joan Dorries, was on the boat with them?'

Ellis's face was genuinely surprised. 'No, I don't know that. I think it's highly unlikely.'

'Why?'

Ellis looked nonplussed. 'I'm sure he would have told me.'

'Did he tell you *everything*? I wonder if he would have told you something that you might have believed compromised his position as the perfect butler?'

'But he was the perfect butler,' said Ellis, beginning to show a trace of emotion for the first time. It was like watching a crack appear in the ceiling. 'This is Mademoiselle Dupont's room,' he added. 'I doubt she's there.'

'Why?'

'She's going home, I think. She was asking me about train times earlier.'

'What? She's going back to France?'

For the second time, a crack formed. 'No. Canada.'

Louisa stopped. 'She lives in Canada?'

'Yes, she's French Canadian. Did you not—'

But Louisa didn't wait to hear any more.

CHAPTER FIFTY-NINE

L ouisa pushed open the door. She could see instantly that Lucie had packed away her things. She wanted to find her passport, but it wasn't there. Hurriedly, Louisa checked under the bed, the chest of drawers and in the wardrobe: no suitcase, only one or two things left hanging. Not only had she packed, she'd packed quickly. Ellis watched her, struck speechless as Louisa pushed past him. She ran down the stairs and out of the back door. The cold hit her but she kept running fast, hoping her eyes would adjust sooner so she could see her way along the path to the dowager's house. The moon occasionally came out from behind the clouds to help her along the way and in record time she was back at the old lady's front door, panting heavily and running up the stairs to the bedroom. Inside she found the doctor, with Deborah, Charles and the duke.

'I know who did it,' she gasped, as they all turned to look at her. The dowager was still lying prone on the bed. Thoughts were rushing wildly through her mind and she tried to clutch at them, to say something intelligible. For a few seconds she could do no more than grip her knees and try to get her breath back.

'It was Lucie Dupont.'

'What nonsense are you talking now?' said the duke. 'Why should we believe a word you say?' The anger was almost palpable.

'I know,' said Louisa, feeling steadier now. 'But it all suddenly makes sense. Lucie is French Canadian. She's not from France.'

'What are you saying?' This was Deborah, more sympathetic than the others though not without wariness in her voice.

'She's twenty-five years old. She's Joan's baby.'

'Joan?' This was Charles. 'How do you know this?'

'I think the butler, Ellis the First, helped Joan go to Canada with the duke. Mrs Airlie told me he was a very nice man, good with children, and we know he went to Canada with the duke. Joan must have had the baby over there. That's why she disappeared and Lucie is the baby. She's come back to take revenge on the family who abandoned her.'

'But how do you know that?'

'Because I remembered the plot of a short story in the book she was reading, an Agatha Christie. The murderer administered poison in wine. It was atropine, found in eye drops. Remember the glass of sherry that Lucie encouraged the dowager to drink every night? And I saw her collect a prescription for the dowager – she said she was collecting her pills. Doctor, did you write her a prescription for eye drops?'

The doctor's own rheumy eyes looked at Louisa. 'Yes,' he said. 'I did.'

'And you said you knew Joan was dead. How did you know that?'

314

He looked weak and pathetic. 'I don't. But she never came back.'

There was a silence while they all absorbed this.

'There's something else,' said Louisa. 'The night Mrs Hoole died, Maisie and I heard the dowager's dog barking, but she wasn't in the house. Lucie told me she always kept treats in her pocket for Rosie. I thought she was being nice but what if she was keeping the dog with her so that Rosie would learn not to bark when she was around? To prevent anyone being alerted?'

Louisa looked at them all, staring at her. 'Deborah, I need you to drive me to the station. I think she's there. She was asking Ellis for train times.'

'Shouldn't we call the police?'

'There isn't time!'

Deborah drove fast to the station, remaining impressively calm and in control as she steered around the corners on country lanes, overtaking a motor-car that was crawling along on the main road to Bakewell. The car's headlights – taped up to narrow slits for the war – lit the way ahead by only yards at a time, leaving Louisa feeling as if they were driving without any navigation to guide them there, but Deborah knew what she was doing. Soon they were turning into the station entrance.

'Thank you,' said Louisa, as she flung open the car door and jumped out.

'I'm coming with you.' Deborah slammed her door. They stood for an anticlimactic moment at the gate. It was late, there were few people around and everywhere, as usual in this damned war, was unlit. Louisa looked at her watch. Guy's train was due in ten minutes. In all the worry, she'd lost track of the time. She didn't know what train Lucie was planning to catch but, at this time of night, there wouldn't be many choices. She had to be there.

'We need to find the station master,' said Louisa. 'Ask him if he's seen Lucie and what trains are due.'

'Right. Yes.' Deborah looked around and, seeing no one, headed onto the nearest platform. They scanned as far as they could see – which wasn't far – and saw a door that wasn't completely closed. Deborah immediately headed there and Louisa saw the sign, 'Station Master's Office'. Giving only the faintest of knocks first, Deborah went inside. No one was there, only a desk, two chairs, a lamp and shelves of books and filing boxes. On the desk were some papers, a telephone, the station master's hat, a pair of thick woollen gloves and a torch.

They were about to leave when Deborah grabbed Louisa's arm. 'Stop. Can you smell that?'

'What?' Louisa's sense of smell had never been very acute.

'It's Lucie's scent. Tuberose. It's very distinctive. I'm sure she's been in here.'

Louisa remembered seeing Lucie come from Mr Formby's with her precious bottle of scent. 'She can't have left very long ago,' she said. 'But why would she have been in here?'

'Maybe she was asking about trains,' said Deborah.

Louisa picked up the torch, and shone it around the room in case there was anything else they'd missed but there wasn't. Just as they were looking at the walls around them, they heard the door close. And then they heard a key turn in the lock.

'What was that?' Louisa spun around and tried to pull the door open but it was shut fast.

Uselessly, she turned the handle and jiggled it while Deborah banged on the door, shouting, 'Let us out!'

There was no response on the other side.

Louisa picked up the telephone and called the police, asking for an urgent message to be sent to DI Tucker, and in the meantime for the on-duty police sergeant to come to the station as fast as possible. She registered the brisk efficiency of the person at the other end of the line but knew it would still take several minutes for anyone to reach them. She looked at her watch again: another five minutes until Guy's train pulled in.

Silenced, frustrated, Deborah and Louisa stared at each other when they heard the sound of a train: was it arriving, or was it leaving? Was that screech from a whistle or the brakes?

'Could it be Guy's train, coming in a few minutes' early?'

'I suppose it's possible,' said Deborah. 'Those timetables never seem to be an exact science to me.'

Louisa pushed her ear to the door, trying to discern whether the train was at the platform they were on or another, but she couldn't. The door was solid, too thick to allow for any clarity of sound. When the station master wanted peace from the whistles, the door must have been perfect. But it wasn't what they needed at that moment.

With no more than a shared glance, the two women started banging on the door again, shouting for help. Eventually, when their hands were sore and their throats hoarse, there was a rattle on the door handle, and a man's voice: 'Hello? Who's in there?'

'Lady Andrew,' said Deborah, in her most imperious voice. 'Please, find the station master and ask him to unlock this door.'

There was a short silence and Louisa panicked that whoever

it was had run away, but then they heard, 'I'll be as quick as I can.'

Louisa put her ear to the door again. She could hear the heavy *thunks* and the metallic clangs of a train's doors closing. Was it about to leave and was Lucie on it?

CHAPTER SIXTY

A t the moment Louisa thought she might pass out from the frustration of waiting, there was the reassuring noise of a key unlocking the door. It was pushed open and they saw the station master, a bemused and curious man beside him.

'What happened?' asked the man.

'There's no time to explain,' said Louisa. 'Is there a train that's about to depart?'

'It's gone,' said the station master. 'Now, look, what are you doing in my office and why is it locked?'

But Louisa wasn't going to stay to answer his questions. She was out. Torch still in hand, she shone it up and down the platform, trying to think where Lucie might be. The train that had gone must have been travelling south, given that Guy's would be going further north, coming from London. Lucie, surely, would want to go south. In London she could hide easily, and perhaps even try to start her journey back to Canada. She'd come to Chatsworth to take revenge and she'd done it – almost. As far as they knew, the dowager was still alive and Louisa prayed the doctor had got her to the hospital in time. At least they would know what antidote to use for atropine.

The people who had got off the last train could be heard getting into cars that had arrived to collect them. There weren't many, though. The station was already eerily quiet again, the reassuring familiarity of signs and timetables obscured by the darkness. The unending, pitiless nights of blackouts in wartime sometimes drove Louisa almost to despair. Wordlessly, she and Deborah climbed the steps to the other platform, no sound or sight to tell them that there was hope of finding Lucie.

'She's gone,' said Louisa.

'What's that?'

'We've lost her,' said Louisa. 'She's got away with it.'

'No. I mean I think there's a train coming. It must be the one Guy is on.'

Louisa heard it then, the soft rattle of an approaching train, and then, only seconds later, the screech of the brakes, the hiss as it pulled in gently. They ran down the steps to the platform, just as the doors were beginning to open, and though she knew she shouldn't, she shone the torch up along the train, hoping she could see Guy from the very first second he appeared.

Instead, what she saw was a flash of a woman's leg as it stepped up and into a carriage. Without thinking, Louisa ran down, Deborah behind her, and pulled open the door that had only just been closed. In the carriage was Lucie.

Not for long.

She shoved Louisa down onto the seat, and barged Deborah with her shoulder, leaping off the train and running down the platform, disappearing into the dark. Still, somehow, clutching the torch, Louisa jumped back down and shone the light, trying to see where she had gone. There were doors banging, footsteps, and then – shouts. Men, a woman. Louisa ran in the direction of the noise, her torch before her, and there was Lucie, sprawled on the ground, her bag split beside her and Guy, with her, apologising, as she started to get up.

'No!' cried Louisa. 'Hold her – stop her.'

Guy looked at his wife rushing towards him, a split-second delay, but his hand shot out and he grabbed Lucie before she could gather herself together.

Louisa and Deborah ran to them, neither sounding as if they had any breath left in their lungs, gasping for air, dizzy with adrenalin. Within seconds of the commotion, they'd been joined by the policeman and the station master, everyone demanding an explanation.

'This is Lucie Dupont,' said Louisa. 'You need to arrest her for the attempted murder of the Dowager Duchess of Devonshire.'

CHAPTER SIXTY-ONE

Once arrested, the fight seemed to go out of Lucie. Pale and tired, she allowed herself to be handcuffed and led off the platform. Deborah returned to Chatsworth, taking Guy's case with her, but Louisa and Guy accompanied the police sergeant to the station, where DI Tucker met them. Lucie was put into a holding cell while Tucker talked to Louisa in his office, both drinking strong cups of coffee to get them through what was promising to be a long night ahead.

'We have no more than twenty-four hours to gather the evidence against her,' he said. 'What have you got?'

'You'll need to talk to Dr Dunn. He can confirm that he wrote prescriptions for eye drops for the dowager, which contain atropine. I imagine her butler can tell you that he was asked by Lucie to prepare a decanter of sherry with two glasses for her and the dowager each evening. Her sons are witness to their mother growing weaker over the last week or so.'

'I see,' said Tucker. 'You've done good work. Will she admit to it?'

'I don't know,' admitted Louisa. 'And the thing I still haven't worked out is why she killed Mrs Hoole.'

'How do you think she did it?'

Louisa sighed. 'The poison? We don't know yet how Mrs Hoole died but that seems a likely way.'

'Right.' Tucker put his hands into his pockets. 'But we have no motivation or evidence to link Lucie Dupont to Mrs Hoole.'

'No. Unless it's something to do with Joan – after all, she's Lucie's mother. And Mrs Hoole was bringing attention to her. Perhaps that upset Lucie?'

'Did she ever seem upset about the story of the missing maid?' asked Tucker.

Louisa shook her head. 'No more than the rest of us. But if she was planning to execute her revenge on the dowager she wouldn't have wanted us to make the link, would she?'

'That's true.' Tucker stood up. 'I'd better go and interview her. We'll ask the doctor, the dowager's butler and her sons to come here in the morning. I'll talk to her now, try and extract a confession – or two.'

'Is there anything else I can do?' Louisa couldn't picture herself going back to Chatsworth to sleep.

'No. I'll ask one of the sergeants to run you both back. We'll talk in the morning.'

Guy and Louisa were silent in the car, holding hands on the back seat. She didn't want the police sergeant to overhear what she thought about Lucie or Mrs Hoole, and as she couldn't think about anything else, she was almost incapable of having a conversation with him. But as soon as they crept in through the back door – it was now midnight – Louisa was fit to burst.

Guy started to congratulate her on the work she had done in identifying Lucie's attempted murder but she quietened him.

'I feel I've missed something,' she said. 'All this time I've been trying to find out who killed Mrs Hoole, and what the link was with Joan, and there was Lucie slowly trying to kill the dowager. What was going on when I was looking in the wrong direction?'

'That's how it is sometimes with an investigation,' said Guy.

'It's only ... If Lucie killed Mrs Hoole, why would she stay in the house after she'd done it? It seems like too big a risk for her to take. Especially given that she tried to leave as soon as she thought the dowager was about to die,' said Louisa. 'It's not adding up properly. What if someone else killed Mrs Hoole after all?'

'Then you need to go back to your initial thoughts,' said Guy. 'Who else has knowledge of poisons, so far as you've gathered?'

'I didn't know Lucie did,' said Louisa. 'The duke knew about poisonous plants in the garden but I'm pretty sure he's innocent. There's Mr Formby.'

'Who is that?'

'The local shopkeeper. He definitely sells black-market goods – maybe he offers something more sinister. There's the doctor, of course. They always know. But Dr Dunn is so old that I can't see him sneaking in to administer poison to Mrs Hoole, and he wasn't in the house that night.' She stopped. 'Max.'

'Max?'

'He's a gardener. He told us – that is, Lucie was there – that he knew about poisonous plants. He was the watchman that night. And there was soil in the bedroom – that detail's been bothering me. I've been sure it could be a clue but couldn't match it up to anything. It must have come off his shoes.'

Guy listened carefully.

'There's more. The night of that air raid, remember? Max wasn't with us – the gardeners were in their own shelter, someone said. But afterwards someone had been in Mrs Hoole's room. That was his opportunity. He must have been in there, looking for something.'

'But what was his motivation?' Guy asked. Louisa looked at him: her poor, darling husband. He was clearly exhausted, his arm in a sling. He'd been through the fright of his life, travelled miles to reach her and Maisie, and all she'd done was drag him through another drama. She leaned over and kissed him. 'What was that for?'

'I'm sorry,' she said. 'I know that what I should be doing is looking after you.'

'No. I'm relieved to be thinking about something else, if anything. And you're so close. Come on, think. Why would Max want Mrs Hoole dead?'

Louisa's shoulders slumped. 'I can't think of a single reason. I've got nothing but supposition, and barely even that. Let's go to bed. Things will look clearer in the morning, and Tucker will have Lucie's confession with any luck.'

CHAPTER SIXTY-TWO

Louisa could not sleep. Even with her husband beside her and the warmth of his body beneath the sheets, the reassuring heaviness of his arm around her waist, she tossed and turned. She thought of Lucie, probably awake too, lying on a thin mattress in a cell, riven by a kind of madness that had driven her to a chilling revenge on the dowager. What had happened to her that had taken her to that edge? Louisa still didn't know the story of Joan. If Max had killed Mrs Hoole, then there had to be a connection between him, Mrs Hoole and Joan – she needed to find out what it was.

She sat up. Ellis's office. She knew the butlers always kept a record of household servants: when they arrived, when they left, why they left, what they were paid. He would hold any papers or relevant information on everyone who had worked under the Chatsworth roof. There might be a clue there. Having thought of it, there was no chance Louisa could stay in bed.

Taking the torch from the bedside table and pulling on a jumper that Guy had thrown onto a chair, Louisa crept out of the bedroom and made her way down to the butler's pantry. Through the window the night sky was dense, only one or two stars glinting, the shadows of trees below. With purpose to guide her, she wasn't afraid of the creaks on the stairs, or what she now knew were the shudders and sighs of an old house in the middle of the night. Along the hall, only the circle of light from the torch ahead of her, she moved silently and came to the butler's pantry. The handle turned – it wasn't locked. She didn't dare turn on a light but shone her torch around the room. One wall was composed of the double doors that led to the silver, locked, of course. Otherwise, the furnishings were simple.

She went straight to the desk and sat in Ellis's chair. Various papers lay on the surface: bills, a letter from the local Home Guard, a book of accounts. Louisa opened the drawer beneath – there was a key in the lock. Inside, more papers, nothing neatly filed, which was a surprise. She was sure Ellis would be meticulous with his paperwork. It didn't take her long to find the large black leather record book for the Chatsworth servants. Her heart beating fast, her ears stretched for any noise, she flicked through the pages. At the front of the book the ink was blotchy, the writing scrawled, hard to read, with ancient names and positions: Evans Ansslow, porter, 1659; Joshua Arnold, master mason, 1701. She turned more pages, and the ink turned from brown to black, the writing a little easier to read: Erasmus Johnson, footman, 1873–8; Madeleine Back, lady's maid, 1881; Henry Bacon, gardener, 1912–22. And then, she had it: Maximillian Landesman, gardener, 1916.

He had been working in the house when Joan was there.

Louisa read the page again and, yes, there was Joan Dorries, 1915–16; Eliza Duffin 1912–16. The fact that Joan's dates had been recorded was interesting. It might have been done to legitimise her departure, as part of a cover-up. Or it might have been someone acknowledging her. Ellis the First, the butler Mrs Airlie had said was kind to children, and whom Ellis the Second had said was 'the perfect butler'. That usually meant loyal to the family, willing to do anything to preserve the honour of the house, and he had gone to Canada. What had he known about Max, Joan and Eliza?

Of all of them, only Max was alive. If he had heard that Lucie had been arrested, would he be afraid that he was next, if he was guilty, too? She put the book in the drawer and accidentally slammed it shut, the noise making her jump. If he did know, if he was afraid, he might try to leave. She couldn't risk it for another minute. Less quietly now, less stealthily, Louisa ran back to her room where Guy slept, as did Maisie in her little bed, holding on to her new doll. Quickly, she dressed and was about to leave when Guy sat up, switching on the lamp beside him.

'Where are you going?'

Louisa had one hand on the door. 'To find Max.'

'Not alone, you're not.'

'You can't come with me. Maisie will wake and be on her own. She'd panic.'

'Then you have to wake one of the maids and ask them to come in here. Or not find Max. Wait until the morning.'

'I can't wait. Please, Guy. I've discovered that Max was here when Joan was here, and when Mrs Hoole was here, in 1916. There's a link between them – there has to be. If Max killed Mrs Hoole, and he's heard that Lucie has been arrested, he'll be afraid. He might leave.'

'Louisa, this is all too much theory and not enough facts. And if anyone's going to apprehend someone for suspected murder, don't you think it should be the police? Not you and me with a broken arm.'

Louisa's hand dropped to her side. 'Yes, I suppose you're right. It's just I started thinking and—'

'You don't have to explain to me. I know the feeling. But it's the middle of the night. Stop. Come to bed.'

'No.' Louisa turned to face him. 'It has to be now. I know I'm right, I'm sorry. I'll knock on Betsy's door and ask her to come down.' With that, she left.

CHAPTER SIXTY-THREE

Her bravado was one thing. Stepping outside into the cold night air was quite another. As if she had been slapped around the face, she realised that confronting a strong man with an accusation of murder was risky at best, life endangering at worst. She had Maisie now: she couldn't take such a risk. But she had put herself into this corner and couldn't quite face returning to Guy and asking him to come with her. She looked at the sky but there was no sign of dawn, the stars still shining, the trees still black below them. To her left was the greenhouse. It would be warm, somewhere to sit and think for a while. She kept her torch pointing low, hoping the batteries would last, and let herself in.

The scent of damp earth and herbs hit her pleasantly and she spent a few minutes simply enjoying the sight of the seedlings, a few hardier-looking plants. It was well managed, with tidy potting tables and the brick floor swept clean. At the back, it looked as if Max had created a small area for himself, with a high table and a stool. She hadn't thought about something like that being there but it made sense: he was usually in the greenhouse. This corner at the back was probably more private than the small cottage he shared with Mr Coates. Alert now, and checking all around – giving thanks she was in a glass house and could see anyone in the distance more easily than they could see her – she rifled through the personal possessions. A couple of postcards were pinned up, one of a seafront, another a photograph of trees. On the table there was some gardening paraphernalia – seeds, twine, scissors, a trowel, some empty pots. An ashtray and a half-empty packet of Player's cigarettes, a box of matches. Nothing of any use.

Louisa sat on the stool and sighed. She was cold, and wishing she was back in her bed in London, hundreds of miles from all of this. She picked the postcard of trees off the wall and looked at it. The message on the card was quite faint, the ink having faded over the years. She made out 'Max' and some general bland remark about having a nice time. It was signed 'Mother'. Louisa saw that it hadn't been addressed to Max at Chatsworth but had been sent care of a post office in some other village she hadn't heard of in Derbyshire. Perhaps he'd once lived elsewhere. Curious now, she shone the torch a little closer to see if there was a date on the stamp's frank and that was when she got a shock. The postcard had been sent in March 1915 from Berlin. If Max's mother was sending him postcards from home that could only mean one thing: Max was German.

As she put the card into her pocket, Louisa's heart was beating at an alarming speed. What should she do now?

But she didn't get the chance to answer her own question. Before she could do anything, she heard the rattle of the greenhouse door opening and was frozen to the spot. Louisa turned off her torch but too late: she had been seen. There were heavy footsteps on the brick, the laboured breathing of a man who had been running. Quickly, Louisa picked up the nearest heavy plant pot and threw it straight ahead as hard as she could.

There was a cry, then a crash and the sound of a heavy body hitting the floor, bringing down several pots with him. Louisa switched her torch on again and saw Ellis lying there, cradling his head in his hands. 'I'm so sorry,' she gabbled. 'I didn't know who you were, I took fright when you came in and I couldn't see anything.'

Ellis groaned.

'Why don't you have a torch?' she continued. She was picking bits of pot off him and brushing soil from his jacket. Luckily there was no sign of any blood.

'I was just coming out to see if you were Max,' Ellis began, but before he could get any further he started giggling.

'Ellis?' Louisa was completely confused now. 'What's going on? What's so funny?'

'I thought you were Max,' said Ellis, almost unable to speak for laughing, then wheezing, then finally 'Ow' as he tried to stand up.

'Are you drunk?' Louisa asked.

Ellis raised both his eyebrows and leaned against a table. 'Well,' he said eventually, 'I might have had a drink or two.'

'What's going on?'

'It's the night watchman, Matthew, he goes to the ... you know.' Ellis snorted. 'You know.'

'No, I don't know. Where does he go?'

'The barrels, in the cellar.' He looked as if he was sobering up now, regretting saying this to Louisa.

She remembered seeing the barrels down there, and that she'd been told Matthew liked a drink. Of all the people who might have joined in on that particular escapade, Ellis was the last person she would have picked. But that wasn't her most pressing concern. 'Ellis, did you know Max was German?'

'What?'

'There's a postcard here, sent to him from his mother in 1915, from Berlin. He worked here shortly after, and I think he knew Joan, the maid who went missing. He must have known your uncle, then, too.'

Ellis looked unsteady but he didn't contradict Louisa.

'Did he? Did he know your uncle?'

'It's possible,' said Ellis. 'I don't really want to talk about all that. I think I want to go to bed.'

But when Ellis turned, he was stopped by someone else who had walked in without them noticing.

Max.

'Yes,' said Max calmly. 'I knew Mr Ellis back then. He was a good man.' He took Ellis the Second by the arm and steered him gently to the door. 'I think it's time you went to bed.'

Helpless, yet somehow not as afraid as she had been before, Louisa stood there while Max waited for Ellis to leave, stumbling out through the door and into the garden.

'The cold'll sober him,' he said. He turned to Louisa. 'What are you doing in here?'

She felt unable to answer. Afraid, she attacked first. 'Are you German, Max?'

From the corner of her eye she saw her torchlight reflect off a sharp-looking tool lying on the table between them, something for pulling out weeds.

He stepped towards her, and she was aware of his bulk, the fact of his strength and the night that lay all around them. 'What makes you think that?'

She wished she hadn't put the postcard in her pocket. Tentatively, she pulled it out, as if it might burn her fingers. 'I saw this. It's from your mother in Berlin.'

Max went to snatch it from her but she held fast. 'That's private,' he said, his voice gruff. 'You've no right.'

'I know,' said Louisa, 'I won't defend myself. But I'm wondering why you kept it secret.' She kept herself as straight as a steel rod, her eye keeping the sharp tool in sight.

'I had to. Germans are not exactly popular in this country.'

'It's not a crime to be German,' said Louisa.

He flinched at that. 'Why are you ... ? What are you saying?'

'You were here during the war, weren't you? This card, it was sent to you in 1915, to somewhere not far from here.' Her heart was beating so fast it was hard to talk, but she had to keep him there, keep him calm and concentrating on her. 'Did you know Joan Dorries, Max?'

Even in the dim light, she could see something flash across his face. Fear? Or anger?

'You're asking too many questions,' he said, stepping towards her again, and it took all Louisa's might not to step back. She could not match him for physical strength: she had to defend herself in another way.

'Did you know Nesbit is German, too? Are you working for him?'

'No, no, I'm not.' She could hear it in his voice then: fear. It soon gave him away. 'What has he told you? Does anyone else know?'

334

'You know him, then.' She said it flatly, trying not to accuse, to draw him out so that he would tell her more. There was a heavy pause in which Louisa heard an owl, cooing its soft sound nearby.

'He threatened to send me back but I can't go back,' Max said at last. 'I can't. I live here now. This is my home.' He staggered slightly, and when he looked back at her, she saw the sadness in his eyes.

'Why can he send you back? What have you done?' She was less afraid of his grief but she still kept that weed puller in view.

'I haven't done anything, I promise. I haven't—' He broke off, and she heard a single sob come from him.

'But what has he got over you?' She spoke more softly now.

'I came here as a low-grade informant, in the last war, to report on the RAF base.'

'And you think he knows?'

'What if the Nazis have found records of those who were here then? What if they want me to do something for them now? I can't betray this country.'

'Has Nesbit approached you?'

'He tried. He started to—'

'When?'

'The night Mrs Hoole died.'

Louisa's heart jumped, like a boxer's punch.

Before she could think about it, she had grabbed the metal tool and was pointing it at Max. 'Did you kill Mrs Hoole?'

Max's head snapped back and he stepped away, his hands in the air. 'No, I didn't. I swear.'

Still pointing the sharp end at Max, Louisa stepped around him until she had her back to the door and he was facing her.

His hands were still up. Louisa walked backwards, slowly, not wanting to trip.

'I didn't,' said Max, plaintively. But Louisa couldn't risk believing him. As fast as she could, she turned in the last few yards and ran out of the greenhouse.

CHAPTER SIXTY-FOUR

Panicking and uncertain, Louisa kept running towards the house. The thin light of dawn was beginning to show at last. She went in through the back door, and up the stairs into the Painted Hall. If Max chased her, she reasoned, she might lose him in the house. But she heard no footsteps behind her. Instead, in the hall, Louisa saw that the lights were on, and there was Guy with the men of household – Billy, Charles, Lord Redesdale, the duke. They were wearing their pyjamas and dressing-gowns, looking rather lost, except for Guy who was dressed. With them, too, was Tucker.

'What's going on?' asked Louisa, as they all turned and watched her come in.

Guy came up and put his arms around her. 'I telephoned Tucker and told him to come here. Then I woke the others for back-up. I've been so frightened. We were about to split up and try to find you.'

'I've been in the greenhouse,' said Louisa, shaking, and realising that she was still holding the gardening tool. 'Max found me in there. He swears he didn't kill Mrs Hoole.'

Tucker stepped forward. 'Lucie Dupont denies it, too. Why did you think it was Max? Who is he again?'

'I'll explain later,' said Louisa. 'He's a gardener here. The short story is, he's German and he's afraid of Group Captain Nesbit.'

'Why is he afraid of him?' asked Guy.

'Because Max came here as an informant in the Great War. He thinks the Nazis must have discovered his records, realised he was still here. He's frightened they'll ask him to work for them.'

'So Nesbit is a spy,' said Guy, and there was an audible reaction from everyone else in the room to this.

'Max says Nesbit approached him the night Mrs Hoole died.'

'The night Mrs Hoole died?' said Tucker. 'Is that the connection we've been looking for?'

'I think so,' said Louisa. 'But not in the way we thought. Right now, we need to find Nesbit.'

'Presumably he's at the base,' said Guy.

'No, he's not.' The voice was clear, and female. At the top of the stairs was Nancy, wearing a silk dressing-gown. 'I had a message from Winston last night. Nesbit's gone AWOL, as of two days ago. There's a warning not to approach him alone.' She came down the steps. 'What are you all doing here? I woke early and thought I could hear something.'

Louisa went towards her. 'I can't explain it all now but we need to find Nesbit.'

'How can we find him?' asked Billy. 'He could be anywhere.'

'This is the only other place he knows,' said Louisa. 'He'd think he could hide out here until he came up with some other plan. And he's got Max here. He'd use him if he had to, or even try to take him back to Germany with him.'

'But this place is enormous,' said Guy. 'How do we even know where to begin?'

'First, we need to get Max,' said Louisa, 'before Nesbit does. Lord Redesdale, you stay here in the hall, and close to the telephone, in case we need to call for more help.'

Lord Redesdale looked relieved at this suggestion.

'The rest of us, let's split between the greenhouse and the gardener's cottage. If he's not at either place, we'll reconvene at the foot of the fountain. Duke and Billy, you had better guard the cars – Max can drive.'

While Charles and Tucker went to the greenhouse, Louisa and Guy set off for the gardener's cottage. Pink light was spreading over the white clouds, and the cold seemed to sharpen in the early morning. At the cottage, the curtains were drawn and there was no sign of anyone there. The back door was unlocked and Guy let himself in. Louisa waited outside but in only a few minutes Guy was back out again. 'The other gardener is still asleep in his bed. There's no sign of anyone else.'

'I've been thinking,' said Louisa. 'About that air raid. It was Nesbit who told us about it, but it turned out to be a false alarm. What if he said it deliberately, knowing it would get us all out of the way?'

'Why?'

'Someone went to the room Mrs Hoole had died in, remember? Perhaps he was looking for something. What if the reason she had lit all those candles was something to do with him – trying to write a letter without putting a light on, maybe? Or trying to incriminate someone else, planting evidence.'

'It's a thought,' said Guy. 'He has the motivation if he thought

339

Mrs Hoole had discovered he was a spy. And he had the strength to smother her.'

'There was bruising,' said Louisa. 'That was in the post-mortem report. Perhaps it wasn't poison at all.'

'He knew you were looking for a connection between her and Joan. So he placed the cap in her hand when she was dead,' said Guy. 'Maybe he put the candles in her room. If that was what he meant, it worked: he kept your focus on another explanation, looking to the past rather than to anything that might have happened that night.'

They'd been walking to the arranged meeting spot and saw Tucker and Charles waiting for them there.

'Is there anywhere outside the main house he could hide?' asked Tucker. 'Any outbuildings?'

'Yes,' said Charles, 'an endless amount of them.'

He looked haggard but he was gentler when sober. Louisa could see what Adele must have liked about him in the first place. 'The Hunting Tower,' she said. 'Max took us there the other night – he knows it well. Oh, my God. The bloody cloth, with the same blood type as Joan's cap – it was found there.'

CHAPTER SIXTY-FIVE

G uy, Louisa, Tucker and Nancy reached the Hunting Tower fast, Charles lagging behind but urging them on ahead of him. Though the sun was rising, the pink had faded to an overcast grey, with rain threatening. They marched in silence, their mouths set in thin, grim lines. None of them knew what lay ahead or what they should be prepared for.

As they came to the tower, wordlessly they divided, Louisa and Nancy staying outside, the men going in. The door was unlocked. Tucker went in first, Guy following. Louisa and Nancy waited, not talking, almost holding their breath. One, two minutes went past and then Guy came out. 'There's no one in there.'

'Any sign of anyone?' asked Louisa.

'Some food in the kitchen, scraps,' said Guy, 'and a pair of brown shoes upstairs.'

Louisa remembered the brown shoes she and Lucie had found in the strange bedroom in the house. They'd been polished clean. Were they Nesbit's shoes, the soil that might have incriminated him brushed off? Was that why he'd had to go back to the house during the false air raid, to find them?

Tucker came out as Charles reached the house, and then they saw Billy running up the hill towards them. 'Lord Redesdale's staying with the cars,' he puffed. 'I couldn't leave you all to this. What were you saying about the Nesbit chap? He's a spy?'

Nancy was about to respond when there was a loud bang from inside the tower. They all jumped. 'What was that?' she said.

Guy, Tucker and Billy ran up the steps and flung open the front door. This time Louisa and Nancy followed. On the floor in the hall, Max was clutching at his leg, crying out in extreme pain, blood seeping through his fingers. Without pause, Nancy knelt down and started tying the belt of her silk dressing-gown around his wound as a tourniquet.

'Where did he come from?' said Guy.

'The tunnel,' said Louisa. 'We should have thought. It's in there.' She pointed to the sitting room, and they saw the chair that covered the hole had been pushed away.

'Don't—' gasped Max. 'Gun.' He'd gone several shades whiter.

'Find me more cloth,' said Nancy, ignoring them. 'A towel or something but we've got to get him to hospital quickly. Can we get one of the cars up here?'

'I'll do it,' said Billy.

Louisa went into the kitchen and found two towels, which she gave to Nancy, who expertly wrapped them round Max's leg, pressing on them firmly.

'Wait,' said Guy. 'Where does that tunnel lead to?'

'It must be an old coal tunnel.' Charles was leaning against the wall, looking almost as pale as Max. 'There's one in the garden by the rockery. It hasn't been used since the last war. God knows what's in there.'

'Go and get the car!' Nancy shouted at Billy, and he ran off.

Guy turned to Charles. 'You need to show me where the rockery is. Tucker and I will go there.'

'Guy, the gun.' Louisa was frightened. 'Please, don't go after him.'

'There's no time,' he said. 'Now, take us there.'

'If you go, I'm coming with you.' If she was with him. she hoped Guy wouldn't take a foolish risk.

After a quick glance at Nancy on the floor with Max, Louisa pushed out past her husband and through the front door. Outside, the cold air and the bright light made it feel as if what she had seen in there was a dream: Max, a gunshot wound, the blood.

They all hurried down the slope as Charles explained where the coal tunnel emerged in the gardens below. 'But there's more than one entrance,' he said. 'Two I know of, but maybe there's more. I used to explore them as a boy but haven't been near them in years.'

'We'll have to split up, then,' said Tucker. 'If an entrance is blocked up at least we'll know he can't get out that way.'

They heard the car coming up to the tower just as they ducked down a path towards the rockery.

'Can a man get through the tunnels quickly?' asked Guy.

'They're not full height and they're very narrow,' said Charles, his breathing laboured. He was not a fit man. 'But they're bigger than you'd expect – they were designed to push a cart through.'

Louisa thought of Maisie sleeping in her bed, not knowing her parents were outside, chasing a man with a gun – a man who was willing to shoot another. Quickly, she pushed aside the image. She wouldn't risk her life, and neither would Guy.

What she didn't know was how close to the edge Nesbit was willing to push the risk to his own life.

CHAPTER SIXTY-SIX

s they approached the rockery, they slowed their pace, making their footsteps as light as possible. If the tunnel ran through this part of the estate, they didn't want Nesbit to hear them. Whispering, they divided themselves – Tucker and Charles to one entrance, Louisa and Guy to another. Guy held Louisa's hand as they half ran lightly through the rocks, the sound of water splashing into the vast pond below. Louisa pulled on Guy's hand and he stopped, turning. 'What?'

She kissed him quickly. 'Please, be careful.' Guy didn't reply but squeezed her hand, and led her on, down some slippery steps. It was then they saw the overgrown square entrance they were heading for.

'What if he's long gone?' whispered Louisa.

'But where would he go?' said Guy. 'Unless he has a car here, he's trapped, isn't he? Stay back now.'

Shivering, her stomach aching from being tensed for so long, Louisa watched helplessly as Guy sidled towards the entrance. She knew he'd been trained for this – he had faced dangerous men before. Every night, in London, they all risked their lives when there was a bombing raid. But she was afraid.

Then, without warning, before Guy had got there, they heard another loud crack coming from the direction of the other entrance. Another shot? Before Louisa could stop him, Guy disappeared into the tunnel. And before she even stopped to think what she was doing, she ran in after him.

It was dark and damp inside. Overgrown with bracken on the floor and coming out through gaps in the walls and ceiling, brushing against her face as they ran. There was only just enough light from the entrance to help them for the first stretch, before they turned a corner and could see almost nothing. Guy stopped, fumbled in his pocket, and pulled out matches. Awkwardly, he lit one and they saw ahead of them another corner to the right. There was no noise from anywhere, only the rush of blood pumping in her ears, their shoes muffled by the lichen and moss on the floor of the tunnel.

Around the next corner Guy stopped again, his hand out behind him, halting Louisa. She could see a line of daylight at the end of the tunnel they were in, faint but definitely there. 'What?' she whispered.

Guy shook his head. Listening.

He started walking towards the light when, out of nowhere, someone was running towards them, unseeing, not knowing they were there – Louisa only knew from the sound, the shift in the shadows. It was so fast there was no time to react, to turn, before the bodies collided, and Louisa knew Guy was down, struggling before her, fighting with the man – it had to be Nesbit. Rage overtook her and she felt before her, reaching to grab something, anything, and pull on it hard. There was a yell and she felt a hand around her ankle, gripping her, and then the crack of bone hitting bone. Her senses heightened, time slowed down. It was as if she could smell every drop of sweat that was shed, the blood that was racing, the skin torn. And yet it must have been over in seconds when she heard a final blow and felt a thump as a body fell to the ground.

'Guy?' she cried. 'Guy!'

'I'm here.' And then she was stumbling as, staggering, triumphant, Louisa holding the feet, and Guy with his good arm hooked under a shoulder, they dragged the body, out of the tunnel, Group Captain Nesbit captive.

CHAPTER SIXTY-SEVEN

In the hospital, hours later, Nancy joked that the drawing room of Chatsworth was looking rather less pretty than usual. Louisa, Guy, Maisie, Deborah, Billy, Kick, Charles, Adele, the duke and duchess, and Tucker were ranged around a hospital bed, in which lay Max. The dowager was recovering in a room not far away. Nesbit had been arrested by Tucker and was being held in a cell while they waited for someone from the government to arrive. So far, he'd been arrested for the murder of Mrs Hoole but, according to Tucker, he was refusing to speak. 'Probably hoping for some kind of diplomatic immunity,' he said, 'but he won't get it. He'll be in a military prison by this time tomorrow.'

'Will you be able to charge him?' asked Guy.

'I don't know,' said Tucker. 'A confession would help. But we have the motive – Mr Landesman has confirmed Mrs Hoole heard Nesbit threatening him in German.'

Louisa looked at Max. 'How did you know she heard?'

'The argument was turning aggressive, and when I raised my voice Nesbit put his hand on my mouth and looked around. It was then we saw her at the end of the corridor – it was only a flash but it was enough.'

'That must have been why she asked Ellis to put her in a room near the family instead of in the servants' quarters,' said Louisa. 'I was so tired and confused at the time I didn't think much of it. She was afraid of Nesbit coming after her. But why didn't you say something at the time, go after her yourself? Weren't you afraid for her?'

Max had been given an analgesic, and managed to rest. Some colour had come back to his face. More than that, he looked as if he had been set free. The burden of his secret for all this time must have been hard to bear. 'I was terrified,' he said, 'but only for myself. I didn't think anyone else was in danger from him, only me. It was the next morning that my worst fears were realised. I knew that if he could kill her, he could kill me. So long as you were looking elsewhere, I was safe.'

'Except that at one point we thought it was you.'

There was a ghost of a smile. 'Even then I reasoned that, if you did accuse me, I'd be safe in prison.'

'There's also the business of the false air raid,' said Tucker. 'It's something we can ask Nesbit about, evidence that will help us when it comes to trial.'

'At least we know now what happened to Joan,' said Louisa.

'That poor woman,' said Charles. 'If my father—'

'No!' called Billy and the duke at the same time.

Charles regarded them levelly. 'I told Louisa everything. Why should we keep his secret for him any longer?'

They started to protest but then Max raised a hand, silencing them. 'The duke didn't have an affair with Joan,' he said. 'He didn't make her pregnant. I did.'

'It was you?' said Louisa. 'Are you sure?'

'Quite sure.' He smiled. 'We loved each other.'

Louisa and Tucker glanced at each other. 'I'm going to have to ask you all to leave,' said Tucker. 'We need to talk to Mr Landesman privately.'

It looked, too, as if Billy, the duke and Charles needed to sort things out between them. Guy firmly escorted out the others, although Louisa could see Nancy was longing to stay behind.

'You need to tell us the full story,' said Louisa. She handed him a glass of water and waited while he composed himself.

'When I was sent to England from Germany, I was hardly out of school. The war had started, and if you were eighteen years old, you went into the army. They knew I could speak perfect English, thanks to my mother, so I was despatched very promptly and told to make my way to this part of the country. They wanted me to report back on the RAF base here, which was being used as a testing site for artillery. But not long after I arrived, I read in the newspaper that eleven German spies had been executed at the Tower of London. I was terrified. Luckily, my role was considered very minor and things were chaotic at the start. I was able to send back some vague reports, and I made the case that I was best placed if I worked near to the base in a big house. That was how I got myself a position at Chatsworth, just as a hall-boy at first – bringing logs mostly, doing odd jobs – and then as a gardener.

'I met Joan soon after I arrived and we fell in love pretty quickly. She was young, but so was I. She was a calming person to be around, a good person, and we made plans for the rest of our lives, for when the war was over.'

'What happened?' asked Louisa. 'What stopped those plans?'

'We were reckless. I don't know if it was because we were young and foolish or whether the war made us behave like that but – we were caught. Charles saw us.'

'And he thought it was his father with Joan.'

Max nodded. 'I didn't look so different from him, in the half-dark and glimpsed quickly. And the mistake suited us. It kept the attention away, or I'd have been sacked immediately.'

'But then you realised Joan was pregnant.'

'Yes. We were happy in one way – it was part of our plan. But we had no money, next to nothing saved, so we couldn't afford bills of any kind. We had no means to set up our own home. She tried to keep working for as long as possible but we knew she'd have to leave eventually. And then she would be a woman with a bastard child.'

'Why couldn't you marry?'

'Because it would have been revealed then that I was half German. It might have come to the attention of the German authorities. It broke our hearts but we decided we would have to hide for a while, and give our baby away. Perhaps, when the war was over, we would be able to get our baby back. Plenty of people did it then.'

'I know,' said Louisa. 'There was no legal adoption process at that time. It was a common solution, as you say.'

'We thought we could work it out. We were young and hopeful. But then she started to get terrible stomach pains and she knew she was beginning to show too much – she was getting looks from the other servants. It was about then that I heard the duke was planning to go to Canada, and ... I made her see the doctor, even though it cost us all the money we had. He gave her a tonic or something. He said that even though the pains seemed bad he thought she would survive. So we made a plan that she should go on the ship, too. She could have the baby in Canada, and when the war was over I would be able to join them.'

'What did you do in the meantime?'

'I went to her room and packed her things. That's why I didn't take everything.'

'And the cap? Where did that come from?'

'She was bleeding a little then. She must have used it to staunch the blood and thrown it somewhere in the room. I don't know why. Perhaps she heard someone coming.'

'Where did you hide?'

'We went to the Hunting Tower. No one went there. It was safe, if we were quiet. I could still work, be at the house, then take her food, and even sleep with her for a few hours in the night. If she heard anyone coming, she would crawl into the tunnel until they left. It was basic, and cold, but it was safe. In some ways, it was one of the happiest times of my life. But her pains never completely went away, and she bled throughout.'

'How did you pay for the passage to Canada?'

Here Max looked ashamed. 'We went to Mr Ellis. We knew he was a kind man and loyal to the duke. If he believed Joan was pregnant with the duke's bastard child ...'

'You knew he would do anything to protect the duke's reputation without allowing any harm to the baby,' said Louisa.

'Yes, exactly that.'

'What happened then?'

'Mr Ellis was as good as his word and he told us when the ship was leaving. He arranged the passage, and as he was travelling too, he was able to make the necessary arrangements on board. There was also a lady's maid travelling with them. Poor Joan, she was frightened to travel so far, alone.' He stopped, caught his breath. 'It was too much for her. She went into labour early on the ship, and although our baby was safely delivered, she died from loss of blood.'

'Which meant your baby was registered as Canadian.'

'Yes, and I lost all means of finding her. You see, Mr Ellis told me the baby was a girl, and that he handed her over to the Canadian authorities.'

Louisa felt very sad for the kind man before her. All these wasted years carrying a burden he had never asked for. 'Why did you never leave Chatsworth?' asked Louisa.

'I couldn't during the war, and then I felt loyal, I suppose. Mr Ellis might not have known the truth but I still felt I owed him for protecting our secret. I was safer here than anywhere, and after a while, it was all I knew.'

'And no one need have thought otherwise, had it not been for Mrs Hoole.'

'I recognised her in the car when I drove her here from the village. I knew she still came back to see her mother and I knew she believed something had happened to Joan. But no one listened to her. Because everyone thought it was the late duke, they hushed her up, prevented any further investigation. That changed when you arrived.'

'The private detective from London,' said Louisa.

'Yes. She saw her chance, and she was going to stir it all up again. I hadn't realised she still had the cap. She must have found a way to hide it before coming to the drawing room.'

Louisa remembered now: she'd arrived without Ellis's knowledge. Mrs Hoole had her memories of the house and would have known where to go.

'Were you worried about what she knew?'

'Only a little. Joan didn't tell her everything – I wouldn't let her. It was too risky. Joan knew I was half German, and she knew it was a secret we had to keep. After Joan disappeared, Eliza – that's what I knew her as then – asked me if I knew what had happened to Joan. I told her we'd broken it off, she'd gone home. At that point, Joan was still alive. She might have been able to come back to work after she'd had the baby.'

'You didn't tell her you thought the duke had done something?'

'No. I was trying not to lie, only to say as little as possible.'

'Did she tell you about the cap she'd found, covered with blood?'

'Yes, and I confess I thought it would cast more aspersions on the duke. It was useful to me, so I went along with it.'

'I see,' said Louisa. She knew fear and panic could make people do stupid things. 'Did Mrs Hoole – Eliza – not wonder why you weren't going to the police too, trying to find out what had happened to her?'

'No. I told her she'd gone home and hadn't left a forwarding address because she wanted no more to do with me.'

'Did she suspect you?'

'No. She knew I loved Joan.'

'But that is no proof of innocence,' said Louisa.

'True. Perhaps she didn't think me capable of it.'

'Yet she was willing to believe it of the duke.'

'Maybe, or maybe not. She just wanted answers and the fact that the duke and his protectors stalled her at every corner made her believe even more strongly that they must have had something to do with it.'

Louisa regarded him levelly. She hoped he was up to the news she needed to break to him. 'Is there any chance your baby was left with any kind of personal possession? So that they might be able to find you later?'

'Mr Ellis told me that he handed her over with a note that had Joan's name on it but I think that was it.'

'On Chatsworth writing paper?' asked Louisa.

'That's very likely,' said Max. 'Not that I thought of it before.'

'So your daughter might have known that her origins began at Chatsworth, and her mother's name, if not much else.'

Max nodded.

Louisa took his hand. 'Max, we know who your baby is.'

He looked at her, and Tucker, confused and hopeful. It broke her heart. 'You mean she's alive? She's here? Who is she?'

'Lucie Dupont.'

There was a silence while he took this in, and then bewilderment furrowed his brow. 'I thought she was French.'

'French Canadian. She's confessed now that she came here to take revenge on the family she thought had abandoned her. With the rumours about the duke, she assumed he was her father. She tried to kill the dowager, with poison.'

'My daughter tried to murder the dowager?' Max closed his eyes briefly, and when he opened them again they were full of tears. 'I never meant for what we did to lead to this.'

'Lucie says she believed the dowager knew what had happened and was responsible for her mother dying at sea, and for her being given away. She came to England before the war to work as a teacher and felt it was fate when there was an advertisement for a French teacher for the school here.'

'I'm so sorry,' said Max. 'I feel as if I've lost her just as I've found her.'

355

'The dowager is going to survive,' said Tucker. 'I'm hopeful Lucie's sentence won't be too harsh.'

'Where is she now?'

'At the police station.'

'Can I see her?'

'Yes, of course. It will be a shock to her, and we'll have to prepare her. But you will meet.'

'I'll hold my baby girl in my arms,' said Max. 'That's all I ever wanted.'

CHAPTER SIXTY-EIGHT

D I Tucker came to the station to say goodbye to Louisa, Guy and Maisie, only to find that Deborah and Nancy were also there. 'It's quite the farewell party,' he remarked. 'I can't stay long, things are moving fast, as you might imagine, but I thought you'd like to know what's happened.'

'Yes,' said Louisa, 'we really would. Did Lucie and Max meet?'

Tucker nodded with a smile. 'They did. I don't mind saying I had something in my eye when it happened. The scene was very touching. I'd told her beforehand that her father was Mr Landesman, and it was a shock for her, as you can imagine. But she knew already that he's a good man, and I think that was a comfort.'

'Nonetheless it means she made a grave mistake when it came to the dowager,' said Guy.

'She didn't actually send her to the grave, though,' interjected Nancy, earning a chorus of disapproval from everyone else.

'It's not the case for that poor Peke,' said Deborah.

'You and your animals,' muttered Nancy, but there was a moment's silence in memory of Rosie.

'What about Nesbit?' asked Louisa.

'That one's trickier,' said Tucker. 'Not one for us to handle. He's being escorted to London but we're being told it will go to trial. There's evidence enough.'

'The false air raid,' said Louisa. 'And Max's statement, of course.'

'I'll hand it to you.' Tucker touched his hat. 'You know what you're about.'

They heard the hiss of a train coming down the track, and Tucker took his leave with a friendly handshake, and a pat on Maisie's head. Louisa was almost sorry to see him go.

Deborah and Nancy remained on the platform with Louisa, while Guy took Maisie onto the train with their cases. With the departure facing them, their manner turned awkward and Deborah started rather formally to say how nice it had been to see each other, but Louisa and Nancy caught each other's eye and burst out laughing.

'I'm sorry,' said Nancy, wiping away a tear. 'I know it's all terribly serious, everything that's happened. But honestly, Lou-Lou, it was supposed to be a quiet Christmas.'

'We all know who Farve would blame,' said Deborah, with a smile.

'Don't start pointing fingers at our family,' retorted Nancy. 'Look at the one you've married into.'

'Everyone thinks their family is the maddest until they marry,' agreed Deborah. 'I've missed Andrew through all this but somehow I'm rather pleased that I'll be able to tell him I managed it without him. I feel as if I could take on anything now.'

'And so you can,' said Louisa, feeling very warmly towards the striking girl, who had everything before her yet kept her humility and her humour.

The guard's whistle blew and then there was only time for a final embrace, the two sisters blowing kisses to Maisie. Louisa finally climbed aboard the train to join her family. They weren't heading to safety – the war was still going on, and who knew when it would end? But they were going back to their home. She leaned out of the window as the train started to move away, waving at Nancy and Deborah until they were no more than dots in the distance. Deborah was going to stay in a tiny cottage on the estate somewhere, getting to know the place, while Andrew was away fighting. Nancy would be back in London soon, and she was sure they'd meet up as often as they could. Nancy said she was determined to write the novel she'd been thinking about for a long time. 'All those family secrets,' she'd said, 'they destroy people in the end. I'm writing mine out.' Louisa wasn't sure if that was a threat or a salve but there was no telling Nancy what to do.

With the train's wheels turning, the rhythmic sound comforting in its familiarity, Louisa looked at her husband and daughter sitting together, pointing and smiling at whatever was amusing them in the distance through the window. It was all she needed, all she ever wanted. That, she thought, and a pinch of the unknown, too.

WHO'S WHO

THE MITFORDS

Lord Redesdale (David, Farve)
Lady Redesdale (Sydney, Muv)
Their children:
Nancy, a.k.a. Mrs Peter Rodd
Pamela, a.k.a. Mrs Derek Jackson
Tom
Diana, a.k.a. Lady Mosley
Unity, a.k.a. Bobo
Jessica, a.k.a, Mrs Esmond Romilly, a.k.a. Decca
Deborah, a.k.a. Lady Andrew Cavendish, a.k.a. Debo

THE CAVENDISHES

The dowager duchess (Granny Evie): her husband
   was the late Duke of Devonshire, died 1938

The Duke of Devonshire (the dowager's son, Eddy)
His wife: the Duchess of Devonshire (Moucher)
Their sons: the Marquess of Hartington (Billy) and
    Lord Andrew Cavendish (Deborah's husband)
The duke's brother: Lord Charles, and his
    wife, Lady Charles (Adele Astaire)
Kick Kennedy, Billy's sweetheart, sister
    of John Fitzgerald Kennedy

THE STAFF (all fictional)

Mr Ellis the Second, the butler
Mademoiselle Lucie Dupont, the French teacher
Mrs Airlie, the cook
Betsy and Anna, the maids

HISTORICAL NOTES

(SPOILER ALERT: DO NOT READ UNTIL YOU HAVE FINISHED THE NOVEL.)

In this novel, I have Kick Kennedy and Billy Hartington reunite for Christmas 1941. At this point, they knew each other. Kick was a debutante with Deborah in 1938 (Joseph Kennedy, her father, was the American ambassador in London), and she was the success of the season, popular with everyone – no one resented her for it, wrote Deborah Mitford, in her memoir *Wait For Me*. Their families didn't approve – the Devonshires were Protestant, the Kennedys firmly Catholic – and it wasn't until Kick had been sent back to America, then returned to work for the Red Cross in the war, that she and Billy were reunited, in 1943. In May 1944 they married against the opposition – although his parents had come around because they liked her so much – but tragically he was killed in the war only four months later. Kick also died far too young, in a plane crash in 1948.

Billy's death meant Andrew inherited the dukedom and the

estate when his father died in 1950 but he and Deborah couldn't occupy Chatsworth immediately because of the need to arrange finances to pay off the heavy death duties. It also desperately needed renovation, which was supervised by the new Duke and Duchess of Devonshire, who finally moved in in 1959.

The real butler at Chatsworth was Mr Simmons, who remained in the house during the war, polishing the gold and silver plate in the strong room, next to the butler's pantry (which really had been turned into a physics lab). But he bore no resemblance to Mr Ellis the Second, and if there is any in this novel, it is purely coincidental.

Lord Charles was married to Fred Astaire's sister, Adele. She was long supposed to be the real star, and better dancer, of the two. For Charles she gave up her film career entirely. Tragically, she suffered the miscarriages Charles describes in this book. Charles died of alcoholism in 1944. Adele remarried, but some of her ashes were scattered beside the graves of her first husband and babies in Lismore Castle, Ireland. (The rest were scattered close to her mother's grave, in a place coincidentally called Chatsworth, a suburb of Los Angeles.)

Nancy Mitford and Peter Rodd separated after the war (divorcing in 1958). Her fifth novel, *The Pursuit of Love*, published in 1945, was a phenomenal bestseller, making her financially independent for the first time. It gave her the courage to move to Paris, where she continued to write novels and memoirs, as well as copious letters to her sisters and fellow lauded authors. She fell in love, too, with a married French general and claimed to much enjoy her life, spending any royalty windfalls on dresses for herself, and antique furniture for her beautiful apartment.

Eleven German spies were shot at dawn in the Tower of

London in 1914, as Max mentions. There was an RAF base close to Chatsworth, at Harpur Hill; it was closed in 1960. And there was a German spy in the RAF, Augustin Přeučil. He was supposedly killed in an accident over the North Sea in September 1941, practising dog fighting with a trained Polish flier. But it was later discovered he didn't die that day, and was the only known German agent to infiltrate the RAF successfully.

I invented the placing and existence of the cottages for the gardeners and the night watchmen.

The records of past servants at Chatsworth are online; all those I mentioned, bar Eliza, Joan and Max, are real.

ACKNOWLEDGEMENTS

This is the last of the planned six books of the Mitford Murders series. It feels quite extraordinary to have got here. But if there's one thing for sure, I didn't manage it by myself. I write the drafts but there's a small army that gives me the time and space to do that, and then turns those drafts into this beautiful, actual book that you're now holding in your hand. That means edits, comments, suggestions (gracefully, sensitively made). Corrections too, of course, but I take the blame for any mistakes that remain. The font must be set, the jacket designed, the paper printed, the books distributed, promoted and sold – all around the world. Contracts are written, ad space is bought, champagne is sent on publishing day. And I rely on everyone's expertise and publishing acuity to make this happen successfully – which, in my very fortunate case, they have done. All of this means that the book is read by readers like you. At this point, for me, it really becomes a book, no longer mine but the possession of its readers. Nothing has given me more pleasure than to receive the many messages from readers everywhere who have told me how much they've enjoyed following the series. Even better, they've gone on to find out more for themselves about the Mitfords.

So that's a lot of people and I can't mention everyone but I'm going to give it a damn good try.

First of all, to Ed Wood, my editor and publisher extraordinaire, with whom this series was first conceived and who has given me what has amounted to a personal masterclass in novel-writing over these last six years. He had faith in me at the very start – when I had written almost no fiction before – and it was his encouragement and belief in me that has seen me through. Thank you, Ed.

Hazel Orme did the most wonderful and sympathetic copy-edit for this particular book. Also on the editorial side, I must thank Ben McConnell, Karyn Burnham and Ruth Jones. For the simply gorgeous designs, Ellen Rockwell. In production, my thanks to Tom Webster. Stephanie Melrose is the very best of publicists, and Laura Vile has worked wonders in marketing. In sales, tireless work has been done by Hannah Methuen, Carly Caulder, Caitriona Row and Rachel Jones. Management – the ones who know what they're talking about and sign off the champagne – are Lucy Malagoni, Cath Burke and Charlie King. What a trio, thank you.

The rights team at Little, Brown are a force of nature, and it's been such a privilege to get to know you and to have you fighting my corner. Thank you, Andy Hine, Kate Hibbert, Helen Doree, Jess Purdue, Zoe King, Louise Henderson and Fern McCauley.

Thank you, too, to Catherine Richards of Minotaur at St Martin's Press, who has not only been my publisher in the US but has given me invaluable editorial guidance, too. We all miss the late Hope Dellon who began this series with me.

For this book, I'd like to thank Edward Mason for his help in vintage car engineering. Also my great friend, Mary Attwood, who came with me to see Chatsworth and the landscape that surrounds that astonishing house.

I'm so lucky that I'm now represented by the magnificent Eugenie Furniss of 42 Management, aided by the efficient and patient Emily MacDonald. Can't wait to take on the world with you.

And thank you to my family, who love me, even though I am truly awful when I'm in the final throes of an early draft. Thank you, my darling Simon and George. And because I love you, I'll thank the dogs because I know you won't stand it if Zola and Benson don't get a mention. So that's it. The last one.

Isn't it?

BIBLIOGRAPHY

Chatsworth: The House, The Duchess of Devonshire. Frances Lincoln, 2002

Murder Isn't Easy, Carla Valentine, Little, Brown, 2021